ANCESTORS

R. Atiba Omar

Copyright 2016
By R. Atiba Omar
All rights reserved
Printed in the United States of America on acid-free paper
Published in the United States by èkíní ink publishing

Book Design by: annakstone.com
First èkíní ink publishing edition, January 2016
èkíní ISBN: 978-0-9907324-9-5
http://ekiniink.com
info@ekiniink.com

Gratitude

IN THE BEGINNING was the Word.

And the Word was made flesh and the flesh embodied a great being named Katherine M. Garry. For many years Katherine Garry was the publisher and editor of an incredible newsletter called (what else?) Freedom Press. She carried the production and financial weight of this powerful, almost revered publication on the end of her purse string which often frayed but somehow never broke.

And then she circulated them nationwide--and almost all for free--even saturating maximum security prisons wherein bad-ass convicts awaited her sublimely sophisticated newsletter almost as eagerly as they awaited parole. Somehow (in between uncompromising community activism, biweekly publication and serving in the office of the Dean of Law of a major university) she turned about five hundred pages of scribbled notes into a carefully edited and almost flawlessly typed manuscript.

And all for free.

If anyone can figure what string of words can adequately thank such effort, please let me know.

Next, i am indebted to a Boddhisattva disguised as a Defense Attorney named Bruce Yerman who tried to single handedly bring Ancestors to fruition. From safeguarding the manuscript to financing production to critique to moral and financial support to introducing me to the cyber age.....

Likewise Renie Morris did not hesitate to provide utterly selfless and complete assistance, often in ways i did not even know i needed. A talented artist widely known for her spectacularly creative use of color [and a being whose face (literally) has been licked by a wolf, almost kidnapped by a horse, and who virtually herds cats and dogs just by walking down the street-- here was no end to the contributions she made to pushing this work forward. Perhaps more than anything she sustained my spirit by giving fully of herself.

But all of these valiant and empowering contributions lingered in the Garden of Possibility until Anna K. Stone--visionary publisher, creative editor, educator, illumined spirit, friend--rained the elixir of her commitment upon their noble seedlings and sprouted the fearsome dragon in your hands.

i wish immortality to all. Ase

DEDICATION

To the living Ancestors: the Dogon, the Traditional Sudanese, the Ba Twa...

And to the Ancestors: the Cheikh Anta Diops, the Fannie Lou Hamers, the Malcolms, the Lumumbas, the Queen Mothers Moore; to those--who because of the Maafa*--are as unnameable as God i offer the libation of this work.

Ase

ANCESTORS

WORK CALL

THE GODS..
   Had they not made my grandfather a womanizer he would not have been killed by one of his beloveds. Certainly, then, his daughter would've had his flighty wing to at least shiver under and maybe her brother would not have died as a child. Then perhaps, as a living man, this elder and only brother of my mother would not have countenanced the monkeyshines of the slick, handsome, heavy-handed, jazz trumpeting mothafucka who was to be my father...and all would've been tra la la. Of course, that might have meant no me–and I am. As indeed all was: tic tac toe/ human souls in a row. The Gods aligned their cosmic dominoes and I had my fate.

   Maybe.

   Could be that all this machination of lives and deaths and might've-beens has only a peripheral something to do with me. In-damn-deed, perhaps the chain of events and DNA which began in the unplumbable reaches before my prematurely departed grandfather is for some other, diviner purpose and I am merely some inconsequential link in the chain of someone else's life.

   I await a sign.

Until then I eat, drink and endeavor to be merry, for tomorrow I might not have eyes with which to see that bad *white* Kerry Washington look-alike sitting at the bar like a sweet, ripe grape on the vine.

Even as the door closed between me and the 5 o'clock rush of NYC foot soldiers and blacktop charioteers battling their way home, I could taste her .Upon that delicious image I clamped down my teeth; looked around. It was supposed to be the happy hour, but of the two dozen or so very fashionable, very white mating-game playing men and women, no one looked especially happy. That might've been 'cause of my black ass. After all, this establishment was nothing so de classe as a bar. Rather it was a *taproom*, a veritable redoubt of leisured yuppiedom. Although, unlike in good ole days of yore, there was no sign above the entrance reading *NO Panhandlers, Dogs or negroes,* my thick lips and wide nose would've been welcomed only if they had accompanied a delivery of booze or a discreetly passed foil of cocaine. As a patron— even in my $600 business suit—I was an invader. .

Maybe. Another reason for everyone's (pardon me) *black* mood might've been the blonde at the bar. For a natural born fact I knew every man (and not a few of the women) hungered for her. I had only just entered the joint and had witnessed nothing. Except that homebaby was halfway through a drink and her demeanor was very relaxed. Several somebodies just had to have tried to gun her down. Yet still she sat alone. Aloof. Unconquered. An unmovable feast among starvelings. No wonder all the gloomy faces!

But I was not daunted.

Mentally I sharpened my knife and fork and forthwith approached the unapproachable one, looked her the fuck up and down. Slowly. So that there could be absolutely no mistaking my raw, animal intent. Indeed, although I did allow her a puff of breathing space, I stood deliberately within the Call-the-cops! Zone,. You know. Closer than custom allows an unintroduced black male to one of the Beautiful People.She pretended to ignore me; while in the mirror visible between and around the Johnny Walker Black and Myer's Overproof she sized me up.

Now, I don't know why bars have mirrors but my guess is to ensnare fools. You know. Prop their ass on the barstool and behind and above and sometimes through the bottles of booze espy themselves. Lonely, desperate, usually unsightly, always narcissis-

WORK CALL

tic self. Narcissistic for no reason other than that you are you. So, like a dumb-ass deer "trapped" by headlights on a highway, you are trapped by your ego in the mirror. Works just like salted peanuts to keep you bellied-up to the bar.

"What'll it be?" the bartender inquired of me.

I ignore the kracker. Partly because his tone was a tad unprofessional. Like, *How dare you come in here and recklessly eyeball this most white of white women who won't even* spit *in our mouths when we're dying of thirst!* But mostly I ignored him, because it further conveyed my purpose. I wanted to emphasize to the elegant lady that *I* ruled and preyed and devoured, and *she* was mere haunch and loin. The fine, dick-loving kracker. She was. My knowing eyes knew and were reassured in their knowledge when our assessing gazes caressed in the mirror like the two ships passing in the night.

"What'll it be?" the bartender asked again in the same impatient tone. I zoomed in upon the mothafucka. What a muscular, handsome bitch he was with his luxuriant ponytail and soap-opera good looks.

"You can fetch when I summon you." He opened his mouth to protest. But to his great good fortune, he saw the promise in my eyes. And I wasn't bluffing—I never bluff. Not that I would've beaten him into a coma for his impudence, but *damn*: I was crashing a white hang out and thereby was in violation of racial etiquette observance #369 blah blah blah. But, since that was *lawfully* supposed to be *nothing*, who could've faulted me had I slapped the handsome bitch for his "unprovoked" impudence? Deeply, like a lover, he looked into my eyes and quite suddenly found some urgency at the far end of the bar.

When I returned my attention to the tethered lamb she was no longer stealing sheepish glances through the mirror but was staring direct, hungry wolf eyes at me. Formerly she had sat decorously facing the ego-traps behind the bar. Now she had pivoted her thick, prime rump so that her slightly parted knees almost brushed my creases.

I was searching my files for the most efficacious bullshit to shoot at her when—in a come¬-fuck-me-now voice—the lady said, "Trespassing, aren't you?"

Well, well. A forthright kracker. *How refreshing*, I thought. So, forthrightly, I replied. "How else could I track you down?"

Her breath caught. Beneath the snug sheath of her silk blouse her proud breasts rose up and served themselves to my eyes, as if for inspection. "Game hunter, are you?"

"*Big* game hunter," I reply.

Just that easy, her breath quickened and I almost fucked up by smiling. You know? She was...agreeable, let us say, but would've been insulted had I too obviously noticed.

"How coincidental," she said. " I have the most interesting trophy collection not far from here."

"Yeah?" Probably the phone numbers of other hunters she'd mounted. If so, I looked forward to expanding her collection. Just to clarify what was what, I clucked my tongue and sighed. "But I haven't even had a drink yet".

She retrieved her purse from the bar.

"I can provide refreshments." She swiveled towards me, got to her feet, "accidentally" brushing against me, but did not merely stand up. Rather, like the proper finishing school graduate she was, she *arose.*

And was not the only thing arisin', I can tell you.

Good shepherd that I am, I extended my hand to help guide the lamb from her tether at the bar to wherever her grazing field might be.

And my damn beeper went off.

Now, people are slaves to all sorts of things. Some to possessions, some to beliefs; TV, of course, is the biggest pimp of all. My master was the Beep. I know. Beepers are passé. But because I wanted to be accessible but not too accessible I stuck with my dinosaur. Anyway, wasn't many had the number and only occasionally did any use it. The hand I had been offering to the lady segued to open my jacket. Like a gunslinger checking his shootin' iron I looked to my hip. *Damn.*

"Barkeep," I called. Almost instantly he disengaged from his glass-stacking and headed towards me. I held a fist with pinky and thumb extended to the side of my face in the universal gesture. Without breaking stride, homebitch swooped up a phone.

"Here you are, sir," he said, apparently decided that being rude to the nigga interloper was not worth a probable ass-whupping. I

WORK CALL

ignored his craven conciliation and plugged the phone into one of the jacks at the bar. Like I said, it was that kind of joint: even in the age of Internet cafes, the taproom retained the quaint accouterments of the pitiable, low-tech past.

To the expectant eyes of the eager lady I made a face, *Won't be but a moment.*, I tried to convey. *Some small matter to attend to and then. . . ..* While as I dialed i was actually thinking *Damn! And I was all ready to slay this pussy. . .*

"Jack?" a distraught voice asked with a Spanish flavor.

"*Si,*" still making my unconcerned expression at the lady. She seemed haughty and independent—I gauged her to be the kind of woman who wanted to be possessed. So, proprietarily, my free hand reached out to touch her hair, as though I always fixed her errant, golden locks. She smiled. Not a strand was out of place, of course, as we both knew. I listened to the voice on the telephone and nodding here and there in response possessed the lady some more.

Down one side of the gorgeous stranger's face, my fingers trailed in an unbroken line, pausing only to massage an ear, rub her neck, her shoulder—beat the hell out of doodling. I listened, as I took the stranger's hand and brazenly nibbled one of her fingertips to a backdrop of huffs and gasps. Jealous huffs at my intimate foray; outraged gasps at her surrender. *Kiss my red/black/and green ass*, I mused and myself kissed the "race traitor's" palm. Then—to further "despoil" her—I fleetingly tongued the inside of her wrist, which, I imagined, the crowd would've loved to manacle and drag off to some dungeon just then. After a few moments. "*No hables mas,*" I said into the phone while peering, ah, with such sweet sorrow into the toothsome mothafucka's eyes. I cradled the phone. Then, without preamble, I cradled the stranger, enfolded her in my arms and engulfed her pillowy lips like she was my very own virgin bride and I was going off to the war. Come to think of it, the analogy wasn't unfitting.

"What an encouraging prefix," she whispered when I finally relinquished her tongue.

"Suffix," I corrected.

"What?" Clearly the lady was befuddled.

"Gotta go."

"But but..." Having never in her gorgeous life been dumped before, she didn't know what to say. I headed to the door without bothering to ask for the number I wouldn't have gotten anyway. Somebody snickered, no doubt taking a pitiful semblance of vengeance in my abandoning the lady who'd snubbed them. To my credit, I stepped onto the sidewalk without dragging the snickerer with me. Bitch mothafucka. He needed to have his spine snapped and I very much wanted to help. Indeed, the image of his body writhing like a partially crushed cockroach on its back was almost as inviting as the image of the gorgeous stranger writhing in mindless lust beneath me. Talk about double whammy, temptation was upon me and upon me again.

But I was on a mission.

I let the bar--pardon me--the *taproom* door close and fished out the keys to my mighty, two-door steed which stood faithfully at the curb. Already I was forgetting the inviting lips: the angelic lips I would never again kiss; the snickering lips I would never split. Already I was forgetting because only what awaited mattered now. It was all that existed, as far as I was concerned. Truth be told, as good a shepherd as I was, I was a better posse. Single minded. Indefatigable. A big dog on a bone.

But not reckless. Automatically I fastened my safety belts after sliding into my ride. "Punk mothafuckas," I whispered, like a mantra, a hex, a vow. Looking dead in the eyes of what summoned me, I sped away.

LOCK AND LOAD

The city ages. Before your eyes, if you look. It started out fresh and vital as I drove away from the posh eastside's manicured flora and trendy taverns. Fresh and vital, bright and hopeful like a joyous young girl in spring. Then as I raced across Park Ave. towards Spanish Harlem, each block I passed was a day, a year, an eon elapsed in the urban continuum. Steadily, as I traveled across distance, I traveled through the lifespan of the city.

On each block the facades of apartments and storefronts declined and dulled. The fresh and vital grew stale, dilapidated. Steadily. Block by block. Until the entire neighborhood had deteriorated into decrepit old buildings with dim lights and dimmer spirits like decrepit old men without ideals. A vast expanse in reality separated where I had left and where I was heading.

But not a whole lot of distance.

It was the tail end of rush-hour and as the September dusk deepened, I zigzagged through the side streets as quickly as the potholes would allow. Zigzagged in my little Japanese import, I should add. Naive me, but I had thought buying a foreign car was a small contribution towards further fucking up the American economy. Yeah, yeah, that was unpatriotic. Especially with all the airwave noise and painstakingly graphed stats about how we're all in this together et cetera. Yea. The Gods know TV never wearies of telling me how much I've progressed. A-mothafuckin-men. And, verily, there is some scintilla of gratification in watching the endless parade of negroes passing out awards to each other...I guess.

However, my reality was that no matter how prosperous the white middle class got or how many black leadership/improvement/we's almost-white awards one negro handed to another, the eternally increasing black underclass still regularly ate wish sandwiches. You know. Mayo and imagination on bread. And so I bought Japanese. Since we were all in this together, my hope was that my small, heartfelt effort would help unemploy some of the steak-for-breakfast-eating krackers into joining us for dinner. Not necessarily at the same table, but the same meal.

I turned off Lexington Ave. into 102nd St. towards 3rd Ave. S l o o o w l y. Lest I crush the cruddy toes of someone among the throngs jamming the street. The *cruddy* street that was part bodegas, part old apartment buildings and all open-air market for drugs. Indeed, throughout Spanish Harlem, clots of drug traffic congealed here and there in the fouled arteries of the city. But here on 102nd was the wicked white heart of heroin in the ten-dollar glasine bag.

And how mightily the sickly heart throbbed!

Elsewhere the city was winding down, but here it surged with people. People from Harlem, Bed Stuy'; from Jersey and the east 50s, with suburban commuters en route home. All openly buying dope from sidewalk peddlers. Wasn't it funny? It seemed everyone but the mayor and the police knew where the drugs were.

I nosed my way through the mob of addicts and chuckled. The only thing funnier than the (ha ha) "secret" location of the neighborhood drug market was my buying Japanese to sabotage the economy of the evildoers. Ha mothafuckin ha. l might as well have got my ride from Ku Klux Autos. The least thing was that my Japanese "import" was largely made in America. More significant was that if the nation-gang rapists of "3rd World" economies were put in a line-up one of the faces would be Japanese. Hell, when most of the dark world was struggling against apartheid, the Japanese were struggling too—struggling to not appear flattered by the "honorary white" status their racist South African trading partners conferred upon them. Stinkin' mothafuckas. Yeah, I was the slick saboteur, all right. Instead of buying from the devil I had

Lock and Load

bought from his brother. Financed my own impoverishment, as it were.

Just like the black and brown morons buying dope from other black and brown morons.

Their mass murder/suicide was going on all up and down the block on both sides of the street and even in the street itself. Could you believe it? I had torn ass from the ritzy east side to el barrio in about 10 minutes. But for the last two or three I'd gotten only a couple of car-lengths into the block. I was supposed to be hurrying. But the cluster of zombies who had spilled off the sidewalk into the street and stopped in front of my car killed my mad dash dead. Apparently someone (probably the young Latino someone staked out on the sidewalk like a licensed vendor) had a "death bag," because folks were mobbing this one dude like housewives at a vibrator sale.

I shifted into neutral and revved my Japanese/American, pan-imperialist engine. Everyone looked my way. Most just to make sure I wasn't the cops. The locals knew I was not. The out-of-¬towners, well, I suppose they deduced that too. Whatever. Even after the neighborhood wretches and thugs saw that I wasn't the law, they dispersed. Those who could crammed onto the sidewalk, quickly queuing in two lines up and down the lip of the curb. Others just vacated, going hither and yon—anywhere but in front of me. The sojourners just followed the crowd. They didn't know why. It was just the herd instinct thing, ya know? In any case, a moment after I'd revved my engine, the immediate congestion vanished.

Except for this one junky who swayed in the street like a big booger in a nostril.

He was so deep in a nod the entire universe had ceased to exist. He just stood there. Ringed eyes closed, ragged knees bent, spittle on his unwashed chin. I revved my engine again and the knees of his holey pants straightened somewhat, but that was all.

Ah, well. I shifted to park and began to unstrap my harnesses.

Just then a young Latina who would have been beautiful if not for her three layers of grime ran out into the street and up to the junky booger. One dirty, still petite hand tugged at his holey sleeve. His Holeyness snatched his arm away. He looked annoyed, deigning to open his encrusted eyelids only to slits through which his doubtless jaundiced eyes peered ungratefully at his rescuer. Some of the spittle on his lips sprayed outward when he mumbled whatever indignation he mumbled to the girl.

Part of his befuddled mind probably resented that someone would dare intrude upon his junkie's heaven merely because he was blocking vehicular traffic. The remainder of his dope fiend psyche--his *larcenous* dope fiend psyche--probably wanted his ass to get run over: what did a broken leg or ruptured spleen matter when, shit, *mijo* maybe he get 'nuff *dinero* out the deal for 20, maybe 50 bag of *montega*.

With some regret, I reached for the door latch. I did want to hurt someone, but this drug addict wasn't the one. I, however, did not have time to fuck around. I mean, I was going to begin civilly. Politely asking the moron why, praytell, could he not stand in the street *after* I drove past. But he looked like he had a very big knife and only a little rationality. I think the girl knew what would happen if I stepped out of the car. I know as she tried to negotiate with the moron she had kept an eye on me. Whatever, when she saw me opening the door her expression of urgency turned to panic and very clearly her lips formed the name: *Gato*. She must've spoken it with equal clarity, because the deeply nodding, utterly zonked, out-to-lunch dope fiend suddenly turned toward my windshield and looked me wide-eyed in the face. Never have I seen a more sober, lucid, alert and comprehending expression. Indeed, you could almost see the cartoon light bulb glowing above his head.

For about two seconds.

Then it and the rest of him jetted into the crowd. He didn't even bother to throw a *thank-you-bitch* over his shoulder to the girl whose mouth hung open as she watched him run away.

Poor girl. She was probably confused. Not knowing whether to yell a bunch of mothafuckas at his fleeing and ungrateful back, or (she turned her glance to me) run for her own life.

I beckoned.

Immediately she proceeded towards me. Fearful or not, no drug addict could ignore a summons from anyone who resembled anyone who looked like he might have a dollar he might let go. Very ungracefully, the beautiful girl beneath the three layers of grime and the lifetime of deprivation shambled to my window. I rolled it down and a monster stink jumped off her and surrounded me. I ate the gag. Even though I thought the stench from her body was the funkiest thing in creation.

Until she opened her mouth. "*Gato*," she spake, not unlike a game show contestant blurting out the really BIG prize-winning answer while her whole family and all of her neighbors were tuned in to her glorious TV moment wherein even the unholy reek emanating from her in huge palpable slabs as if from the very bowels of Hell was a laudable thing against which I was not holding my breath.

Whew.

In more ways than one she *transmitted* so much when all she said was *Gato*. Cat. Although I was Jack Kerwin (for god's sake) Moore to my dearly departed mother and a few intimate others, I was Gato on the Puerto Rican streets wherein my red/black/and green was raised. Actually, Gato *la Piedra*. Cat the Rock. No one ever called me such a mouthful to my face. But you know how it goes. Catch a bullet, dodge a bullet; catch a bullet, dodge a bullet. Perform the feat long enough in the same street theatre and the audience, ever eager to adore, will name you a name. Especially if those cast as your antagonists can not do encores. What I'm saying is I had a rep. And (may the Gods bless her wayward soul) Chunk-O'-Funk was acknowledging it when she intoned what was more my street honorific than my name.

I try not to inhale. "*Como esta, mamita?*" say I. That's Porta Rikken for *What up, baby?*

She preened. In that quintessentially womanly gesture, one (*sigh*) needle-scarred hand flew to her hair, as though to assure herself that the three or four quick swipes she had taken at it with her apparently dirty brush were still holding up. Even her smile, which began as an artifice to mask her uncertainties, a tool with which to inveigle from whatever chance whatever scrap of possibility, even her smile deepened and became—however fleetingly—genuine.

"Ah, I ain't doin' too bad--*Gato*." she said, working the name some more. She leaned a little farther into my window and a great block of funk the size of a pyramid stone banged the shit outta me. "But," she fingered a flick of snot from her nose, "if you could hit me off with a lil' somethln'. . ." She sniffled an I-ain't-had-a-shot-all-day sniffle and smiled her fake smile again, thinking, I am sure, it was beguiling.

Funny.

Just a moment before her vestigial innocence had surfaced and made her smile radiant. Now it was just a bunch of bad teeth on display.

I handed her the ten-dollar bill I'd extracted when I called her. "Oo!" Her eyes alit like a thousand diamonds in a dazzle of sun. "Thanks, baby," she cooed, taking the money. *Taking* it, did I say? No Weed Hopper ever snatched a pebble from any Shaolin master's hand half as quick. "I really 'preciate it, man," she said, clearly ready to make tracks—away from me and onto her arm. My nostrils, if not my heart, rejoiced at the prospect. But I had to ask her a question.

"*Un momento,* little girl."

"*Whaaatt?*"

I suppressed a smile. Even the infamous Gato was a mere annoyance when a junky was trying to get to her junk.

"*Mija,*" say I. *My daughter,* rather than *my sister;* a colloquial streetism for establishing pecking order. I tried to lock eyes with her but she fidgeted and looked down the street, apparently hoping a fleet of cars would come and nudge the annoying obstruction (me) the fuck outta her way. But—*damn* her luck—not a single car turned into the street. "Look at me," I say softly. Reluctantly, she glared in my direction. "Look *at* me," I suggested with just a tad more force. She did. And oh how beautiful her eyes *might* have been. But they were sluttish and old—though she was young—and red and cunning and unhealthy and, just then, quite resentful.

The mothafucka.

Had she been a man, I would've slapped her. But her gender put me at a disadvantage. I wouldn't let her predacious ass know it but—damn *my* luck—barring murderously exacerbating circumstances, I considered women a protected species. Including that obnoxious subclass belonging to the genus *thattimeus ofthemonthus* and other related, equally obnoxious subdivisions. Like damn ass snotty drug addicts who smelled like opened graves. Nah. Unless she was trying to put a bullet in me, I couldn't lay unloving hands upon a female of the species, even if the specimen was a rarity of sorriness and funk who needed a lesson in respect. And so I did the next best thing to rattle her chain. That is, I told the truth.

LOCK AND LOAD

Which was—"I need your help."

The heart went out of her resentment so fast, had I not known what to look for I would've missed it. But in the blink of an eye (which is literally what she did) surprise, suspicion and pride rippled beneath the grime on her face. Surprise that such a one as me would need such a one as she. Suspicion because my needing her was too flattering to not have a string attached. Pride from realizing that I just *had* to be serious because, hell, she ain't had nothing a string could attach to. Now don't get me wrong. Ordinarily, people are as moved by truth as the mountain was moved by Muhammad. (which, of course, was not at all). But because the "people" who was standing at my car window making me wish I had bought a lot—and I mean a *lot*—of air freshener was so taken with my rep, the unexpected truth I told was a very boss *juju* indeed.

But she was a homegirl to the bone. She struck a nonchalant pose and leaned into my window. "Oh, yeah?" she said. Coolly. As though she side kicked for antiheroes everyday.

"Yeah," I squeaked, trying to breathe as shallowly as I could. Lawd help me, but I was on the verge of displaying my agony. Because I was in a rush, that would've been counterproductive. I mean, homegirl knew every ripple of the streets she prowled as thoroughly as a Vietminh knew her jungle. So no one could better tell me what I was rushing into than this junky. And she would, if I didn't antagonize her. In desperation, I pawed the dashboard vents towards my suffocating face and punched the fan to HIGH and COLD and MAXIMUM. *Aaaaaah.* The cold blast of recycled smog and car exhaust was so refreshing. It didn't quite relieve the choke hold homegirl's proximity put on me, but at least I could inhale.

Quickly. before the wind shifted. I began probing. "What you been up to today, *mija?*" I asked, as though making small talk.

Homegirl grinned. "Ah, not much." Her head drooped and wobbled side-to-side like a shy doofus trying to ask his first date for a kiss.

I was enchanted.

She was ragged, cutthroat, drug addicted, *ssstankin'*. And utterly ingenuous. Once again her smile had turned genuine and, in consequence, radiant. I hated manipulating her. But what was I to do? Say, *Homegirl, I need some info?* That kind of wording smelled like snitch. I doubt if she would've thought that I, the notorious Gato, had flipped like a pancake-Mafiosi angling for Witness Protection. But she would've thought something: *What's the right answer? Who will it hurt? What can I get?* Whatever--and then tailor-made an answer. But a contrived response was useless to me. Equally important, I didn't want her thinking she had something to wag her tongue about later. So, to elicit a direct answer. I asked an indirect question.

In stages. "Just holding the street down, huh?" I inquired, moving a little closer to the point.

"*Sí*, Gato. All day. Tryin' to score."

"All day?" I ask matter-of-factly. "So what's been happening?" She squinted at me. Puzzled at first, but then with suspicion--because she realized she was being pumped, despite that that realization was not what I wanted, ultimately it didn't matter. Poor child, but in her desolate ghetto, the inhabitants filled the emptiness by watching each other. Especially the zombies. Since most had long since smoked or snorted or intravenously ingested their TV sets, their soap opera was the 'hood. And not only for entertainment. When you measured happiness by how many cc's you had in a syringe, every slight occurrence on the neighborhood set was a potential additional unit of joy. No addict was gonna miss that chance—especially one who hadn't scored all day.

"What you wanna know, man'?" homegirl asked outright. She sounded surly and I didn't blame her.

"Nothing, *mija*." Which was true: her unguarded, quizzical expression of a moment before had the response I needed.

A horn honked behind me. How convenient. I shifted into drive and looked in my rear-view. A bunch of well-scrubbed white kids filled a teenmobile—a teenmobile with Jersey plates. "Be—" careful out here,I was gonna say. But homegirl had spotted them too. I chuckled as I pulled away. There were five faces visible in my mirror—and five hands covering five noses as Home-stank *malodorously* ran down where the killer dope was and the really good price she and she alone could get them for it. I wondered what her name was as I cruised down the street looking for a parking spot. I wondered if she would trick that carload of youngsters outta their money without getting them anything but the blues, or if she would sucker them out of an exorbitant amount and send them off happy. I wondered, oh, about many things.

Lock and Load

But not about who might call me in to 1-800-SNITCH.

After all, since Home-stank hadn't noticed that anything had jumped off, I was reasonably confident that *no* one had. Then I was sure of it: dead in front of the tenement I was going to was a parking space. And just my size too. Had to be a sign from the Gods. No longer concerned about snitches, even though I expected there'd soon be much to snitch about, I pulled to the curb. Like a conspiratorial wink from the Right Eye of Osiris, night's shadow fell across the sky.

*****

Forgive my morality, but I just can't grasp what the hooplah's all about. A woman—35, not unattractive; law-abiding, gainfully employed, respected by her peers, liked my her neighbors, loved by the neighborhood kids for whom she occasionally bakes goodies and from whom she faithfully purchases Brownie and Girl and Boy Scout stuff and who, further, is active in community to-dos and almost never misses Sunday in church—fucks a 14-year-old boy.

So what? So mothafuckin what?

You would think she'd be praised for her sense of civic responsibility. After all, who better than a woman to teach an impressionable young boy how to please a woman when a man? But do you think her sacrifice is appreciated? Does anyone commiserate with her for the nascent sexism and insecurities she has to overcome? Who sympathizes with her for the many, many premature ejaculations she has to endure day after clandestine day before the eager pup learns to not wolf the meal? In short, does anyone mourn for the seductress?

Hell no. Though if it had any sense, society would provide a federally funded Adult-Male In-Training program wherein every pubescent boy is assigned a passably sexy older woman as a very personal trainer, thereby nipping male chauvinism in the you-know-where and putting battered women shelters out of business. Amen (Ra). But no. Instead of praise and financial assistance. the poor woman is arrested by the local DA's office and pilloried by the press for, (try not to laugh) *scarring* the innocent young boy for life. Kiss my *cajones*. Like he's gonna be traumatized for actually living what all young boys wet dream. No one considers how edified he becomes, how deepened. Or, not inconsequential, thinks of the 14-year-old *girl* spared the rampages of his mindless hormones.

Which brings me to the point.

I was sitting in *Senora* Magdalena Orona-Reyes' tenement living room. Not that it was dilapidated or anything. *Au contrair*. The walls looked freshly painted; the undisguisedly commercial furnishings well-maintained. The inevitable, forlorn crucifixes hung forlornly here and there. Everything was clean, orderly. But that indefinable tenement quality obtruded. Perhaps it was the smell of some neighbor's frying grease invading the *senora's* apartment. Or maybe it was the two or three different hubbubs riding in with the cooking odors like a gaggle of idiots on a magic carpet, or (perhaps) the forlorn crucifixes hung here and there. Whatever, had you been abducted and blindfolded immediately thereafter, the moment the blindfold was ripped away and you saw Magdalena's living room you would know you were in a tenement. That's why the calfskin-upholstered Italian sofa seemed pretentious. It was too elegant for its milieu. It belonged somewhere else.

Not unlike Magdalena her self. "I don't know what else to tell you. Jack," she said.

My heart fluttered when she spoke my name. A conditioned reflex, I suppose. There was something languid and sensual in how she pronounced it. Always was. From the time I was 14 and she was...28, I think. Certainly no more than that. And *boriquenna*! You know what a beautiful people the Puerto Ricans are. Well, she was *very* Puerto Rican, and oh the promises my young ears heard when she would call me and say something like: *Jahock! Where is Julio? You put that basketball down* now *and you find him and* both *you get up here for dinner. And I mean* right *now. You hear me?* Ain't no telling what I was doing with a basketball, I didn't play. Probably took it from somebody to give to Julio. Julio. My partner; her son. Together we stormed through the streets fearless and fearsome, giving orders, making noise; ruff and tuff, taking no sh—*Don't let me call you again, Jack! Si, Miss 'Lena*, I promptly yelled up (all meek and goo-goo eyed) to the fourth floor window which now, twenty years later, was closed and curtained behind the still *bonita mamasita* sitting erect upon a couch that matched nothing in the room but her.

Me, I sat across from her in a straight back chair I had pulled bumper up to her knees. For one thing, it was conscientious to sit within a consoling distance. You know. Able to reach right out and lay a comforting touch upon one of Magdalena's slim, pianist hands, if required. But also I sat right in Magdalena's face because

LOCK AND LOAD

I always sat in Magdalena's face, my unresolved schoolboy crush being what it was. Shameless, isn't it? Instead of monomaniacal resolution to rescue the damsel, my chivalry was burnt round the edges by the fire-breathing infatuation of my youth. But (boil me in oil) tragedy didn't blind me to beauty . And just now Magdalena's ageless own was looming large all over the place. Her luxuriant hair was a thick braid nearly as long as she was tall. Black and gray-flecked it fell between the two palmfuls that were her breasts, forcing her chubby nipples into prominence beneath her sweater.

Woe is me, but I yet suffer from the trauma I experienced when as a boy visiting her son, I accidentally saw uncovered the rare twins now sitting outlined across from my studiously averted eyes. Indeed, I am quite certain I haven't recovered because to this day fat-nippled women discombobulate the fuck outta me. Word. in fact, my staid proximity to Magdalena's, er, memorable, er, things was probably therapeutic. Least ways the re-exposure caused me no anxiety.

Unlike the long, gray-flecked serpent braid coiled in the nest of her lap. I swear: I was grim, as befitted the moment—but that didn't stop the mothafucka from speaking: *Entwine me*, it said, most indecorously. *Entwine me, wind me, pull— Get thee behind me, Satan* , thought I, and shifted the whole of my focus to *Senora* Orona-Reyes' demure posture.

That did not help.

I am certain Magdalena meant no harm, but it was impossible to not notice her sleek and sculpted hips were *wearing* them jeans just right; a TV commercial come true—and they had not become a whit less telegenic just because I was worried and angry. Neither did the age lines tracing her exotic features promote platonic ruminations. They only deepened her mystique, etching her exquisite womanness into a high relief your hands ached to read as a blind man would braille because to touch her was to see forever. Egads. Magdalena Orona-Reyes was technically old enough to be somebody's granny, for crying the fuck out loud, But invariably, inexorably, I found her...interesting.

Nonetheless, beauty didn't blind me to tragedy. That's why I was elated when Magdalena explained, "...they said they would kill Lizette like they killed Julio." Though outwardly I only raised an eyebrow, my inmost heart cavorted. More than a month had elapsed since Julio had been butchered, autopsied, buried and farewelled and still the cops had no suspects.

That, of course, was because they did not care to have a suspect. The "case" wasn't manhunt material, ya see. Wasn't even media material. After all, no white citizen had been harried or panhandled. Julio was only Julio: another dead New Yorican in the drug war. So if no one was fool enough to mosey into a precinct and confess, the cops would never know whodunnit. But now I did. That's why the triple hallelujahs crept upon me. When Magdalena conveyed what the incompetents had unwittingly disclosed I *knew*. I instantly knew the face of Julio's killer as well as Lizette's...well, *only* kidnappers, I hoped. Pardon my sexist reckoning but a woman and a boy was one thing; a man and a girl quite another.

"And you're sure they were Dominican?" I asked, which was what she'd said when I had phoned. Or *not* said, actually. The wire taps had probably ended with Julio's demise, but Magdalena—the uninvolved if not wholly uninformed mother of a notorious if minor drug lord—still spoke on the telephone in vague, unincriminating circles. Thus my double check.

Calmly, too calmly, Magdalena answered. "*Seguro*, Jack," I am sure.

"But you say they wore masks," I said, and immediately realized that of the many things I should've said that was not among them. Magdalena was looking at me like I was stupid—extra stupid, in fact. But on second thought, I didn't mind. Indeed, I was glad to see her displaying some emotion, even if derision for the village id'jit. "*Lo siento*," say I.

She sighed heavily, accepting my apology? and motioned weakly towards the coffee table and her cigarettes. I retrieved them. "*Gracias*."

"*Por nada*," I replied and flicked my trusty Dunhill into flame. I didn't smoke, of course, but many beautiful barflies did. So the lighter, together with my files of bullshit, was part of my pick-up kit.

Magdalena puffed the cigarette to life; thoughtfully exhaled the cloud of carcinogens towards the ceiling. "There is no doubt they were *dominicanos*," she said, sounding as animated as a supermarket cashier voice-checking groceries. Her lips gestured a smile. "Their clothes were tight and pointy. You know," her sad, exotic eyes looked at me askance. "Like *jibaro* John Travoltas. Like—"

Lock and Load

"Dominicans," I finished for her, and smiled a little. I know it was amateurish psychotherapy, but somehow I hoped my little smile would wrap around her little smile and kind of help keep her together. But she was already looking pass me again.

"They spoke Dominican *Spanglish*," she was saying in that too detached cashier's voice. "Their accents were Dominican too." She extended an arm and the ashes from her cigarette dropped onto my approximately $300 worth of pants. Neither of us cared. "They came right in behind Lizette," she said, pointing over my shoulder to the door. "She was scared, Jack. She *must've* seen those two masked *maricones* waiting in the hallway but she was too scared to run and—"

I moved to the couch to put my filial arms around her just before the first quaking sobs erupted. Deep sobs, wrenching sobs; sobs enough for two. And they were. For the life of her only daughter, of course, and—at last—for the death of her only son. I was relieved. The way she had been withdrawing and dry-eyed since Julio's funeral had scared me, and I'm pretty close to fearless. Hell, most mothers adore their sons. But *boriquenna madres*? The only thing that made her loss less than utterly devastating was Lizette. And now Lizette was gone. The dudes who had taken her hadn't wasted a moment negotiating or ransacking. They just stated their case: "We want one million dollars," they'd told Magdalena. Then nonchalantly, as if ordering fries, one added, "Your daughter will be our collateral." Before that first shock could register, the same spokesthug dropped a second. "If you don't want to come," he said to Lizette, "we will kill your mother." That, Magdalena recounted through her own tears, is when Lizette had started to cry.

I was heartbroken. *Senora* Reyes' anguish was hard enough to bear. But the image of Lizette terrified and in tears . . . How can I describe my displeasure? The daughter was her mother in delicate youth. I mean, all children are beautiful, so Lizette's beauty was no thing. As a human being, however, she was a wonderful, rarefied blossom. And that such a rarity should blossom in the streets! Even though such flowerings were infinitely more routine than you'd guess from the incorrigible-little-monsters portrayals the news media presents of ghetto children, the flowering was always extraordinary. And these dogs would trample that. Avuncularly the spokesthug had put an arm around Lizette's petrified shoulders and pointed his gun at her head. "If you won't let her come," he said to Magdalena, "she is no good to us and we will kill her now."

"*Take* her," Magdalena had said, almost pleaded, "Take her." They did. But not without a parting threat: "And if you call the cops, we will kill her like we kill her brother."

After the kidnappers had left the apartment Magdalena had composed herself enough to go to the window. Looking out, she saw the two gaudily attired men wearing baseball caps and dark glasses, putting a big cardboard box into a van.

Now I may not be the most versatile of men, but I could walk and chew gum, as they say. Meaning I could be emotionally wrought *and* offended by the bad guys' ineptitude: the fools *killed their ransomer* and *then* took his sister for ransom. Essentially the idiots had a viable idea: relieve Julio of some of the drug loot everybody knew he had. But the methodology stank. What the nincompoops *should've* done was to kidnap Lizette from the giddy-up, when Julio was *alive*. Shit. Magdalena, I am sure, had a few pennies tucked away. But she could no more produce a million than she could deduce the identity of the culprits from the fact that they were Dominicans: she was Julio's mother, not Julio's confidant. Only Julio could've managed the amount required. And he would've, to his last quarter if necessary—and then tracked and slain everyone involved. But shaking down Julio himself was the Effort in Futility incarnate. The certain way to get him to buck was to demand something. Word. The magnificent mothafucka had a hundred hearts— all of them courageous. And therein lay the annoyance. Now that all of them were murdered, *now* the self-defeating murderers kidnap Lizette.

"What?" Contemplating the mothafuckas' flabbergasting ineptitude had made me miss what Magdalena said. "What?" I asked again. Needlessly. Now that I wasn't woolgathering, I saw that her whole being spoke her meaning: *Find my baby*. Then she bawled like one herself.

Ah.

I squeezed her tight and was suddenly very angry with Julio. I told him and I told him to get outta the drug game. And what was his response? *Stop nagging me—dad*. The mothafucka. Always teasing me about having a hard-on for his mother. And now look what his hard-on for money has spawned. The fool. Fancied himself a boss player but couldn't play himself outta the script the slums had written for his ass while it had yet slumbered unlettered in the cradle, the stupid mothafucka. Not that I was much better. Indeed, my only claim to self-actualization was that I fell only into holes I knew awaited me. But fall I did. On occasion I did totter over the possibility that maybe there just might be another option. But if the momentum of conditioned behavior was not hurdling you over one precipice, the big foot of socio-economics was shoving you over another. When you got down to the bone, we were all suckers. All the thugs and hustlers and gangstas from all the 'hoods. We controlled jack, least of all our own lives. The goo-gobs of blood loot stashed in tenements hither and yon gave (to some few) the sense of vitality. But it was a sickly vitality, as sustainable as a vampire sucking off itself. Nonetheless, that's what we did; that's what we were in our Transylvanian *bantustans*: suckers—just like Julio.

At last Magdalena quieted. Good. Gently, I pushed her away. Although I'd've consoled her till doomsday, it was past time to get busy. "Magdalena, you're gonna have to be okay."

She reached past me to discard her partially smoked cigarette then wiped at her eyes. "Lo *se*," she said, *I know*.

Damn it. She was so valiant my heart ached. I don't mean just that she was bucking up and all that, but rather that her spirit was so much finer than the crude thing her circumstances would make of it. Straight away I got up from the lady's couch, my game plan laying itself out for me like a red carpet for a head of state. "Just stay by the phone. When they call, agree to whatever they say." I was almost out the door.

"Jack."

"*Si*."

When I turned to face her I was a bit surprised. Someone had stolen the despairing woman who had sat on Miss 'Lena's couch a moment before. Upon it now was wrath and vengeance. "If they hurt my baby..." she said, her teeth looking quite like fangs. I nodded, thinking, In that case I'll have to kill them twice. Because of Julio—no matter what befell Lizette—they were already dead.

KNOCK KNOCK

F lies are stupid.

Kill one dead and set its pulpy speck of a corpse in some conspicuous place where other flies can see it, and what happens? Instead of buzzing off to safety some damn where, one dumb diseased fly after another dumb diseased fly flits carefree passed its squished cousin just long enough to be surprised when it gets squashed. Ain't that the stupidest something?

I know if I were about to enter a neighborhood and saw some dead black guy on display like a scarecrow in a cornfield, I'd put my brakes on with the quickness. Sheeit. If priorities allowed, perhaps I'd even stop seething long enough to altogether rethink my itinerary.

Which could not be said of coke heads.

Of the many things they could be accused of, circumspection was not among them. Granted, there was no sign in the sky above Washington Heights warning *Abandon hope, all ye who enter here*. But anyone with half a brain (well, maybe, half an *unfried* brain) could see that venturing into Little Dominica for its community resource was not a propitious thing. Still mothafuckas came. Like lambs longing to become veal patties. Like Muslims on pilgrimage to

Knock Knock

Mecca. But then, I suppose, why not? For the zealous devotees of the Coke God, Little D' offered deliverance in any which way you chose: brick flake grams kees to shoot or toot or smoke. However you cared to be anointed, Little Dominica was the sea of dreams.

And afros. I hadn't seen so many since 1974. But these throwback hairdos to the days of Cultural Awareness were decidedly not crowning glories. Admittedly it was dark, my sweat hood was laced tight over my baseball cap and my gaze seemed locked onto the pavement. All I had was the peripheral view. But damn if every `fro that trudged ugly down Amsterdam Cocaine Ave. did not resemble the burr head of a runaway slave. Indeed, walking among them seemed like the Night of the Living Dead, because dead is what these horror flick versions of an Old Soul Train rerun were, the Legion of the Dead Flies Walkin.

And one was about to collide with me. His zombie eyes, downcast like his spirit, swept the pavement as he shuffled slowly along in search of something, *any*thing, he might exchange for *one* mo' hit! Just *one* mo' hit, *one* mo'. . .

Closely I clocked his approach. Was hometown trying to play chicken? You know. Asserting some imbecilic right of-way like a little dog defending his pissing tree. Was he, my victimized and treacherous bruhda, truly just zonked into stupefaction? Or, mayhap, was he trying to get close enough to cold-cock my "unsuspecting" ass? So I clocked him. Lawd, he was greasy, and his particularly gruesome "afro" looked like a wet mutt had just curled up on his head and died. He was two paces away and showed no sign of acknowledging me. Imperceptibly, I readied up. Then almost immediately relaxed.

He was just another zombie, I saw, when we were mug-to-mug, just another oblivious fly. I sidestepped out of his way, but do you think he noticed my existence? He just proceeded metronomicly eye-sweeping the sidewalk for whatever scrap of salvation it might yield.

At the corner of 140 St. and Amsterdam Cocaine Ave. I deferred. A *marenge*- blasting jeep load of Dominican drug dealers was rolling lordly up. They paused momentarily before me, their haughty eyes at the level of my dick. While they deigned to favor my merely pedestrian person with their scornful, en-vehicled glances, I occupied myself by looking down what was less a city street than a shit streak buzzing with flies: look-outs and steerers;

dealers and guards—and burrheads, burrheads galore. After the lords of the realm cruised off, I crossed and put my hands casually into the pockets of my sweat hood.

The two 9s I'd picked up when I jetted home from Magdalena's had slipped a mite.

Always happens when you step up and down from curbs. I readjusted them in my waistband. Adjusting my gats when they slipped was a second nature because I've always been disdainful of holsters. Perhaps it was just a thing peculiar to my anatomy, but even drop holsters impeded my draw. So I lugged my guns in my belted waistbands and could right them in the middle of a cop funeral undetected.

I cut doggedly through the streets, at one with my guns. Actually distracting, however, was that I was only a few blocks from where I'd find out about Lizette, or (I hoped) find Lizette herself. So, I was on red alert. Ironically, more than for cops or point men I was worried about acquaintances. You know how that goes. It was so depressing, but thieves just didn't honor the code anymore. So, alas, if some "stand-up" gangsta saw my infamous ass and then shit coincidentally happened in the vicinity, I might as well pack my bags for Attica. That's why I was hoofing it.

My trusty steed was parked several blocks away by City College. Good lighting and frequent patrols made it unlikely my unpretentious yet widely known ride would be seen by any of my friends. Or would-be enemies. I say would-be because the dudes who murdered Julio and kidnapped Lizette didn't quite qualify. True, they had put the serious hurting to me and to people I cared deeply for. But that meant only that I must attend them. Otherwise, they were as much my enemies as the dog shit that sometimes got on your shoe. I mean, if you had any self-worth, your enemies had to be worthy of at least a modicum of respect. And how could you respect someone who follows useless murder with reprehensible crime?

And *then* inadvertently leads you to his door?

Which is where I almost was: Amsterdam Cocaine Ave. betwixt `43 and '44. As though I belonged there, I entered the first apartment building that seemed like its door was unlocked. That, of course, meant the first apartment building.

Knock Knock

Quietly, I mounted the stairs, smiling...ah, derisively, I suppose. The situation was comedic. Indeed, I almost experienced a twinge of guilt, as if I were taking advantage of the handicapped or something. See, the dudes I was relentlessly bearing down on were not satisfied with being just stupid. Rather they strove to be extraordinarily stupid by not knowing I was coming. That of course was the great grand pappy of numbskullery.

I reached the roof door. Like its mate downstairs it was only a symbol. I had been undoing the lace to my hood as I ascended. Now I paused to roll down the stocking from beneath my baseball cap. I adjusted the eye holes, relaced my hood, put on a pair of surgical gloves. While I listened I slowly, silently pushed open the door. While my vision adjusted to the night's dark, I listened some more. If there was something to hear I didn't hear it, so I unzipped my sweat' and leaned my gats just-so. Each already had a round in its chamber. Now they were tilted for a cross-draw even Doc Holliday couldn't beat.

I stepped onto the roof. It was deserted, as I had assessed. Not even a dope fiend getting a fix. I proceeded. Catlike. Moving nimbly over the dividers between the buildings; keeping low. The last thing I needed was to be spotted by a lookout. They were in the buildings. They were on the streets. They were all hi-tech, with their walkie-talkies and cellular phones and night-vision goggles. And had they seen me creeping on one of their rooftops they would've all taken me for a stick-up kid. And *that* wouldn't've been no fun, getting chased by a hundred well-armed Dominicans protecting the integrity of their cocaine traffic. Funny thing is that while others would've stood over me wondering who the dead *moreno* had been out to rob, Felito would've known his *compadres* had killed me for the wrong reason. For which he'd done a thousand *Ave Marias*, or whatever it is good Catholics do when they sense a miracle. At least as surely as water allegedly turns into wine, Felito would've known it was his ass and not some drug dealer's stash the dead *moreno* had been coming for.

Very gingerly I stepped over the divider onto the roof of Felito's building. He didn't live in it, of course. It was instead your average Little Dominica drug dealer's version of the business office: an untenanted apartment furnished just enough to prop up an electronic scale and a sack or two or cocaine. And an altar. Damn if they all didn't have altars. Replete with candles and icons and offerings of fruit and I know not what.

What a strange god, I always thought, *to be expected to bless such an enterprise.*

Several months prior, it was to this same sanctified cubbyhole Julio had come. The shortsighted mothafucka wasn't content to ravage his 'hood with just heroin. He wanted to diversify and do damage with *perico* too. And so he'd come to Felito's "office" to purchase stock.

The deal went ga-ga from the gate. Tribalism certainly didn't help. I mean, anyone without cataracts could see that someone did profit from the antagonisms between Puerto Ricans and Dominicans—but it was not Puerto Ricans or Dominicans. Of course, you couldn't tell them that. They were too smart to be manipulated, you see. The helping (itself) hand that strangled their national economies subsequently—ineluctably—strangled their human relationships. Somehow they imagined the debt-restructuring hand didn't touch them. Neither as peoples nor as individuals, let their *machismo* mouths tell it. If Puerto Ricans and Dominicans didn't like each other it had nothing to do with all that abstract geopolitical stuff. How preposterous! Rather, it was just because... because... Well, they just didn't like each other. Which was not to suggest that contrived antagonisms could not be put aside for business: Felito welcomed the opportunity to take some of the fucking Puerto Rican's *dinero*; and Julio welcomed the possibility of a discount on the fucking Dominican's coke.

*****

"But he's trying to play me, Jack," Julio had confided in me. "The first package was mothafuckin' primo. But now, if the quality's not off, the quantity is—but the cabrone always wants more dough, like he got a right to squeeze me 'cause I'm Puerto Rican."

"So what's it gonna be?" I had inquired. Julio smiled. Self-satisfyingly, I noticed. I didn't blame him. He had expected me to unhesitatingly offer to get his back. And I expected him to be satisfied that he was right. "Chill, homey. Felito bailed out of our deal when his material got funny. So I'm just gonna bail out on him and shop elsewhere."

Of course, neither of us imagined what that would come to: him in a coffin; his mother distraught; me on a rooftop looking for his sister..

Knock Knock
*****

The spangled dark of the city night covered me. I pressed my ear to the roof door for a long, long minute but heard nothing, so I tried the knob. Most uncooperatively, the door was locked. But the way it gave a little, clearly it was secured by a padlock affixed to one of those hinge jobs. Precisely what I'd expected, so (I wasn't new to this) I reached beneath the back of my sweat hood and extracted the six inch crowbar I had stuck down my pants for the eventuality.

I inserted the crow between the door and the jamb at the point the hinge seemed attached and very gently, steadily, exerted pressure. I was trying to be meticulous. You know. Listen for the sounds of the screws (or nails) coming loose from the door so that they wouldn't tear out too audibly, while also listening past that for whatever was to be heard. But, frankly, now that I was so close to a possible resolution it was hard not to headtrip. For one thing, the closer I got to Felito the more distinctly did I taste anger. Indeed, as I had been walking to the building, rage had been but a vileness in my mouth. Yet now that my quarry was only a lunge away I could feel the weight of its broken body clamped between my teeth; could taste its life oozing out, sliding in thick, dizzying globules down my throat. Verily, hate and anger were a hunger threatening to blind me.

As was guilt.

The door gave way under my practiced ministrations, but I only half-noticed. Most of my attention was kicking me in the head. Didn't I tell you? It was *I* who had led Julio to his grave, because it was *I* who had told him about Felito. Like most serious errors it seemed appropriate at the time. Why not? For a brief period I myself had pilgrimaged as a runny-nosed worshipper to the Mecca of Little D. Although the Gods had saved me from becoming a full-fledged zombie, for a while I had very definitely *not* been unentranced. Consequently, I saw a lot of cubbyhole altars. And eventually discovered Felito's, where the coke god poured out heart stopping bounty without unduly taxing your budget. So when my number one honcho insisted on expanding into coke, why shouldn't I show him to the purest deal in town?

Because it might get him killed, I answered myself just as the hinge gave way. *Him killed, his mother two-cigarettes away from a meltdown, and his sister...*

Thinking of Lizette made my hand hasty and the door opened with a creak. *Shit.* If anyone was in the hallway, no way they could've missed the noise. So I did the sensible thing: yanked the door open, rushed inside and peered over the banister as I poured swiftly down the stairs. If someone was out and had noticed me, I wanted to notice him back. So I flew down the stairs; my stocking-capped mug hanging over the railing for all the world to see. But either some hidden mothafucka had turned into a ninja the moment my lapsed attention had let the door creak, or there was no hidden mothafucka. Least ways, no one yelled as I silently but very openly glided down the once regal staircase, flitting from one now dingy, broken tiled floor to the next dingy, broken tiled floor.

It was only a five-story building, so I descended from the roof landing to the second floor in one noiseless motion in only a few seconds without straining my heart or, happily, encountering a challenge. On the second floor, I put on my brakes. I didn't have to look to know that two or three steerers were perched on the stoop like vultures perching on a limb. Included among them was no doubt, one from Felito's mob, eager to steer some new worshipper to the coke shrine in 14D. For the nonce it seemed the Gods were with me. There was no traffic into the building: no cocaine cowpoke, no besieged resident in the lobby.

Very, very gingerly I leaned over the banister. Millimeter by millimeter the figures on the stoop came into view. They were upside down and obscured by the dirty glass of the lobby door, and all I could see from my surreptitious angle was legs and some torso. But the legs and torso were chillin'—not guarding the entrance until reinforcements could come for the intruder someone had noticed in the building. Just as gingerly as I leaned over I straightened up, lest the sudden movement of shadow catch someone's eye.

Realigning the guns in my waistband, I headed up to 14D.

BANG BANG

I was wishing the mothafucka would hurry up.

I was standing in front of Felito's coke shop with my hood on and my head down—but with my stocking cap rolled up—anxious for someone to respond to my knock. Yo, if a neighbor exited her apartment just then and even just glimpsed my face, I would have problems. That of course is if i survived. Oh, I would do the damn thing anyway--no doubt--almost regardless to whom or what. But I'd flow better if my attention was uncluttered. That meant not having to worry about witnesses or alarm-raisers. Hence I stood there looking at the scuff marks on the door of 14D, anxious as a coke head to be welcomed.

My feet ached to fidget, so to quell the agitated mothafuckas I raised my hand to knock again. But footsteps approached. Immediately the peephole opened and an eyeball kind of appeared. I smiled at it. "It's me," I said, very *sotto voce*. Somebody grunted and the eyeball I could not quite distinguish disappeared and the door opened just enough for me to slip through. *"Que paso?"* say I to the familiar but nameless dude who held open the door.

El Nameless-o stuck the giant fucking .44 mag he was holding back into his shoulder holster. "Nuhtheeng up, man," he said, and turned to lock the door.

I took the opportunity to see what was to be seen. Still and forever, the living room was unfurnished, except for the candle lit altar in one corner on the floor. Still and forever, while one or two presided over the sacred stuff in the kitchen, and one or two caught forty or a video in the bedroom, one dude admitted the worshipers attended by only himself. So, while Alone-n-Nameless re-did the locks, I jiggled my arm and the butt of the knife I'd slid up my sleeve while waiting at the door slipped to my palm.

"Felito here?" I asked, working the knife fully free—rather deftly, if I do say so myself.

"*Si*," Nameless turned to face me. "He een back." His thumb was on its way to sticking out like a man hitching a ride when I grabbed a handful of hair (which, incidentally, looked and felt Africoid to me despite the Dominican fantasy about being not being Black) and quite violently yanked his head back.

Good thing he doesn't fade his hair, I thought, as my right fist— clutching the knife—banged hard into his throat.

"I'm glad he's here," I said loudly, but not too loudly, while homebuddy struggled to wheeze a breath passed his brutalized larynx. Valiantly, the mothafucka pawed at this holster. Admiring his courage, I punched my knife into his heart and gouged it around a little bit. "I'll meet you in the kitchen," I said, in the same audible volume as I helped the dude's dying body settle quietly against the door. I let his chest hold my knife for awhile, pulled out and cocked my 9s. Cautiously, I entered the living room. "I hope you're right," I said, still feigning conversation with the now dead thus really nameless doorkeep.

The bedroom door to my left stayed shut, but through the doorless kitchen entrance I saw a little movement, heard a little shuffling. Apparently someone was bestirring himself to welcome me, so I hurried along. I beat the greeter to the doorway by a step. He was a big burly mothafucka with two shoulder holsters over an orange shirt. Unfortunately for him he had a sandwich in one hand and a soda in the other. Both they and his mouth dropped when he saw me. He tensed visibly, quite wanting to tear me a new asshole.

"Don't try it, hometown," I advised.

Seated in a rickety-looking chair behind a folding table, a dude I knew as Hector (or was it Hernando?) had been in the midst of setting up shop. An electronic scale, not much bigger than a calculator, sat alone atop the table, and in Hector/Hernando's many-ringed hands was a knotted plastic bag of cut cocaine.

Apparently he had been preoccupied with undoing the knot when Big Burly's sudden mess startled him. *"Que pasan—"*

What the fuck is up? he was in the process of saying. But at the sound of the warning I'd just given to Big Burly he looked up from the spilled-soda-on-bologna or whatever and instead exclaimed, *"A dios mios!"*

Guess I'm not as sharp as I need to be. I mean, both the seated man and the dude standing but a pace before me were already entirely in my range of vision. And what do I do? Shift my eyes to Hec-nando when he exclaimed. Big Burly thought that was a good time to go for his guns.

It was not.

I plugged him once in the face just as his surpassingly quick hands were pulling his roscoes loose. Hec-nando felt...I dunno. Maybe that he should try his luck too, figuring, perhaps, I was gonna kill him anyhow. Frankly, that was a correct figure. But regrettably for him his effort was poor. I think he was meaning to momentarily divert me by throwing the folding table at me. But just as his hands perceptibly budged it, I aired out his head.

Post-mothafuckin'-haste I turned to face the bedroom. Right on time, because Felito's right-hand man had opened the door and peeked out. I never did learn his name, but I knew him to be a bonafide mean mothafucka. One of them dudes who would kill somebody for a snack. The moment he saw me seeing him he withdrew. Instantly, I began sidling towards the bedroom. My gats led the way. The right one I held somewhat sideways, shoulder level in my fully extended arm; the other I held at my waist, pointed slightly downward. I was still several feet away when the mean mothafucka made his move. Inevitably. He appeared in the doorway like an awesome presence—a bare ass naked awesome presence, I saw, now that he stood fully in the doorway. Nonetheless, his Uzi aimed competently at the area I should've been in. I wasn't, of course. Instead of being over *there* (where he had the right to expect me) I was over *here* squeezing off on him.

It was so easy, I almost felt I was cheating.

As I said, the man was a mean mothafucka, a true killer with tremendous courage. And, let us not forget, *machismo*. The question, then, had not been *if* he was gonna try me but *how*: straight up or crouched down. *Which* I didn't know; that's why I approached the door with my guns arrayed for either possibility. Had I time to ponder, I should've guessed the haughty mothafucka would try to do me standing up. But I was operating on instinct. Lucky thing, too. Homeboy had materialized in the doorway like a ghost, every molecule of his naked but nevertheless deadly being committed to slaying my ass. Indeed, it was a great testament to his spirit that he actually fired a spurt at where I was supposed to be before I hit him. Four times. Because I was so startled by his astonishingly quick response, I fired both guns at once.

But I wasn't mad: the lower shot caught him in the thigh, I think. The other shot went square to his chest. That gave me my bearing, and so I fired only my right gun twice more into his body. Talk about dying without your boots on. He fell like the proverbial tree and I leaped forward, dropping to a crouch on one side of the bedroom doorway, guns again aimed north and south.

All my primal focus was on the doorway and at whoever might there appear, but my mind was everywhere. Who heard the shots? Did "who" know whence the mothafuckas came? Would "who" call the cops? Mind their/her/his business? Or—happy prospect— was a goddamn drug posse on the way? Lawd, lawd, but my inquiring mind wanted to know.

Before a semblance of an answer could form, Felito called out. "Sheeit, *mi pana*, why you have to kill my friend?"

I stood up and shifted position slightly. "Because, *mi pana*, your friend was trying to kill me." The moment I finished, I dropped back down to a squat.

The rustling I had heard even as I spoke a moment before stopped abruptly. "*Gato?*" Felito asked, unbelievingly.

"*Como estas*, Felito," I greeted, imagining he was standing there momentarily stunned, only half into his shirt or pants, yet (I cautiously assumed) still fully dressed to kill.

Angrily, he huffed something in Spanish I couldn't understand. "Goddamn, Gato," he then exclaimed. "You go crazy? Why the fuck you shoot up my house?" As he spoke, the telltale rustling resumed.

I stood up again.

"Because you took the girl."

Quickly, I returned to where my voice hadn't fixed my ass as a target.

Guess that I had come for Lizette was also a surprise to Felito because again the sounds of his dressing seemed to stop prematurely. "So," he said, "her brother was a friend of yours?"

I felt like an instructor in a Jane Fonda workout video, but I got back to my feet again anyway. "A good, good friend, *mi mothafuckin' pana*." The getting-dressed sounds resumed then ended a second before I did. I hurried up and duck-walked to safety, not in the least surprised that he hadn't bothered denying his guilt.

"Gato, Gato," he cajoled, "why you no tell me from the beginning? I woulda treat him much, much better if I know he a friend of yours." That polite assurance conjured up the image of Julio's tortured body—and I almost did a Mean Mothafucka myself. You know. Stand straight up in the doorway and blast away. But getting myself killed would've been a terrible disservice to all the victimized parties involved: the Reyes family—my family.

So I curtailed my impulse and in a calm voice lied, "That doesn't matter now. All I want is the girl."

The bitch grunted. "You hear that, *chulita*? Gato say he come for you."

For a fleeting moment I thought, almost wished, he was faking, just trying to fuck up my head so he could move. But I had supposed the worse was true when homedog had appeared naked in the doorway. Then I knew it when I heard a small mewling and then, faintly, Lizette's frightened voice. "J-j-j-jack?"

"*Si, linda*," I blurted, totally forgetting my diversionary knee-ups, her plaintive voice so painful to hear, "I've come to take you home. Everything's gonna be all—"

"I no know, Gato," Felito interrupted. "You come to my house, kill my people—I think if you no drop you gun now I kill the girl."

Instantly, I made myself guffaw.

"*Wha*?" Felito's consternation was unmistakable. "You think that's funny, *amigo*?"

"Sorry, homeboy," I replied, trying to sound amused. "But you been in America too long." Felito sputtered. "This ain't TV," I explained. "I ain't dropping *nothing*. But if you kill the girl, you know what happens?" I continued quickly, lest the idiot answer the rhetorical question. "First, I kill you. What do you think, *amigo*? I just killed four of your *honchos*, so whaddya think? Think maybe I might be able to kill you too?" I paused, both to listen for his movement and to hear from his response if I was getting to him. But he said nothing. I took that to mean I was hitting a nerve. So I pounded it some more. "*Dead*, Felito. That's what you'll be—I'll kill your dumb ass dead. You know what that means?" He tried to interject something. Probably bluster. But I just bulldozed him to silence. "No more Big Macs is what it means, mothafucka. No more *chocha*—no more nothing. Just you in a hole in the ground with worms crawling out of your mouth." Again he tried to mouth a defiance and again I mowed him down: *I'll be sure to put that on your tombstone*, and so on I said.

And then (my back pressed to the wall) I inched away from the doorway, because I expected him to be plenty mad when I said: "Then I'm gonna kill *all* the family you have in *Nueve* York— including your *madre*." I squatted even lower, waiting for a volley of bullets to blow chunks of plaster out of the wall. But the only thing to drop around my head was a barrage of curses. "Yeah," I said, when his tongue lashing was done. "Yeah yeah yeah. But kill that girl and you can be sure I'll tell your *madre* you're the reason she's being tortured. And you can watch it from hell, *amigo*."

And that was that. Truthfully, I didn't know if I could rationalize killing his family. The only thing I was sure of was that if I un-assed my guns Lizette and I were dead. Hell, we might be dead anyway because there was no guarantee that my shots had not invited attention.

I wanted to get the hell out of there so I tried to hasten things along. "So what's it gonna be, *mijo*?" I inquired. Sincerely, too: all my chips were anted up. The next play was entirely his.

He was silent so long I got to thinking maybe I should try to prod him some more. Then he blinked. "If I let the girl go, how I know you no kill me?"

Bang Bang

Well. Bless my soul. I was so relieved I almost promised to tattoo a guarantee on my dick. Instead I told another lie. "Because we're even. You killed my friend; I killed yours."

"My friends, *amigo*," Felito clarified. "You killed more than one of my friends."

"But you raped the girl, " I countered, as though the fact were but another feather on the scale .

A moment passed. The longest moment of my life.

Then he sighed. "Ho-kay."

"Okay," I said back, and heaved a sigh my mothafucking self. Standing up, I started backing up through the living room to the front door noting, as I proceeded, that the floor didn't creak. I was rather exposed now, but to get ass he had to bring it, an exchange for which he'd shown himself uninterested.

"She come out now, Gato. Ready?"

"Ready."

"No funny beezness, my friend."

"No," I say, both my guns pointing to where I prayed his torso would appear. "No funny business."

"Any funny beezness, I shoot her in the back, Gato."

"No, no. Just let the child go and we're outee."

I damn near shot Lizette, he shoved her out so suddenly. She stumbled a few feet into the living room, having tripped over a leg of the dead dude sprawled half in the doorway. Peripherally, I noticed she was disheveled and very wide-eyed; her thick, beautiful hair—so like her mother's—was a soiled tangle. Her blouse was buttoned crazily and half tucked in her jeans. Her hands indifferently clutched her socks. Poor child; she seemed so lost. Lost and entirely lost.

"It's okay now, Lizette," I said, my eyes locked on the bedroom doorway, though—peripherally—I watched her. Watched her turn to look at the naked dead man; watched the socks slip from her hand and fall unnoticed to the floor; watched her move stiffly towards me like a toddler newly arrived at upright mobility. "That's right, baby," I said as soothingly as I could, as though she had not noticed the dead bodies when she passed the kitchen doorway. "It's all gonna be all right," I reassured, as though the wide, frightened eyes looking past me were not seeing the dead dude slumped against the door behind me. "Your mother's waiting for you at home," I said, and some of her tension eased, I saw, though, of course, my eyes never left the bedroom doorway.

Lizette had nearly reached me and was threatening to walk straight into my arms—which meant straight into the line of fire. My guns waved her curtly away. Before hurt could fully replace the dazed expression on her face I scarcely whispered, "Go to the bathroom and close the door loudly." Then, louder: "Okay, Lizette, let's get out of here." Quickly I looked from the bedroom door to Lizette. *Go to the bathroom*, I was about to mouth again. You know, for clarification. The child had to be disoriented mentally, emotionally—in all respects—and here I was telling her *Go to the bathroom* and *Let's get outta here* in one breath. But, bless her indomitable soul, when I tore my sights from the bedroom to look at her, instead of the confused, quizzical expression I expected, the brave little girl wore a knowing face. *Don't worry,* it reassured me. *I gotcha.* Dammit—she even gave me a wink before resolutely heading for the bathroom.

I, in turn, headed for Felito.

Swiftly, 'cuz like I said, I had noticed that the floor did not creak. The second I reached the bedroom doorway I pressed my back to the wall. And looked across the room. Lizette was staring at me from just inside the bathroom.

"Hurry up and close the door, Gato," she said, as though I were standing right next to her and as though she called me Gato—the name Felito knew—everyday. "Hurry up and let's get out of h—" and then she slammed the bathroom door just loudly enough.

I smiled the kind of smile your lips approximate when both admiration and sorrow grip your heart, like what you feel for dead heroes. And to think that her beautiful promise was imperiled by these animals! May the Gods forgive me, but in that moment I felt I could indeed kill Felito's mother and children—even the roaches that had fattened on his food; anything that ever marked his existence. So I smiled and waited eagerly for the demon to appear.

Wasn't long. His movements were as unstealthy as they were impatient. I wasn't surprised. After all, he was a drug dealer and a rapist, which was tantamount to saying he lacked finesse and self-control. So I was not in the least surprised when two minutes after Lizette slammed the door his jerry-curled mop began appearing in the doorway. That gave me several options. Like, subduing his clearly dimwitted ass and then doing him as he'd done Julio. You know. Mutilate him. But I didn't think I had the time for self-indulgence. Or else, as his forehead slowly appeared past the door frame like a greasy sun over a horizon, I could've waited for him to see me and then shot him, so if there were an afterlife he'd know who to curse for his being nose-deep in hell shit. But it was a miracle all the gunfire hadn't already brought a stampede—a couple of stampedes. I didn't wanna press that luck no more by firing na'y another shot. Indeed, could've been just my imagination, but already I was hearing sirens and commotion and a passel of footsteps in the hall. So, I took the most expeditious option: as soon as enough of his forehead emerged I whacked it with one of my *pistolas*.

Extremely hard, of course.

Before he could say ouch I was through the door. The windowless room was just large enough for the queen size bed and nightstand it contained. And it was upon said bed that Felito's soft, stubby person was falling when I helped it along by jumping upon his chest.

Immediately, the bitch showed his colors. I mean, I know he was hurting. I had, after all, banged the *shit* out of the trigeminal nerve running through his forehead with a steel pipe; to wit, the barrel of an automatic pistol.

But was that any reason to drop his Uzi?

Hell no, of course. Hell *fucking* no. To the contrary, now was the time to *eat* pain, dig deep; to cut his mad dog a-loose. Instead the bitch dropped his gat. In fact, had the air not whooshed out of his lungs when I landed on him, I'm sure the soft mothafucka would've whimpered. As it happened, he couldn't even get around to a death rattle. The moment we hit the bed—him on his back, me straddling his chest, which was just as flabby and weak as his spirit, by the way—I thudded the butts of my 9's into his temples. While he pondered this new arena of pain I let my guns fall to the mattress and grabbed his head. Before he could comprehend what was happening, before he could beg or draw a decent breath, before he even knew my hands were upon him, I snapped his neck.

It was the most unsatisfying moment of my life. I alit from the corpse like a nympho alighting from the arms of a premature ejaculator. Word. Killing Felito appeased nothing. True, you could argue that I'd saved Lizette's life. But nothing was *un*done: Julio was still dead; Lizette was still ravaged; and Magdalena Orona-Reyes would still be aggrieved and guilt ridden. Perhaps the abstract something that yet hungered within me would've been appeased had I extracted more from the murder by…. I don't know. Torturing him; making him beg; somehow killing him again. But I didn't and I couldn't; so however satisfied quintessential justice might've been, for me Felito's death sated jack.

A siren interrupted my lament. It was distant and could very well have been an ambulance. Nonetheless, I took it as a sign—a sign to get the fuck out of Dodge.

I stood over the dead creature and contemplated spitting in its face. But DNA testing being what it is, I contented myself with the fact that it was I who was tucking my guns away and Felito who was just lying there with his head hanging funny, waiting himself to be tucked into a body bag. Hurriedly I rifled the room for whatever; even taking the gold crucifix from the pants the naked dude had left neatly folded on the nightstand. Then I went to the kitchen and robbed the dead some more. The coke I emptied into the sink and then carefully rinsed away, though I balled up and pocketed the empty bag. I'm sure there was more coke around, but when the police found it, my expectation was that they would think that the robbers were just too inept to find it themselves. Then I retrieve the socks Lizette had dropped. Finally, I went to get my knife. I stood on the side of the once brave doorkeep now slumped haphazardly against the door and pulled my knife out slowly, lest I get blood all over my sneakers. Could've saved myself the trouble, though, because when I unplugged him, a cloying clot dropped out of his chest and he was done. Indifferently, I wiped the blade somewhere on him and returned it to the sheath I had secured to my calf. To my surprise, the only sounds I could detect in the building came from the noise Mean Mothafucka's carcass made as I dragged it by the ankles across the room. You know. To get it out of Lizette's sight. True, she had already seen it, but that didn't mean she had to see it again. I heaped homey in the kitchen with his *compadres* then hurried to the bathroom. And knocked. Yeah, knocking on the door was at least comic under the circumstances, but it was a closed *bathroom* door, for crying the mothafuck out loud, and I am *not* an unsocialized being. Anyway, I knocked only once before I called, "Lizette?" and I didn't wait for an answer before I entered.

BANG BANG

It was dim and cramped and the inside of the toilet had not seen a can of *Cleenee Bowl* in a long while. Part of the dingy bathtub was visible. The other part was mercifully hidden from public view by a half-drawn, stank-ass excuse for a shower curtain. I spoke softly. "Lizette?" I reached for the shower curtain, wincing at the nastiness despite my surgical gloves. "Lizette," I said again. "It's me, little sista. Everything's all—"

—right now, I was, of course, gonna say. But when I drew the curtain aside and saw Lizette—meticulous Lizette; Lizette of the Dainty Sensibilities—scrunched down in a filthy corner of a filthy tub like a cowering animal, I knew everything was not all right. Indeed—if such a diminution as I was beholding was possible—perhaps nothing in creation was.

Slowly I descended until I was fully upon my knees; slowly I removed my gloves. "Aah, little sista," I said. Very calmly. Hoping that neither my voice nor expression betrayed the exceedingly acute anxiety that wanted to bolt from my heart like the enslaved from a plantation. I was hoping I was cool enough but I didn't know. Frankly, it was difficulty to gauge myself, to clinically evaluate my on-going performance as though I were but some actor in the thick of an audition. Yet I had to try to be cool because Lizette was so close to the edge of some abyss it seemed that just a single more thing out of the ordinary would push her irretrievably off.

I remained on my knees, lest the terrified child feel menaced by my height. "Your mother is gonna be so happy to have you home," I said in an offhanded tone.

But looking at Lizette's face my heart's desire was to pound the dogshit out of Felito's corpse. Pound it and slam it around the room. Her *eyes!* Her eyes were so huge. Huge and full of agony, terror. I wanted to reach out to stroke her reassuringly as you would a trembling bird, to gesture towards the first step in the long road of her healing by letting her again feel a human touch that did not abase or hurt.

She seemed, however, just a cringe away from buggin' out. Proceeding carefully was definitely in order. You know. Things that passed for men had just touched her most hurtfully. So my own compassionate but masculine touch, rather than pulling Lizette from the brink of trauma, could easily push her deeper in to it. Thus I neutralized my hazardous inclination to wrap the battered child in my arms by resting them on the tub.

Why'd I do that? Slimy muck instantly saturated my sleeves and slicked my skin in clamminess. Clamminess from the sewers of Hell, so it felt. My god. My Almighty God. I mean, I knew the tub was gruesome but I had not expected it to be *alive*. But I didn't flinch. Even if you had flunked Psych 101 it was not hard to figure that flinching would've reminded Lizette of *what* she was sitting in. And that was not a helpful idea because it would remind her of *why* she was sitting in it, which of course was a reminder her sanity did not need.

"Lizette," I said reassuringly, as though speaking to a suicide with a gun in her mouth and her finger on its hair trigger. "Your mommy's gonna be so, so happy to see you." I spoke calmly, though I was so convinced of the power of this evocation I practically announced it, like I was bestowing a large inheritance or something. So I spoke calmly but with an upbeat inflection and smiled a cheery, infectious smile. Lizette stared through me. Earlier, reminding her of her mother's concern reanimated her a bit. But apparently that button had just one push in it. Lizette seemed utterly unaware of my existence. She was just a blank, unmoving shell propped in a corner, drawn up into a tiny ball, as if she had tried to curl herself into a nonexistence where no one could find or hurt her anymore. The spark she had earlier displayed was no more; snuffed out, perhaps, by whatever nightmarish possibilities she had imagined while she cowered in filth, helplessly awaiting her fate. No wonder her unseeing eyes stared through me, as though expecting that any moment the door would burst open and—

Realization caught me so suddenly I almost grabbed Lizette. "Lizette," I whispered. "Homegirl: *they're all gone now—no one's* gonna hurt you any more. You hear me?'" I asked, and I thought she did 'cuz her eyes seemed to perceptibly focus. "No one's gonna hurt you any more, Lizette. *All* the bad men are *gone*."

Slowly, as if emerging from a fugue, she blinked.

Hurriedly, I stuffed the surgical gloves I'd been holding into my pocket and reached out to take her hands. "That's right, baby, everything's...," I launched into a babble, too relieved to know whether I was actually helping to draw her out further or if the worst danger had receded and I was only making noise. All I did know was that a mighty exhalation escaped Lizette's little lungs and if I did not quite see the palpable tension she thereby emitted, it was because the moment she released it I sprang into the tub, dropped into a crouch, attacked her with an embrace. I know it was psychosomatic, but it reassured me to hold her. Like, if I held her in my arms, I was holding onto whatever part of her sanity that'd beamed the fuck back down. She trembled: another step back into the land of the living.

Then—joy of joys—she spoke. "Did you kill them?" she asked in her musical, child's voice. "Did you kill them, Jack?"

My brain froze for a moment; started to lie. But, alas, she had already seen the bodies.

"*Si, preciosa*," I admitted.

She pulled away from me a little and my heart sank. Of course I told myself she had pulled back because I was holding her so tightly she couldn't breathe, but I feared that the real reason she tugged away from me was.... I dunno. She was horrified by what I'd done; horrified and thus now afraid of me. But she was neither.

"*All* of them?" she inquired—in the same *hopeful* tone I had been too relieved to notice the first time. I looked at the little tear-streaked face looking up at me but could not meet her eyes,

"Yes."

"I'm *glad*," she said, but she did not sound glad.

Still I fidgeted. It was so confusing. Hers seemed a healthy attitude, was probably essential to her healing. But was I to encourage her to rejoice in death? Should I validate the lesson impatient life had all too soon taught yet another child? Lizette had come back from the edge, but clearly not all the way. Should I bridge this critical limbo by apprising her of Perspective, of "necessary evils"? There was no comfortable position on the horns of that dilemma so I fidgeted.

The child misunderstood. "Don't worry, Jack." she assured me, "I'll *never* tell."

I sighed; smiled the sad smile. "I know, precious, I know." I un-hugged her so I could reach into a back pocket for the last rabbit I had in my hat. "Put this on," I said, shoving a bandana into her hand. I knew the mothafucka was gonna come in handy. Either to help hold in my bullet-ridden guts or to veil Lizette.

She seemed to not know what to do with it.

"Let me help," I said, and extracted it from her uncomprehending grasp, folded it once into a big triangle and placed it over her head like a scarf.

"Did anyone see you come in here?" I asked, while tying the ends under her chin.

Her eyes fell. "No," she said softly. "They had me in a box." I helped her to her feet and before I could stop myself said,

"Well, they'll be the one's in boxes now."

I had one foot on the rim of the tub and was holding one of Lizette's hands to gallantly help her over and out when her dainty, little damsel fingers clamped down on my mitt like a vise. Alarmed, I stopped and turned quickly to her, thinking her in pain or properly aghast at my remark. But when I looked at her I saw beneath the makeshift scarf hooding her face the same fierce expression her mother had worn just before I'd departed. "I'll *never* tell," she all but hissed.

I suppressed a smile. The intensity of her gaze was so grown-up and so impossible to doubt. I nodded; squeezed her hand. She nodded; squeezed mine. Like two thieves, we stole into the night.

LAST LAUGH

"It's so terrible, terrible—why do people do such terrible things?"

I do not answer. The question, I think, is too weighty to be anything but rhetorical. So, though I hear it, I do not look up from the coffee stain on the cheap carpet. Strange, but in the stain's Rorschachian contours (probably caused when my not ungrand inquisitor was reaching for a bagel) I find a place upon which to project my own weighty, unanswerable questions. Silently, I try to attend them. But the inquisitor will not be ignored.

"Well?" he prods.

I look up. The insistent man has a Bozo-the-Clown halo of hair and is so short the average size desk he sits behind seems too big for him. As does the overlarge *snozz* protruding *way* out to perdition from beneath a set of eyeballs that are a little popped, a little red and all penetrating and unafraid. I wet my whistle from the non-biodegradable styrofoam cup o'cafeteria mud my host has thoughtfully ordered up to help pry my night-owl eyelids open.

"Damn, Marty," I say around a wince, because the black coffee is still too hot, "how the fuck can I say?"

Marty Feldstein, looking like a B-movie mafioso in his black dress shirt and tie gets up from his desk and heads for me with arms outstretched. *He always looks like the Bride of Frankenstein when he walks like that*, I am thinking. In fact, his extended hand is almost upon me when I realize his intent.

"Don't pinch my cheek, Marty," I warn, wondering if I can park my full cup on the table without sloshing a new stain onto the rug before he lays his trademark oh-what-a-cute-baby touch upon me. Before I can work out the vectors involved in getting Object Coffee to Point Table from Point Hand, Marty has struck again.

"*Try* to understand," he exhorts, giving my head a vigorous waggle.

"You're gonna make me spill the coffee," I protest. Marty lets go of the handle he has made of my cheek and stands fully erect. Although I am seated, we're still almost eyeball-to-eyeball.

"*Spill* the coffee. Go downstairs and knock over the whole coffee urn already. But *try* to understand this incomprehensible thing." He throws up his hands in exasperation and stares up at the ceiling a little distastefully, as though looking in the unwashed morning face of God.

"Why," he asks of the opaque plastic sheet covering the overhead florescent light, "*why* doesn't anybody try to understand?"

He drops his arms, hangs his head; turns and trudges back behind his desk, looking every bit the picture of a defeated man.

I ain't fooled.

His lament to the heavens is genuine enough. Indeed. One person's *oh wow!* might be another's *so what?*, but not to Marty Feldstein. He would experience your wonder as intimately as if he were a Zen Buddhist striving for *kensho*. You know. That *I am you/You are me thing*. Likewise with your pain. It so bothered him to see people hurt, he threw himself on their agony like a hero on a grenade. And if it *KABOOM*ed in his face, whatever pieces of himself remained would get up and hug the world. Word. That's why I smiled at the dejected walk he was walking. He maintained it, no doubt felt it—dejection—in every step he stepped until he reached his seat. He even sighed dejectedly when he plopped down. Then—what did I tell ya?—he cast down into the well of himself and drew forth a reason to brighten.

"But we're kicking this problem in the keester," he said, holding up a professorial finger.

Last Laugh

I smiled and nodded. Sipped my coffee. Eyed the man over the styrofoam rim. Funny how the mystical crops up in the most ordinary places. Looking at Marty through the steam rising from the 50-cents cup of coffee was like peering through a haze, a veil of time. I suppose the fact that the man hadn't aged a day in 20+ years encouraged my reverie. If he was any different it was only that he and his humanity had relocated. Once he had been *Counselor* Feldstein (or Counselor Marty, as we familiarly called him in the corridors of Juvenile Detention).

Now he was *Director* Feldstein, overseeing an array of social services in a private agency that was almost as poor as its clientele. Who knew who or where he'd be tomorrow, this Traveling Bodhisattva, after cutbacks or burn-out folded his current tent. Tryin' to heal him somethin', that's for sure. Trying to blow with his inexhaustible benevolence into one burst bubble or another.

Unfortunately, my own optimism was less extravagant. "You know I hope you're right, Marty, but I don't know."

"*What?*" he exclaimed, as if I had said gefilte fish wasn't kosher. "What's *not* to know? She's been here only a week and already she's better. So what's not to know?"

He was talking about Lizette, of course. Almost three weeks had passed since what Lizette referred to (quietly and with her head down) as *that time*. Talk about going from the frying pan to the fire! No sooner had we escaped from Felito's and Little Dominica then we almost got kidnapped again. By the staff at the hospital we detoured to. Naturally, they'd wanted to report the rape of a minor to the police, so—naturally—I had come prepared with a concoction for them to report. To wit: I just found this girl and she ain't got no I.D. Then the minute Lizette was treated we were outee. I mean, what was the point in reporting Lizette's rape to the cops when there was no one to prosecute but me? But that was the least thing. Far worse was that Lizette had been only physically liberated. Her spirit, her self-worth and faith, was yet kidnapped, trapped in some wretched psychological place from which neither her mother nor I could free her. So I had brought her to Marty. Years before he had taken a paternal interest in my wayward ass because he thought it precocious. Along the way—despite that I was now a wayward adult—the would-be saviour of my misguided potential had settled for being my friend. Thus his especially personal concern for Lizette.

"I guess you're right," I conceded. "At least she's stopped acting like everybody's speaking Martian when they talk to her."

"And tomorrow she'll *sing*," he almost sang himself. Word Didn't take much to charge his battery.

"But—"

"But button your mouth, already," he interrupted, apparently thinking he was preempting my doomsaying. "I've got the best therapist in our rape counseling service working with Lizette. Hmpf," he snorted; waved his hand to encompass the world. "Milagros Dixon is probably the most innovative rape counselor anywhere. We're lucky she's willing to work here for the pennies we pay. So if you're not counting a blessing, shush your mouth."

My my. My mothafuckin' my. He looked like he might leap over his desk if I even hypothesized a disagreement. Fortunately, that was not my intention.

"Thank you for rallying my morale, sir," I said. "However, sir, I wanted merely to inquire why the fuck my presence is required here and at this time. Sir."

"Oh." When he saw I wasn't calling forth evil spirits with pessimistic remarks, he relaxed.

"Well, I...," he began. I leaned forward expectantly. Now that the ritual coffee sipping—and cheek pinching—was done I was eager to know why I was in his office in Queens instead of in my bed in Manhattan. "Well, I...," he repeated.

I waited some more, poised in my seat attentively, expectantly, as I said, even though I was really more asleep than present. "Well, I...," Director Marty damn Feldstein ventured—yet a-damn-gain.

Through the thick curtain of my drowsiness a slight impatience shone. "Marty," I said quietly, "you call me at 7 a.m. after I had just pulled the cover over my head. You tell me Lizette's recovery hinges on my presence here this morning. You tell me you'll explain when I arrive. Well, Marty—" Mindful not to spill my coffee, I stretch out my arms, putting myself on display "—here the fuck I iz. Please, sir, tell me why."

Marty tugs at his black, Mafioso collar with a finger. "Well, Jack, I don't *know* why you need to be here, but—"

Last Laugh

"I think I'm gonna have to report you. Marty."

"*Report* me?" he said, as if he'd never heard the word.

"Yeah." I sit the styrofoam cup on Marty's battered desk and get to my feet. "Surely you're my *gumbani* and all that, but if you call me at 7 a.m. again and have me drag my weary ass all across town without a reason I'm gonna report you to….." I stroke my chin, look up at the ceiling then shrugged and look to Marty. "Who is it you report somebody to for calling before business hours?"

"The police."

"Yeah?" I am surprised. "You don't say. I had thought there was some special agency or something."

"It's the police, Jack, but—" I hold a hand up like a stop sign and Marty screeches to silence.

"Yo, hometown, yo. I ain't never been a morning person, especially not after gallivanting till dawn, so if you'll excuse me—" I mosey to the door, convinced now that Marty has summoned me for some laudable but cockamamie purpose, like calling down the power of *Love* through our combined presence. "—I'm gonna get on my pony and ride."

"But Jack—"

"Tell Lizette I'll drop by her house later." I meant her new co-op in Long Island. *Senora* Orona-Reyes was abandoning the east side almost as soon as Lizette, traumatized and hurt, had stumbled through the door. I was reaching for the doorknob, already fantasizing about pulling my bed sheets over my head and falling all the way away from the world, when Director Feldstein lassoed me.

"*Goddamn* you, Jack."

I pivoted, quite surprised. Marty just didn't use de lawd's name as an expletive. When I turned to look at him, his smiling face was almost upon me. "*Goddamn'?*" I inquire.

His smile broadens. "Figured that'd get your attention."

"It did. But I'm still ready to vamoose." He clutches me by a sleeve and—because he is so small and kind—I let him herd me back to his desk.

"That's what's wrong with the world," he pontificates as he sits me down and stuffs the cup o'mud back in my mitt. "People just don't take the time to listen."

"Well, I'z a-listenin'," I announce and take a swig of the warmish brew. "Make it good."

"What I was trying to tell you is that *I* don't know why you're needed for Lizette's therapy, but her therapist does."

"Her therapist?"

"Yes, you lug head. Milagros Dixon is a dedicated professional. Aside from me and the janitors, she's here at 7 or 8 a.m. every day. This morning she bushwhacked me when I stepped off the elevator." He swings a fist through the air as if to convey that she'd actually jumped out of a tree onto his back and clubbed him. "She has a session with Lizette today, Jack, but she's insisting that she absolutely must see you first." The smiling mothafucka really smiled at me now. "The choice was between calling you at an unlawful hour or rescheduling Lizette. So…."

"So I lost?" He nods his smiling Bozo head up and down. "Well, why didn't you say so?"

"You didn't give me a chance."

I opened my yap to challenge that but could find no denial worth a damn.

"Well, whaddya expect from me at—" I check my watch, "—8:47 a.m.? Coherence?"

Marty picks up the phone, hits three numbers. "Coherent or not, Ms. Dixon insists conferring with you is crucial to helping Lizette, so you just have to—Milagros?" he asks into the receiver; listens. "Yes, he's been here about 15 minutes. Okay." He puts the receiver down and looks to me. "C' mon," he says cheerfully. I follow, feeling—presciently, I discover—like a lamb going to slaughter.

*****

SERVICIO DE CONCEJERIA/COUNSELING SERVICES, the sign greets or warns when the elevator doors open onto Floor 3 of Helping Hand Social Services. Dull and peeling, the long plastic shingle informs you of your whereabouts from above the long reception counter that separates the large waiting room from the offices of the staff like the threshold to Nirvana. Some standard institutional color that strives for neutrality but is invariably depressing coats the walls of the waiting room itself. It's scarcely 9 a.m. but the scarred wooden benches that are equally institutional thus equally depressing, are crammed with people.

LAST LAUGH

Marty Feldstein marches through them dispensing smiles. I follow tight on his heels. Because my own face remains impassive and my eyes look only ahead I seem, I guess, disinterested. I am not. In fact, though I look politely at the cracked lettering in the bilingual sign and I'd much rather be zeed out in bed, I am interested enough to see every one: —the cluster of middle-aged homeboys and homegirls free, for today, of drugs;—the subdued, indifferently made-up young women free, for today, of their batterers;—the groups of children elated by the cheap and worn-out agency toys free, for today, from the Gods know what.

I see them all and know them at a glance because I see their poor, unloved faces everyday.

Are they not sublime?

I think they are. I follow unassumingly behind Marty. Marty the Loving. Marty the Humane—Marty the Blessedly Officious. At every step he dispenses smiles like benediction. No doubt he means to hearten the downtrodden supplicants of his agency's Head Shop Dept. You know. A little pre-counseling prep, as it were. And that is all cool and wonderful. And superfluous as hell. Word up. The only meaningful thing either of us could do for these outwardly bedraggled folks is run out and get them donuts. I may be sleepy, but I ain't blind. That is, my spirit is not. So clearly my eyes see what Marty, smiling like an alacritous missionary, does not: here in this drabby ass waiting room among these discounted people, an imperishable spirit prevails. It is nothing so ordinary as the generic "human spirit" white folks are always blathering about whenever some other white folk triumphs over a sex change operation or some such. That shit is hysterical. Some soccer mom is traumatized because she heard about a hold-up in the mall parking lot. After which, she receives four months or ten years of federally funded counseling, and a TV mini-series is done on the Triumph of the Human Spirit. Ain't that nothing?

In bonafide contrast, the human spirit I sense here as I am towed along through the seedy natives by the benevolent Great White Father, is nothing so commercial. What I sense, rather (if you'll pardon my melodrama) is that *fathomless* something. You know. That *essence*, I suppose, which the builders of pyramids and science and religion called forth to enable them to build pyramids, invent science, establish the Mama Ship of religions Do you know what I'm talking about? That *ESSENCE*. *The* ESSENCE. The *pitch*

blackness that is the matrix of the multiverse: the Dark Matter of dark matter. The Dark Matter that even Western physics now calls Spirit. The *vital force* its science once decreed nonexistent when its chemists could neither find nor replicate it in their test tubes. The *infinite imperishability* that stowed away in the cramped death holds of slave ships. *Here* in this dilapidated waiting room that is the stillborn descendant of the slave hold; *here* among these discounted people, that same imperishable spirit prevails.

No wonder most everybody looks at the nice white man like he's daft.

They don't comprehend his smile, you see; though if they did, they'd feel insulted. For how can he dare imagine that he might impart encouragement to those who have forever encouraged themselves and imbued all of human consciousness with the eternal flame of hope? In-goshdamn-deed, millennia before the first Cro-Magnon mutated from the Nubian Grimaldi above the 51st Parallel, the Spirit that is essence and pitch blackness and infinite imperishability sustained them. When the pale mutants laboriously multiplied and forthwith started murdering each other both on general principle and for the scrawny pickings of their wasteland—utterly unaware of the bounty to the south— the Spirit sustained them. For eon upon eon, the Spirit sustained them. Unfortunately, the Cro-Mutants got sustained too— by dumb luck, most probably. Whatever. Instead of having the decency to self-exterminate as they seemed destined, the mothafuckas evolved. Into missionaries, among other things—and then were inconsiderate enough to venture forth! Can you imagine? Bearing nothing but the salvation they brought from their *exceedingly* unsaved lands, the haughty, unwashed missionary presumed to save "the native" from real paradise now for a fabricated paradise later. Yet in the immediately resultant hell, the unnameable Spirit—the One, the All—sustained and sustains them. Props their despised and beleaguered persons up, goshdamn, whether they kneel as impoverished subjects in their native lands or sit as bedraggled clients in agency waiting rooms. It is all the same, you know; 3rd World and waiting room. They help themselves to your paradise and throw you the gnawed-over bone—then call you "welfare mama" if you take it. Tagging along behind good hearted Marty Feldstein, I think how alike are missionary and capitalist and (sigh) compassionate social service director. Some are arrogant, some are kind, but damn near all are paternalistic. That is why Marty's well-meaning and compassionate smile was insulting. When it comes to black independence—biological, spiritual, cultural, whatever—whites think that the native cannot exist without their encouragement. And they're right. The mutants might be right. I mean, I ain't no paleontologist but neither am I a Neanderthal. That is to say, the evidence is abundant and unequivocal and available to anyone with no racial delusions to cherish. And damn if it doesn't say that the original inhabitants of the earth—The Mother People—had harnessed fire, planted food, established art and culture from southern France to Sango Bay in Uganda and beyond. And all before a single white Cro-Magnon had erupted on the face of the earth like a putrid zit upon your countenance.

But the "*native*"?

Doesn't matter if he or she lifts a bale or totes on safari, or says *bwana* or *sahib* or *kimosabe*, the native you always see with flies on his lips holding an empty bowl in TV commercials is a *white creation* that would *not* exist without their love.

"Good morning, Mr, Feldstein," a receptionist greets cheerfully.

"Good morning, Gloria," he with equal good cheer replies. We glide on by her to the offices beyond.

"I'm just gonna introduce you two and be gone," Marty says over his shoulder to me.

'Cool, *mijo*," I warmly reply. And sincerely. Despite my ruminations I am not in the least perturbed with Marty. He is, after all only an above-average product of Western culture, not an escapee from it.

He knocks on a slightly ajar door and pushes it open before anyone can respond. Ever gracious, the good Feldstein holds it open and stands aside so I might enter. The room is a bright, spacious contrast to the dull, cramped waiting area. Flowers and sunlight and furnishings that look comfortable and unintimidating fill it. At first I see no one, then Marty enters behind me and closes the door.

"Mil—" he calls, but stops abruptly when the now closed door reveals a woman at the far end of the office. Apparently someone's life is utterly engrossing because the woman is kneeling before an open file drawer reading the folder she'd extracted from it a second or a minute ago.

"Hi, honey," Marty says to the top of her still bowed head.

Almost casually *honey* marks her place with her finger. Almost casually she raises her eyes. "Good morning," she replies, but to Marty alone, for her eyes have yet to touch me.

But I see her. And am smitten. Smitten to the blessed damn bone. From the giddy-up and the break-away and with room for maneuver I am smitten. Partly, of course, because I am a sucker for braids and this glorious mothafucka has a shimmering waterfall cascading down her back. But what really hoisted my red/black/& green was her headband. Did you know that the designs of many African fabrics, like the asoke and bokolanfini and, of course, the renown and venerable kente, have names? They do. Like, *"The Ancestors Will It So,"* and, *"We Have Awakened the Possibilities,"* and *"A Thousand Shields Will Protect Me."* See? Glorious and profound stuff like that. Certainly, the multitude of patterns made it hard to know for sure, but the stylized black birds and suns on the vivid purple strip banding my future homethang's waterfall looked to me like *"The Occasion is Solemn ."* Did that forebode something? Perhaps. But I was too enthralled to be bothered with augury. Baby was in motion, you see. In a single stream she snaps shut the folder, as she closes the drawer, as she arises, as she walks towards us—towards *me*—with her long Nefertiti neck inviting my lips. Lawd, but even in mundane gestures her grace was uncanny to behold, her each movement unfolding into movement like the petals of a flower in the morning. Pardon my coarseness, but my immediate impulse was to suck the flesh from her bones.

But I had to play the game.

Which is to say I was expressionless as the lady spans the ten or so feet between us. Yet as I watch her I think, *nyoka*. Snake. Because that is how the mothafucka moved. Liquefied. So soft you could pour her, as though warm butter over bread. And never-damn-endingly did she flow. 'Cuz even when she reached us and only stood still something about her continued to move, continued to surround and enrapture me. Lawd. En route to her office I had been trying to figure what the fuck a Milagros Dixon was, and I'd concluded Latina. (After all, Milagros is *espanol* for miracle.) Now this particular miracle was jet black and surnamed Dixon, but still I could've been right. I mean, in just Panama alone there's no shortage of jet black Spanish-speakers with surnames like McPhee. Nonetheless, however accurate my surmises, the *verification*, shall we say, killed me dead. Outwardly, the child was perfect. A woman to inspire poetry. A love for whom you'd build a *Taj Mahal.* And she was her own adornment. Her face was as naked as her dress was unrevealing. But all her utter lack of make-up and stylishly unprovocative attire did was make her womaness more distinct. Verily, verily, homegirl was all that and a slice of pie—*and* a dollop of ice cream with chocolate chunks. I drooled discreetly. But damn if 'n my teeth didn't ache to sweat rabidly all over her ... carpet. Marty, however, seemed impervious to her spell.

"Milagros," he said, craning his head back to look up at the long, tall drink of water that she was. He poked a thumb in my direction. "This occasional gentleman here is the culprit you've been looking for." She winced. Too imperceptibly, too fleetingly for Marty to notice. Hmph. For that matter, I didn't really notice either. I mean, I stay on automatic. So of their own accord my keen eyes saw her soulful ones squinch ever so faintly when Marty jestfully called me culprit. But I was too distracted to interpret the observation. Marty pivoted his craned head to look at me. "Jack Moore—Milagros Dixon," he introduced.

Slightly, I inclined my noggin. "My pleasure," I said, twice overjoyed. Once for being brought into the radiance of her acknowledgment, then again for not being introduced as *Kerwin*.

Two or three of her meticulous braids had escaped the corral of her headband when, I suppose, she had stuck her gorgeous head into her file drawers. In a gesture that was as serviceable as it was graceful, one unpolished but neatly clipped fingertip tucked the dangles behind her ears. To my eternal gratitude, the masterfully sculpted lines of her Nubian face came fully to my scrutiny, an unveiled work of art to an esthete. And did baby have lips! Full and pouty and kissable irresistible. And I—personally and directly— was about to be addressed by them! Perhaps, I dared to hope, they would speak my name or say (with the underlying, suggestive tone I was already scanning for) how much the pleasure of our introduction was hers. In happy anticipation I started formulating a charming rejoinder when (at last) my proud beauty spoke.

She looked at her watch. "It's almost time for Lizette's session," she said impatiently. Then she looked to Marty. *"He* should've been here." Brusquely, without in the slightest acknowledging my existence, the lady brushed past us to her desk.

Marty started speaking to her back. "But he drove all the way from Manhat...." And fizzled the fuck out as Milagros Dixon seated herself and glowered at him.

Some champion. His token defense of my worthy cause routed by a gaze. "Well. I'll just be off then," declared my hero, beating a full and undisguised retreat to the door. "See you, Jack," he called over his shoulder. Before I could even mumble a good-bye he was gone.

I was confused. Not by Marty's summary departure. That, clearly, was just a matter of his knowing when his precious therapist was in need of therapy her-mothafuckin-self. Instead, what confused me was why she was relapsing over me.

"Please be seated, Mr. Moore," she said, and not too very sweetly, I might add.

Warily, I approached and obliged. "Ms. Dix—"

"You are the *man* who took Lizette to the hospital?" she interrupted, saying man like a dirty word.

"I am. Now—"

"*And,*" she emphasized, looking to the open folder on her desk, though (I think) more to avoid looking at me than to check her info, "you did not report the very violent sexual abuse of a minor to the police."

"Well, I—"

"You also were the *person* who *found* her, Mr. Moore—is that not correct?"

I almost smiled. Talk about extracting the most from the least. You felt almost ashamed to be a person, the way she said it.

"This is a true thing," I say.

Shrew Dixon slapped the folder closed, startling me somewhat. "Mr. Moore," she said, at last deigning to cast her soulful and hostile eyes upon my mug. "Did you rape Lizette?"

Well, well. Bless my soul. So that's why shed been regarding me like I was her monthly cycle—the faggot-ass mothafucka. Certainly the deduction was understandable, even inevitable. But that didn't stop me from wanting to tell the heart stopping beauty, whom I still wanted to slay, to suck her mammy's dick.

Last Laugh

"Ya know," I said really calmly because I was really angry, "my heart breaks. My inmost desire is to accommodate you, but the very first thing you ask me and I must tell you no."

The lady blinked. It was so unfortunate, but unless given reason to assume otherwise, even black-thinking black folk expected other black folk to speak thuggish—which I was, even as I was not.

But my beloved was not nonplussed for long.

"Really?" the punk ass mothafucka says, her voice full of raised eyebrows. Raised eyebrows and scoffs.

I nod my head Milagros Dixon looks at it as though sizing it up for the axe. Very deliberately she pushes back from her desk and leans back in her chair.

"Mr. Moore," she says, "the only reason you are answering questions here instead of in a police station is because of Lizette."

"I—"

"Her recovery to date is tenuous, Mr, Moore," her sultry voice interrupts. "At the moment Lizette finds the thought of your arrest distressing."

"She—" The punk mothafucka does the stop-sign thing with her delicate little hand and looks away.

"Don't find too much refuge in that, Mr, Moore. It's common for sexually abused children to protect their molesters." Then, like a sinuous river, the woman flows to me—which is to say she leans forward in her seat, as though to whisper conspiratorially into my ear. I inhale her as her soulful eyes look at me—murderously. I bask in her as her kissable irresistables delicately part—and snarl. "But that misguided protection never lasts, Mr. Moore," my *preciosa* threatens. Her silence after seems to be pointed, as though expecting me to panhandle her for a stay of' execution or something. I just look at her. "Well?" she prods.

I use my most innocent voice. "You mean I may speak now?"

She recoils so suddenly the braids she'd tucked behind her ears fly out like serpent tongues. "Don't toy with me, Mr. Moore. Despite the setback it might mean for Lizette, I'm *that* far," she snaps her fingers, "from turning you in. So I very strongly advise you to cooperate with me." Then she wags a finger under my nose to be stern, I imagine, though all I see is something to nibble. "So spare me your attempts at wit. Do you understand?"

I tell ya, baby made my knees weak and was utterly beguiling even while implying I could go to hell. Still, enough is a-mothafuckin-nuff. "I understand you think your outrage has a leg to stand on. But actually, Ms. Dixon, *never* did a more crippled thing *ever* hobble the planet." The lady's mouth plopped open like a fish. "Don't get your gall bladder in an uproar," I console. "Actually I think it quite a good thing that you assume the worst about me." I guess because she didn't know what to do with that, she looked stupid. You know. Like a jackass stage actor who's forgotten her lines. Of course, one monkey, one fish, or one jackass could not be permitted to stop the show, which in this case was my explanation. Thus I continued. "Too many children are abused. So suspicious people like you who ruthlessly seek and destroy are needed. But, Ms. Dixon, occasionally you should examine the throat you've put your death grip on before you squeeze it." The dumb-critter look an instant of doubt had a moment ago put upon her face was now a knowing smirk—which didn't know a damn thing and so was equally dumb. I mean, her expression declared she'd found a cure for AIDS when all she really had was a recipe for bullshit. "Don't look so triumphant," I advise. "I speak truly, even if one—" *like you, you gorgeous punk ass mothafucka* "—might construe my remarks as defense."

Annoyance flits across her face and away. Evidently she doesn't like being anticipated. *But that's your problem.* Somewhat methodically, Milagros picks a pen up from her desk. Both her lovely hands fingerfuck it as she takes a moment to rally her momentum, contain her annoyance. Whichever. There was room for elbows and some more stuff in the space before she spoke.

"Now that you mention it, Mr. Moore, that's precisely how I construe your remarks."

Now I know it's supposed to be true that to be forewarned is to be forearmed. None-the-damn-less, I was disappointed. When I came through the door I was a child molester. Now that I had spoken I was a *lying* child molester—*that* was Milagros Dixon's position. And since I don't argue people out of positions, I, with prodigious reluctance and disappointment, had to un-ass my fantasy about fucking her. And instead had to fantasize about being far outta Dodge before my beloved called the cops.

"Well," I said quietly, as though not planning a thing, "that's your prerogative," *faggot ass mothafucka*. My unvoiced addendum was not without a little justification. After all, I risk my life to save somebody and gotta take it on the lam in consequence.

Not that Milagros cared a lick.

"You fucking *monster.*"

See what I mean?

"I am *sick* of your charade." Angrily, she snatches up the phone.

I look around for a hogtie. *Who're you calling?* I almost blurt. But Milagros would've correctly translated that as *Are you calling the cops?* Since I had no doubt that she had no problem lying to me, I struck my nonchalant pose and spoke calmly in a hurry.

"Be sure you inform the police that I appeared here voluntarily." She looked up at me with her angry eyes and I prayed she wouldn't compound my disappointment. I mean, hers were lips to be bruised with kisses—but she was one wrong word away from being gagged with her exquisite headband.

"Oh, don't think I wouldn't love to explain that in a court proceeding, *Mr.* Moore," she said, making Mr. sound like a mouthful of horse shit. "But my first duty is to the child you brutalized. You will confront her. Right here and right now."

Ah. No cops. Now there was a response I could live with. As discreetly as I had tensed I relaxed. "Ain't that unorthodox?" say I, as though binding and gagging her had not just a nanosecond ago been my agenda.

Milagros answers by again flashing the stop-sign palm in my face.

"Casandra?" she says into the receiver. "Is Lizette Reyes here yet? Good. Would you send her in now, please." She hung up, folds her hands atop her desk and, well, *scrutinizes* me. Literally. As if I were some especially nasty microbe on a glass slide *Probably looking for a squirm or a facial tic,* I deduce and suppress a smile.

"Aren't you afraid that actually laying eyes upon the monster will traumatize Lizette?" I ask—provocatively. But then I never did have a lick of sense. Steam trickles outta Ms. Dixon's Thousand Petal Lotus. You know. The energy center the Taoists and Buddhists and Yogis say emits from the middle of the top of the head. But, maybe because Lizette was on her way, she puts her boil on simmer.

"The sight of you might unsettle her," she conceded. "But frankly, Mr. Moore, Lizette's progress is impeded by her refusal to acknowledge your role. Confronting you unexpectedly like this will no doubt make her afraid—but that will be an acknowledgment and perhaps the basis for Lizette's genuine improvement."

"Perhaps?" I say, before I realize my mouth is opening widely enough for my foot. "How generous of you to play Pig In the Poke with somebody else's psyche."

From the way her face screwed up and her eyes started going ga-ga I am absolutely certain that that observation from me, the "culprit", was over boiling her kettle again. Mercifully, however, before the lady could do more than swell the fuck up with apoplexy, the door opened.

Isn't life ironic? Once a door opened and a lion rescued a hare. Now another opens and the hare rescues the lion—from the consequences of his big mouth, among other things. I wasn't mad. Indeed, thankful for her timeliness, I swing around in my seat and watch my diminutive saviour damn near tiptoe into the office looking all school girlish and shy. Until she sees me.

"Jack!" she exclaims, and sprints a blue jeaned streak across the room.

I barely had time to unseat myself. "*Hola, manita,* "hello, little sister, I say to the top of the plastic butterfly hair clip holding Lizette's coif in place. That was all I could see of the little girl. The rest of her face was buried in my solar plexus while her boa constrictors hugged me to death. Poor baby. Her tremulous hug conveyed vast relief, as vast as her spirit was heavy. Gently I extricate one of my arms from the child's gorilla vise.

"Hey!" Gently I tug at her hair clip. "There's a butterfly in your hair."

Sluggishly, hollowly, she sort of giggles. "Silly rabbit." She looks up at me with her sad smiling face and holds me in half a hug. "That's to hold my `do." The hand that composed the other half of the hug resettles the butterfly in the nest of her hair with a fussy exactitude, which I note is a joyous shade of the finicky, self-respecting self she was before Felito.

"Well, so it is," I acknowledge. Unobtrusively, I steer her to the chair I just vacated. Lizette sits very primly and looks at the floor. I stand very watchdoglike and look like I'm not looking at Milagros.

LAST LAUGH

And suppress a smile—again. From the befuddled look on the good therapist's face, her expectation and Lizette's behavior are pieces from two different puzzles. See? The good therapist was all set to watch a psycho-drama and a PG movie comes on. But if the quandary did knock her to the mat, she got off her butt, which I knew was a gorgeous dew drop even though I'd yet to see it, nimbly.

"Good morning, Lizette," she says in a pleasant, unruffled manner. Lizette, still looking at the floor, is conspicuously subdued.

"Good morning," she whispers. Both my beloved antagonist and I wince. *No child should sound so forlorn*, we separately observe, and so, at last, finally do something together: we make pained expressions. Of course, partly because of my socialized male consciousness I hide my pained expression behind a blank face. However, as the female of the species, Milagros has not been socialized into emotional fakery. Thus her aching heart gets flashed—momentarily. For therapeutic reasons, I imagine, she tucks her emotion away almost as quickly as it appeared.

"Your hair looks gorgeous today," she says gaily, *distractingly*, because she is, after all, a good therapist. "Did you style it yourself?"

Lizette continued staring a hole in the floor. "Yes."

"I'm impressed," Milagros gushes. Her voice rings with rainbows and flowers, but I hear the sucker punch inside. You know. The Confrontation Lizette's gonna get hit with when she blinks. "It couldn't be lovelier...," and so on Milagros lullabies. Seemingly forever. Like she was gonna pour the *whole* bottle of *Ain't You-Mama* syrup on this one pancake.

Lizette's lovely little face turns up to me. Searchingly; inquisitive child to sagacious father. "Do we *have* to listen to this stuff?"

Milagros' mouth drops open like that sucker fish again. I am charitable enough to not guffaw.

"Don't be testy," I say and mush her chidingly in the head. "She's trying to help you," I playfully mush her again. "You should—"

"That's right, Lizette," Milagros cuts in, retaking control. "I'm sorry if I've annoyed you. I want only to help."

I steal a glance at her and a tiny bit of the smile I've been on-and-off suppressing squeaks out. From the strain in her features

I see how terrible it is for her to find herself siding with me, even if for the professional need to assert just who's running the show.

But our adult shenanigans don't interest Lizette. Huffily, she twists away from my touch. "But she's trying to make me tell her, Jack. She's trying to make me break my promise. She—"

"But you *must*, child," Milagros beseeches. Mama-like she reaches for Lizette. Probably meaning to snatch the child from the clutches of Misguided Loyalty. Whatever, Lizette wasn't having any.

"*No!*" she shouts, recoiling from Milagros' hands like they were dripping with the heebeegeebees. In a breath she slips out of the seat and hides herself behind me. "I don't wanna come here anymore, Jack." Her delicate arms snake around my waist. "Please, can we go home now?"

I turn slightly so I can put a piece of a hug back on her. And to further refine my spirit and enlarge the annals of my good deeds, I even give no indication that I see the look on Milagros' puss. Gone is Mighty Righteous Woman, able to leap to ugly conclusions in a single bound; come is Soopa Stoopid. Apparently, this is *not* how The Confrontation was supposed to go.

"Tell you what, *manita*. Why don't you wait for me in the—"

"With Casandra," Milagros suggests. I look to her askance. She sits hunched and tensed on the edge of her seat. It was difficult for her, I am sure, but her whole posture was a begging bowl incarnate imploring me to concur.

So, what the hell, I throw the proud beauty her alms. "How 'bout that?" I ask Lizette, and tuck a finger under her chin to hoist her head up so we could do the eye-contact thing. "Would you mind waiting with Casandra?"

Lizette's glance evades mine.

"Hello, down there," I tease. "A little cooperation from your eyeballs would be appreciated."

After a stubborn moment more, which I welcome since it heralds her returning egostrength, she attends me. "O-*kay*," she whispers, most begrudgingly. "But can we please just go home afterward, please?"

"Certainly," I prevaricate. See, I don't mean quite what she means. *She* means five minutes after Casandra. *I* mean if and after the good therapist Dixon nips the bait I'm'a set for her. But my reassurance is essentially true and, anyway, gets her gone. Together Milagros and I watch her trudge away. Out of the corner of an eye I look at my now somewhat wilted passion flower. Damn if I don't feel like we're a couple of hand-wringing parents. You know. Ambivalently watching our first-and-only trudging off to Summer Camp Swamp Dog. *Don't fret, dear. She'll write,* I wanna say. So (what the hell) I do.

"Don't fret, dear. She'll write."

"What?" inquires my beloved.

"I was saying that we should speak bluntly. Is that all right with you, Ms, Dixon?" The outlines of the anger she had so painstakingly nurtured for me try to reappear in her face.

"Mr. Moore," she intones, again stuffing a stink bomb inside the bland wrapping of my name.

I tilt my head and eye her quizzically. Damn. Her anger might've been all dressed up but (after Lizette's behavior towards me) where, pray-tell, could the gussied-up mothafucka go?

Happily my would-be nemesis is...I dunno: gracious, honest— *something* enough to accept when the party was canceled. "Very well," she concedes, like a whining kid saying *all riiight.*

But the concession does not appease me. I shake my head. "I'm not sure you understand, Ms. Dixon. I mean, raw dog talk. No niceties, no bullshit of any sort." I stare my hardest stare at her. "Like, don't say 'ignoramus' if you mean 'bitch mothafucka.' Are you capable of such a thing, Ms. Dixon? For the sake of the child you seem so concerned for?"

Fear overcame her for a moment. I didn't fault her. After all, she was no longer convinced I was a maniac animal, but she wasn't sure I was not. Hell, when you add to that ominous possibility a disconcerting stare and a construably "sinister" request, the lady would've been stupid to not be fearful. She was, however, also an intrepid mothafucka. Thus fear bound her like a straight jacket bound Houdini.

"I don't think candor requires vulgarity," she firmly asserts and thrusts out her chinny-chin-chin. A thousand pardons, O God of Gender Equality, but once again I found myself suppressing that same persistent smile. I mean, the woman was meaning to look resolute, I'm sure, but all my eyes saw was adorable. In any case she was saying, "…for Lizette's sake I'll accommodate you in substance, Mr. Moore."

"Fine," say I, not incidentally noticing that this time she hadn't made Mr. Moore sound anything like Mr. Dog Shit. "Now let's see if I have this right: you think I raped Lizette because she won't talk about what happened." I can see that her clinical mind wants to nit-pick so I open my mouth to protest.

"All right," she forestalls, because she sees that I see. "That is essentially correct."

"Good. Now here comes the tricky part, Ms. Dixon," I say, as if I've got it all figured out. I don't. However, the only reason I don't wonder what the hell I'm doing is because, like I say, I ain't got a lick of sense.

Or why else would I prepare to confess multiple homicides to a stranger?

Indeed, to underscore how dumb I can get, my face smiles at the grave risk to which I, with every appearance of rationality, am recklessly delivering my ass. "The tricky part is speaking the truth. Not logical conclusions or facts or what side of the prevailing custom you're on, but speaking truly—saying *exactly* what you feel. Whaddup wid dat, Ms. Dixon? Can you pull that breed of rabbit outta your hat?"

She smiles, and (I must tell you) never did a more glorious thing illuminate creation. "I'm afraid the distinction you're positing might be a bit too philosophical for me—homey."

Homey? I do a mental double-take. First she takes the nasty out of *Mr.*; *then* she favors me with a smile; *now* she lapses into the intimacy of our native tongue. *Could this,* I wondered, *be the start of the crossing of our swords? Were our sabres gonna rattle? Were we moving towards The Duel?* You know. The clash *we* win when I run her through and she surrenders for victory. Inquiring minds wanted to know. And *would*, by the Kinky Naps of Moses—if the next feint I survived.

"Well, let us see if we cannot learn by doing," *my beloved.* "For example," *(you fine ass mothafucka)* "how do you feel about child molesters?"

The softness that her smile had left on her face like a rainbow after a delicate shower vanished as though it had never been. I mean, like, *poof!* and the tender beauty had become a gargoyle with

LAST LAUGH

a bunch of rocks in her jaws. *Damn if she don't look like she needs an exorcist*, think I. *An exorcist with a BIG damn cross*. But I am cool, and in any case, my question is answered by her transformation. "Wonderful," I say in response to her expression. "Now—specifically—what would you suggest for such a one?"

"Castration," she spits right out. Then, after a thoughtful pause, her musical voice continues to regale me with her vision. "Brutal castration. Something along the lines of Loraina Bobbit with a can top." Somewhat cunningly she looks at me and her smile bursts with great good humor. "And of course no anesthesia." Through their own volition, my balls retreat into my lower abdomen. Milagros Dixon, however, is oblivious of my agony. I think. At least the way she smiles and casually tucks another of her errant strands behind an ear suggests that telling the rabbit how lovely his foot would look on her key chain is perfectly all right. "Furthermore, Mr. Moore, I would additionally recommend that such a person's last meal consist of his genitalia." Angrily, laughingly, her eyes inspect me. She is looking for something, but (significantly) not for that squirm I cheated her out of earlier. "Is that blunt enough for you, sir?"

I smile a little smile. What a damnable world we live in, wresting the worst from even the best of us. "Only if you mean it."

She smirks and throws back her head, a wild and glorious stallion. "Have no doubts about that."

My gangsta heart weeps. The genteel lady's surety is right and necessary but as apropos as a butterfly with fangs.

How unfortunate, I think. "How wonderful," I say. "But, ya know," I take a moment to sneer, "I bet if you had a Catholic priest or one of those other mass molesters we're always hearing about all trussed the fuck up right here," I thump her desk with a fist to help convey the emotion I don't feel, "you wouldn't do jack." Then I appear to size her up. "You wouldn't do jack *bone*." Naturally, the right honorable sista went through the offended routine. She drew the deep breath, looked the affronted look, parted her kissable irresistables to issue the Indignant Denial. Then, alas, undid herself. I mean, all her reflex indignation deflated like a pricked balloon.

"Well," she began, very undefiantly, "you may be correct, Mr. Moore." She smiles a wry smile. "If I had the stomach to do it, the legal consequences would deter me."

Thoroughly let down, I smile back. "So you just talk," I say triumphantly, as if my plan was not routed by her acquiescence.

Clearly irritated, Milagros shakes her head. "Not at all. You asked what punishment I think fits the crime and I answered. Whether *I* could impose the punishment." One elegant hand gestures negligently. "Well, that's another question entirely."

I slap both hands on her desk and lean forward in my seat until I am quite in the lady's face. "So let me see if I have this straight: you're a coward. You think guilty molesters should lose their balls as long as someone else does the cutting."

The lady blinks. "And the penis too," she says—a little personally, it seems to me. "Don't forget that part, Mr. Moore." Pointedly, she withdraws her gorgeous self away from me. Just in time too. I mean, I had got ringside to her eyelashes because in war the least nuance the enemy communicates is helpful. So if any part of her said no while her lips were saying yes I wanted to see it. But (I gotta tell you) the near hand-to-hand proximity was too delicious. Indeed, to my thirsty eyes my irate, somewhat erstwhile foe had begun to look like a Slurpie, but—more importantly—a *sincere* Slurpie. I relax my intense act but still play.

"But wouldn't execution be kinder?"

"*Too* kind," she says, sounding annoyed. And impatient. In fact, I would've been surprised had she not next asked: "But what is the point of all this?"

To see how you feel about dead rapists, is what I think. *To get you the fuck off my back.* But: "Call for Lizette," is what I tell her. "She'll explain."

STICKIN' TIGHT

Alabama looked evil. You might think that at 3 a-mothafuckin-m. there were other places his big, bald headed ass would rather be than hiding behind the front passenger seat of a minivan. On the floor. He probably did have other druthers, I'd mothafuckin' bet. But the fact is Alabama looked evil because it was the only face he had.

Right now his one-and-only was looking through a smoked glass window across a two-way street. "That's six," he said.

Bakari's six-foot-five was scrunched down between the second and third row. His gaze had been following Bama's. Three flashily dressed Al-Capone class mothafuckas were disappearing into a modest two-storey house. "Check," Bakari confirmed. "That's two. One to go."

Bama watched the screen door kick the last of the three thugs in his pasta fazul. "Check." he said quietly. "Six—and three to go."

Bakari returned to wiping his fingerprints off the last of what had been a handkerchief full of bullets. Lovingly, as though gently, gently fingering some sweet thang's clit, his surgically gloved hands eased each newly polished slug into a jumbo banana clip. "Check," he said. "Two and one."

ATIBA OMAR

Me? I sat in the van's ass end on the right tire hump like the ignoble bump on the log. Very unprofessionally, I might add.

Oh, I was sufficiently attentive to the police scanner peeking at me from a partly unzipped bowling ball bag on the floor between my feet. Hell, how could I not be attentive when the damn Miracle Tech receiver plug ("for that discreet and comfortable fit!") was jammed into my ear and was not a comfortable fit at all? And in a further professional discharge of my duties, I was the spirit of the patrol cop ("Help! Send back up! Three teenage blacks congregating! Help!") on his Bitch Button. Which is to say, I had a hair-trigger finger poised to transmit on my walkie-talkie. But dereliction of derelictions, when from the dark recesses of the van's ass I had looked out through the dark glass clearly, instead of seeing six gumbas as 'Bam had (because he was counting *all* arrivals). or two gumbas as Bakari had (because he was counting *only* capos), I recalled seeing just the last group of three.

And Milagros Dixon.

What the fuck she was doing here (*all* up in my head), I dunno. I thought I had shaken her loose when I'd left her office yesterday... All right: I thought I had shaken her loose when I had awakened this morning... Well, all *damn* right: I thought I had finally shaken her loose when the first crew of three Mafiosi had swaggered by. Despite my most extricating effort, however, homebaby was dogging me like New York's Finest dog payola. I guess her dogging me was inevitable. Without question the last expression I'd seen on her mug was quite memorable. Something like an embarrassed fish with frightened, admiring eyes. That's after I'd coaxed Lizette into telling her what'd happened. Bless the child's soul, but my little Lord Protectoress had refused to rat me out even at my insistence. Only after I'd convinced her that omitting particulars (like body count and location) was better than having Milagros turn me in, only then did my miserly Lizette dole out a pinched penny of a story.

It was edifying to see Milagros look stupid.

All at once the heavenly mothafucka seemed human—hence vulnerable, hence even more desirable, hence unforgettable.

Hence here she was in the back of a van unforgotten.

Stickin' Tight

Huh, woman? I asked again of the smirking mind-image intruding into the moment. *Huh, woman? Whatcha doin' here?* But all the image did was wink at me and smirk some more.

"Another ride comin'," Alabama whispered, the swoosh of a Saracen's blade slicing through the night.

I looked up. A long four-door had pulled up to the house. It seemed to want to park but couldn't. For one thing, there was no place. For another, had there been a place this car couldn't've fit. Parking spots tended to match the size of average vehicles, a driver's instinct, I guess. That generally meant compact, which completely x-ed out this Mafia-mobile. Word. It was longer than our van. A classic gas-guzzler. Probably the last such Mohegan Buick had manufactured when all the patriots started buying imports. For a long moment the car's occupants just sat there. The nerve! Like they were staking out the house—the house that *we* had staked out first!—the weaseling so-n-sos. Soon enough, however, they decided something because the front passenger door opened and a typical homegrease got out.

Immediately his quadrant of the car raised about 15 degrees. It was no wonder. To the delight of the Buick's chassis, this triple Fat-Paulie type Mafioso had dislodged his extra-meatball-and-sausage hero from the car. Ponderously. Yo. Watching homegrease a'struggle out the car was not unlike watching a fat newborn hippo struggling turd-like outta its mama's ass-quarters. Made you wanna scrunch up your nose. But I was not so contemptuous as to be allayed. To the contrary, as homefats took two Sumo stomps to open the rear passenger door for his master, I thanked the Gods that my 9mm rounds were Rhino Bore. However, if Fat (but not to be "slept on"/taken for granted) Paulie was a regular at the Mo' Mozarella restaurant, his boss was a *live*-in at said establishment. Verily, you could almost hear the Buick's axles scream *Thank you, Jesus!* when this other triple Fat-Paulie type removed himself from its rear.

"That's Little Bones," Bakari observed.

I nodded, but actually what I was understanding was that it was neither for nostalgia nor patriotism that these dudes were riding a "classic." Their choice was based on fit. The car idled (probably to get its breath). Fat Paulie One helped the squatter, softer-looking Fat Paulie Two wheeze his way to the sidewalk. Having thus gotten his waddle jumpstarted, Little Bones (a veteran capo of the

D'amato family) waddled the rest of the way to the house under his own choo choo.

"That's a cold muddafudda there," Bama apprises us.

Mentally I hmph. "And rollee damn pollee."

Fat Paulie watched until his boss was safely shoehorned through the door of the private house, Then he stepped back to the car, spoke through the passenger window. The car moved off. Fat Paulie straightened. And looked dead the fuck at our van. He just stared for a moment. Possibly tripping about the vantage point it had of the house. Whatever. I didn't wait for his pinball to drop.

"Down," I whisper and zip the bag with the luminous police scanner all the way closed.

Bam slides under the front seat; Bakari slides under the second. I pause only long enough to check that the flaps are down over the back legs of the specially rigged car seats. Quickly I note that neither gun butts nor butt-butts protrude, then slide my own McDoogle under the third seat. Some mysterious how one of my 9s has materialized in my left hand. What the fuck for, I dunno. My forearm is pinned to my chest and if I pull Little Sista's trigger I'll blow my jaw off. Still, holding her makes me feel better.

Being under the seat, however, does not feel better, does not feel good—is a mite damn tight, in fact. Empathy for my *compadres* explodes in my head: Alabama was big and Bakari was long. I mean, we had prepared the van for this disappearing act and it worked just fine. But even after a dozen rehearsals cramped was still cramped. I imagine they felt like a couple of dead Pharaohs all wrapped up and sarcophagused . Or, perhaps, like bound warriors in the belly of a slave ship. But I had no attention to spare for analogy. Sho' nuff, the light sprinkling of gravel I'd laced discreetly around our vehicle and (for verisimilitude) all up and down the street crunched. Then crunched louder as the behemoth approached. I chided myself that if I ever do this hide-under-the-seat shit again I'll have my head at the street-side of the van so I could better hear what's going on. Indeed, when the crunching stopped I was just fit'n to wonder if I should start imagining that Fat Paulie's face was pressed inquisitively against the smoked glass window. Then he saved me the trouble. The whole van listed to port. My God. What (I gleaned), what a *humongous* mothafucka he was. Just leaning incidentally against the vehicle to peer inside it and

STICKIN' TIGHT

the whole mothafuckin mini-van leaned to one side like a Homburg cocked ace-deuce-trey.

We waited. Bama, Bakari and I. Without rustle or audible breath. Like three babes in the cradle—or heap big Injuns in the grass. You know how it goes. When a true warrior is trapped like a helpless babe, it is still a coin-toss as to who has the drop on whom.

The van righted. Part of my mind screamed, *Now, mothafucka! Jump out and blast!* because my imagination just knew that Fat Paulie had either pulled some anti-aircraft guns from under his big half-a-slab-of beef armpits and was fixin' to wet us down or that he was signaling for a posse to encircle us. But— crunch crunch crunch— the van rocked backward. Evidently Sumo-san was now peeking through the rear. I could imagine the facial imprint he'd leave. Probably as high and wide as one of those giant boulder heads those ancient Afrikan mariners left all over Mexico. I scoffed. *Look on, mothafucka.* See. That's exactly why we'd chosen a van with windows, so if inquiring Mafiosi wanted to look they could. Certainly a commercial van without side windows would've hidden us better. But then the mothafuckas—unable to see in—might've imagined we were the Feds or something. And since when was spooking your game how you bagged it? The van stayed pulled rearward under the weight of the behemoth, but the gravel went crunch Crunch CRUNCH. That meant that somebody else was coming.

"Whatsup, Bobby?" that somebody asked. The van righted.

"Just checkin'. Where you park? You know Lil' Bones don't like to walk." They moved off, the gravel crunching informatively under their feet.

"'Round the corner. But I could always drive up to the fronta the house when he's ready to leave."

"Yeah." Bobby's voice was growing fainter. "That's right."

I inhaled, slid from under the seat while my well-behave gat (the female of my twins) put on her safety and tucked herself away. Very very very slowly I sat up—all eyeballs, more than ready to draw forth both Sista and Bruhda like lightning bolts from hell.

Fully intent, I steal a look. Bobby Behemoth and his human-size companion were entering the house. "Everything cool."

"'Bout damn time," Bama grumbled, but softly.

"Word up, man," Bakari concurs, but softly.

I smile. They would've stayed there all night had I not sounded the all-clear. That's how our thing went. We divvied every job into what were effectively "theaters of operations," and whoever got what was its "general." I suppose that made me General Run-and-Hide-Everybody. If so, the troops would humor me to death. As I would them. Obedience came easily when you knew that the person you trusted was competent and cared about your ass.

"Wish I could smoke," Bama said.

I felt Bakari 'look' through the car seat at Bama. "It ain't bad enough you let them kracker sticks be the death of you, you want 'em to be the death of all of us, lettin' every Eye-talian in Queens know we in here."

Bama sucked his teeth. "I said *wish*, fool, I *wish* I could smoke."

I picked the Miracle Tech plug that dangled outta a hole in the bag off the floor. It worried me that I'd left it sitting there in my hasty dash to refuge under the car seat. Not because Bobby Behemoth might've seen it (he'd've had to have cat eyes to discern it in such dark and then have beau coup deductive acumen to make sense out of what it was). But as a child I'd contracted a nasty ear infection that even now I took pains to not re-experience. Vigorously I wiped the mothafucka off then squeamishly stuck it in my ear.

I looked up to see Bakari smiling at me. I think he winked. I was about to ask whaddup? when his head ducked back out of sight.

He whispered in his Watusi bass. "Yo. Bama."

"Whaddup, man?"

"If you kickin' for some nico-demus why don't you chaw on some tabbacky?" Bakari sounded quite concerned and reasonable, even if he was talkin' like a yokel.

"'Cuz I ain't got no chawin' *tabbacky*," Bama said testily, 'cuz he just knew he was being mocked.

"Well, pull your knees up to your big mouth and chaw on them." I swallowed my guffaw.

"Go 'head, muddafucka," Bama warned. "Go 'head 'fore I blast you."

STICKIN' TIGHT

Bakari was the voice of incredulity. "Blast me?" he asked. "The way you blasted that floor last month?"

He was talking about an accidental discharge during our last fund-raiser. Deliberately I laughed a little. Mostly to help Bakari twist them screws deeper into Bama. But partly because it was somewhat funny. Alabama—big, evil looking, country-talking high school exile—was an arms expert and meticulous planner. And he never wearied of flaunting it. That's why we good-naturedly enjoyed that during a getaway the master technician and weapons god had almost shotgunned himself in the foot.

Very loudly in the quiet confines of the van, Bama worked the slide on his Uzi. "I'm warnin' you," he, well, warned.

The top of his silencer peeked over the seat and my heart constricted. Not 'cuz I gave jackbone for his threat. But because it jarred a memory. Earlier in the week Bama had offered to thread the barrels of my twins for silencers. I had been appalled. To me that was tantamount to offering to change the sexual gender of my children. Bama and Bakari, however, were not as neurotic about their guns. Consequently their silenced gats spoke in tongues (so to speak), whereas mine just spoke, which was somewhat all right 'cuz I always shot economically.

Bama was still carrying on. "...don't wanna heah *one* mo' word outcha."

No doubt his gorilla antics would've menaced almost anyone else into cardiac arrest, but we paid them no mind. Indeed, though we never actually sat around and analyzed the psychodynamics, in the ineluctably tense moments before show time, somebody always ribbed somebody. You know: to ease tension, because more heads have been blown off by tension than by purpose.

"'Notha ride," Bama said.

We all sank lower, prepared to either count bodies or hide our own. But the ride rode up and on. A bunch of late-night revelers, it seemed to me, when the not especially steady, jam packed sports car cruised past my line of fire.

Made me think—

"I wonder if Skins' folks still on the road," Bama said.

—yeah. That. That is what the lone car on the quiet street made me think.

Bakari hmphed. "Should be in Antarctica by now, if they kept drivin' like they was supposed to."

"Should be," Bam agreed.

"Yeah," I two-cents-ed with some conviction, and I surely hoped I was right.

Pity poor Skins' grandma if I wasn't.

To lay their cross-signing, holy-water-sprinkling hands on Skins, crews of Mafia soldiers would've put the Catholic Inquisition to his granny, his mother, three sisters, younger brother, and whatever other 'moolie' was luckless enough to happen by the Collete family's plushly laid tenement apartment. In pursuit of a dollar, the Mafia would do anybody—that was their *raison d'etre*. Indeed, hadn't they gotten their start by doing their own? Shaking down mama and poppa store keeps, vegetable merchants, organ grinders and the mothafuckin monkey too. Prostituting little Anna from downa the block and Maria from arounda the corner. Charging unpayable 'vigorish' to all their *pisanos* just offa the boat? Ain't that how the American Mafia got its start? Honor? *Omerta*? *Omerta* sounded all good and noble in the movies. That's because the movies had changed and glamorized its meaning. But historically *omerta* (that is, "Don't snitch!") had been concocted only to keep Italians from telling the cops how they were getting roasted by other Italians. Off-screen, where script writers held no sway, organized crime families considered it their prerogative to dial 911 on rivals. Except that wasn't snitching because it was business. The honorable Mafia? Pa-mothafuckin-tooey. They started out as poor, ruthless and unscrupulous criminals. Now that they'd amassed googobs of money they (like the Kennedys and Rockefellers) had some legitimacy—because they were *rich*, ruthless and unscrupulous criminals. The things they'd done and continue to do to their own would make a knowledgeable white man volunteer to crush his own nuts in a vise rather than submit himself to their mercies. So you don't wanna think what they'd do to a 'moolie'.

Why in the fuck Skins thought he could play with that fire and not get burnt, I dunno. The dumb mothafucka even had some delusion about being 'made' honorarily. Can you imagine? Just because they used him. Mostly to set up other black dealers who dared to get their product from the Tongs. Just because of *that* he thought they might make his black ass an honorary Mafioso. The

STICKIN' TIGHT

sucker. Probably was ready to dance a jig when Don Vespuci (via a lowly underling) had asked him for a favor.

"Sho'!" Skins had said he'd said, too stupid to first ask what.

But after being told what the favor consisted of, he was not too stupid to know that his mouth had walked his ass into a corner. If he did what was asked they would have to repay him—with a bullet. If he didn't do what was asked, well, now that he knew the details, they would have expressed their disappointment—with a bullet. "Ya'll can count on me." he had enthusiastically assured them, figuring, I suppose, it was better to be killed later than just then. Forthwith he'd hightailed it to Bama, his 'enforcer.'

That was another joke.

See, Alabama shook down several dudes who'd gotten fat dealing crack or whatever. To him, a punk with money was just a punk with money. Dat all. Skins, however, thought he and Bama were kind of homeboys (Skins was from Mis'sippi). So he told himself that the weekly stipend he paid Bama was for riding shotgun on his territory and wasn't the punk dues everybody else was paying.

Anyway, Bama agreed to do the 'favor'—but with different flavor. "Best you get drivin' now, Skins," Bama had told him, "and be sure to take yo' fam'ly."

Skins had been nonplussed. Apparently he'd expected 'his' (ha ha) 'salaried' enforcer to rally an army in his defense. Not even after Bama let him keep the weekly fifteen hundred was Skins happy. But he did have some sense. He knew if the 'favor' wasn't done on schedule 'pizza deliverymen,' 'gas meter readers,' maybe even real NYPDs moonlighting as henchmen would be a-calling at his door immediately. If mission were accomplished, however, Skins would have at least one mo' day before the expectant good fellas stopped laughing wait-until-that-sucka-moolie-gets-here. Because every moment counted, Skins took his family and his refunded extortion payment and ran.

While Bama, Bakari and I ended up in a stolen van all tricked up for the occasion. I didn't quite like it. Skins was a weak link and a loose end. Bama had to know that, but bringing this fund-raiser to the table wasn't acting like it.

So I'd taken the time to point out the obvious: "Bama," I'd said, "if we do this stick-up and Skins gets caught or starts thinking he can bargain, whose ass you think he's gonna give up or trade?"

"Skins too scared to get caught and too smart to think he could sell us out. Anyway this's a *mama*-load, man." Bama had grinned—and still looked evil. "I'll take muh chances."

I could dig that. For two million cash (plus assorted mafia pocket change) and 20 kees of Mexican Mud, I could dig that plenty deep. But let me be clear. For different reasons no one in my crew wanted the dope. It just happened to be the reason the two mil was now sitting across the street.

Or was it?

I checked the time; searched for headlights; watched the occasional shadows pass behind the windows of the house. None of us knew just which of the three crews was bringing our goodies. All we knew was Don V. was crossing somebody. We didn't know why, though I, particularly, would not have given a mothafuck if I did. Hell, the cross (Brutus, Machiavelli, Rudolph Guiliani) was a routine Italian thang. It is, in fact, what they do. Not all Italians, of course, but enough of the mothafuckas so that you knew that the Back Stab was their systemic condition. So I cared not a whit why one Italian was wanting to cross another. What did get me, however, was that Skins' (ha ha) 'people' had been subcontracted into the mix. Ain't that a bitch? Like we couldn't figure that getting robbed by the 'nigga stick up men' was supposed to be the insult to the injury. Injury to the Italians getting crossed, I mean. Our insult was that we were afterwards expected to tra la la with the loot into some secluded place and wait around for Don V's people to give us shares —as handouts, I guess, 'cuz standing in welfare lines for USDA cheese had conditioned us or something. You know. To stand around and wait for handouts. Don Vespuci was gonna be upset. Instead of waiting around like the welfare recipients he expected, the 'nigga' stick up men were gonna take the loot and (like the Energizer Bunny) keep going and going and...

That's if the last batch of mobsters ever arrived. To distract myself I did my job. Which is to say I flipped the dial of the police scanner and scanned and scanned and—

"This gotta be it," Alabama said.

Sho' 'nuff, a Mercedes was rolling slowly up the street as though—

"Look like they checking for house numbers."

STICKIN' TIGHT

—yeah. What Bakari said.

At last the car stopped in front of The House. Two more gumbas emerged.

"Yep," Bama whispered, "that's the one we been waitin' on."

The 'one' he was referring to was Anthony 'Tony Beans' Salerno. Now that was interesting. Everybody and their mama knew that Tony Beans was a Vespuci soldier. He and a henchman walked up to the house carrying a valise. Wasn't that interesting? Didn't matter if it was drugs or dough—good old Don V had, apparently, sent us to rob himself. That was a subthought, however. When, like Fat Paulie's chauffer, the driver dropped his boss and pulled off to park I knew we had to improvise.

"Change of plans," I said. Because this was my assigned department and we were all just one big old clock, B and B just looked at me expectantly. "Because that last driver couldn't park," I explained while pulling on a ski mask, "what we gotta do is...."

*****

The dapper young man walked briskly to the house. You could feel his excitement. He was newly 'made,' I am sure, and so probably felt he'd miss out on something if he didn't hurry. Indeed, he bounded the steps to the porch door as if to keep the mothafucka from escaping.

His knock was cheery. "It's me, Gino."

I didn't hear anyone approach—but I did hear locks being undone. So did Bama and Bakari. Like twin bolts from hell, they streaked from the side of the house and put the bum's rush on Gino.

"What the—" something, he said before helping the door open by slamming into it. Me, I pushed a button.

"Yo," I whispered into the walkie-talkie.

Immediately, "See ya" came back.

I dashed like Jerry Rice for yet another touchdown and a heartbeat later slip into the house and am not surprised to find Little Bruhda in my right hand. I drop the walkie-talkie where it will fall and close the door behind me. From the way blood was oozing outta his skull, Gino's enthusiasm had carried him as far as it was gonna. The doorman (who was one of the other two remaining

Vespuci soldiers) would, like Gino, also never get to be a capo. I felt nothing, though passingly I wondered why Bama (or had it been Bakari?) had killed them. Usually our fund-raisers were clean. But no matter.

I stepped past the bodies and headed for the stairs. Before I got halfway up, I half felt/saw a blur on the floor below. It was Bakari. Headed for the kitchen and Bama. That meant of the seven remaining Mafiosi none was in the living room. On general principle, however, as I climbed the stairs I presumed that all seven were not in the kitchen eating linguini. Girlfriend, uncle—whosever house this was was gonna be aghast when she got home and found all the mess we made. More importantly for me, however, was that I had reached the second floor unaccosted and found the two bedrooms and bathroom exactly where Skins'd said they should be. But all the doors were closed. Decisions, decisions. While I paused to ponder the possibilities, my Spidey senses got to tingling again. I glanced back. Like a smoothly ascending shadow, Bakari was comin' up the stairs to join me. That meant someone was indeed in the kitchen with Bama—but (as I'd assumed) not all seven someones. Briefly Bakari released the snoze of his silenced Uzi to show me two fingers, meaning two greasers were somewhere about. I acknowledged the info by gesturing with Little Sista (now who had let her out?). Momentarily I felt like a contestant on Let's Make A Deal.

But only momentarily.

Before the game show host inside my head could ask, *What'll it be, sir? Door #1 ? Door #2? Or Door #threeeeee3?* some idiot whispered, "Shit! My phone's out!"

"Shut the *fuck* up!" a lesser fool warned, though (alas for him) too late. I put the brakes on my rice-paper walk by the first bedroom door. Without query Bakari, the tick to my tock, poured his shadow next to me.

"Fuck this," the first idiot whispered. "I'm gettin' outta here." I guess he had been looking out the window at the backyard because even as he spoke we heard a window sliding open. Guess he figured he could make the drop.

Why he also did not figure that he might run into a guy with a cell phone jammer and who had cut the house's phone wires, I dunno.

Stickin' Tight

However, his shortsightedness provided opportunity. While the dead man was 'escaping' (and thereby engaging the attention of his homedoggy), I stepped across the door and squatted down until I was damn near sitting on Bakari's size 14s. Of course, he understood right away (the Bowery Boys weren't the only ones with set 'Routines'), and took one giant step around me to stand directly in front of the door. Even before his feet were fully planted his silenced Uzi was going clack clack clack as he sprayed high and middle and low. See. The door opened inward and to the left. Anyone directly in front of it was now bear meat. Anyone to the left of the door was (for an exploitable moment) out of the game. The only thing to stop entree was if a mothafucka had painted himself on the wall where the door didn't swing. That's where I was headed. While the clack from the Uzi's housing mechanism was still resounding from bullet 19 or 20, Bakari kicked the door open and (tick and tock, baby) I frog leaped inside, even as his Daddy Long Leg was recoiling. I wasn't worried about the door rebounding into my back. Indeed, soon as I was in, Bakari shot it, The impact stopped dead as a door...nail, but he kept firing, entering as he did. Me, I was down in my Japanese toilet bowl squat. My gats ,like the stone giants of Egypt peering eternally into distance, looked the way before me. While I myself looked up at Bobby Behemoth. He was painted on the wall, all right. And his big knockwurst (or Genoa sausage) mitts clutched a big .44 that reminded me of that doorkeep at Felito's. Except in this dude's hand the gun was more a rosary than a weapon. In fact, he could've been praying because his eyes were squeezed tight and damn if'n his lips weren't moving. In one jump I was at Bobby's side while obligingly Little Sista tucked herself away. My left hand moved to grip the heaven-pointed barrel of Bobby's roscoe. Little Bruhda parked his nostril against Bobby's temple.

"Let go the gun," I suggest.

Bobby's eyes flew open and—more importantly—his hands did likewise. Without taking my eyes off Bobby, I passed the .44 back to Bakari. "Just be easy," I advised, and massaged the whale-size mothafucka for a back-up piece. "Turn very slowly and very slowly put your hands on the wall." I moved out the way so Bobby would have turning room for his 18-wheeler. Once in the Position, I massaged him some more. He had a wide damn sweat streak running down his ass but dat all. No gun or knife or anything. Unless you counted the hog-gagging roll of large denominations he had in his pocket. I passed that to Bakari too.

"Bobby," I say. His face clearly showed surprise at being addressed by name.

"Yeah." He speaks into the wall but his voice was clearly showing something too: that his balls (which had been shriveled little pitted prunes when the shooting had started) were re-inflating again. That's precisely what I'd been afraid would happen.

"Yo," I say, "you's one big mothafucka." I had one hand on his back as I spoke and damn if I couldn't feel pride and self-confidence undulate beneath his tee-pee size suit jacket like a sea monster rippling beneath the waves. Then I popped the question. "But do you know what Rhino Bore is?" The sea monster resubmerged—and I didn't blame it a bit. Bobby Behemoth (and his sea monster persona) probably ate .38s and 9mms for breakfast. Might even nosh on a .45 slug. But as every self-respecting gun toter knew, Rhino Bore was the trade name of unlawful fragmenting hollowpoint bullets. They'd kill the devil if you could hit Her. "That's right, Bobby, and I got a clip full of the mothafuckas pointing at your head. So whaddya say? Do you think we could go to the kitchen without any problem? Even though you're so big?"

"Sure," he said right a-damn-way. "Whatever you say." I back off. Thoughtfully Bakari had cleared the path of door fragments.

"Okay. Let's do the whole thing slowly. Out the door, down the stairs, to the kitchen—*slow*."

We proceed smoothly enough. Oh, he did stop a little short when he got to the doorway and saw a long, tall faceless Bakari-demon backing up just ahead of him. But dat all. We managed the route (down stairs, past dead bodies) sweetly. Bakari in front, me behind—just one big cookie with extra cream. We entered the kitchen. Five men sat around a table with their hands on top of it and their heads down.

"Took y'all long enough." The ski-masked Bama spoke without turning to look at us. I raise an eyebrow. *We weren't exactly getting crackers from the grocery store*, is what I want to say. Instead I suggest to Bobby that he lie face down on the linoleum and please keep his hands on his head.

"I'll start cuffin'em," Bakari volunteers.

Stickin' Tight

"Gonna haveta tie the two fat dudes up," Bama observes.

Businesslike. No slur meant. Just pointing out that our cuffs wouldn't fit around their calf-size wrists. But Little Bones misreads it.

"Who in the fuck ya think you're talkin' 'bout?" In a fury he raised his head. "Fuckin' moolie—you're not gettin' a-fuckin-way with this, I can tell you."

"Shut up, Bones." Tony Beans, keeping his head obligingly lowered, prudently advises. Bones sputters in his direction.

"Don't tell me to shut up. I know who this big nigga is." He glowers at Bama. "It's that goddamn country boy some of them jig dealers been squawking about. And when my people get through with him—" Bones now glowers at the masked Bakari. "—I'm gonna know who you are too. So all of youse, you'd better start hikin' back to Africa right now, you fuckin' moolies."

Beans looked sick. "Shut the *fuck* up," he said.

Bakari, however, was already putting the handcuffs he was holding back into his pocket. Part of me saw it. While part of me noticed (not for the first time) that contempt does give one a certain courage—and a certain stupidity. Ah, well. Into the waistline of my Sean Jean jeans I tucked my loud mouthed children and strode up to the prudent if inefficacious and trembling Tony Beans. The way his face was bent down towards the table the back of his neck could not have been more perfectly exposed. Without hesitation, I drop a hammer fist onto his medulla oblongata. He plops onto the table, lights the fuck out. On general principle, however, I turn his head backward, just to make double sure he's dead. Bones' jowls went slack when he saw his suddenly dead homey scromey. They were all 'made', for goodness sake. Didn't we moolies know we couldn't kill them?

I didn't—and apparently no one had informed Bama either. Because even before I'd made Beans look like Linda Blair in The Exorcist he'd already blown the recumbent Bobby a new head hole. Not to be excluded from the ranks of the uninformed, Bakari wet the flummoxed Bones and another dude at the table.

That left only one.

"Sorry," Bama apologized, "but yo' man got a big mouth." Shabataka! (that's one of my exclamations; 25th Dynasty for "Son of the Cat Man") but the soon-to-be departed mothafucka looked impassively at Bama and inclined his head. As if to say, *Sure. Business. I understand.* Before Bama could do him I looked away. No doubt the mothafucka would've just as stoically fed my moolie guts to his dogs. Still, I could not help hating to see a fearless cat like him depart.

"Got the loot?" I inquired of Bama, largely for distraction.

"Yeah." For portability, he started unscrewing his silencer.

"I'm gonna get the walkie-talkie and roll the two dudes in the vestibule," I inform him.

Bakari headed for the back door. "Yo." I paused in the kitchen doorway and spun to face him. "You didn't haveta do that," he says.

I shrugged. He was talking about killing Beans . "You know how it goes," I said.

He nodded. Easily I could've hid behind the fact that I had no silencer. But it was reassuring to my gumbanis that all our hands were equally dirty.

I stepped off to retrieve the walk/talk and rob the dead. When I returned, Bakari was just coming through the back door with Skip, who was as short as Bakari was tall. Between them was the half-dragged, half-carried remains of the would-be escapee.

"I see you got him," Bama said.

Our little phone-line-cutter-cum-cell-phone-jammer-cum-waylay-er huffed and puffed under the load. "I'm glad it was just one." Soon as the body was inside they unassed it.

"Now that they's all accounted for….." Bama hefted the valise onto the table that Tony Beans had been carrying. He opened it and there they were: 20 kilo bags of gimme-some-mo'. With a butter knife from the dish rack, Bama stabbed a bag, rolled up his mask and gingerly licked the dab of powder from the blade. His face went blank. Immediately I'm alarmed. *Poison!* And I actually start to reach for him when he bursts out laughing.

"Shush your big ass down, mothafucka," lil' Skip sensibly suggests. Bama winds down to a chuckle.

"Don't tell me," Bakari said.

For answer, Bama jabs the knife into another bag and licks a whole mess of the stuff off the blade. "You know I got a sweet tooth."

Stickin' Tight

"Why that—" I got out.

"Yeah." Bama smiles some more and shakes his head. "Don Vespuci is a dirty mothafucka."

"Well, what about the money?" Bakari asks.

"Yeah," I kick in. "That's a *good* mothafuckin' question." Bama shoves Beans' valise off the table, and the milk sugar in the open bags powders Little Bones' nose and the cavity in his head. With a little flourish Alabama put a second valise onto the table. And, I tell you, we gathered tighter round that suitcase than Lincoln's army around Dred Scott when they marched the courageous brother back to Dixie.

Bama's gloved thumbs poise over the latches. "Is she is or is she ain't my baby."

"*Stop* fuckin' around," all three of us said as one.

Bama laughs and—pop!—opens the lid. Me and Skip and Bakari heave one sigh. Bama threw the five assorted wallets and money clips he'd collected on top of the Ben Franklins and Co. When the rest of us added our finds, Bama closes the case and shoves it at me. I shove it across the table to Skip.

"You and Bakari ride together." Skip's face screwed up like he ate something nasty.

"Shit, man, I ain't climbing that fence again." Everybody chuckled. He meant the fence he'd have to climb—again— to return to his car.

"Short ass mothafucka," Bama said, "you can ride with me." Happily Skip shoves the case of money back at me—which meant I would have to climb the fence to get to the cleanest of the cars we had.

I sigh. "All right, hometown. Give me the keys." Skip hands them over.

"Don't break no traffic laws," he warns.

I pick the suitcase up off the table. Damn. Two million *dolores* was heavy. "Don't worry," I say, "If we get pulled over, we'll buy a precinct."

Bakari holds the back door open for me. "Or even better, shoot a cop."

NEVER A DULL MOMENT

White folks and their Star Trek mentality kill me.

During the Slave Era they ran into an irreconcilable contradiction: the need to prove that Afrikans were jigaboos—*and* the discovery that these very jigaboos were the architects of the pyramid culture, hence of Graeco-Latin civilization. Their solution to the Enigma of the JigabooSphinx?

Run from the past for their plagiaristic lives on a forced march to futuristic conception.

You know: all eyes *only forward* towards the new god Progress, while studiously ignoring the 'irrelevant' past.

Now, however delusion-salvaging the motivation, a march towards progress would be Christmas candy if the march were humanistic. You know. A beneficent pilgrimage through space-time. A systematic procession towards higher human development.

Instead, whadda we got?

—A demolished kitchen.

—A charred pan-thing.

—A proudly grinning seven-year-old boasting, "See, ma—I made it myself!"

Never a Dull Moment

That (kindly) is the metaphor of modern (that is, white) science as it microwaves its way through existence. Science for profit, science at any cost, science as cold and soulless as the lunar wastelands it extols. White folks, as they trek through the "final frontier" on a fancy without waste disposal problems, deny this. But one good size glob of spit entirely covers the whole speck of truth in their disclaimer. You know. The disclaimer they call history but is really psycho-cultural damage control. Don't take my word for it.

Just *look*.

Dat all. Forget 'expert commentary,' 'official version,' the prime-time self-adulations of a science without humanity. Just *look*. See what you see Are toxic wastes/dumps/household goods everywhere or not? And *see* all the experiments on unsuspecting people. *See* the radiation, the syphilis, the psychotropic drug, the testing of pharmaceuticals on dark skin children; *see* the biological weapons tests on GI Joe. AIDS? Nature unequivocally did not produce it. Ergo, a laboratory did. And isn't it strange that the CDC (which normally tracks down whatever mouse dropping or flea bite caused whatever disease), isn't it strange that the CDC has abandoned the search for the source of AIDS? And what about Ebola? Is it really mere coincidence that the Ebola outbreak started right smack dab up side against a US Army Biological Research Laboratory in Liberia? Hmm. . . To be polite, science in the hands of western quote civilization unquote has been a loaded gun in the hands of a child. That's why you can't freely eat the fish, the *vegetables*, for chrissake, and is also why a smog index is a normal (!!) weather report feature. Word. Every time you turn around white science goes, *"Oops! Sorry! Let's settle out of court!"* If it ain't radioactive fall-outs it's DDT; non bi o de gra da ble is a household word and you *expect* pharmaceuticals to cause law suits. Indeed, books and seminars and tv newsmagazine specials on *Is Your Workplace Killing You?*, and *How to Detoxify Your Home* are depressingly commonplace, and people ain't drinking bottled water because it's fashionable. *Shabataka*! You can't even be sure what you're *fucking* these days, or what genetically mutated abomination is in your shopping cart. Tell me I'm lying. As a *byproduct* of *white* scientific progress the ozone layer is doing the Energizer Bunny and the whole earth is on the verge of being a chemical spill.

Horrifically, as it is on earth it's getting to be in heaven.

Shitting its mighty shit on nature is not enough for the computer enhanced surround-sound orifices of the Science, the Progress and the Unholy Future. A god-complex fuels this Unholy Trinity. A god-complex that is really just the flipside of profound insecurity. Problem is this god-complex has an insatiable programming to despoil and is covetous of the very stars. *What a terrifying prospect!* Leastways every time a space mission blasts off I shudder. Fear of 'space junk' and its unpredictable aftermath is one dread. Global warming and pollution are others.

Mostly I worry for ET.

It looks good on the Big Screen (*every* whimsy looks good on the Big Screen), but the noble Star Trek 'Prime Directive' forbidding interference in alien social orders is (after make-up removal) doo doo. See. It ain't just the USS Enterprise that's 'seeking new life and new civilizations.' NASA and its euro-counterparts are too.

Therefore, ET is in trouble.

I mean, I don't ever recall pale-face sea voyagers respecting life and civilization on other continents. Do you? If anything, they've rampaged through the 'Old World' and the 'New World,' the '3d World' and the animal world like Kligons on warp drive. Now they wanna pretend they're Capt. Kirk. Ergo, God save the aliens.

Heck: God save *God*.

All these monster telescopes and space probes pouring megabucks into black holes are not entirely unmindful that there might be a Supreme Something out there. And Lawd help Her if they find Her. I know this is the United States of Denial, but even Republican subconscious can't dispute that white folks have an historical m.o. that puts Her Supremacy at risk. First they'll claim they discovered God (and you know what commercial jockeying that would mean). Next they'll tell God they want to trade. All the while they'll be sizing God up. *Hmph*, they'll scoff behind their treaties and trade agreements, *Her Infinite Person doesn't look so omnipotent after all. Mayhaps a few neutron bombs. . .* Yo. If the Supreme One has been blinking on European history She'd better have an Exit.

"Because damn if'n them devils (after causing widespread and severe adverse impacts in the environment of the universe) won't try to make a pot for Your goose."

NEVER A DULL MOMENT

I was warning the Beyond, of course, just in case She wasn't listening to the morning news. I was. Some cheery, prideful newscaster had just informed me that another space shuttle had successfully blasted off and how happy we all subsequently felt. *Why* she presumed that I dunno because what *I* felt was appalled. In effect the newscaster was telling me: a. Yet another venture to profit the coffers and curiosities of an elite economic subclass of white dudes has been undertaken at my financial and environmental expense; and b. White folks still ain't figured it out.

First, the b.s. about "…one giant step for all mankind" is b.s.

Jet propelling through the mesosphere might inflate mindless national pride—but *dat* all. The practical result of space missions were just another seven-year-old's pan-thing. Like atom splitting, their environmental, human and financial cost far, far exceed their gain—though not, of course, the insanities splitting atoms entails.

Second, white folks still have not learned: Just because you *can* do a thing doesn't mean you *should*. Like, just because you *can* manufacture genetic abominations doesn't mean you should; just because you can enslave people, exterminate nations, fuck a man in the ass doesn't mean you should. Likewise, just because you *can* punch yet another hole in *EVERYBODY'S* ozone layer doesn't mean you should.

But white folks (who prattle about justice but practice might-makes-right) still haven't figured that out.

"…mission will conduct experiments that may have some future application," the newscaster informed me.

Oh. A few billion definitely needed on earth today for a space-maybe tomorrow. That explained everything.

But I still didn't understand how these mothafuckas had the right to routinely damage the ecosystem without consulting anybody, as though the devastation the white minority inflicted on the earth left the innocent majority untouched. *That* I didn't understand at all. But then that was only me. The weird weather patterns which always followed space blast offs and landings bothered me too. Of course, the one weather report I'd heard that mentioned the spaceflight/weather tandem assured me that the supposition was childish. But then what other 'analysis' could you expect from the United States of Denial?

"Not admissions of guilt," I muttered as I puttered about my task.

It was a little after 6 a.m. I was shoving stuff into the pouches and pockets of a back pack squatting amid odds and ends on my bed. Into the center of the sack I'd already stuffed the rich filling: half a million cash *dinero*. Now I was affixing the nuts and raisins. Little Sista went into one pocket; a dozen loaded clips and several boxes of *Rhino Bore* filled a pouch. Here I put a .380, semi-automatic handgun, two clips and a box of ammo. There I put a small drawstring bag containing several wallets full of fake I.Ds. After finishing with a miscellaneous sprinkle (my trusty knife; a gun cleaning kit; handcuffs and what have you), the only stuff left on my bed was grenades. Four concussion. four frags, four incendiary. I paused, uncertain. All the pouches and pockets were full. I picked up a concussion (distinguishable from the other types by its smooth surface) and bounced it in my hand. I looked at the bag. Then at the grenade. Then at the bag again. *Hm.* If I took out the gunkit and cuffs…

"Fuck it," I said.

Like so many eggs upon a nest, I rested the grenades on the cash. Then zipped, snapped and velcroed ev'thang closed. The bag had a little heft to it, but it was my 'flight' bag, after all. You know. If the untenable occasion arose and I had to get gone, my adrenal glands would carry some of the load. Humming some old plantation tune, I moseyed over to my closet.

And to the open trap door in its floor.

Gently I set the bag down into its accustomed place. I made it myself, you know. Took me five months. One month to do the labor; four to find a suitable apartment. That's 'cuz I'd needed a vacancy above a vacancy. How else was I gonna cut through 5E's floor and keep cutting through 4E's ceiling? Sheeit. Come crunch time, God might not have an exit ready, but I sure the hell was gonna. The couple now residing below me of course had no idea that the 'sheet rock' ceiling of their bedroom closet was covered plywood. Although a rectangular frame of the original ceiling remained (because my bag did need a firm ledge on which to rest). if I dropped just-so through my opened trap door I'd be able to try on Mr. 4E's shoes. As though setting a baby in a cradle, I lowered the lid. Ordinarily I left it open when I was home, but ordinarily I didn't have more than a half million dollars. Until I got used to it, baby was in deep stash. I unscrewed the thumb-thick rod that was the trapdoor's handle. Into the subsequent 'knothole' I placed a sized bit of wood and—voila!—the floor was just a floor. I put my shoes and thangs back in place and (hoping that I wouldn't need a quick exit the one time shop was closed) headed for the shower. The screw-handle went into the trashcan between my bed and nightstand and my shoes and clothes went where they went as I peeled myself naked en route to the bathroom. I stepped a grateful foot into the tub.

And my beeper beeped.

"Motha*fucka.*"

Part of me wanted to pretend I was mishearing (the beeper was, after all, on my dresser in another room). But my ears were as attuned to the sound of my master as were a mother's to the cry of her child. So I'd have to find some other bullshit to sell myself. Muttering imprecations, I backtracked and retrieved the clothes I'd flung damn hither and blessed yon. I'd considered burning them, of course, but then realized that disposing of the 'evidence' was pointless, in this instance, 'cuz if the cops ever did get around to *thinking* about looking for carpet fibers or Mafia DNA on my clothes the party would be over. Yo, acquittal or conviction, if anybody just *accused* of wettin' and robbin' them mobsters turned up he'd end up in a tuna can.

I dropped the pile of incriminating clothing by my bed and bowed to my boss The Beeper. The number surprised me. Could it really be—

Reeeng. I picked up the phone, still squinting questioningly at the familiar number that, lo, these many years had never before shown its digital face therein.

"Jack!"

"Marty! So it was your beep. What's—"

"Jack, meet me at Mother Immaculate Hospital soon as you can. Ruth is dying."

*****

"I don't know what I'll do without her, Jack."

I groped for an appropriate response. It was now 12:30 p.m. and once again I was a sleepy and reluctant visitor to Marty's office. *It's too soon to worry about that now,* sounded about right. *So that's what I said.*

"It's too soon to worry about that now." Marty just stared at his desk, the past, the future....

Suddenly he jumped up. Walked resolutely pass me; headed for the door.

I turned to watch him. "Where ya goin'?"

"I gotta go back." He spoke as if entranced.

I got up and overtook him in two strides. Forthwith I draped an arm across his shoulders. A comforting gesture, *certainamente*, but also a practical one, for thus I steered him back to his desk and parked him behind the mothafucka.

Then I parked myself. "Marty. The doctors said her condition has stabilized."

He looked through me.

"They said there's nothing you could accomplish by remaining there."

He looked through me.

"And you yourself said you should keep busy to keep from falling apart."

At that he stirred.

"For Ruth, Marty. You've gotta keep yourself together for Ruth."

Marty's nostrils twitched.

Ah, shit. He's gonna cry. I whipped out my handkerchief—

Ah CHOO!

—and wiped a spray of snot off my hand.

Marty was aghast. "Oh! I'm so sorry."

I waved away his solicitude.

"Think nothing of it. In fact—" I pause to rub away a really tenacious glob of mucous. "—I bless you *personally*."

And why not? It was all cosmic. The sudden embolism in his wife's brain. The frantic call to me—of all people. How responsibly I went through the motions..... And motions is all they were, I confess: noises, gestures, customary responses. I mean Marty was my man, for real. For that matter, I (a black thug) was the closest thing he (a Jewish law-abider) had to a living relative on the entire eastern seaboard (and wasn't that especially cosmic?). And I loved

NEVER A DULL MOMENT

him to death. But I didn't even like his wife. Ruth, frankly, was a bitch. To know her for a moment was to fully understand why her parents had orphaned her ass (though one could of course argue that she became herself because she had been orphaned). Anyway, I myself never forgot her birthday or their anniversary and was always faultlessly polite. But that was for Marty. Spare me the folderol about not speaking ill of the dead (or near-dead, in this case). Ruth was a bitch on wheels when she was healthy. Now that she was comatose she was a bitch on life support. Dat all. Nonetheless, I had said a heartfelt prayer on her behalf, (maybe you heard?).Because Ruth Feldstein might've been a real and true bonafide bitch but (after all) she was *Marty's* real and true bonafide bitch.

"…..thanks for being there for me," he was saying.

I gestured. "Just keep your head on straight, hometown. That's how you help Ruth."

"I will, and—"

"Oh, Marty."

Ah. Now *there* was a voice. It came from behind me. I turn. And as I expect, Milagros Blow Me Down Dixon is hurrying her prime time into the office. She rushes to his desk.

"I just heard, Marty," she coos and wraps her consoling arms around him as he stands to get deluged with that cornball stuff women do so wonderfully well. It was all so touching.

"Well." I got up. Clearly Marty—the *lucky* mothafucka—was in better hands (and arms!) than mine. "Guess I better vamoose."

Milagros shut her floodgate in mid-coo.

"Wait!"

I slam my brakes on, utterly surprised. I mean, just because I was smitten with her didn't mean I expected she'd start talking to me. "What's that now?"

I guess she misunderstood my tone.

"Please wait," she amends.

I move to resume my seat.

"Your command is my wi—"

"Out *there*!" she screeches. Like I was stealing her chickens or something.

"Good gracious." I back towards the door, a bowing supplicant exiting an audience. "A thousand pardons. A thousand times a thousand pardons."

Baby looks contrite. "I'm sorry, Mr. Moore." She wipes at a braid dangling in her face. "I'm just so distraught. Would you please give me a few moments alone with Marty?"

"Certainly." I spin and truck. "See ya, Marty," I call over my shoulder.

"Thanks again, Jack."

"Por nada. By the way….." I pause at the door. "I just came into a little *dinero*, so if you need—"

"I'm all right, Jack."

I continue like he ain't said shit. "—if you need help with the bills, I'll be happy if you let me know."

*****

"Mr. Moore."

I kind of open my eyes.

"Mr. Moore."

I open my eyes some more and suddenly wanna jump to my feet and wrap my arms around something. But I'm cool. "Damn." I swipe at my mug. "Never dozed in a waiting room before."

"Sorry I kept you," says Milagros. "Would you come with me to my office?"

I gets to muh feets. Like I'm not thinking, *I'd rather come with you in your office*. Negligently I gesture.

"Where thou leadeths...."

*****

"I wanted to reassure you about…" She trails off, unsure of how to refer to the grisly thing I've done.

I save her the trouble. "I quite understand," I say helpfully, noting how comfortable the seat I was sitting in had become now that it wasn't hot.

"Mr. Moore—"

Never a Dull Moment

"Ain't that something."

Her soulful eyes look quizzical.

"You know all the secrets of my life and yet refer to me as a stranger."

Distantly she smiles. "Very well—Jack."

"Ah."

"I feel my position was inconclusive when we parted."

I nod—in agreement that her position was inconclusive and not in agreement that we'd ever parted.

"I want to be clear Mr.—Jack, that although what you did was…"

"Illegal?" I suggest.

"Yes. You need never worry about my reporting you."

"I wasn't worried."

"No?" She looks at me askance. "Were you planning on killing me too?" I smile.

"The 'k' word at last. How liberating."

"Well, were you?"

Almost imperceptibly I sigh and shake my head. "You disappoint me. Whaddya think I am? The Mafia?"

She chews on that a moment. "Point taken. I also want to apologize for the horrible things I suggested."

A slight smile gets away from me, but I succeed in not looking sly. "And don't forget the terrible way you treated me." I say. Like Thoth (and Legba), the Opener of the Ways, I wanna open me up a little something here.

The lady seems sympathetic. "Ahhh….," she says/sings. "Did I hurt your feelings?"

My hand flies over my heart. "I've yet to recover."

Baby hints at a smile. "And I suppose you expect me to nurse you to health?"

Ow! Now *there's* an image. "You devastate me further," I protest and try to look innocent.

Milagros looks stern—or would if her eyes weren't smiling. "Good. Because—"

"But now that you mention it, I wouldn't mind a little consolation this weekend."

"I'm afraid I can't."

I'm taken aback. At least I try to look like I'm taken aback. "'Afraid'?" I repeat, inflecting it *way* the fuck outta context. "So then all your talk about understanding and apology was just talk."

She sizes me up. I mean, I could actually feel her clinical mind a-turnin'. "I'm not sure you believe that. In fact—" She grins. "—I'm sure you're trying to manipulate me."

Manipulate? *Shee*it. The image the word evoked gave my thumb and forefinger erections. Ma-ni-pu-late—I would *love* to do that, I think.

"Now why would I do that," I say.

Baby huffs. "Are you going to persist?"

The question is so raw I stare dead in. Past her eyes, her mind—as far down as I can get. "'Til the damn cows come home, I'm gonna persist."

Her grin falters. I'd bullshitted so much she was unprepared for such a serious response. But how nimbly she recovers. "You'll be persisting in vain. I didn't wish to divulge this but you leave me no choice: I'm a lesbian."

Forthwith I crack the fuck up. See, men who have trouble with even compliant women are intimidated by lesbians. As if they had dick-withering, extra-resistant pussies or something. Other cats resent dykes because to them each woman turned lesbian was another item removed from the male food chain. But me? When I saw a lesbian I saw double-pussy. But anyway, not for a second did I believe Milagros' 'admission'. Consequently I 'confessed' too. "Well, whaddya know. And I bet you thought I was a man."

Homebaby's mouth dropped open. The suggestion that I was transgendered befuddled and surprise her.

"I was only joking."

"Well, whaddya know," I say. "So was I."

Milagros stares blankly at me then shakes her head, as if to say *look at this fool.*

NEVER A DULL MOMENT

"Well, whatever your gender or sexual orientation, you'll have to remove it from my office now."

Immediately I rise. *See?* (I am thereby saying) *Even though I've killed people, I'm just an alacritous gentleman.* "Client coming?" I venture.

The lady removes her purse from a drawer and rises with me. "Therapist leaving."

I check my watch. "It's only 2:30. What happened to the dedicated worker?"

"The dedicated worker has been here since 6." She goes around the office turning off things.

"Well, let me save you carfare and hassle." I whip out my car keys.

"I—"

"Not another pass, overture or intimation," I interrupt, "Just a ride."

Milagros smirks. "I was about to accept unconditionally. But now I will accept with those terms."

Ordinarily cutting my own throat would've made me feel stupid. Now, however, I didn't mind because I was too sleepy to try to talk her skirt up anyway. "We have to walk all the way around the block, though. It was the closest parking place I could find."

"No problem." Milagros locks her office door. "The service elevator will let us out through the back."

*****

We stepped out into an alley filled with dumpsters.

"Be sure you close that door securely," Milagros advises.

I shove the fire door closed and we proceed from the building, which is the back end of a cul de sac. About one hundred paces to the street, I saw. Wasn't bad. One hundred paces through a gamut of trash bins on a bright afternoon. Still I said: "I hope you don't come through here alone."

I felt Milagros steal a glance at me; felt her smile. "Well, well. Aren't we the mother hen."

We've walked only a half-dozen steps when I stick my arm out like a barrier.

"*Oje!*" she exclaims, thinking, perhaps, she's made a terrible boo boo and I really am a maniac after all.

I motion for silence and (very out of character, I feel) she acquiesces. I am grateful 'cuz I wanted to *hear* and I mean like *right* the fuck then. Having bushwhacked many a mothafucka myself, I knew the sounds. The ones coming from *there*, between two dumpsters just ahead.

I turn to Milagros. Hold up a stern finger. Poor child. The fright is visible in her eyes, so to reassure her, my stern finger taps her playfully on the nose. *Stay here*, I mouth, and point to the ground so that she'll be quite sure to understand which here I mean. Without seeming to, I catwalk towards the end of the bin on my left, my ears and eyeballs leading the way. As the space between it and the next becomes visible so do two scalawags hovering over a crack pipe. One is puffing anxiously away. The other watches him hungrily, awaiting his turn. Both had been dividing their attention between the pipe and the alley, however, because as surely as I'd heard them a-hidin' they'd heard us a-comin'.

However, it was the third mothafucka who'd most interested me. He was in full ambush-mode, you see; pressed close against the side of the bin intently awaiting my arrival, looking like Edward Scissorhand with four broken nails. But *oh* that fifth one.

Eddie Knifefinger jumped dead in my path, like Robin Hood confronting the Friar on that log.

I hold up my hands. "Chill," I say. "We're just passing through. Puff to your lungs content."

The two scalawags join Eddie. Thus bolstered, Eddie speaks: "Gimme your watch and empty your pockets."

"And the bitch too," one dude demands from behind him.

"Yeah," the remaining dude chokes down his swallow of crack smoke and concurs. "The bitch too."

I hear Milagros approaching but I don't turn around. "Stay where you are."

She stops. "Just give them the mon—"

"And keep your voice down," I tell her, because nothing so provokes a robber as noise—I oughta know.

Never a Dull Moment

Still and forever I watch Eddie and his Finger. For the first time he raises it menacingly. Scruff and Scrags spread out on cue, the percussion section responding to a conductor.

"Kick it out, nigga," Eddie demands. "I ain't gonna tell you again."

At that moment, I have to tell you, I was 34 years old. Still youngish, by some measures, but already I'd outlived Nat Turner, Sam Cooke, George Jackson, Akhnaton—Jesus, if you believe he existed. Even so, I was not quite ready to cash it in.

That's why when Eddie Knifefinger (tired, I suppose, of my procrastination) tried to give me the finger I broke his arm.

Actually he broke it himself. I just allowed it to happen by shifting into Empty Stance and doing Separate Palms. Indeed, the only reason his thrust didn't kill him was because Milagros was watching. Probably watching more closely than Scruff and Scrags, because soon as Eddie lunged for me and caught a bad decision they still sprang at me. Meaning to overpower me, I guess, and then move on to the Helpless Woman, etc. But they were not paying attention. Either that or they couldn't put the brakes on their momentum. Otherwise they would've realized that instead of attacking me Eddie was actually hurling towards a trash bin and I had his knife and his arm was hanging funny. BANG-clangalang! the empty bin went when Eddie's *cabasa* crashed into it. Whether the alarming sound their leader's head made against the metal jarred them to realization, I dunno. Was too late for realization anyway. Scruff, on my right, ran hellbent into Flash the Arms and had yet to complete the aerial circle that would land him on his back when I used the energy generated thus to let Lotus Leg Swing happen. The counterclockwise circle of my left leg lightning flashed through the air and struck the side of Scrags face just as the arc was descending.

My *sifu* would've berated my ineptitude only slightly.

Anyway, if Scrags jaw was only dislocated when he gave his face to my foot, it was sho' as you born busted when it broke his fall. All from just a little *wu wei*. Non-effort. Beingness.

That's one reason, without turning to look, I knew Scruff was shaking off his daze. Slightly, I turn to my left. Then—I spin. Casually, it appeared. But the imperceptible twist in one direction unleashed from the hinge of my waist through my arm to my out-held palm a force that would make the county coroner wonder what strange manner of weapon had been put upside Scruffs haid.

Or maybe would've but for Milagros. I didn't want her bothered by dead bodies. *Shee*it, I'd just barely managed to *un*bother her, lawd knows I wasn't fuckin' up no more. Besides, I wasn't all that sure he needed to die just because he tried to rob somebody. Consequently as Scruff rose to his knees, I kind of only skimmed Press Palm off the top of his now doubly numbskull. He still flew a few feet before prostrating. But (thanks to my doubt and Milagros' presence) he'd rise to smoke again.

When I finally looked at Milagros I'm sure it seemed an afterthought. It was not. Throughout the entire spinning of my wheel she'd been my center. Yet it was the damnedest thing. T'ai chi Chuan—'The Grand Ultimate,' 'The Dance of the Gods'—induced a meditative state; indeed, was a moving meditation. Thus one whupped ass and felt serene.

Whatever. I moseyed up to the rescued damsel. "I know. It was unsporting to hit that one dude when he was on his knees and his back was turned. And it was stupid bravado to not just give up the money and be done."

Milagros stands there with her mouth open, looking like a fish again.

So I told her, "You always look like a fish when your mouth drops open like that."

Self-consciously her mouth snaps shut.

Mine, however, yatters on. "But a melt-in-your-mouth fish. Like Beluga on Beluga. And the way your bottom lip presents itself when it hangs makes me wanna suck it off your face." I tug at her hand. "Come on."

Baby blinks. "Wow! *Que eso?*" (What was that?) "Karate?"

I laugh. She'd hadn't heard a word I'd said. "T'ai chi Chuan—watch it," I warn. Milagros peels her mesmerized eyes off me just in time to side step Scrag's head. Finally we make the street.

"Can you drive?"

Wondrous eyes look upon me. Gorgeous head nods up and down.

Never a Dull Moment

"Here." I hand her my keys as we approach my car.

She takes them and looks me a question.

"I gotta shut my eyes," I explain. We slide into my ride and (a moment later) that's exactly what I do.

*****

Next thing I know some chump is shaking my shoulder.

I open my eyes. "Oh. The chump with the rump."

"*Que to dice?*" (What did you say?) she asks, though her tone says she knows perfectly well what I said.

"Nothing. The tail end of a dream." Get it?

Milagros, sitting kind of sidesaddle, holds a finger out to me. My teeth, ever ready to sink into something sweet, sweat like Pavlov's dogs. But, alas, she is only holding out my keys. And scrutinizing me again. I reach for the ring.

And Milagros snatches it away. "You're in no condition to drive." She starts exiting.

Suddenly I feel refreshed 'cuz I just know she's gonna say—

"Come upstairs."

Yeah. That.

*****

We stand before her apartment door. She opens her purse, extracts her keys. Nothing in my demeanor suggests eagerness. Except maybe that if I tailgate any closer I'll be ramming the lady's bumper. She shoots me a quick look. I try not to appear smug, but could you blame me if I did? Yo. It's difficult to speak about oneself without sounding like the megalomaniac all of us creatures with egos to one extent or another occasionally are. But—raw dog: I liked women. I mean I liked them a *whole* lot. And—I'm happy to say—almost the entirety of the species liked me back ... and forth.

But I digress.

The point was that Milagros Evasive Pussy Dixon was (for all her extraordinariness) about to be another notch on my gun. Dat all. And I knew it. Philosophically I appraise her while she opens the last lock on her door. *You were wise to surrender now, my love hostage,* I muse. *Succumbing was as inevitable as resistance was futile,* and so the fuck on I go while the magnificent animal in my sway undoes the last of her door's triple locks. At last she steps in and aside so that I, the conquering hero, might enter. In a final gesture of capitulation, she locks the door and faces me. I, however, am a merciful predator and don't fall upon my quarry like the ravenous wolf I can be. Rather, I invite her to her feasting by extending a hand. Realist that she is, seeing her fate and knowing there is no escape, Milagros extends her own hand above mine.

And plops my keys into my mitt.

"*Madre*," she bellows and turns away.

The hinge to my lower jaw gives way. Partly in surprise; partly to provide egress for my rapidly deflating ego.

A slim, graying woman in jeans and joggers comes into the living room drying her hands on a dish towel. Disjointedly, something far in the back of my mind wonders if (because my mouth is hanging open) I look like a fish.

"*Hola, Mila,*" *madre* greets, though it is I at whom she looks.

"Weeth your mouth hangeeng open you look like a feesh. Close it pleez."

I obey, not incidentally noting how gleefully Mila (I *like* that) reacts to her mama's observation.

"What is thees you have here?" mama asks of Milagros while keeping me warily in her gunports.

Ain't that something? What is *thees*, not *who*. As though I'm just a ... well, a *feesh* Baby's brought home from market. I wasn't mad. Obviously mama was an earthy woman and (I'm sure) the reason she depersonalized me in English and not in Spanish was so the fish wouldn't feel slighted by being spoken about in an (ha ha) "unfamiliar" language.

I waste no time brown-nosing. "*This*," I say, "is only a man struck dumb by your ageless beauty."

Mama beams.

Mila rolls her eyes. "Actually he is only a man too tired to drive himself home." A little huffily, the mothafucka trounces out the room.

"Yeah," I say, interestedly watching the really interesting way she trounces. "That too." But I wasn't entirely just sucking up to

Never a Dull Moment

ma, I must tell you, 'cuz the woman was truly striking. Indeed, my immediate thought upon seeing the graying *mamasita* was *If this is a glimpse of Mlilagros-Future I might stick around.*

La senora waves me to the couch. "Pleez." Then she calls after Milagros. "So who will drive him home?"

Milagros yells back from wherever. "He can drive himself after a nap."

"A nap!" mother and I say in unison.

I'd been moving to the couch but at the sound of that demeaning suggestion I put my brakes on. Had these women no regard for male superiority? First I'm a *fish* to be haggled about like I ain't got no ears or identity. Now I'm a ... a ... a *baby* to be given a nap! Milagros reappears. With a pillow and blanket the impudent mothafucka reappears!

I pivot to *madre*. "*Senora* Dixon?" I venture.

"Pleez, call me Lydia."

I clasp her hand, dishtowel and all, in both of mine like I'm giving her the howdy-do. "Lydia, I feel blessed to have met you. My sun will now shine forever. I hope we meet again and soon. But now—I'm outtee." I turn to go.

Milagros puts the bedding on the couch and (how embarrassing) fluffs the pillow. "Then you'll have to take the subway."

I stop dead. Revelation dawns. But on general principle I check the keyring in my hand. Of course, the ignition key is missing.

"Don't be difficult," she preempts. "Better to rest here a few hours than wake up wrapped around a road sign."

I twirl my lightened keyring round a finger like it's a shootin' iron and I'm Dead Eye Mothafuckin' Dick. You know: That black cowpoke everybody thinks is white. Momentarily I contemplate the mudda. "Well," (varmint) "since you've already taken me hostage, I could stand to sit down a minute."

Mama (still openly amused at what a hyperbolizing fool I am) spectates. You know. Tries to gauge by the interplay 'twixt Mila and the Feesh if we have a Relationship and what the shape of it might be. It occurs to me that I should say something clever but I'm too tired to figure what. So I just mosey up to the couch and plop down—on the end *opposite* Mila's nappy-poo kit.

"I don't need your pillow," I announce, "'cuz...hmm." *'Cuz all I'm gonna do is perch on the edge,* I was gonna say. But the couch (I sink back and relax) is surprisingly cushiony. Embracing. Kind of like a big fat woman's bosom when she puts her arms around you and you press your head...

*****

(Mmm. My Third Eye never felt so loved. Something mystic is giving a full body massage to the Orb which hangs around or in or (maybe) is my pineal gland. Straight like that—but not straight but is...but is...but—Sorry, Morpheus, but soothing as you iz something outside is more soothing still.)

I open my eyes to see what it is. Milagros is leaning over the back of the couch, wisping a feather across my forehead. Now that I'm awake it feels only good, no longer otherworldly. Still I am sorry when she stops and (strange thing) when looking inside the waterfall her hair makes as she leans over me, I see a sun shining. It is her smile of course and it is slight, so the radiance of the sun I thought it was is faint—but damn if it doesn't illuminate my every shadow, my every hidden place. *Damn.*

"Time to...." She frowns. "What is that word you say?"

Takes me a second to catch up to her. "Mosey?" I hazard.

She shakes her head no.

"Get-gone?"

No again.

"Vamoose?"

"That's it!"

I stare up at her. My head and heart working double quick.

"Time for you to vamoose."

"But I just sat down," I protest.

She laughs then vanishes from sight. "Check your position."

Huh? Well kiss my red/black/and green. The mothafucka must've blindsided me or something because (mortification upon mortification) I discover I've been *napping*. Hurriedly I sit up and fling the blanket off. To further my *unmacho* disgrace, I've been relieved of my jacket, tie and shoes. *Mothafucka.* Here I'm trying to be Mr. Wonderful and instead I get my diaper changed. Hurriedly

Never a Dull Moment

I slip on my shoes as if slipping back into my suave persona and gaze balefully at the bedding. Least it ain't baby-boy blue.

"Here you are." Milagros has returned with a cup and saucer. I rise to meet her.

"But I don't understand."

She thrusts the saucer at me, as though to keep me at bay. "Don't understand what?"

I take a strategic sip of tea. You know. So her attention will have another moment to settle and she can better read between my lines. "Why I have to vamoose. I like it here." Conspicuously I eyeball the place to (ha ha) show that I really mean *here* and not *with you*, though *with you* is what I mean. "I like it here a lot."

Some of everything is in her laughter. "Sorry, but the 'dedicated worker' has to go to bed."

"All the more reason for me to stay." Sorry. But how could I resist spelling that out?

Then it hit me. *Bed?*

I hold the cup of tea (which is some intriguing Milagros-like herb) in my right hand and check my watch. "Nine-fifteen!" I can't believe five hours have passed.

From across the distance of her fully extended arm, Milagros sticks out my key. "Thank you for almost getting me killed then saving me and for the ride home."

I pluck it from her fingers and bow a little.

"You are too gracious—even though I know you think me juvenile for fighting." But I cannot tell her it was a matter of principle: con men don't buy bridges; gunmen don't get robbed.

"If you care to splash some water on your face—" She points in the direction whence her party-pooping mammy appeared. "—the bathroom's that way."

"Nyah." I politely drain the cup and return it to her. "I'll just be off." I look around. "Where's my jacket?"

"Oh." The lovely lady with the mystic touch flows away.

My eyes follow and hunger, but it's just as well I'm getting evicted. Her mama was home, if you remember. Thus I'd've had to sneak me some and I wasn't into sneak thiefin' pussy. Verily, I don't care how refined a lady Milagros was, my plan was to have her make a *lot* of noise, and I mean in multiple octaves.

She returns with my jacket and (I completely forgot) my tie. I drape the tie around my neck and slip into my jacket. "May I have my heart back too?"

Very unromantically, I must tell you, the mothafucka *stares* at me.

Undeterred, I stare back. "Your eyes are getting to be my favorite place," I whisper. And don't think I didn't notice that deadpan though she was she wasn't hurrying me out the door. Indeed, her *aura* yielded. So I step within it. She does not step away. We were only a breath from a kiss.

And my thrice damned, spell-breaking nuisance of a damn beeper mothafuckin' beeps. Through the swiftly receding mists of romance I reach for the faggot and espy the number. "Uh-huh," say I, in lieu of *What the fuck?*

"How opportune," Mila *confesses*, and starts herding me to the door before, I guess, her knees get weak again. "Good night, Jack."

I treat myself to a visual lick of her triple thick Junior's cheese cake. "It most certainly was."

Was, see? 'Cuz of the beep I just received I knew the rest of my night would be all kind of things. But good was not one of them.

INDIGESTION

C onquest through kindness is conquest.

Okay. These days the Christian US (unlike Islamic countries) is too economically developed to import you into slavery. They no longer lash you to the bone and pour salt into your wounds. Castration, they now admit, is insane. Generally, neither do they anymore rape your little girls while you watch, nor hustle their pink faced children out to have their pictures taken beneath the feet of your father/son/mother who is a'dangling (all bloodied and battered) from the tree. Indeed, they even let some of us work in their stores. You know. In Shopping Mall USA. As drivers, celebrities, doctors, cops—in whatever capacity will help ring up more and ever more of them white hegemony deposits. We can even buy from catalog New World Order NOW! Order today! Order New World Order! Yeah, they even let you work in their store. And we (because we do not know history) think that progress.

But that is what they set out to do.

When the first unsuspecting Afrikan was plucked from Eden by the Catholic Majesties of Portugal and Spain, having you work for them is what they had set out to do.

Am I to be grateful for that?

That the very status quo my forebears so ferociously resisted has been accomplished? They've destroyed my cities, obliterated my universities, slaughtered my scholars, my holy ones, erased my civilization from the annals of world memory—they have uprooted me from my being and allowed me a *job*! A *position*! A *career*! Am I to be grateful for *that*?

I laugh and laugh.

Certainly if one looks no further than the grammar school point of departure Abe-Lincoln-and-the-Slaves, receiving your disproportionately lower income seems progress. Yet go back. Back before the nigga breakers and slave ships. Back before Papal Bulls. Back to ancient roots—*then* (given that unedited context) all their multimillion dollar sports contracts and accolades and titles seem, in contrast, dogshit.

Yo. That's why white folks say, are always saying, "*Forget the past! Let bygones be bygones,*" because they don't want you to know history. Because then you would know what they've done, would know you've been robbed and raped and are being played. You would, in short, know the Truth. Then you'd not do what you do (killing each other; using drugs; selling drugs to anybody's child) because you'd be too angry. If you knew what was taken from you, you'd be angry. If you knew the atrocities, the crimes committed against you, you'd be angry. If you knew, if you knew, if you only *knew* you'd weep.

And rage.

To the marrow of your soul you'd weep and rage and every molecule of your being would scream to the heavens, 'These motha*FUCKAS*! These *thieves*, these *monsters*, these *evil* dogs from hell!' because just as surely as ignorance is bliss knowledge is...ah, so many things.

Including perspective. See, to me the negro appointee who keeps a (ha ha) discreet watch on me and Bakari (as though we're gonna steal the salt shaker off the table) is the end product of this conquest I muse about. Manufactured to exact specs, he knows nothing of the world that was and so accepts the appearance of the world that is.

Which means (among dumber things) black man plus jeans equals petty thief. To Bakari, however (who is steeped more in immediacy than in history), the assistant manager or resident token

INDIGESTION

or whatever the surveiling negro has been told he is is just a fool needing to have his jaw 'bruck.'

Bakari glowers at the menu. "I'm about ready to accommodate that sucker and go to Mickey Dees—after I kick a mud bone out his ass."

Somewhat lazily I look up from my studious contemplation of my menu. "Wha'? And commit another black-on-black? Tsk tsk, Bakari. Tsk mothafuckin tsk."

"Well, that mothafucka is pressin' on my last nerve. Why'd you wanna come here anyway?" he accuses. Like it's my fault and not his social programming that is making him feel uncomfortable.

I chuckle. We are seated in a corner of a (drum roll and ta da) *trendy* Broadway eatery. On the other side of the spotless window, trendy people pass over spotless sidewalks to and from trendy shops and trendy things like brunches. *Why'd you wanna come here?* he had asked. *So we can watch this live-action tv commercial*, I almost say.

Instead, I tell him what he already knows. "*Uno*. Because we've never been here before so, *dos*, anybody trying to clock us would stand out like a sore thumb." I show all my teeth. "Just like we do."

From his lofty height, Bakari drops a placated nod.

"Good. So fuck Secret Eyeball back there and tell me the bad news." Of course that's what it is. Why else did he beep me and then insist that we meet this morning? He rests the menu he wasn't reading anyway.

"Bama's busted," he whispers.

"What?" I say too loudly.

Distracted, I've lowered my menu too and instantly a waiter (trendy in a white jacket, bow tie and designer jeans) appears. Because an army doth indeed travel on its stomach, neither of us hesitates to order. Nominally, anyway: Bakari requests pineapple juice, scrambled and rye toast; I opt for mud and melon.

Soon as the waiter takes his ears away I jump on Bakari. "Why in the fuck didn't you tell me when I called you last night?"

He shrugs. "What would've been the point? We couldn't've talked on the phone and I couldn't get free to see you. So—" He shrugs again, "—why fuck up your night with mine?"

Mentally I scratch my head. That shit sounds like a case of good intention gone astray. But what, now, does it matter? "What they got him for?"

Deadpan, Bakari says, "Selling two oh-zees to an undercover."

My brain does a triple-take. "That's gotta be b.s. Bama don't....."

Bakari's nodding as I speak. "Yeah," he says, "but they still charged him with selling two ounces."

Funny how things reveal themselves. It is said, for instance, that satori comes not only from performing rites or reading scripture or from sitting at the feet of sages, but also suddenly and all at once from inconsequentials. A broken dish. A burp. A stone reflecting (or not reflecting) the sun. In like manner I all at once knew the real reason Bama was in jail. What I didn't know was: "How'd you find out he got knocked?"

"Some sista called me."

I raise an eyebrow.

"Yeah." Bakari concurs. "But I guess he had to put her in the mix to get word to us."

"Still a weak link, though, hometown."

Hometown nods. "Could be. But from what she says, our drawers ain't all the way down. She went to visit him on Riker's Island and he whispered my number in her ear."

"I hope you moved." He smiles.

"Why do you think I couldn't meet you last night? But I ain't mad."

"You did kind of ask for it," I acknowledge. See, while Skip and I had been satisfied with our homesteads Bakari was forever talking about abandoning his 'dump'. Ergo (probably), that's why Alabama chose to make Bakari's crib potentially hot by giving the woman his number.

"Funny thing too." he says.

I grimace. "I'm dying for a laugh."

"Nobody in the precinct laid a hand on him."

At that my eyebrow raises an eyebrow. "How you figure that?"

"Janet—that's the sista—she said they kept asking him about some money. They didn't wanna hurt anybody—they said—or even

INDIGESTION

keep him in jail. All they wanted was some money he was supposed to know about."

"Ah. So not breaking him up is supposed to prove that if the money turns up all will be tra la la-ski."

Hometown's long Afrikan mask-head bobs up and down. "Guess they think country boys are stupid."

"I guess, You know what else is funny?"

"Sure do," Bakari says. "They didn't ask him shit about his partners."

Emphatically I nod. They can't know who we are because nobody knows there is a we. Indeed, not only is our professional relationship unknown, when we socialize it's infrequent and way off the beaten track.

"Apparently somebody thinks he's got a plan." Bakari observes.

"Well, we gotta get one too. Let's round up Skip and bail Bama outta jail."

To my surprise, Bakari shakes his head. "You know Skip always said as soon as he made some real money he was cuttin' out."

So much for that wind in my sails. "I see."

"Yeah. But in all fairness, when I called him last night he was already in the middle of packing up his girl and baby. So it ain't like he's runnin' out on trouble."

I mull that a second. "Okay, I'll go for that."

"Me too. Skip ain't no punk, as you know."

"Probably wise for him to get his family gone anyway,"

"Sure is. Anyway he says as soon as he gets his family set up half-assed he'll call you to see if we need him."

"That's good to hear," I say because, well, it was good to hear.

The waiter comes with our order on a platter that sure looks silver if it ain't. I pour Bababowski a cup of complimentary mud. "Savor this flavor, me bucko, because after we pay Bama's ransom I won't be buying drinks for awhile."

Bakari raises his cup in a mock salute to Secret Eyeball. "You won't haveta worry about that."

Hm. The coffee is delicious. Definitely fresh ground. "Why the fuck not, praytell?"

"'Cuz Bama ain't got no bail."

I guess I probably fulfilled the guardian negro's *de clase* expectations of us 'cuz I slam the cup on the table, sloshing the white folk's quality java everywhere. "I thought it was only a *sale* beef."

Bakari butters a wedge of toast and slops some egg on it. "You know how it goes. The cops whisper to the D.A., the D.A. whispers to the judge, and the defendant gets a *date* for a bail hearing."

That's unconstitutional, I wanna say. But when it comes to Black folks, white folks wipe their ass with the Constitution. Unlike the mesmerized herd, I know I *still* ain't got 'no rights a white man is bound to respect,' especially not if they're inconvenient. So I hush my mouth and (following Bakari's warrior lead) attend to my own meal.

And huff a bit. "Just wait till I get my craw dogs on that mothafuckin' Skins." Angrily I chomp the bejesus out of a melt-in-your-mouth cube of just-ripe enough fresh honey dew. Homeboy chews his toast, as if I've said nothing. And I suppose I hadn't. Given the particulars, who else but good old Skins could've sold Bama down the river?

"There's one good thing." Bakari refills our cups. "At least the faggot didn't give him up to the cops."

I scoff. It is of course true that the police who are involved are only agents of the mob, otherwise they'd be talking murder. It is of course advantageous that Bama is not officially connected to what the press has described as yet another "Family" thing. Nonetheless I do not feel overwhelmed with gratitude.

"Well, Ba." I spear the last succulent cube on my plate."Whenever I get through killing Skins I'll be sure to thank him for that."

UPGRADE

"I can't believe you did that to me."

"Did what?" Milagros Babe-in-the-Woods Dixon innocently inquires.

We are seated at her desk, brown-bagging lunch in her office. Fully a week has past since I saw her. Seven days of learning about Ionging. And if that ain't blues enough. Bama *still* ain't had his bail hearing and Skins (neither as corpse nor reconstituted Mafia flunky) has yet to materialize. The sole bean on my rice was that Skip had phoned home— from Kansas ("So that I can see a muh'fucka comin' a mile away"). But dat all. Verily, the pall of gloom was my shadow, and heavy burden weighed down my heart. Or, as my prematurely departed granddaddy reportedly used to say, *if it ain't one thing it's two.*

Yet one can not wallow in morbidity. Thus while I fended off tribulation with one hand, I shot full-auto at Mila (I *like* that name!) with the other. I look at the genuinely uncomprehending lady like I think she knows perfectly well what I'm agonizing about.

"Didn't you just tell me that your mother said she was sorry she had to leave before I woke?"

"Yes?"

"Because she didn't wanna miss her bus?"

"Yes?"

"To her home in Randolph, NJ?"

Mila (what a *lovely* sobriquet!) has not the temperament for my circumlocution. "And?" she demands impatiently.

Suddenly, I stand, throw up my hands. "And you *evicted* me," I declare, as though ready to fling myself on the stake. Solemnly I point the finger of condemnation at homebaby. "You were *un*chaperoned," I accuse, "and you *evicted* me."

Slowly, slowly as the sun rises, a bright smile arises in her eyes. But not to her lips. "I don't understand what you mean." her lips say, though, of course, they do.

I slide back into my seat. "Milagros—Mila," I say, I *invoke*, as though her name were a spell. Perhaps it is. I know my intention when I resumed my seat was to fall into my spiel. You know. The glib bullshit elegant ladies lap up by the troughful. Yet when I spoke Mila's name the sound flowed from my crux and engulfed me, stilled the noise my tongue would make, released my heart. Yo. Kiss my red/black/& green but the child's name just felt so unsullied my conniving ass needed to speak truly when I said it.

So, bless my soul, I did. "Mila," I said, utterly without humor now, for who in the hell feels humorous when he's scared to death? "Do you know who I am?"

Her eyes search mine but (I am relieved to see) without fear. "What a peculiar question." Wanly, she smiles. "Unless you're some *in cognito* celebrity." I laugh.

"That is not my curse: I am only myself—or was. And that's why I ask if you know me. Until a breath ago—" which (being an animated mothafucka) I indicate with a wave of my hand, "—I knew fully who Jack Kerwin Moore was. I—"

"You're joking."

I give an inquiring look.

The fag grins. "You mean your name is actually Kerwin?"

The only reason I don't turn red is 'cuz I'm black. "I don't know what the hell my mama was thinking." Or what *I'd* been thinking for letting that countrified shit slip out.

Upgrade

Before she can get her sensitivity training in effect, half a giggle gets away. "Sorry." Prettily she bites on her lips and (probably) down on a rip-roaring belly laugh.

But I forge ahead. "You know how women say 'all men are dogs'?"

The lady snorts. "In English and *espanol*."

"Well," I drop my head in shame, "I used to try to be King Fido."

De lady snorts again. "And I suppose you're going to tell me you're rehabilitated." She tries to say this incredulously, but is that a note of hopefulness I detect in her voice?

Quickly I raise my head, search her unguarded eyes for confirmation. And find her searching my demeanor for the same.

"Yes," I tell her. "It's the corniest thing I ever did say, but because of you…."

And on I prattle. True to my extremist nature I was not content to be just a sap, I had to be a sappy sap, confessing ev'thang. From the first palpitating moment I laid my eyes upon her to how she's haunted me (though not where) to, well, *now*.

"I am *zapped*," I finally conclude, though by now I'm feeling such a sucker I'm talking to Milagros surrogates. The side of her PC's VDT; the carpet; a spot beyond her shoulder—anywhere but her eyes. "Milagros." I say to the top of her desk. "I've never in my life been serious about a woman. But damn if I'm not now."

The only reason I don't sweat bullets is 'cuz I'm very consciously diverting my energy into counting deep breaths. *Hm*. Now that I think of it, a lot of them have puffed in and out and still Mila ain't replied. Very curious, I look up.

Into rapt eyes. I *believe*. Could be I'm seeing with my heart. So to be sure, I cast a line into the quiet.

"Last I heard, silence is consent."

Baby blinks, hastens to regroup. "Well, I—"

Reeeeng.

Damn. Automatically I reach for my beeper. *One of these days*, I swear, *I'm gonna get rid of*—

Milagros silences the alarm clock on her desk. Puts it back into a drawer. Busies herself with disposing of sandwich wrappings and soda cans.

"Lunch time's over."

That, of course, is not quite the response I'd hoped for. So I try to interpret it. "And our time begins?"

But Mila has checked out with the end of the lunch hour. In her place is the Good Therapist already reviewing the file of the next psyche to be massaged.

"Sorry we can't talk," she says dismissively.

My heart sinks. My ass arises. I am about to spin to the door—and mothafuck saying goodbye to the punk ass, heartless—

"But I'll be free at 6:30."

—precious adorable rnothafucka.

"So I guess you'll be wanting a ride home."

Briefly the professional recedes and Mila the Most Lovable reappears.

"Yes." she says, confirming her decision: acknowledging my offer. *Yes.*

*****

"Just a cup of tea, Jack, and then you'll have to vamoose."

Vamoose? Clearly Milagros has a case of the Jacks already. But my face reveals nothing, though my mouth says, "I hope the infection is systemic."

Mila hesitates a hair's breadth in locking us into her apartment. Her eyes convey much. *All right*, they say, *I have been thinking about you.* Yeah. The lady's eyes convey much, search mine for much. But my face stays blank and I stare straight ahead. Like: *I don't know what's going on, lady. I'm just standing here waiting for this door to get locked.*

Apparently satisfied that I ain't gloating, she finishes doing just that. Then: "*Madre,*" she calls, "I'm home."

I grimace, exposing (thereby) an emotional chink in the armor of my deadpan. Disappointment flashes on my face as I look expectantly for *madre*.

But *madre* doesn't come.

UPGRADE

So then I look at Milagros—who is looking amused. The mothafucka. I dip my noggin to the worthy trickster. "I can tell we're gonna get along fine."

Her eyes concur. *I think so too.* Or so I care to translate. She turns and walks away. Without thinking, I follow.

The mothafucka pirouettes and shoves me. "*You* go over there."

"Sorry." I mosey over to the couch Milagros has indicated and with which I am embarassingly familiar.

From out of the mysterious recesses just denied me, her voice comes. "Play something, if you like."

Obediently I detour to the wall unit. Surrounding a fairly phat sound system is the inside of the lady's head. That is to say, her music. Neatly arrayed in stacks and racks is some of *ev'*thang. Reggae. Soul. Euro-classical—jazz. I trace a forefinger down a row of CDS as though skimming through Mila's secrets. I *am*, to an extent. Nina and Coltrane, for example, suggest that Baby's river ran deep. And the absence of that watered down commercial stuff confirmed it. You know the stuff I mean. That castrated, bleached stuff you hear on CD 101.9. To the contrary, not only did Milagros have depth, she had ears. Which of course meant she had Charlie Parker.

"But not now," I say to the Birdman. On the computer screen *Instrumental* was showing. So I hit that.

The third cut is playing by the time Milagros shows. "Good choice."

I stand and turn.

Milagros (barefooted, wearing an oversize tee-shirt and jeans so nicely hung you wanted to rush out and buy shares in the company) approaches with cups and saucers.

"You're forever creeping up on me."

She extends one service.

"How so?"

I nod a thanks. "First on my heart; now on my person."

I get what I am realizing is her usual answer: silence and a searching look.

To relax the pressure, I sip my tea. "Mm. This is excellent," I say—'cuz it is. "What is it?"

Balancing her own saucer and cup Milagros sinks to the couch. "A little this, a little that—something my mother blended."

Much against my druthers, I sit a respectful distance away. "You needn't have bothered."

"Bothered?"

"You're potion enough for me." Well, I said *relax* the pressure, not cease it altogether.

Baby sips her tea. Over the rim of her cup her eyes, wary but hungry, search mine. When she finally deigns to speak, it's from outta the blue. "Both Lizette and Magdalena think so much of you."

I shrug. "We're family."

She rests her cup and saucer on the coffee table and, well, eyeballs me. I try to interpret the body-speak. Let's see. One foot folded under her plump rump—that means relaxed. Arms folded across her inviting little bosom—that means defensive. Shit. I don't know what to conclude. As if to help the dunce, she explains.

"Without meaning to, they've convinced me you're a good man." *Even though* (she seems to imply) *you're a killer.*

I take no offense. See, I've long ceased to require other people's understanding. Kind of like the Buddhists. They so revere life some actually sweep their paths when they walk lest they inadvertently squash a bug. Yet during the Tang Dynasty they and the equally life-affirming Taoists murdered each other in droves and didn't worry about being understood. Yet who can deny they were good?

I rest my own cup on the table. "I want to be an even 'gooder' man," I say and am surprised because it's true.

"May I pry?"

I look at her oddly. *You're already all the way inside me. How can you pry?* But I don't wanna spook her with heaviness. "Woman, haven't you probed enough psyches for one day?"

She shakes her head. "That's not what you mean."

Now I really look at her oddly. "No? Okay, my little clairvoyant." I retrieve my cup and take a swig. "What *do* I mean?"

UPGRADE

Baby also gets her cup and takes a thoughtful sip before replying, "From the expression you gave, I'd say you thought my question about prying absurd."

"No wonder Marty raves about you," I make no effort to hide my astonishment. "That's observant."

"It's part of what I do."

"And pretty damn well, I see." I finish the tea and set the cup on the table. "And that was pretty damn good."

"My mother will be happy you liked it. Now tell me: You're always well dressed and you seem to keep whatever hours you choose. What do you do for a living?"

Naturally her Hubble telescopes were locked on my mug, on the lookout for prevarication. But she could've spared her eyes the strain.

"I'm a freelance mothafucka," I kind of confess.

"What?"

"Actually," I amend, remembering the half mil in my stash, "a freelance mothafucka emeritus."

Mila comes to a seated attention, as though regarding a snake which may or may not be venomous. "Emeritus, eh?" She drums her fingers on the knee of her outstretched leg. "And exactly what motherfuckery did you retire from?"

I laugh. "*Motherfuckery*. That's cute."

"Well?"

"Armed robbery."

"God!" Milagros springs up and grabs her head, like she has an extra strength Excedrin headache.

"Occasionally, though, I've run paper games. Forgery, bank fraud, that kind of thing."

"*A dios mios!*" Visibly agitated, the lady collects the cups and heads out of the living room/for the kitchen/away from me.

"But I've never sold drugs." I say cheerily to her departing back. Stiffly, it disappears. No question, she is one upset mothafucka.

I could not be more pleased.

Because, sho' as you born, her upset was in inverse ratio to her affection. Which, apparently, had had its flame on high. I give Milagros a moment to get where she's going. Then I give her another to get pass the initial shock.

Then I get up.

The hallway leading pass her bedroom and bath is a straight line to the kitchen. She doesn't turn around when I enter, but then I did not expect her to.

"So who are you most angry at?" I say to her back. She puts one washed saucer in the dishrack and commences washing a cup. But (did you notice?) she did not say I was intruding.

"Is it I?" I say very formally 'cuz, hell. this is a *very* formal occasion. "Are you more angry at me for 'betraying' you by being a crook? Or," I inquire of the top of her head, "is it yourself? Are you mad with yourself?" I ask and notice with delight that the braids I expect to spend a lot of time playing with are not extensions. "Does it bother you that your observant eyes let your heart crash into me?"

She puts the last saucer in the dishrack and turns off the water but makes no move to face me. She just stands there. Her glorious head hanging down, her hands resting on the edge of the sink like dainty birds perched on a branch. I step closer. More frightened than a sissy at a shootout I take the deep breath and—*exhale*—cover her hands with mine.

Slowly, gently, my fingertips caress them. "Your hands are lovely. When you do dishes, you should wear latex gloves. Or keep a bottle of lotion nearby."

Despite herself, though I know not the reason, she sighs.

"Of course another option is to let me do your dishes."

At that she goes through the motion of snatching her hands away. But a semblance of pressure keeps them still.

"And of course for that to work you'll have to have me over for dinner and lunch and—"

In a move so fluid it was almost tai chi, Milagros the Downcast whirls suddenly around and puts the Ironhand Deathgrip to my lapels.

UPGRADE

"Swear to me it's over," she demands looking up at me with her impossibly soulful eyes.

I start to laugh. *How melodramatic can you get?* But the tear streaks on her face put my brakes on. Poor child. Seems I wasn't the only one who'd been secretly smitten. Sad for her and happy for myself, I kiss her eyes.

Then permit myself a smile.

"We can open up a mom and pop store right now, if you want."

But what she want is more serious assurance. "*Swear* it to me," she demands again and tugs so hard on my lapels I'm ready to just give her the whole damn jacket *and* the pants too. In any event, I open my mouth to speak—ecstatic at the chance to accommodate this lady, more than eager to please

—and not a damn thing comes out.

What a revealing moment that was. *Swear*, she'd demanded. And I wanted to.

But to what?

The yearning in my thug heart as I did my thug things was far less alloyed than that of the pious Christians who love God and hate man—*dat* was sho' for sho'. Verily, my gangsta soul sought the Cosmic Connection, too.

But to What?

I hadn't embraced the Five Pillars or been Born Again or shaved my head Krishna Krishna because just because I wasn't clear on other options didn't mean I had to settle. So there I was. Delicate hands all but ripping off my lapels, soulful eyes laser-beaming my skull, kissable-irresistables (without realizing?) demanding that I reach into the mystery and draw forth Answer. A pivotal moment. See, even if I could've slipped some sham vow by her I wouldn't've tried. Love required truth. And I, alas, had no truth to give. Ah well. *Sorry, my love*, I again open my yap to say, *I know nothing of vows.*

"On my mother's grave," I said, "no more stealing for a living."

Now where did that come from, my inquiring mind wanted to know and would. Soon as I confirmed something with the Awakener of Mystery who just now had her head buried in my chest and was squeezing the breath outta me. "Guess this means we have a contract."

I feel her head move up and down. I feel her smile.

"*Si*, Jack, *si*."

Well, idiot, my mind informs me, *you may hold her now*. Oh. Alacritously I convey the command to my arms but (whaddya know?) they've already completed the circle of our embrace. Easily, naturally—in point of damn fact, her every contour had been sculpted for my arms and my arms had always held her. Then— Mother Mary and Joseph—I at last entwine a hand in her mane. I pull until her face upturns and (feeling quite the vampire) drink her lips.

And my thrice damn beeper beeps.

I tense but ignore it. This is our First Kiss, after all. The stuff that women make anniversaries out of—and *woe* to the man who forgets that on October 19th or whenever it happened. Whatever it (according to her) happens to be. Thus I kiss on.

For another fifteen seconds.

"My pardons." I disengage. Kind of. One hand rests territorially on one magnificent swell of a hip. The other extracts my beeper. Takes me a second to recognize the number. That's 'cuz it's from a pay phone. "A thousand pardons, but I've gotta make a call."

Milagros doesn't understand. "Phone's on the wall behind you," she says, making absolutely no effort whatsoever to unwrap me.

"Thank you, but I've gotta make this call from outside."

Shabataka! One second she's clinging to me like she expected me to hump her whole sack of potatoes across the room to the phone. The next second she's peeled away and down to a french fry.

I watch her stalk away. "It's not what you think."

Halfway to the kitchen doorway she spins around. "If it's not some criminal thing or some woman, why can't you call from here?"

Slowly, as though to a skittish colt I'm trying to bridle, I walk towards her. "*Muneca*." (Doll.)

"Don't call me that." I keeps walkin'.

"*Mi amor*."

Upgrade

"I am *not* your love," she refutes. But only with her words, for now we stand so close again if she tiptoes she will kiss me.

"Years from now you'll be glad you had faith in me."

"But how can—"

"Trust me, Milagros," I interrupt. "I've given you no reason not to." Then I play my big card. "Haven't you learned to disbelieve the obvious?" Reminding her about the last assumptions she made about me hit her just right.

"That's a low blow."

See? Wha'diditellya? Hesitantly, I touch her hands.

She grips the bejesus outta mine. "You owe me an explanation."

"And you shall have it." I release her hands so I can grab her body. I kiss her forehead, her lips. Then I kind of drag her to the door. "I'll call you if I can't make it back." I step into the hall.

Smirking, Milagros crosses her arms and watches me depart. "Yeah?" she says. Like calling her is the most outlandish promise she's ever heard.

I'm halfway down the hall. "Of course I'll call," I firmly announce.

Then walk meekly back.

"555-09i3," she tells me.

I hug and kiss her. "Thanks."

She touches my face. I tug a braid. Out came a smile from inside her. And (before some bad or dumb or too high somebody insisted Bakari un-ass the phone he'd beeped me from) I got gone.

INSIDE OUT

The world is upside down. No shit.

First off, I do mean literally. (*Why is Europe and north at the top of the map, when the Egyptians, who knew more than everybody about everything, showed that all flowed from the heart of Afrika in the south?*)

But figuratively, too, the world is upside down.

How come, for instance, when a wet-behind-the-ears 13-year-old shoots another 13-year-old, the shooter is a vicious monster. But when a highly trained adult police officer shoots a 13-year-old (in the back with his hands raised—four times) it's an accident? Does that shit balance? Or when some poor uneducated slob who ain't got a can of jackbone to his name burglarizes a store to provide for himself he gets 25 years in prison. But when a wealthy Ivy League alumnus 'misappropriates' millions—out of sheer greed— he pays a fine. Explain that to me. And what moron ever thought to assert *blacks are equal to whites,* or the *black* contribution to world history? For, praytell. what in the fuck have whites *ever* done to demonstrate that they are equal to the rest of humanity? What have *they* contributed to world civilization? I mean, Aristotle suddenly 'authors' scores of books on diverse subjects—*after* his alcoholic fuck-toy 'Alexander the Great' conquers Egypt and allows his pederast to peruse for twenty years. And let us not forget

Inside Out

the French, who suddenly *discover* metric, et al.—after Napoleon gives Egypt to French science. And look at the Washington Monument—then do a double-take of 'Cleopatra's Needles.' Indeed, the white man is an ungrateful child. There's not a solitary worthwhile thing he takes credit for that was not originated, influenced or improved by his Afrikan forebears. From architecture to physics to Kim Bassinger's lips. Word. *You black ape*, they're quick to snarl, as though they had a tongue-load of shit. But *we* ain't the ones who are ethnologically hairy and, like the ape, lipless. Word the fuck up. Draw aside the white curtain of damn near any worthwhile thing and damn if'n it ain't black therein, as black as Egyptian temples. But what happens? We are made to think it's understandable that whites cross the street when they see us, when given their consistent criminal history and ongoing m.o. it is *we* who should cross the street—the river! the continent! The *galaxy*!—when ever we even think we see a white man.

But the world is upside down.

Ergo, we remember the Alamo but have forgotten Elmina.

And Bama's "—bail hearing is postponed another two weeks."

I shake my head disbelievingly. "Because his court appointed attorney 'missed' the hearing?"

Bakari stirs his rum and coke with a finger. "Because his *cop* controlled attorney missed the hearing," He flicks the drops onto the booth's table or wherever. "For 'Bama," he says absently.

I raise my snifter (but not too high, lest the waiter think I'm ordering another round). "I'm not sure I stand corrected. 'Court appointed'. 'Cop controlled'. Where's the difference?" Only half-consciously, I tilt the glass till a bead of cognac drops from its lip. "Bama," I mutter.

Bakari swigs from his highball. "He wants us to retrieve his money."

I haveta hmph. "I guess hometown was looking down the road."

Bakari nods. The cops had dismantled Bama's apartment and found jack. As usual, the 'dumb' country boy had played ten moves ahead. This time by having stashed his cash deep when all seemed well.

"I don't want you with me when I get it, though."

I shrug. "Okay." Shrug and sip.

Bakari's looking at me questioningly. "Ain't you gonna ask me why?"

I shrug again. "There're only two possibilities and I know them both."

The mothafucka sips his rum and eyes me coolly. "Yeah? And what might they be?"

"One, you wanna take the money and run. Knowing Alabam-boy, he's got way more than that half a mil in his stash." I fingerfuck the snifter while I speak. Of all the assorted goblets and thangs, it has the most interesting feel: indeed, is probably part of cognac's appeal. "All that loot is tempting, Ba, even to a friend."

"But," Bakari offers.

"But if that were your intention you would've *been* got outta Dodge."

He smiles. "You forgot to say 'my Dear Watson'."

I smile back. "That's 'cuz I ain't finished deducin'. The other possibility is you're thinking like me: they got Bama: Bama's been in touch with you, however indirectly. Ergo, if any ass is next for de auction block it's your'n."

Hometown beams, a professor glowing at his prized student.

"Therefore—" I conclude, pointing my snifter eruditely at the mothafucka. "—your long ass might need a friend the way Bama needs one now, my dear Watso'."

"That's why you should keep Skip outta the picture."

Petulantly, I suck my teeth. "Mothafucka, why you think I told him to keep his ass in Kansas?" Of course at the time I'd thought Skip would be *our* hole card. Now I see he's to be mine.

As I am to be Bakari's.

"One thing I do wanna know."

My *gumbani* stuffs about five complementary pretzel nuggets into his big mouth. "Wha'dat?"

I cover the mouth of my glass until the fussilade of crumb missiles spraying outta his attack muzzle has subsided: "How'd he tell you where it is?"

Homeboy laughs. "That 'Bama. Know what he did?"

Inside Out

I shield my snifter from another attack. "It is my dream that you might tell me."

"On three different days he had three different visitors—and gave each one a piece of an address."

"And of course none of the...women?" I venture.

Bakari nods.

"None of them knows each other'?"

He nods again.

"But how did they get the info to you?"

"First through Janet. You know I call her everyday."

I nod.

"When she told me Bama needed a number to reach me, I gave her a pay phone number and a time to call. Then another calls with a piece of info and a request for another number." He waves one of his long hands in a graceful arc. "And so on down the line."

"Shit still gets me mad, though." And to show my agitation I swig too big a swallow and almost gag, which made a lot of sense.

"Me too," Ba says.

"If they'd a charged him with homicide I could see them jerkin' him around like this. But for a routine sale?"

His face becomes a grimace of disgust. "Blind justice ain't supposed to work like this."

I snort; raise my glass in mock salute. "Welcome to America."

KILL ME AGAIN

Oprah Winfrey is not physically unattractive. Indeed, she looks mighty svelte these days. However (my prodigious esteem for the sista notwithstanding) the reason Oprah initially got action at her job was because of her original package. Which (in the typecasting eyes of racism) was large part pancake box. Her will and prodigious talent counted for much, no doubt.

But her appearance was *not* irrelevant.

Once upon a time the unhung sign above Hollywood read *Only Light Skin Coloreds Need Apply*. But the times changed. Or was it just that the *appearance* of the times changed? Either way, our beloved Oprah had the right look for the repainted historical moment and thus was cast as Aunt Jemima. You know. The big black bosom full of mammy's milk. Least that's what old massa saw when (after his lust was spent) he looked at the black woman: breasts at which his pink cherubs might suckle-- *And jus' lay your own pickaninny in the ditch, gal.*

Oprah ingenuously provides the same function.

But with a psychological tit: feel-good TV for white pseudo conscience, feel-good TV unpasteurized—and never mind the malnourished black psyche a-hungering in the ditch of American society. The sweat from your brow, the milk from your breast, the reassurance from your media tits--it's all the same. *And is all for massa!* Who sucks it up prime-time five days a week and never comes away unfortified. For who better to absolve them, to lullaby their guilt than a perceived mammy-type from among their slaves: *"Dere, dere, you po' lil' ol' devil you. You taint really no monster, dere, dere...."*

Certain vignettes encapsulate things, are freeze-frames of the human drama. Like, check it: the death of Dr. Charles Drew, the Afrikan who invented the means to bank blood plasma but died because a hospital refused to transfuse him with "white blood" after a car accident. Or how whites receive celebrity status and financial awards after murdering unarmed Black children like Trayvon Martin or Michael Brown.

And Oprah Winfrey.

There are many mysteries in the world. But whether or not the good hearted Oprah was gonna play to the commercial appetite of white folks ain't one of them. She is. Thus her talk show's become a vignette of sorts; a way to instantly establish whether or not a person was in or out of The Box.

That's why I was elated when Mila (did I tell you I *love* that name?) told her voluble colleague,"...to tell you the truth, Shelly, I never catch Oprah."

Shelly's prattle, at joyous last, braked to a halt. Yo. In a perfect world nature would confer the power of speech only upon those with something to say. In which case America would abound in mutes, one of whom would be in this elevator sign-languaging *My name is Shelly and I can't talk 'cuz I ain't got shit to say.*

We were descending to Mila (and Motor Mouth Shelly's) floor after a mini-celebration in Marty's office. Yeah. Bitch Ruth recovered (and thank you, by the way). The three of us had been on hand with Marty to help in the unholy event. According to the attending physician, company would stimulate her recovery. So rather than let the bitch wallow in the emptiness she had made for herself, Mila, Shelly and I had gone with Marty to take up space and make appropriate get-well noises, speaking for myself anyway. Unlike Shelly, who until a second ago had been regurgitating the view of all humanity—according to what she'd heard on Oprah.

And what do you think about it? Shelly's National Enquirer's mind wanted to know. *To tell the truth,* my beloved highbrow (showing fine therapeutic form by answering the moron with a straight face) had said, *I never catch Oprah.*

Shelly seemed speechless. Speechless? *Decapitated,* is what she seemed. Like not watching Oprah was unAmerican. (Hm. Mayhaps it was.)

Anyway I stood behind them, leaning nonchalantly in a corner. Gloating (I'm ashamed to say) when Mila deigned not to stoop into Shelly's small talk.

Then a thought so horrible hit me I sprang off the wall. "And you don't record it."

Milagros and Shelly look at me like I'm crazy. Shelly (perhaps because she espied my agony) smiled broadly. "My, my, but you look stricken."

For Mila's sake I bit my tongue. "Well?" I ask of my mothafucka.

The punk toyed with me. "I do have a programmable DVR."

"*And,*" Shelly declared triumphantly, "she uses it to tape Oprah!" *Because she can't get home in time to see it live, so there!*

"Actually I've never bothered to work the thing." The doors open onto their floor. "All I use it for is videos," she explains and gets off.

Shelly looks betrayed. I step past the id'jit and make a show of being humble. And (shucks) she hurries off the elevator just before the doors close. Happily I watch her scurry off to wherever airhead counselors go. Probably to gleen some therapy tips from the Oprah videos you just knew she had in her office. Me, I follow the hips.

"Don't get comfortable," Milagros says, "I have an appointment in ten minutes."

I sit down anyway. "So I assumed."

She had just turned on her PC, was no doubt about to access a file. As though she were a little doll (and she was) I pushed her and her seat back from the desk ("Hey!") and then pulled the whole kit and caboodle right up to my knee caps. Bless my soul but between her startled expression and the way she clung to the arm rests of her chair she looked just like a little girl on a carnival ride holding on for dear hallelujah. My heart ranneth over with delight.

"All I want is just three of your pre-appointment minutes." My position thus clarified, I scoop her glorious ass up and deposit it upon my lap. *Whew!* A lot of *chi* and upper body strength went into that, I can tell you.

"*Jaaack*," she objects, but drapes her arms around me.

I help myself to an earlobe. "Sorry," I say between nuzzles of her neck, "but you looked like you belonged over here." And wasn't *dat* Sojourner truth. Delicately I suck and tongue a corner of the lady's lips. Inevitably she *mmms*. "So," I ask 'twixt nips, "what time should I fetch you?"

"*Mmm*," she croons.

And then vanishes from my lap.

Shabataka. One second I had her right where she was supposed to be, the next she'd beamed outta by battle zone like one of them Kligon space vessels with its 'cloaking device' in effect.

"Don't bother," she says, wheeling back to her terminal. "My sister's giving me a lift."

"But..." I say hopefully.

She favors me with a glance. "But you can drop by for tea around 6:30."

Tea? methinks. *How coy*. Conspiratorially I reduce the outward size of my smile by half. "Bet. Wouldn't miss your *madre's* brew for the world."

*****

Having long been a conscientious thug I knew something was different even as I raised my mitt to knock on Milagros' door. Call it hood sense or keen observation or whatever. All I know is that thieves without it spent a lot of time in jail (if they were lucky) or died young (if they were not). Thus—instinctively askant—I knocked warily 'pon de do'.

"Who?" a little girl's voice inquired.

Ah. So that's why my antennae had got to waggin': I'd overheard/ sensed/hood-detected an unexpected voice without realizing it.

"Jack," I say, without (I hope) conveying the dejection I felt for not having Milagros to myself.

"It's *him*," the little obstructor of my designs calls excitedly. She undoes the locks and opens the door wide, like she's expecting King Muckamuck's whole entourage or something. Doesn't take but a second to see she's Mila's little sister, for the child was as exceedingly swanlike and black, though (alas) her long hair was treated. You know, 'Silken', weak—false, in a word. Kind of like Robin Givens'. However, I didn't bother wondering how such a little sister could've legally given Milagros a lift home because arrayed on the couch like exotic birds on a limb were four of the *baddest mamasitas* I ever did see—*peripherally*—including another sufficiently older version of the Milagros miniature who'd let me in. It was obvious Milagros had put them on point about the *moreno* who was to come a-callin', 'cuz *ev*'thang came to a standstill when I came in. Indeed, all four of Mila's assorted girlfriends and kin had craned about on the couch and were smiling the biggest *oo-we-heard-about-you* smiles you could fix your mouth for. Still, I cast not a direct eye upon them. You know. Because when a man looks directly at a beautiful woman for more than one parsec he looks like he looks interested. And in the South of male/female relationships that constituted reckless eyeball.

Mila was just turning around from tuning something into her sound system. "Hi, Jack," she says—*musically*, quite (I am sure) without knowing.

"*Hola*," I reply.

As I proceed closer to the couch where I will be poked and prodded by assessing eyeballs like so much produce at the market, a song begins. Some Latina singing something about love in words I only half understand.

But I understand the music wholly.

I walk up to Milagros, who again is barefoot and wearing a loose tee and jeans. She extends a hand. I take it.

"Jack, I'd like you to meet—"

Lightly I turn her, lightly I enfold her, lightly I kiss her lips. *Oos* and muffled giggles come from the couch.

I maneuver Mila into swaying with the music. "Dance with me," I whisper in her ear.

Instantly her arms encircle my neck, as though they always have. Like water my hands fall to their natural places, as though they always have. To a song I never heard before we dance, as though we always have.

"Isn't he *handsome*?"

KILL ME AGAIN

"And he can *dance*."

Out the corner of an eye, I see little sister make a throwing-up face. "I think I'm gonna be sick."

"*Gijate la boca*," (hush your mouth) three or maybe four voices say as one. Little sister contents herself with a giggle.

But I barely hear it, for truly they and all else have fallen away. Slightly I pull back so that I might bless my eyes while I speak. "Pardon me, *senorita*, but have we met before?"

Baby is a little entranced. "I don't think so," she plays along, but as if from far away.

"Ah then. Must've been a dream."

She smiles. "Must've been."

I pull her close again, til her head rests against my shoulder. I whisper so that no one else can hear. "But it's real now."

Milagros clutches me tighter.

Too soon, the song ends. Mila is somewhat breathless. One arm around my waist, she turns to face her *companeras*.

"*Girls*," she all but announces, "this is Jack."

The four seated women burst out with applauds so (fuck it) I take a bow. Little sister rolls her eyes. "Oh *please*."

*****

While I awaited Bama's court date, my life was just the two sides of a coin. By day I sowed: Cleaned my gats. Worked out. Practiced at this and that.

And beat the bush for Skins.

Ah, but at night—at night I *reaped*. Kind of. At least being so often in Mila's company felt like bountiful harvest. She was a wage slave, true. But every night I cajoled her into something. Dinner out, dinner in, the park, a jazz club—something. And no matter what I was doing during the day, she never needed a napkin to wipe the lunch crumbs off her lips—a treat as delicious as Tassili's Raw Reality Vegan Tomato Chips, I can tell you.

The problem was I was devouring her no further.

Bless my beloved's cowardly heart, but except for noon interludes in her office the nimble sprite never let me get her alone. Seemed like her whole family and all of her friends were working in *shifts*. You hear what I'm saying? If I was at Mila's apartment somebody—and sometimes *every* somebody—was too. Yo. Call me paranoid but I knew a conspiracy when I saw one. Moreover, I knew the motive of the plot.

See, I've had to be my own father (which has made me a better man 'cuz—to tell the truth—my daddy didn't know shit). And one of the many things I had to teach myself about was women. Now I don't pretend to understand them (there ain't a god with enough heads for that). But probing into their mystery firsthand has given me a certain...grasp of the subject, shall we say. Kind of like a paleontologist who's done his own primary research. Ergo, once I realized that Milagros was deliberately ducking the dick, it wasn't hard to figure why. See, the way to a man's heart is through his stomach.

But the way to a woman's heart is through her pussy.

Spare me the shrieks of indignation, please. I have the deepest respect for women (after all, my mama was one). But ain't no question that for the female of the species sex is an acutely emotional experience. That's why they're so stingy with it. They give up the pussy like it's love because (for them) it is. Of course there's always the conditioned exception, like women socialized to become hoochie mamas. Most generally, however, what to men means orgasm to women means commitment. That's why afterward women wanna cuddle and men wanna go to sleep. A biological reflex. you understand. The foot bone's connected to the ankle bone; the ankle bone's connected to the leg bone--.

And the pussy bone's connected to the heart bone.

Dat all. Get mad if you wanna, but the man who did his 'homework' could do no wrong. That, alas, is one reason so many women accept abusive relationships, the kind Aretha used to sing about. You know. Wherein *every*body tells the woman, *"Girlfriennnd, that man ain't no damn good!"* But no matter how many times he leaves her, here she comes again—looking to *cum* again. Further, pussy originally comes with a seal and double airlocks for one reason and one reason only: to keep them hearts from dropping out or (once the seal is broken) from being easily accessed.

Hence Milagros Slippery Eel Dixon's conspiracy against the dick. The little girl was afraid she'd fall in love more deeply than she already had.

Kill me Again

This particular TGIF she was yanking my chain with both hands, quite inadvertently (?) of course. See, her magnificent braids were afire with golden beads and threads. Thus bejeweled and beguiling, the thousand snakes of her hair dispersed from a nest of headband even more vivid than the one she'd first lassoed my heart with. *The Gods Have Blessed You With This Vision*, it should've been named and much with reason, I can tell you. Moreover, the black silk shift baring her strong arms and proud shoulders flowed down her haunches like shimmering black light illuminating every corner of my hunger, my soul; and oh, how I envied the birds on her patterned black stockings as they fluttered around her dancer's legs and vanished upward and alit, perhaps, somewhere near a garden of delight. And if that weren't taunting enough, she assailed me with the purity of her beauty. Which is to say that aside from the golden vipers threaded into her braids and a hint of gloss, the proud beauty wore no jewelry, was again her own adornment. *What jewel can compare with me?* her jewellessness seemed to say. *No jewel*, I think. And indeed it was she who would enhance a galaxy of suns.

Thus (thoroughly fucked up) I stood behind her and her exquisitely sculpted ass as she unlocked the door to her apartment, one impulse away from swallowing her whole.

Utterly oblivious of my reaction and designs, Milagros opens the door, steps inside, holds it open for me. I step towards her and the open portal.

Then sat down on the steps across from it.

Baby tries to appear puzzled behind her smile. "What's this now?"

I check the time. "It's after one a.m. I figure you can bring my tea out here. This way I won't disturb your sisters."

"Neither of my sisters is here."

I pinch my pants legs just above the knees and tug slightly. You know. Just 'cuz I was murderin' the seat of my pants was no reason to fuck up my creases. "Well, your aunt then."

She bestows her laughter on my ears. "My aunt isn't here either."

"Well, she's coming."

"No, she's not."

"Well, somebody is."

The stamp of one of her slippered feet smacked sharply in the quiet. "Will you get in here, Jack?"

I cross my arms, determined to be petulant. "Why? So we can play three-handed whist with your friend Yvonne again?"

She lowered her voice, trying another tactic. "Jack," she drawls seductively, "don't you like my teas?"

"Yeah. Love your teas." Then (under my breath): "But what I want is some of your honey."

She blows out a noise of frustration. "That does it." Before I of the divinely swift hands could even think about doing Fend, baby was pulling me up by an ear.

"Ow!"

Thus towed I stumble sideways through her door. She kicks it shut behind us.

Rubbing my ear, I glower malevolently at the luscious outline illuminated by the street lamps streaming through her living room windows. "I bet you practice that on children at your—"

She cuts me off by sticking her tongue in my mouth and encircling my neck with her arms. But though my lips cooperate my arms hang like they were uninterested at my sides,

That'll show her, I told myself, though, truly, if anything was showing her anything it was the telltale activity down my pants' leg. When she finally stopped assaulting me, our lips still touched.

So I speak into her mouth. "Aren't you worried your mother might find us not enjoying her tea?"

For reply, she took one long-legged step back and with a sinuous movement made her dress pool around her feet.

I flew into motion.

"*Oh!*" she gasps, surprised, no doubt, at the rapidity with which I'd scooped her ass up in my arms.

Never before had I entered her bedroom. But having had cast my wistful eyes on its door en route to the bathroom whenever *senora* Lydia's teas had compelled me to attend to my bladder I knew exactly where the mothafucka was. I strode for it like a warrior triumphant carrying his spoils in his aims. Boldly I strode. But carefully. My left arm was happily draped with legs, my right arm was just there for her back. But my hand cradled her noggin as preciously as you would an infant's because, take it from me, bumping a woman's head on a doorjamb is very unromantic.

Once inside I let her legs descend—slowly—while keeping her close so that her pantyhosed loins slid down me like a fire-gal down the pole. And (I gotta tell you) once the lady was upon her feet my hands alit on the exact kind of ass for which black women are justly renown.

Milagros reached past me to turn on the light. "My sentiment exactly," I say, for I had been looking forward to *seeing* her eyes roll up to the whites.

My fingertips slipped into her waistbands. Impatiently she rears up, as though she would leapfrog out of her underthings. Ever the gentleman, I endeavor to help, splaying my fingers inside her panties, sinking down, taking them with me as I went. All the while as I descend, the tip of my tongue cleaves her in two. From her forehead, pass her nose, pass her chinny-chin-chin, her throat. Slowly. Much too slowly for her taste, I can tell you, for already her breath has quickened and little frissons, faintly suggesting the quakes to come, pulse against my tongue. Surely the lady has been getting it less and was needing it very much more. So naturally I slowed further—and wasn't that an homage to my mightiness, 'cuz, yo, her panties were down past her crotch and her exposed womanness all but blared in my face imploring me to hurry up and enter. Succumbing, however, was not one of my things. For her own greater good my tongue stopped its suggestive descent and segued to her breasts. She made a little mewl of protest. *Oh how I suffer so*, it said. And, impatient still, her hands went to my bowed shoulder to encourage me down.

Until my tongue swirled around one blessedly long fat nipple.

"*Ohh.*"

Ain't that somethin'? One minute she's trying to push me down to the yonder; the next she's trying to force her torso down my throat. Yea. I was more than willing to accommodate the lady, to stop skirting and engulf. Indeed. I did stretch my mouth wide and covered one breast so as to bend its nipple against the back of my tongue. But that was only to see if I could. Before she could settle into the sensation, I released her now moist breast to the air that thus (I imagine) felt cold and empty. More cruelly, like the almost-touching fingers in the Sistene Chapel, the tip of my tongue just whispered pass the tip of her now engorged nipple. The poor baby groaned in torment, but obliviously down I went. Into the valley of her navel. Over her mountain veneris. My hands caressed her calves with her bunched stockings. My tongue frolicked around the lip of her garden. But dat all.

With a groan of exquisite anguish, the famished beast fought her legs out of her stockings and pulled me to my feet. "Please," she whimpered and bullied my jacket off my back.

It fell where it fell and I got at my shirt and tie because she (not surprisingly) went for my pants. In a thrice I was as naked as Milagros who instantly lifted one leg and tried to climb aboard. I grabbed her by her buttocks and lifted her up, pretending to help. Her arms went round my neck; her legs went round my waist. Faking further, I held her aloft with one arm and held my turgid self with the other. All the while I consumed her expressions. Her slack mouth, her unfocused eyes, the acuity of her hunger; all were to me as blood to the Vampire Lestat. How delicious. how intoxicating when her ethereally lovely face contorted with lust. She moved her bottom searchingly and I revealed my whereabouts by lightly grazing the petals of her flower. From deep in the pit of her being a quintessentially animal sound came and forcefully she thrust herself downward.

To slide along the shaft of the target I had moved just outta her line of fire. Mila, of course, whimpered in frustration and tried to raise herself back into the necessary position. But my arms entrapped her now, letting her raise her parted self only so high and no higher.

"You're killing me," she groans.

Or so I think. Her voice was really quite unintelligible as she slid up and down against my shaft like Sisyphus up and down the hill. Only difference is Milagros was accomplishing something. The contact, you see, was enough to turn her initial frustration into at least a couple of mini-Os. I looked to her face and (I saw) I wasn't even there. I was only an instrument for what (at least for the moment) was the sole function of her existence. Ain't that something? I and all my human elements—my rights, my needs, my meanings—had been reduced to a mere thing, a mere object upon which the lady was getting her jollies.

I could not have been more pleased.

Kill me Again

Once, when her tremors had registered markedly higher on the scale, I kissed her brutally. And indeed that did help her along. But dat all. Otherwise just letting her appetite get wetter—that is, whetter—was chill with me. In-damn-deed, had my legs not started getting tired I would've parlayed the foreplay into five. But they did, so I headed for respite which in this case meant the lady's bed. Mila's legs remained wrapped around me as I lowered her to her back, though I'm sure she did not immediately notice that we were no longer perpendicular. Hell, had I not done the lowering I may not have noticed either. Both of us, you see, were too startled. My God! But corny as it sounds, when our eyes met our souls entwined as palpably as an embrace. I was so distracted that before I realized it I had entered her slightly. That was not the plan but Milagros had taken advantage and locked her legs around me and melded us together with a thrust—the quick muddafudda. But I was quicker. Fleetly I withdrew and raised my hips until (let us say) I was just peeking in her door. She whimpered and arched higher. But as earlier my tongue had just encircled her nipple, I now just traced her outline. The poor child had conniptions but I just watched. Like a matador with his whole being awaiting the bull to show him the Moment of Truth, I waited for Mija to show me the limit of her frustration. Thus just before her excruciating craving dissolved into mere annoyance, I impaled her.

She froze utterly. Then thrashed like someone had dropped a lamp into her bathwater. In fact, had I not been compelled to stifle her prodigious scream (clasping her head still and engulfing her mouth with mine), she would've bucked me cold out the saddle. Was too much, even for my bronco-busting ass, and all at once I myself was bucking like a pony on loco weed. I guess that was all right. Leastways Milagros Dixon's sometimes critical, always soulful eyes had rolled up until their pupils had disappeared. And after all (in both love and war) that's when you're supposed to shoot.

WRONG NUMBER

Nicky Barnes—heroin distributor, rat—was still King of Harlem and hence of NYC.

Personally i despise him for both his *raison d'etres*. But the function of one (drug dealing) and the not functioning of the other (snitching) had a humanitarian value. See, when Nicky was King of New York and rode roughshod over heroin distribution, the trade was very strictly regulated. And cocaine, the flipside of the dope game, was so rare as to be exotic.

Then unsaintly Nick got busted.

Once he and his iron hand network stopped controlling the flow the dope trickle rapidly became a flood. "Junkies' Paradise" (the infamous stretch of four or five city blocks that teemed with drug users and dealers all day in, all seasons and was formerly *unique* to Harlem) sprang up everywhere.

And concomitantly old Nicky turned rat.

Yo. Hard and unforgiving as the drug game had been, up until Nicky Barne's arrest and betrayals a very concrete code prevailed. Of course there'd been snitches even during his heyday. But just as his control of drug distribution kept heroin and other shit to a trickle, his reign over The Code he'd inherited and (in the great

Wrong Number

Cyclopean eye of thugdom) The Code he *absolutely* exemplified kept a meaningful honor among the thieves.

Now imagine what would happen if the Catholic Pope publicly renounced Christianity. Well, that's precisely the impact Nicky's flipping had. Do you understand? Nicky Barnes was a living legend. The *Pope* of Standing Up. The *Pope* of Being True to the Code.

So when *he* broke down and became a government witness the *code* broke down with him.

Ain't *nothing* speculative 'bout it.

Street folk were devastated, and not just locally. Just like, say, in rap or clothing style, mothafuckas everywhere take their cue from New York, so too did NY influence the rat trend.

And the result of the undammed pestilential tributaries that were the Dope Traffic and The Broken Code? A deluge of drugs and fleets of people selling and being sold down the river. And high tides of blood. The drive-bys, the gun downs, the just general viciousness that is now the ghetto norm stem directly from Nicky's betrayal. People simply became devalued. See, if it was all right to send someone to prison (and it was 'cuz Nicky did it) then all other bets were off. Intimately related is the fact that mobs of unrestrained, unprincipled children now call the shots. That's 99% of the problem. The proliferation of the drug trade without even its veneer of conscience has made children filthy rich in a culture that esteems filth and richness above all things. And therein is the answer. Children are by nature immature and irrationally self-indulgent—*and* impulsive *and* egocentric. Now they've got automatic weapons—without a tempering code of conduct—and all the loot in the world.

Do you see?

Unschooled kids (who think the purpose of life is to party) have taken over. And these dumb children (if not killed by other children) grow into dumb adults. But dat all. No wonder our communities operate like kingdoms ruled by spoiled brats. They are. Except instead of *one* adolescent or adolescent-adult on the throne, we've got a *million* of 'em, each trying to out-mis-rule the others.

Except they weren't.

'Cuz in my dream Nicky Barnes—heroin distributor, rat—was still King of Harlem, hence of NYC. And so you *still* hid the joint and fanned the smoke when *any*body's ma came into the building; old folk *still* sat on their stoops and children played in their concrete jungles unafraid….

(*But what was this intrusion?* It was quite random, quite unrelated; failed to fit the scheme of my dream in any fashion. Gradually I left the REM state for a somewhat more conscious brain wave pattern and the intrusion made a bit more sense. I was dreaming about drugs and violence, after all. Consequently being poked under the chin by what my long experience recognized as the cold barrel of a gun was not all foreign to my dreamscape…A gun?)

My eyes flew open. Yep. There it was. I could just make out its silver body if I stretched a glance down. Then I thought I was still dreaming because attached to it (sitting naked astride my chest, pinning my arms) was Milagros.

I smiled. "For a man recently retired from my line of work, this is not a good joke." I start to rise.

She pushes the steel up into the underside of my jaw. "Do I look like I'm joking?"

I take a moment to check her out. *My, my,* I think. *Now that you mention it, no, you do not.* So I say. "Now that you mention it, no, you do not."

"Good. So you know if you try to think of anything I'll blow your motherfucking brains out. Do you understand?"

Motherfucking? A hint of a smile returns.

Milagros digs into me with the barrel. "You find that funny?"

"I thought you were such a lady."

She pushes my head up another notch. "What? And a lady can't kill you?"

"Oh, anyone can kill me." *But only you can break my heart.* And, you know, that hit me harder than the possibility of my imminent demise. "Question?" I appealed.

"Make it quick."

"What nationality are you?"

Fierce pride flashes on her face.

"Dominicana, maricone."

WRONG NUMBER

Ah. From good old Felito's *patria*. So that explained it. Somewhat. But now wasn't the time to figure. Wearily, my head shifted into battle mode. Never mind that my antagonist was naked and beautiful and I (alas) loved her. Once again it was just a fight for my life.

And that's why, though my head readied, my spirit idled. Life? What life did I have to fight for? I went from one gratification to another without purpose or accomplishment. like an aimless cockroach from one crumb to the next. Life was a circle, all right. One of them circular treadmills the caged mouse walked round and round. If occasionally I got a speck of cheese I gave it back, was just another nigga spending a dollar--a black dollar in some white place. i was just another nonentity passing through, being done to but not doing. So feverishly I searched about for reason to fight for life. And wasn't that funny? The one thing I would live for was threatening to kill me. So I groped. And Bama came to mind. You know. His plight; the danger to him. All right, then. Saving Bama would be my reason for saving myself. Yeah. Okay. Bama.

Feebly my spirit clutched at that and (because surviving is what I do) my being determined to survive. Imperceptibly I gathered my *chi*, prepared to all at once hurl Milagros violently into the wall behind me, putting all my money on one bet. I relaxed.

And (perhaps in response) the lady with the gun pulled the trigger. I blinked.

And saw the bluish butane flame of the "gun's" wick.

"You punk ass motha*fucka!*"

The laughing faggot toppled to the bed when I bolted up. Straight away I straddled her. But gently, gently. Far from angry, I felt like a man who'd had a terminal disease and was suddenly diagnosed as cured. I know. Many another male would've broken her jaw. But did you hear what I'd said before? Last night, in a lightning flash of something, Milagros and I had touched souls. Hurt her? I'd kill and die for the magnificent beingwith equal alacrity. Thus when the punk pulled that trigger and instead of lead flame shot out, all the possibilities of the world again re-opened, were illumined in her light.

Overjoyed at the dirty trick, I wrestled the gun from her hand. "If you wanted some more dick,. all you had to do was take it."

She looks at me like I was stupid. "*Well?*" You know: *well what do you think I'm doing?*

"And where did you learn to say 'motherfucking'?" I push her thighs firmly against her breasts.

Ever the gracious lady, Mila clasps her knees in place for me. "From you," she says a little huskily.

"Yeah?" I descend on her, my willing victim, like a rampaging angel of doom. "Well let's see what other bad thing I can teach you."

*****

More than a little time elapses, I stare at the ceiling. Mlla was curled kitten-like in my arms. Quiescent, appeased; her cerebral cortex fucked into a stupor. The whole day was ours, we'd already agreed. And then—*again*—the night.

"How long have we known each other?" I ask out of nowhere.

"I don't know," she distantly murmurs, "months."

"No. That's how long it's been since we've met. I asked how long have we known each other. And the answer—"

"*Ow!*" Milagros rubs her glorious butt, which (to ensure her attention) I'd pinched.

"The answer is 'always'." I incline my head and find her looking up at me. "Whaja say to that?"

True to her analytical nature, she attacks the question. "I think you're a classic 'incurable romantic'." Then she smiled her magnificent smile. "I think I like that a lot."

"And I think you're a repressed romantic afraid to confront her feelings."

She laughs. "And what does that mean?"

"That we should get married."

"Fool," she says, but not with her eyes.

"Yeah, anybody who knows me will tell you that I ain't got a lick of sense."

Lovingly she strokes my cheek.

"Harass me with your confessions later," she murmurs, then returns to her sated repose.

Wrong Number

I return to contemplating the ceiling. Wasn't I a lucky mothafucka? I mean, how in the world men had let this one get away I don't know. Maybe one day she'd tell me. I'd never inquire about her past, of course. I mean, I was curious, but idly. Although I knew for a natural born fact Milagros was a person of great dignity, it wouldn't have mattered to me if she'd been selling ass on 9th Ave. If I dug you I dug you. Dat all. Indeed, already I felt so indistinguishable from the woman lying serenely at my side, I knew nothing could tear us asunder.

Beep beep beep...

Except that.

"Pardon," I say. Gently I try to extricate my arms, but I needn't have bothered:

Milagros has all but snatched herself away. "Your master beckons," she says sitting up, looking...afraid?

I tried to make a joke of it. "Now you know all of my secrets." Bare-assed I mosey to retrieve my shamefully discarded *pantalones* from the floor. I didn't bother unclipping the pager. I just pick the whole mess up and looked. "Do you have any coffee?"

Milagros' soulful eyes looked a look at me. Something along the order of a Louisville Slugger and a hard swing. "In the kitchen."

When she got up, she took the top sheet with her. You know how women do that. Like it's a triple extra large bath towel. Never could figure it. I mean all night you say and do things with and to each other. Then come daybreak the woman gets this modesty. I believe it was more paradox than hypocrisy, but sho' as you born the woman who sits with her knees primly together and is perfectly demure in the light of day is the same wanton trying to break your dick off whenever she makes it disappear *(Look, mom! No hands!)*

But I digress.

Still bare-assed, I start gathering my clothes; look around for a place to put them; settle for a chair. Then I head for the bathroom with my undershorts in hand. The door was closed—and locked. Expecting the worse, I knock. "Open up 'fore I huff and puff, et cetera."

"Wait til I'm done," she says, though from her tone it may as well have been *fuck you, mothafucka*.

"And you too," I say to the door. Obediently I wait. And wait. And bemoan my fate. A beautiful Saturday morning we should be spending together and I got to get beeped to a mission. Ah well.

Milagros emerges. Huffs pass me carrying the sheet; is wrapped in a real towel now. I am very inclined to just reach out and touch me somebody but already I've delayed too long,

I hustle in and do some quick ablutions; jetted back to the bedroom and my clothes. Milagros sits at her vanity removing the gold from her snakes.

I dress. "Milagros, we never did get around to that explanation." I am of course in motion while I speak. "But as soon as I tie this loose end you'll have it."

Baby kept at her chore. I moseyed up to her flawless back and (looking over her shoulder into the mirror) straighten my tie. Then I pick her and her chair up and turn them to face me.

"Your feats of strength are so impressive," she says nastily.

"And your impressive feet are so strong." I squat down. "A kiss before I go?"

Of course she turns her head away. "Just go."

I sigh. "I am really overdue so I'm gonna haveta leave you to your irrational assumption. But when I return I'll accept your apology."

"Just *go*," the mothafucka insists—rather vehemently, I might add.

So go I did.

FLUCK IT

"Fuckin' mutant," I mumble.

And justifiably. I mean I'm just sitting there sipping coffee, watching the sickly Hudson flow by Riverside Park. Dat all. I wasn't even noticing the bitch jogger until she made a show of noticing me. She'd been approaching at a good clip, see, when suddenly she'd done a double-take at the bench upon which my red/black/& green was parked. Since mine was the only ass sitting on the mothafucka I figured it was I who'd made her abruptly slow, swing into an arc, then burst into a sprint for her life.

Ain't that something?

I mean, my suit wasn't *that* crumpled. The racist bitch. Like all black men go to the park for is to lie in wait for bitch white joggers.

How *dare* the fuckin' mutation react fearfully to me! If anyone had a right to be fearful it was I and my people of her and almost all of her mutant race. For it is written (or should be if it ain't): *By Their Cliches Shall Ye Know Them* because by their very matter-of-factness cliches reveal what a people are really and truly made of.

And what are the cliches of the bitch jogger's mutant culture?

Dog eat dog.

The rat race.

ATIBA OMAR

Every man for himself.

The end justifies the means.

And what is this shit about *The struggle against nature*? How could the idea that *nature is the enemy* be so widespread and commonplace as to become *cliche*?

For that one, you've gotta be a fuckin' mutant living in a mutant culture.

No wonder their botanists can pervert the seeds out of an orange and think it a good thing! No wonder their ideal of the future is a space station. No wonder they say they love nature while reveling in a lifestyle that destroys it. Then a wonderful thought hit me.

"You look happy." I glanced up at Bakari, whose long, wide presence I'd sensed before he'd spoken.

"I just had a lovely thought."

Hometown looked like an NBA player in the pretty warm-up suit he wore. He sat down. "I'm list'nin'."

"You know all those fluorocarbons whites are always spewing into the air?"

"You mean through spray cans and fossil fuels and shit?"

I nod. "That shit's fuckin' up the ozone layer."

"Who don't know that."

"Well, I was just thinking." I eyeball homeboy. "You know how the sun hates them?"

"Sho'. That's why outside of their natural caucasoid habitat they gotta glob on sun block and shit."

I nod vigorously. "So wouldn't it be wonderful if all these extra UV rays they're unleashing gave all of them skin cancer and they died?"

Bakari laughs uproariously. "The cosmic chicken coming home to roost, huh?"

"Yeah." The possibility of white extinction makes me grin hugely, 'cuz--let's face it--that's the *only* way to stop the destruction of humanity, native societies, killer cops and the world..

"Well, I got more joyful stuff for you to chew on."

Fluck It

"Wha' dat?"

"They pushed Bama's date up."

"Yeah?" My already wide grin widens. "That's a good damn sign. When's it now?"

"Wednesday."

Then a not so wonderful thought hit me. "Yo. I'm very happy to learn that Bama is closer to the door—but that ain't no emergency. You could've told me this on the phone."

"Hmph." Bakari looks me up and down. "I can see you come straight from a high old time. But that's still the stupidest thing I ever did hear."

I opened my mouth to protest but jack came out. Old Ba-ba-dee-ba was right, of course: it was stupid to undervalue detail, especially details of security. Like, when Bakari beeped me from a pay phone, I returned the call—from a pay phone. And when he'd answered all he'd said was *four/eleven*. That's where we were now. Location four. And (I glanced at my watch) the time was 11:05. We always kept five or six randomly selected meeting places up our sleeves to be used once and bye. Kind of like toilet tissue. And we did a lot of hocus pocus to get to them undetected. You know. To make sure we weren't followed. Yo. The pains we took were always tedious and usually unnecessary. Probably. But it was elementary that the first time you didn't overkill security precautions the laxity would kill you. So, as Ba-da-ba-ski had implicitly said, talking shop on the phone only once was as sensible as sticking yourself with an AIDS infected needle only once.

Thus I conceded. "Yeah. You're right. I'm just talking."

Hometown smiled knowingly. "She must be a double-humdinger."

"*Triple.*"

"Well, here."

Only after I pocketed the two keys he'd extended did I raise an eyebrow.

"That's where me and the money is staying, mine and Bama's."

Quickly but clearly and twice--like I was retarded or something—he whispered his new address and where in the apartment I could find over two million cash.

"I hope it don't come to that."

Ba shrugged his mile-wide shoulders.

"General principle is general principle." Suddenly he stood his long ass up and started going through a warm up routine.

I was a wee perplexed. "You act like you're getting ready to jog." He had his right leg bent up to his butt.

"Figure since I got this suit on and I'm in the park….." He changed legs.

"Well, what about *me*?" *Sheesh*. That sounded whiney like a *mothafucka*.

"All I know is I'm gonna run on down this track. But if I was you—" He started jogging backward down the self-same path the bitch mutant had jogged. "—I'd get on back to that 'triple'." Spinning forward, he trucked away.

See ya, I yelled at his back. Or started to til I got distracted by what was on it. A bull's eye inside one of those red circles with a diagonal slash. Printed above was JUST JOGGING. And beneath: DON'T SHOOT.

*****

I was a fool to press my luck but (as I'd told Milagros earlier that day) I ain't got a lick of sense. That's why I was knocking on her door.

After I'd left Bakari I was just a hop, a skip, and a jump from home so I hopped, I skipped and I jumped. Soon as my apartment door was locked behind me, I undid my tie with one hand and reached for the phone with the other.

"Yes?" Milagros said.

"*Hola, mi amor*, I—"

Click.

I expected that. Personally I thought her reaction excessive. But because she imagined some justification I expected she'd be acting soopastoopid for a while. Ahl well. I showered. Thereby giving her some time to locate whatever piece of brain she could find. A half hour later I called her again.

"Yes?" she said. And never was a more seductive sound ever reproduced by fiber optics.

"Milagros, I—"

"Do *not* call here again."

Click.

Now *that* fell outside my anticipations. I mean, I didn't quite expect her to fall prostrate at my feet, but I did figure she'd let me get a beg in.

Ah well.

I pressed play on my answering machine. A couple of brawds had left messages indirectly asking for the dick. A couple more had spat the request right out.

And Marty called (*Just want you to know that Ruthie's doing fine and sends her love*). Love? *Rattle snake venom*, he means. But for him I am happy. For myself, well, I was feeling somewhat bereft. So to quell my blues I moseyed to the kitchen to make a sandwich.

Then I clicked on the radio.

"...—ternational Criminal Court issued another warning to Israel against what some are calling 'ethnic cleansing' of Palestinian communities," someone regurgitated. With just the right note of seriousness in her voice too.

I open the frig. *Poor oil-less Muslims,* I think, whilst peering contemplatively at the options. 'Cuz—let's face it—without oil reserves or strategic locality, the Palestinian Muslims could forget about the West finding the outrage it feigned for the oil-rich Muslims in Kuwait.

Now let me see. What's it gonna be? I had a lot of cheese, I noticed. So tentatively I pulled a few out. Swiss, American, Monterey Jack. Then, my bearings established, I start pulling out stuff with unfailing ease: horse radish, lettuce, tomato, onion, garlic—now that my mission was clear, my hands knew exactly what to do for my tongue. By the time I found a jalepeno pepper the news had narrowed to national. "...potentially positive, many questioned its leadership." That made me smile. Bullshit always did. The same newscaster (now inflecting just the right amount of distaste) was talking about the Million Man Marches and, of course, Farrakhan.

Now don't get me wrong. I'm hardly a lover of Rev. Louis. To tell the truth, he's so in love with himself the autograph line (if you were so inclined) is too filled with him to wait in. However, just because he's a meglomaniac doesn't mean he can't do something progressive. Like organizing a MMM. Yeah. The event missed targets and tripped and fell short. The mojo had not quite arisen. Nonetheless, it was ... intriguing. Not unlike stirrings in a graveyard.

I moseyed over to a cupboard and took out some prepared mustard powder. By the time I'd heaped a big spoonful into a bowl (I liked it flaming hot) I was really smiling because now the bullshit was really rank. The newscaster (that is. the white male supremacists who proofed the script for the affirmative action white female newscaster) was reporting 'candidly'. And t'weren't nothing funnier than a candid face spouting bullshit. You know. Like a Barbara Walters. "...couldn't in good conscience be associated with a self-avowed leader who declared Hitler even 'wickedly great'," some after-the-fact negro had said/would always say. You know how it goes. Stick a mike into a negro's puss and he thinks career opportunity. Mayhaps the table spread of fixin's to be diced, smeared, layered and lathered was too dizzying an array.

But I believe what actually confused me was the implication of all the commentary on Farrakhan's Hitler remark.

Both white and black eurocentrists loved to misquote it. It was all so peculiar. Not unlike that neat trick Caucasoids love to do. You know the one. Sometimes to promote themselves they hide in a crowd (like in the notion of "reverse racism" which they think enables them to say, *See! We're not so bad 'cuz you can be racist too).* But other times to promote themselves they single themselves out.

Neat, huh?

Like, to let Jews tell it, Hitler exterminated non-Jews incidentally. Only *they* and *they alone* were *real* victims. Indeed, whereas gypsies and homosexuals receive passing acknowledgment, the unspeakable crimes done to Africans (both captured troops and kidnaped North Africans) are, well, never spoken. Maybe it's some kind of lunatic jealousy. You know. We had a *really* long running horror show all to our chattel slaveselves. So can't we just get off the holocaust stage, already? Whatever. Though others seem unaware of Nazi crimes against Original People, I am not. Thus Hitler is no friend of mine.

Fluck It

Nonetheless, the ballyhoo about him "wickedly great" confuses me.

See, I know of this dude who enslaved people, then physically and sexually exploited them. It is abstractly conceivable he was a 'good' master. But we know that to the enslaved human being that meant only that on the 'good' plantation sadism required pretext to indulge itself: reckless eyeballin', shiftlessness, being uppity, too slow, too black...you know: pretext. In any event, I know that this child molesting enslaver and (at *least*) condoner of torture made a *fortune* through his evil enterprise--and doubtless not because he was squeamish about cracking the whip.

But who is allowed to say that the bestial, perverted, wicked George Washington was not great?

Thus I am confused. Irrespective of what he did to my people and to Jews, Hitler was a great man to the Germans. So if we're supposed to get appalled because Farrakhan acknowledged that, let's get appalled when an evil monster like Washington is lauded. Hell. The only real difference between George Washington and Adolph Hitler is time. Dat all. Like in a hundred years Newt Gingrich (who is Rush Limbaugh in disguise who is David Duke in disguise who is Jeffrey Dahmer) will be touted as a champion of Afrikan-American rights. But what do I know?

Why, how to make a righteous sandwich is what.

I sat back and eyed the as yet open-faced construction. Dagwood Bumstead would be so proud! Then, having paid my handiwork proper respect, I resealed the bag of multigrain bread (careful to squeeze as much air out as possible, as any true sandwich maker would) and prepared to do what even the master Bumstead had never conceived in any of his comic strip thought bubbles: I reached for a *different* kind of bread. In this instance, a thin slice of bakery pumpernickel. My god, I was nearly atremble in anticipation as I plopped the top on the heap. With a very sharp bread knife (sharp because it was almost impossible to dull a bread knife if you used it only for bread) I sliced the mothafucka diagonally. Eating slowly, I listened to some more white edited white interpretations from the white newscaster.

And cussed Milagros.

By the time I'd finished chomping the first heavenly mouthful into babymush, I'd concluded that had Bakari not beeped me Milagros wouldn't be giving me the blues.

So I cussed him.

Mm! My next chomp was a dee-*lux* chomp. I mean I got it all: garlic, jalepeno, mustard, horse radish, onion and a *big* old glob of mayo my arteries would be paying for for a week. *Mm!* Sweat beaded my forehead and reverentially, slowly, I moved the head-exploding taste from tongue to esophagus. By then I'd realized that if only Bama wouldn't've gotten I-D-eed…..

So I started cussing him.

Then Skins for ratting Bama out to the mob.

Then all three of us (Bama, Bakari and me) for not killing Skins on general principle *before* the robbery, though that's something i contemplated now only 'cuz of hindsight.

Hell. The first wedge wasn't half-swallowed and I'd left a string of *if-not-far-yous* almost back to the Celestial Throne. So I got up, stored the remnants of my masterpiece in the 'frig and tried Milagros a third time.

"Hola," she said pleasantly.

"Milagros, don't—"

"I'm not home right now but if you….."

Now it was my turn to hang up. Sort of. Truth was I was hung up *on* her and I was starting not to like it one bit. I mean love is cool when it's requited. But this one-sided shit wasn't working. I had no idea how to fix what I was feeling. So I did the psycho-emotional defensive thing and—*poof!*—tried to make it not exist. The crumbs on the table existed. So I took care of those. The plates existed, so I got at them. Yeah. This was good. Between washing the mustard bowl and the utensils there was no room for what's-her-name at all. So continuing not to think about She-Who-Does-Not-Exist I moseyed on to my bedroom for a baseball cap and my car keys. *Gonna hunt for Skins some mo'*, I told myself. And to my credit I made convincing gestures. I sought out two of his main lieutenants and tried to buy some product. But shop, they said, was still closed—which meant the proprietor was still out on bitch-leave. Then I tried his apartment—for the fourth or fifth time that week.

Fluck It

But some kind of mysterious how I swerved onto the Van Wyck Expressway and ended up at Milagros' door.

Feeling like a sucker, of course. I mean, was I not a True Player? Had I not seen *The Mack*? *Seen*? I had so many notches on my gun I was damn near sawed through the handle. So what the fuck was a lady killer of my deadly calibre doing acting like a hard-up stalker?

"Trying to suck up," I muttered. "Trying to kiss me some ass." That settled, I knocked upon the door.

Milagros answered almost instantly. "Who is it?"

"Milagros, it's—"

"*Go* away."

Now who didn't know she was gonna say that?

I did. Verily, all the time I'd been denying her existence my subconscious had written a script. It ended *And they lived happily ever after.* But it began *Go away.* I smile. Even her tone, I realize now, is what I'd imagined. Confidently I prepare to launch into the next lines my subconscious had rehearsed.

Then baby shut me down. "If you knock on my door again I'm calling the police."

That poleaxed the fuck outta me. Snitching, of course, was the blasphemy of blasphemies, like returning a captured fugitive to the plantation. From anyone the threat was grievous. But from Milagros, who I thought cared about me?

I back away from the door like it's a rabid dog on a frayed leash. "You win," I said loudly enough to be heard. Then under my voice, "Irrational mothafucka. Should kill your ass." Because who knew? The crazy mothafucka might indeed rat me out on all that shit I'd been stupid enough to confess to. A coldness tightly enveloped my heart. I paused and touched one of my guns. Then quickly, fleeing from myself, I hurried away.

*****

In *tai chi chuan* (which teaches how to rupture organs with a touch, hurl people across rooms with a gesture) force is abhorred.

Yo. You can subdue a dozen Mike Tysons in one whirlwind encounter, but if you use strength to do it the 'players' pity you your ineptitude or are offended. Verily, the *chin*, that is, the Tao school, was finesse city where no brute stuff was welcome.

That's why I'd taken my angry ass to the gym. I may have needed the calming effect of a Taoist moving meditation, but I wanted exactly the kind of violent workout their serene brows frown upon. So when I'd left Milagros', instead of going to the temple as I should've I indulged the uncultivated thug part of my second nature and went where no Taoist had gone before. To one of them private co-ed gyms where crude strength is extolled.

I'd just finished a routine that was in keeping with the vulgar spirit of the upscale place. To be sure, I used only punk weight, did scarcely more than 300 for squats. But the high rep, virtually no rest intensity I maintained was murderous. Yo, when I threw down you could line up ten bad mothafuckas and maybe one could hang. Not surprisingly, then, I was drenched, even though I'd been winding down with stretches for the last ten minutes or so. I was in the section of the vast gym consisting of a padded surface for floor exercises. Just now I was doing a split, palms pressed together prayerfully, eyes closed. But clear as day I saw (? felt?) a presence drop down in front of me. It did not feel menacing, it felt…..I dunno. Indifferently, lazily, I opened my eyes.

And peer into the dazzling green orbs of a Cover Girl.

Now there are many things that come from black folks that de white folk benefit from: monotheism, hygiene, the traffic light, refrigerated cars, elevators, cellular phones, ice cream and potato chips ad infinitum.

But what I like best is lips.

Yo. Show me a Kim Basinger or Diane Sawyer or whoever and I'll show you a 'tainted' gene pool. Right now the beautiful face of the technically white girl was faking a blank, though her Irish eves are smiling.

Apparently oblivious of me, baby of the wild red tresses mirrors my posture. Not badly either. Yo. Only difference between us was that I was barefoot wearing gym shorts and a muscle shirt while she had one of those spandex girlie outfits on a physique so sleek you wanted to run out and renew you membership. Other than that, she held the split with depth and ease like my very own mothafucking twin. Impressed, delighted, I tried to do the eye contact thing. You know. To convey appreciation, etc. But her dazzling greens danced away.

Well, if she won't acknowledge me directly....

FLUCK IT

Maintaining the split, I lowered my torso until my nose touched the mat and my arms outstretched in salaam, my fingertips 'inadvertently' (ha ha ha) a sweat drop away from her spandexed vulva. After a moment I raise my head till my chin is on the ground and look a gloat at baby.

Who has *her* chin parked on the ground and her outstretched arms salaaming me *back*.

Her eyes still smiled but her expression was yet blank—like she's thinking these stretches up all by herself and I ain't even on her mind, much less in front of her. I chuckle a little and slowly raise up until again seated in a forward split. Then, smoothly but carefully, I turn in to a right side split.

Baby does likewise.

So I raise up a little, turn left and grab my foot and touch my head to my knee. Discreetly I stretch my eyeballs at baby to see what's what.

The colleen (looking bored!) has matched me.

I sit up, still facing leftward in a side-split. Raising up slightly, I swing my right leg around (my foot just so happening to brush the lass' thigh in passing) and park it next to my left. I pause. Exhale fully. Then put my right leg behind my neck. Very gingerly I sneak a peek at O'Baby.

Who naturally has her right leg well down her shoulder blades— the mothafucka. Took me ages to get that loose and here she comes and does it like it ain't jack.

But I am not deterred.

Like the arc of God I drop down (leg still behind neck) and touch my head to my outstretched knee. I stay there a while, holding the tension, overcoming the pressure (*That'll marinate her sauce*).

But when I finally squeeze a look-see Baby O'Baby (who was doubtless waiting for my attention) yawns.

What a darling little rascal!

Slowly I sit up, make a nominal gesture of doing the same exercise for the left leg. But that was for symmetry. You know. What you do for one side….. Of course O'Baby followed even *that* perfunctory movement like a heat-seeking missile would a target.

By now a crowd has gathered to watch our shoot out. Yo. At least a dozen people have stopped working out to spectate this heretofore unseen kind of battle of the sexes. I (the champion) smile acknowledgment.

O'Baby (the contender) looks blase.

Maestro-like I gesture the growing throng to stand back. It obliges. A hush descends. Expectation mounts. Trumpets— Oh. That's another story. Anyway, I kneel, palms and forearms flat on the mat. Then, as if in abject obeisance, I rest my face on the back of my hands. I inhale. Hold the breath. Slowly, smoothly—all my weight on my forearms and palms—my face lifts, my head tilts back, my legs go up, up and over until my toes almost touch my upraised head. I stay there in the Scorpion an effortless moment then triumphantly (riskily) sneak a look at the gorgeous upstart.

Whose painted toenails (where'd her sneakers go?) are actually *touching* her mane.

That did it. I descend. Like a Samurai in a frenzy I fold this, arch that, twist, bend, flow like water into one intricate maneuver after the next, pausing only long enough to display each *shih* or *asana* clearly. But I feel like Bugs Bunny trying to outrun that tortoise 'cuz *every* time I look up, there is O'Baby doing what I'm doing and often better.

I come to a pit stop on my knees, chest heaving. O'Baby still has her blank mask on but (praise the Gods!) her shapely little bosom belyingly heaves with mine and her face is flushed, her sexy mop tossled. She looks, in fact, much as I imagine she would if she were wrapped around me in bed and half recouped from orgasm and—

But there were too many people around for that erecting line of thought. So to displace the sexual energy I sprang all at once from my knees to my feet, startling the white folks (who doubtless feared the entertaining nigga was reverting to lunatic type). But when they saw my violent outburst was only in the force of my movement the cowards murmured admiration. We all then looked expectantly at O'Baby who was still surprised on her knees. But bless her brave self, you could actually see her intelligent face working out the mechanics of how to go from kneeling stillness to erect motion in one explosive instant, as though it was a math problem or something. When she hit upon the solution (which, simply, was to just do it) her face alit a moment before she exploded like a starburst to her feet.

Fluck It

She bows. Folks applaud. I smile; stroke my chin. This was one *bad* mothafucka—and she knew it, the delectable so-and-so. In fact, now she even looked at me, her Africoid lips at last smiling with her eyes. Her still slightly heaving bosom thrust up and out as if to challenge, *Any more rabbits in your hat? Well* bring 'em out.

So I did something I'd never done before.

While *oos* and *ahs* were yet being thrown at O'Baby like so many flowers at her feet; while O'Baby basked and gloated and dared, I (without knowing what the fuck I was doing) bent my knees, tightened my dangling hands into fists and from my standing position leaped myself into a backwards spinning ball that touched down in an Olympian 9.5.

Stunned silence followed a moment. Then: "*Wow*!" "Bravo!" "Did you see that?!"

Gracefully I accepted my cheers then waved a your-turn at my worthy foe. All eyes ping ponged to O'Baby. She looked shook. But of course the intrepid mothafucka prepared to give it a go anyway. She bent her sturdy little knees until (wreck me, baby) her pert butt jutted out as invitingly as a moue. Her hands clenched, her body tensed and even I watched to see how she'd do it so I would know how I did. Thus attentively I observed O'Baby tense and tense.

And deflate like a stuck balloon.

She shakes her glorious war bonnet of a hairdo. "Uh-uh." Smirking, she walks to me--and *what* a walk it was. I mean it was only a few steps between us but her strong, feline legs kicked out each step like Bruce Lee knocking down bad guys.

When she poked me in my chest my heart reached out and (Milagros *Who?*) wrapped around her electric touch. "You win," she says, as gracious in her imagined defeat as she'd been graceful in her performance.

The crowd started to applaud me. But it was too entirely undeserved. Before even I knew what I was doing, I picked O'Baby up by the waist and rested her butt on my shoulder. The little girl in her squealed with delight and I was suddenly overwhelmed. With her scents, her heat; with the electric touch of her intimate flesh against mine. Easily I held her lithe body in place with one hand.

With the other I gestured at O'Baby, the big prize on the *Price Is Right*. "All hail the conquering hero," I boom.

ATIBA OMAR

Boisterous *hoorahs* and such erupt, as much (I'd like to think) for my magnanimity as for O'Baby's razzle dazzle. Slowly I spin around so that all who encircle us might gaze on the triumphant beauty—who now hams it up with mock bows and things, the little darling; clinging to me with one arm, gesticulating sinuously with the other. Once the round was made and the crowd began dispersing, I used my free hand (somewhat familiarly) to help O'Baby slide off my shoulder, down my arm. Soon as her feet touch the ground she's walking away with *nary* a backward glance.

Before her arm, which trails negligently behind her, can slip out of my grasp I clutch her hand. "Wait." Only when she turns to face me do I release my hold. She looks surprised. "How can you just leave me like this?"

"*Leave* you?" Just then an admirer hands her the sneakers she'd toed off when the stretches had gotten funky. "I'm only going to change."

Now I look surprised.

"My name is Katherine," O'Baby says. "And if you give me about 10 minutes I'll be very pleased to meet you."

OOPS

The swell of her recumbent hip was what helped me figure it out.

Three days had passed since Kat baby and I had had our now legendary showdown in the gym. Three days of discovering other synchronicities:

She was an anthropology major/I dug jumping her bones.

She was vegetarian/I found that vegetarians were tasty.

She liked to recover curled up on her side, one majestic hip thrust to the heavens, perfect and splendorous like the veiled and secret mountains of the moon/And I…Well, I just liked looking at her ass.

Curve flowed into curve like sea into sea. As smoothly and effortlessly as a vessel caught in the Gulf Stream. You know. That natural watercourse that carried sailors of antiquity from the West coast of the African mainland to the Americas.

And that's when I figured it out.

If not for those ancient black mariners, I wouldn't be lying here trying to pretend I was not bewildered and heartbroken. It was all so simple. Now that archaeology and linguistics and so forth have uncovered the bridge between ancient African colonizers and Olmec civilization, making the leap from Katherine O'Grady's shapely butt to comprehending my doldrums was easy. See. Sailing more than two thousand years before a manjack in Europe knew what longitude was, Africans landed in the Mexican Gulf Coast and established such incredible civilizations they were deified as (among others) Quetzalcoatl, the feathered serpent, who sailed away to his eastern homeland promising one day to return.

That's why when the Spanish Constipators arrived with their verminous bodies and hellish designs the devils were greeted as Gods. Alas, so much time had elapsed between the Africans' *going* and the Spaniards' *coming* the Aztecs and others had forgotten that Quetzalcoatl's jet black color was not *entirely* symbolic. So instead of slaughtering the Constipators as they needed to be, the grievously mistaken Incans and what have you actually handed the Constipators their children for the fucking. By the time they realized, *Hey, these guys don't act like the ones who were here before*" they were almost as extinct as their culture.

Thus came to pass Mexico, NAFTA.

And Milagros Dixon.

It was that Cosmic Domino thing again. Just because some ancient black folk thought it a good day for a sail, the world ends up with a Panama wherein a Milagros could be born to break my heart. And drive me cold outta my m.o.

And I mean really.

Katherine was indeed cotton candy, but I'd been consuming her in my Sunday suit. Which means I'd been fucking a *stranger* in my apartment, for crying the fuck out loud. And without condoms! Though to tell the truth that fazed me only slightly 'cuz condoms are for people with futures, you see, and I didn't have one now that Milagros was gone.   Indeed, my Post Milagros purpose was to just indiscriminately give all womankind what it wants: multiple Os—and I don't mean a multigrain cereal. To me there is nothing so satisfying as satisfying a woman. That stemmed from my insecurities, I suppose. Whatever. Take Katherine. I had! Again and a-goshdamn-gain. After our very friendly competition that afternoon we came to my homestead—and her lovely thighs had opened to me like the petals of a flower to the morning sun. But now they were clamped so tightly together a hydraulic jack couldn't pry them apart. I know because just for fun I had tried, had trailed a finger here, gripped her body there. But Kat baby, worked to hypersensitivity, repelled each spurious advance with sweet pleas

OOPS

and quadriceps so strongly exerted they would not admit the egress of an ant dick. So for the past fifteen minutes of so I'd left her alone, a ball of contentment, and was just in the midst of commending myself on another job well done when the door flew off the hinges.

It was the cops, of course.

Instinctively (or with the conditioned reflex that is much the same) I grabbed the gat I keep on hand for just such an eventuality and rolled my ass outta bed while Katherine O'Grady (anthropology major, totally alive human being) took the bullets that were, perhaps, meant for me.

I say *perhaps* because who knows? Katherine had *lain* with me, you understand. In the eyes of the cops—and much of the white public which gives them their cue—that was on a par with bestiality. So, who knew? Could very well be that the copsters who killed her thought it nothing more than what the 'nigga-loving slut' deserved.

Like with Fred Hampton's wife. Both the Feds and the Chicago PD had had maps detailing each room and who was in 'em when they stormed Fred Hampton's apartment. The informant (aka snitch lackey dog bitch mothafucka) who provided the maps also provided assurance that everyone was duly drugged with the sedative the upholders of the law had supplied—including Fred's pregnant wife.

Then they went and tried to murder everyone inside. These facts are incontrovertible. Some miraculous how Sandra Hampton survived the fusillade. The Gods know that even if the expectant mother had done something to get those cops mad, that almost-born baby ain't did jack. But they tried to kill it too, for the same reason they tried to kill its mother: *they were with Fred.*

Now I ain't no Fred Hampton (who was a Black Panther, by the way) but that doesn't matter 'cuz most cops (and all copsters) hate all of us equally. So maybe the bullets that tore into Katherine's nigga-loving body were hers after all. I tried to console myself. Maybe she had a father with some clout. Maybe she died happy. But the truth of the matter was I mourned.

I mourned as I rolled, firing along the way. Like so: roll—*blam blam blam!* Roll—*blam blam blam!* Roll—*blam blam blam—blam!* just in case some smart ass was thinking he had me figured.

Now I know that in my hasty roll to the closet the chances were slim that one of my hasty bullets would hit something. But if I did not fire the chance was absolute I would not. Additionally, if I provided no deterrence the bitches would come charging in like they always do when the pickings iz faggot easy like it was for the USAF in the first Iraqi invasion. So I sprayed and rolled and rolled and sprayed.

And was rewarded by another sort of carnal satisfaction: a scream followed by a thud.

"Oh Jesus, I'm hit!"

Of course the other police officers ceased firing and (shades of Larry Davis) got with their wounded attempted murderer. For one thing they were doubtless genuinely concerned. (As I continued moving inexorably to my escape in a fraction of the time it takes to tell it, I heard what sounded like a body being dragged outta my blind lucky line of fire.). But their attack on my skeedaddling person paused for less selfless reason too.

See, nothing will make you slam your brakes on quicker than the sudden reminder of your own vulnerability.

Until one of my desperation slugs had found itself a mark, those cops had been bearing down on my ass like it was the big hog at the county fair.But soon as the lead hero bit the dust the rest of his co-pigs instantly shifted off of stupid: *Uh oh*, they realized, *we can bleed, too.* It was so funny. Even though a few of them manage to get themselves needlessly killed every year, they're still surprised when death pops up in the script. You know the script I mean. The one written at the police academy that tells about all the fun they'll have swaggering through ghettoes, shaking down drug dealers in hallways and taxpayers everywhere via inflated salaries and benefits and monster OT. Nope. They never understand that scripts contain *dialogue* until a response to the line they like to deliver falls whining *Oh Jesus* at their feet.

Such a reality check was very welcomed, though. 'Cuz while they rescued their brother pigster and contemplated their own mortality, I got to my hatch. A splinter lodged in my butt but I ignored the terrible *ouch!* it wanted to evoke and instead yanked open my bag and fumbled for what I hoped was a concussion grenade. But between the cops beginning to pour into the bedroom in between my trigger squeezes and my anguish over Katherine—to say nothing of the long splinter in my ass—I didn't know what kind

Oops

of a grenade I was grabbing, tactile though I usually am. Trusting to the Gods, I pulled the pin on the first one my hand touched and (dropping through my hatch) let it fly. Bare-ass naked I crashed through the ceiling of the closet, appearing (I guess) like some unholy Santa out a chimney. Mrs. 4E, I noticed, was equally naked and in grinding sexual union—but not with *Mr.* 4E. I had no time to chide her for her infidelity. What I *did* have time for was a dash across the bedroom of the terrified couple (picking up homestud's pants and shirt en route) when the grenade above exploded.

Bbb-DOOMMM! it went just as (I hoped) the cops had regrouped and were talking that *We've got your black ass surrounded* shit.

Surround **that**, *mothafuckas*, I thought happily, even as the reverberation bounced me off a wall.

Plaster fell in a blizzard and the now hysterical Mrs. 4E got dislodged from her even more hysterical boyfriend. The only thing that held tight was me to my semi-auto. Indeed, I clutched it and my juju bag (and homeboy's I hoped not too funky clothes) for what was left of my dear little piece of life. Battered, dazed, emotionally wrought, I got the mothafuck gone.

CURIOUSER

"So why didn't the mothafucka go back?" I accuse. As if it's his fault. As if he had an answer. As if he were hard of hearing.

"Hold your voice down," Bakari whispers.

"*What?* Hold my *voice* down?" Angrily I cast my eyes upon the impudent mothafucka: *How dare you suggest such a thing,* they say. *Now we gotta fight to the death.*

But Bakari's eyes stay glued to the movie screen, utterly unconcerned with my attitude, as though the reason we came to the movies was actually to watch one. In fact, while I had one gun on the seat under my thigh ready to fight for my liberty and the money bag between my feet, hometown munched popcorn from the (what else?) *extra* large bucket perched on his knees, a soda in the empty seat on his left. To tell the truth, the whole of his demeanor was so nonchalant and dismissive of my bullshit it compelled me to consider that maybe holding my voice down was not an unreasonable suggestion after all.

So I compromised. "Fuck you," I whisper.

Relaxing into my seat, I try to look as composed as Bakari. Still watching the cornball B-movie, his silhouette nodded approval. If we held our voices to the level of my *fuck you* we could talk without

CURIOUSER

disturbing any of the clods who really wanted to see yet another white man single-handedly make the world safe.

For other white men.

So I resigned myself to whispering and looking composed, though actually I was quite eager to kill something. See (we should remember) Katherine was more daring than a horde of lemurs and just couldn't be dead.

But she was.

And as long as we're remembering shit, remember that even as I sat there all my worldly goods (both demolished and unscathed) were being inventoried by hateful strangers who sho' as you born had taken a bloodthirsty moment to put an APB on my head. Neither let us forget that splinter fragment in my butt (*damned* if I could). Nor the fact that I had to tear my ass outta Manhattan, raggedy and barefoot—with a backpack full of arms and loot and the not unjustified impression that all the cops in the world were on my ass. And if that ain't enough fuel on my fire, what does Bakari tell me when I meet him? Alabama's bail hearing date had been suddenly moved up. From Wednesday (tomorrow) to Monday—*yesterday*.

And somebody had bailed him out.

"Why didn't the mothafucka go back in?" I ask again, though this time in an accommodating whisper.

Bakari sucked a swig of soda and reseated the cup before answering. "You know Bama." He speaks while looking at the screen. "He ain't afraid of shit."

"Good sense ain't got jack to do with fear." It was difficult to not shout. "If I would've gotten bailed out at three in the morning under the circumstances that prevail, the minute I stepped outside and didn't see one of y'all I would've turned my ass back in and fuck who thought I was a punk."

"That would've been wise," Bakari allows, "but you know Bama."

"Mothafucka--you already said that."

Ba finally looks at me. "Well, whaddya want me to say?"

"How 'bout what the fuck happened to him."

Homeboy turns back to the screen. "That ain't hard to figure."

All too regrettably, that is true. The second those cops crashed my door I did rather figure that (since life ain't TV) it wasn't great detective work that'd led them to my address. So while I tore ass from Manhattan for my natural born, I made opportunity to call Bakari. I had to warn him, of course. But also I wanted to see if he knew who had given me up.

Never did I suspect it would be Bama.

Not that I blamed him. See, some folks used popcorn and nonchalance to distract themselves from the unthinkable. Me, I hid behind anger and doled it out indiscriminately. At Bakari. At Bama himself. Alas. Better to be mad at him than to contemplate what had made him talk. Though, as Bakari suggested, it wasn't hard to figure. He spoke around a mouthful of popcorn. "And you'z a *lucky* ma'fucka."

"Yeah?"

"Well, if them cops would've been official, your building would've been *surrounded* and your lucky ass wouldn't be sitting here insulting me."

"Ah," I said. Which was as good a response as any when you're wrong. Now that he mentioned it, I had had no idea what those cops had planned to report to their precinct. But from the giddy-up I'd known it was sure for sure not gonna be jack—until *after* they had murdered me and looked for the money.

"But congratulations anyway."

I look inquiringly at the mothafucka. No shit, but in the dimly lit theatre his boldly chiseled face could've been one of them Ghanian masks wrought so fearsomely in gold. "Congratulations for what?"

"Five cops paid you a visit," he explains. "Only two survived the trip to the hospital and one of them ain't expected to live."

"Wonderful!"

"Hold your voice down."

"Sorry," I readily whisper, more than happy to accommodate this wonderful bearer of wonderfully good tidings. "But it's not often I receive such joyous news."

"Don't get too overjoyed. The minute they find a decent picture of you, your mug'll be all over everywhere."

CURIOUSER

I sigh. Heavily. The thought of being featured on snitch-TV could make you do that.

"And," Bakari reminds me, "we still gotta find Bama."

Now that really gets me weary 'cuz it's a nigh impossible task.

"I'm open for suggestions." I say, well, wearily, 'cuz impossible or not, we've gotta do it.

"So am I," Ba responds. "Any suggestion would be nice." And for the first time I see what I pretty much knew all along: Bakari's nonchalance is only a mask for his sorrow, rage and confusion.

"Well, first thing I wanna do is stash my cash," I spit this out quickly, so hometown wouldn't know that I'd seen his fortitude-gauge slip past E. Not that it really meant anything. True heart, as every self-reflecting bad-ass could tell you, was not the absence of fear and confusion but perseverance in spite of them. Thus an occasional wobble as you shouldered the load didn't mean shit.

"Already took care of my dough," Bakari pats his waist, "Except for the ten thou' I got under this vest."

"Good," I say, meaning good that his dough is secure, and good that he was so quickly back to his resolute self, as though his dismay a scant breath ago had never been. "Have you told Skip yet?" I ask.

"Nah. But what we should tell him is to keep his ass where it is."

Secretly I smile. With each developing detail of our course of action, Bakari's always deeply rooted self sinks deeper.

"I'll go for that," I second. "But we absolutely gotta put him on point."

"No doubt."

"Then we find Bama."

"No *muh*thafuckin' doubt."

Now I smile openly, infected by my brother's resolve to get busy. "Well, let's get this party star—" Beep beep beep. Angrily I silence the pager and stuff Little Bruhda back under my thigh having whipped it out as quick as a devil's forked tongue.

Bakari chuckles at my overreaction. "You better be careful of that thing."

"I wasn't gonna blast nothin'." I protest. "I was just getting ready."

Ba laughs. "Sure, sure. You wasn't startled a lick. But what I meant was be careful the cops ain't paging you."

I unclip the eternal disrupter of ten thousand lives so that I might clearly gander the luminous digits. "If I don't like the number," I say, cupping the pager in both hands, "I'm crushing this mothafucka now." With murderous intensity (like if I peered hard enough the face of the caller would appear), I squint at the numbers. "Well. kiss my ass," I whisper.

Bakari sounds worried. "Who is it? Something suspicious?"

"Very." I fidget around until the pager is once again stuck under Little Sista.

Bakari reads me perfectly. Which wasn't really an accomplishment since my face was all teeth. "Must be that double humdinger."

"Triple, hometown, *triple*."

Ever conscientious he starts gathering his trash. "If you can trust her with your loot, that's two birds with one stone."

"Depends on how she acts. But what's the other bird?"

"Your ass needs to be off the street." He gestures at me with the bucket of popcorn that now contained a few hard kernels, a soda cup—and an empty box of Goobers. The *mothafucka*. He didn't tell me had any of those. "Your disguise won't fool any of the six dozen 'friends' the mob and the cops got looking to turn you in. So even if you can't trust your heart-throb, stay with her til I call." He stood up.

Hastily I stick Little Bruhda in my waist. "And what are you gonna be up to?" I stood.

One of Bakari's big baseball-glove hands clumps me on the shoulder. "First I'm gonna tell Skip what's what. And then—" his whisper quieted, "—then I'm gonna give Mr. Vespuci a call."

FAIRY TALES

Women say men are dogs and we are.

I know because I was en route to Milagros on the elevated subway, as chipper as Little Red Riding Hood a-tra-la-la-ing to Grandma's. Of course the Big Bad Wolf might've been waiting for me too. You know. With a NY Eye-talian accent and an offa I couldn't refusa—or with an arrest warrant, if the Big Bad Wolf wore sheep. For the nonce, however, the prospect of seeing Milagros had me too stupid with joy to worry about that scenario.

Yet I was not without anguish.

For Julio and Lizette. For Katherine and Alabama. And (to a lesser degree) even for the murderous now dead strangers I'd beaten here and there to the blizmo. Also I worried a-plenty about Bakari, whose necessary effort to contact Vespucci was like a rabbit seeking dialog with wolves. And of course I had the perennial worry for the planet.

But most immediately I worried for myself.

Yo. Mightily I strove to appear but another fuck-the-world New Yorker as I chug-chugged along on the train. But within my facade were nerves so frayed, every child or old lady who didn't look like a cop looked like a mafiosi. And the rest of the passengers in the half-filled subway car? They looked like cutthroats with x-ray eyes. Yeah. All the indifferent seeming, apparent working stiffs could try to look indifferent if they wanted. But I knew: they'd all seen right through the bag sitting next to me in the corner seat and were just waiting for me to blink so they could steal my half mil. And if that weren't perturbation enough, every time I shifted the urge to drop my pants and shoot that splinter outta my butt was driving me cold crazy. And what happens? Out of all this angst and love and paranoia and rage, what do I do?

Salivate over the woman sitting across from me, woof mothafuckin' woof.

Yeah. She was an intelligent and skilled human being, I am sure. But serve me a large can of Alpo, baby, 'cuz I just wanted to slay her.

I consoled myself that the drooling bow-wow yet within me was strictly a conditioned response. See, *it was not lofty* I, I told myself, who was a-barking over the black-stockinged, jet black girlie girl who should've been riding a limo but (to my gratitude and delight) had parked her pedigreed doggie treat on the #7 to Queens. No, it was not I who wondered if her thighs were as firm as her muscled calves, or what sounds her slackened lips would emit if I tenderized her loins. Nor was it I who noticed that I could swallow her— succulent bones and all—in one carnivorous gulp. No! It was the unsettled ghost of the varmint inside me and bow wow yippy yi yay.

The train pulled into a station and I turned dutifully alert. Sho'. It was highly improbable that anybody gunning for me would just so happen to board. But I sized up anybody anyway. That turned out to be two teeny boppers and a geezer. Harmless, I guess. Nonethe-damn-less I watched to see if any of them looked like they wanted to kill something. Didn't seem so. Mostly because they'd chosen seats at the far end of the car. So (since I'd weary of reading the ads about zit removal and psychic hotlines) I indulged the dog some more. It was all Milagros' fault I—I mean *it*—was still hungry.

And what a morsel Black Stockings was. Very *today*. From the tips of her expensive fire red flats to the top of her short blonde 'fro. That pumped my heart both ways, I confess. My diastole dug the blonde contrast to her jet black razz matazz. My systole wondered what she saw when she looked in the mirror and—

worse—what the recesses of her psyche wanted to see. Yet though I vacillated over how I felt 'bout her 'do, I was rock steady over how she stretched her dress. Did I tell ya? If there's one thing I'm crazy about it's hips. And lips. And fat nipples, don't forget. And legs and—what the fuck: the Gods created pussy and it (and the entirety of its life support system) was good. Dat all.

"But bless whoever invented hips," I mumbled as the train pulled to my station.

I stood, grabbing my bag and straightening my gats in the process. I'm sure I seemed carefree (despite that splinter in my rump) as I moseyed to the doors. But I was primed for even my beloved Black Stockings to try to back shoot me. Happily, I saw through the doors' reflection, neither she nor anyone else reached for a gat. I stepped onto the platform—onto Mila's platform, I might add—and all else (the cops, the mob—all else) fell away.

Until I got to Mila's door.

I'm not saying the Manhattan District Attorney is working for the mob. I'm not saying he ain't. What I *am* saying is that the D.A. sure moved Bama's bail hearing around like the hand of the mob was afoot (ha?). Anyway, *somebody* knew there was beau coup loot just waiting to ransom Bama. *Somebody* didn't want him ransomed. And *somebody's* want was abetted by Bama's coincidentally mobile court date.

Somebody like Don Vespuci.

Where, I wondered, would coincidence abet him next? At Milagros' apartment, mayhaps?

Now that I stood before her door the euphoria I'd felt since I'd called her was …on the street? the subway? Beat the bejesus outta me.

All I knew is I was suddenly hoping I wouldn't have to kill her.

Quietly, sadly, I let the backpack slip from my shoulder and set it on the floor. *What'll it be?* I ask myself and unzip my jacket. *The Lady when I choose the door, or the Tiger slash Big Bad Wolf slash mafiosi slash cops?* My inquiring mind all aquiver to know, I thumb back the hammers of my automatics and position myself on the hinged side of the door. Was no point in bullshitting. When it opened I wanted the most immediate view 'cuz at the first sign of unfitting company I was blazing.

Head level too.

A vest *might* stop my Rhino Bore (shucks and be damned). But if one of my slugs slammed into your bulletproof hat, you wuz a dead muddafudda in a bulletproof hat. Dat all. Trusting to the Gods (and my 15-shot 9-ems, Amen), I knock.

The door flung open so immediately I almost drew and fired, and what a faux pas that would've been! Milagros was frightened enough, you see. And that was so uncharacteristic my heart ached. She wore her usual housegear. Her loveliness, as usual, wore only itself. And though I'm sure I gave no indication, her naked beauty squeezed the breath from my heart (even as I discreetly squeezed down the cocked hammers on my roscoes).

I pretended not to notice the frightened, un-Milagros look in her tear-riddened eyes. "So you finally got your door unstuck." I say. Pleasantly, I think. And to further ease her I unleash my irresistably infectious extra-extra reassuring grin.

Milagros bursts into tears.

"Wha—" I manage to get out.

Kind of groppily, she's thrown her arms around my neck and pulls, it seems, as hard as the law allows. To keep from getting my back broken I stumble into her apartment, off balance figuratively too. I'd been elated to be seeing Milagros only because I was elated to just be seeing Milagros. But when I'd called her her tone had suggested…I dunno: *Let's-be-adult-for-Lizette's-sake* or some equally formal thing. So this was hardly the reception I expected.

Like a commiserating parish priest in front of his congregation, I press against her. "Why are we crying?"

Llike a commiserating parish priest *privately* consoling a parishioner, she returns my press. Which meant of course not a molecule of air cold fit between us.

"Mimttentink (something something)," she mumbles into my chest.

Gently I palm the back of her coconut and tug. "What?"

Reluctantly she unburies her face. "I (sniffle) didn't think you would come."

What? methinks, *I didn't think you gave a fuck*. So I say, "I didn't think you gave a fuck."

Fairy Tales

Her kissable-irresistables get to quivering like she's gonna bawl again, so I hasten to reassure her. "But wild horses couldn't've kept me away." Of course, the NYPD might've, but there was no point in mentioning that.

Milagros lets go my neck and (much like a little baby) the little baby wipes her eyes. "Oh, Jack," she says around a sniffle, "I've been such a fool."

Now that's true. So I say, "Since you mention it, that's trite but true."

She stops in mid-sniffle and eyes me suspiciously, "Did you say 'tried and true'?" Her tone, I notice, is suddenly very Milagros again.

I rejoice at her recovery. "'Fraid not, divine lady. I said what you know I said."

For a long second she looks acutely displeased and I am sure she's gonna explode. But she surrenders to a smile. "A *foolish* fool," she concedes.

I smile back. "Well, as long as you're confessing, maybe now you'll explain your motive."

Her expression drips into a grimace. "I wanted you to feel what I felt."

"If you mean rejection—"

"*Yes*, rejection."

I try not to make a face. "You succeeded."

"Almost too well." She squeezes my hand. "I'd begun to fear that I'd pushed too far."

"Threatening to call the cops on me kind of helped."

Milagros has the decency to drop her eyes. "That was a terrible thing to threaten but—" (both her hackles and her eyes arise) "—it was a *terrible* thing you made me feel."

"Well, had you given me a chance to explain—"

"Idiot," she interrupts. Then softly she touches my face. "Beloved idiot. No explanation was possible. Don't you see? I felt I'd be first with you as you were first with me—and then you made me second. There was no reason I could accept."

Now that was so welcomely mushy I dropped my eyes and squirmed. "I am overjoyed you felt so strongly. Overjoyed and overjoyed.

"But piggishly unromantic."

"Me? Me, unromantic?"

Before she can think to respond I swirl her around, a cloud swirled on a breeze. With feathery touches, I caress her and kiss her face. "How's that for a love story?"

She rewards me with a languid smile. "I'm ready to read the sequel. Please carry me away."

Instantly I pick her up, kick the door closed, take one hungry giant step towards her bedroom.

Then put her down.

"What?"

I run the two steps to her apartment door, snatch it open and grab my bag as though it was trying to escape. "Forgot something." I display the bag as explanation.

The interruption was just as well, however, because now I act like I have some sense and lock the door when I close it. Jauntily I march smack dab up to her face. As though narrating one of them supermarket romance novels, I say, "And just when they wondered if they'd been only a lie they'd told themselves...."

Her arms snake round my neck. "They discovered the truth of themselves," she completes.

"Hm." I raise an eyebrow. "That's pretty good," I commend and pick her up because women so like to be carried--*and* it's fun to carry them.

She sighs with contentment.

"We're definitely writing the same story."

Her voice is playfully self-congratulatory. "My line did fit your line rather nicely."

I size her up geometrically. *But not as nicely as my line is gonna fit yours.* Because, as I've said, I don't like apologizing to ladies for ramming their heads into doorjambs, I angle us a bit sideways at the open entrance to her bedroom. Nimbly I slip us in.

"I love you," she whispers.

Fairy Tales

"Shucks. And I wanted to be the first to say that."

As I carry my meal—I mean *Milagros*—to the table—I mean to her *bed*, I glimpse my reflection in her vanity mirror. Lo and behold, I'd been right. There *was* a Big Bad Wolf in the plot after all. But—what *great* big eyes I have!—it is I.

THE BEGINNING OF ALL POSSIBILITIES

...thus (as you might expect), I devoured her.

And when her lips, ripened into fullness from a million kisses, said *devour me again*, I obliged.

Now she lay in my arms, reconstituting, as it were. As for me, well, my soul picked its teeth and burped. Not that your ears could hear it. We had, in fact, been quiet for a time, speaking in glances, touch, an occasional sigh. True romance, I tell ya. Just like in the movies.

Inevitably, however, even the heart needs voice.

So: "I'm never going to leave you," Mila does not *say* but *declares*.

My own heart quickens. First in abject trepidation, then in surprise at myself. See, normally when a woman tells me that she's never gonna leave me I take it as a threat. And like any mouse—I mean man faced by a cornering feline, I flee for my life. Only now I didn't. And that's what surprised me. She 'threatened' to never leave me and not the least of me wanted to run.

Careful not to dislodge my *preciosa* from the snuggery she's made of me, I grip the tip of one magnificent braid and circle one magnificent nipple. "You know how I know I love you?" I ask. Casually. Like I've no idea how I'm distracting her.

The Beginning of all Possibilities

"No," she says, but so distantly and so high up on the scale it is more a musical note struck than a word.

"Because being with you a lifetime doesn't scare me."

"What?" Her voice is grown husky but she makes nary a squirm or an arch, the self-possessed little darling.

"See," I explain, myself seeing how rapidly her wee nib stiffens and grows. "When a woman tells a man she'll never leave him he usually hears the rattle of chains."

Lightly, from deep inside whatever else she's feeling, she laughs. "And what do you hear?"

"Before? A threat. Now? *And they lived happily ever after.*"

Milagros pushes me away and suddenly arises. A nymph arising from the water. But with her knees drawn up and her hands clasped around her legs she could not be more demure. Still my *kundalini* gets to stirring. Not that Mila's interested. Point of fact, she eyes me through the curtain of her hair with a look suggestive of much. Sorrow, dejection, curiosity, fear—but not interest in my, er, *kundalini*.

So I sit up Indian fashion and drape a bit of sheet over the activity. "You know," I explain. "*Happily ever after.* Like in the fairy tales."

The better to see me, I suppose, Mila throws a bunch of braids behind a shoulder. "I don't recall the handsome prince having guns."

Shit. And I thought I had undressed discreetly. I do the hang-dog.

"I'm not angry."

I still don't look at her. "And I am not smart."

Featly, like the graceful Goddess-animal she is, Milagros rises to kneel before me, takes my face in her hands. "I'm just wondering what role they play in this lovely story you tell."

"If all goes well, no role."

"If?"

Forthright and matter-of-factly, she plops down in my lap and crosses her legs behind me, as though I'm only a more comfortable seat. At first I don't mind. At all.

"What do you mean if?" she demands and digs her fingers into my shoulders.

"I have a loose end to tie."

She digs deeper. "And what does that mean?" She sounds—and acts!—angry.

So I say, "I thought you weren't angry." I am grateful her nails are short.

"That was before you got evasive." I evade some more. This time by keeping my mouth shut. "What's wrong? Afraid of incriminating yourself?"

I snort. "But that's strictly a reflex, I assure you." All at once her anger vanishes and (praze da lawd) she unearths her nails from my person.

"Fool," she whispers. Her lips, I notice, are barely a kiss away from mine. "If you'd kill me because I might know too much, you're behind schedule."

"Don't be stupid," I say, like (forgive me) the thought couldn't cross my mind. I mean, I didn't mind being a sucker for a dame as long as she didn't try to cross me.

Then I realize what she said. "What you think you know anyway?"

Mila leans back, swings a leg over my head; scoots back under the sheet. Half reclined against the headboard, her naturally proud (if covered) bossum jutting out pridefully further when she props her head on her arms. Silently, she regards me.

I half jest. "I can see you're in the therapeutic mode."

A breath passes. Then: "You see correctly."

I nod. "So, Sherlock, whaddya think you know?"

She gives me the silent eyeball a second before almost blurting. "The names of the five men who kidnapped Lizette."

I try not to blink. How tactful of her to not say *the five men you murdered*.

"Yeah?"

The mothafucka scoffs. "*Yeah*. You think it was hard finding them?"

"Well—"

THE BEGINNING OF ALL POSSIBILITIES

Her laugh interrupts. "I'm Panamanian, Jack. Why do you think I said I was Dominican when I pulled my cigarette lighter on you?"

Now that she's asked, I see. But for rec' I say, "Because you wanted to give Dominicans a bad name?"

"Maybe--*fool*. Or maybe the only multiple homicide that occurred the night Lizette was raped involved Dominicans."

I hold my wrists out. "So cuff me, baby."

Like a jungle cat, Mila bolts upright and siezes them.

"*Fool*," she hisses, "I haven't turned you in and I can't. What more do you need to trust me?"

She is on her knees again. And because the sheet has fallen away she wears only her fierce (if gorgeous) visage. Still, as she squeezes her palmprints into my wrists ain't jackbone vulnerable about her. And her eyes! Despite her mood and what she means to convey, her eyes beguile me.

So I say, "You have the most soulful eyes."

The lady makes a little ugh of disgust and takes a swing at me. With no thought and less effort, I pluck her mighty blow from the air and pin her to the bed.

"Okay. You win. You are absolutely right." I'm looking down on her, nose to nose. Indeed, with just a change of attitude and a shift of hips we'd be fucking.

"No more secrets?" she asks/demands. For answer I get up and head out the bedroom. In a jiffy I'm back with my bag.

"And what's this now?"

To my disappointment, she's covered herself. "Woman, I wants to see ya." My free hand beckons. "Unveil thyself."

The faggot pulls the sheet up to her chin and faintly, faintly smiles me a challenge.

"What have you got there?" she chimes. Briefly. Musically. So that you hear the resonance more than the words.

"Should trade you a peek for a peek," I mumble, and rest the bag on the foot of the bed. "You wanted to know why the prince carries guns."

Bare-ass naked, I mime shoving up my sleeves, a magician 'bout to magick. Reaching into my bag-o-tricks, I pull out a stack of crisp

100-dollar bills and rifle them like a deck of cards. "For one thing," I continue, "the prince used to be a frog."

Before she could ask what or why, I start throwing money all around her. Yeah, it was germy, but it was *money*-germs. It is so unfortunate. I mean, alas, that money is the stuff of dreams. That's why even nonacquisitive Milagros sat the fuck up when the bills began to rain. I mean the pile already seemed enough for a dream state the size of Nebraska—and I was still throwin'.

At last I groped around for a errant sheef of bills but felt only grenades. I closed the bag like I had nothing to hide and set the mothafucka on the floor. "Well, that's that." Milagros finally snapped closed her mouth and (shucks) pulled the sheet back over her breasts.

"All right, Jack." Mila slumps against the headboard. "I'm all ears."

Of course I look her up and down, "I wouldn't quite say that." I sit near her. "But what I will say" (a-fore your monthly cycle drops outta the blue again) "is I have *not* come out of retirement."

Milagros laces her fingers in her lap. "I did rather wonder about that."

"Fret not, *mamasita*." I gesture at the loot spread hither and yon. "This came *before* my promise."

She pronounces her belief with a nod. "And this has something to do with your guns. I suppose."

"You suppose correctly." And without flinching from anything but what would incriminate others, I tell her things I never dreamed I'd say aloud. About sticking up mobsters. About killing them. About Bama, the cops and my bombed up apartment and the inevitable and very current APB. *And* (though I admit I paused to swallow) even about Katherine. Of course I observed her as I spoke. Of course emotions kaleidoscoped across her face. Shock, fear; things that shamed me. But resolutely I proceed to my conclusion.

"Now all I want is to find my partner then—*presto!*—" (I make like I'm chucking a gun) "—the ugly ducklings drown in a lake and we live happily ever after."

Mila smiles so forlornly it breaks my heart. "You needn't expurgate the story."

The Beginning of all Possibilities

"Expurgate?" I ask, like I don't know that she's read between my lines.

"What if you find your friend dead?"

I shrug. "I won't be happy."

As if drawing behind a curtain, Mila drops her head to her knees. I give her a moment to at least partially digest the unpalatable mess I've dished up.

"So," I venture, "what sayeth thou?"

She sighs. "Nothing," she says to her knees.

"Not even gonna try to talk me out of it?"

Her head is still buried in her knees. "Could I, Jack?"

"Look up, child. Look up when you speak to me."

She does, "I *said*," she says very loudly, "*could* I talk you out of it?"

Well, well, I ease closer to her. Enough so I can brush away one of the tears she was hiding. "No, my love."

"Well, then," she snaps, though (I'm relieved to say) she does not move from my touch, "let's pray you find your friend alive."

I slide within kissing range. Seeing how her face was all tear streaked, lightly smooching up her eyes and cheeks was the fitting thing to do. Besides, it might've been my last opportunity to lay lip upon my love. See, I had yet to ask if she could accept my position. And if her answer was I had to choose either our romance or Alabama's life ...well, I was just gonna have to live with a broken heart.

Almost as if I'm speaking sweet nothings. I pose the question. "What if I have to get my hands dirty once more? What if i gotta take care of stuff because they murdered my brotha? Would you evict me again or what?"

Milagros shoves me away with such suddenness I'm still hearing my question mark when I hit the bed.

"Don't you understand." She's on her knee, shaking her fists at me; the sheet a forgotten pool around her legs. "Don't you understand that I love you?" Clinging and crying, crying and clinging, the angry-looking woman falls upon me.

Gently I puts the squeeze to her. When her sobs abate, I sit up and drape her across my lap like the little baby doll she is. "I'm glad your love conquers all," I say, " 'cuz then you'll have no problem accepting my dough."

She might've. Even highly intelligent mothafuckas like Milagros turned stupidly righteous about blood money.

Stupidly righteous and unwittingly double-dealing.

See, the white man isn't interested in truth. He's interested in maintaining his privilege. Often that requires not examining things too closely. Like, if you *really* look at chattle slavery you find a bank. Look at child prostitution the world over, find a bank. Look at the conditions that create US crime, unemployment, malnourished children in the midst of white southern hospitality and find a bank and a bank and a bank again. Hell, wherever a dark belly distends with hunger a fat white bank counts its profit margin.

But what do the devils have us see?

How other white men parlayed a purseful of sixpence into multi-billion dollar financial conglomerates. But through wisdom and industry, not blood and plunder. Hence the stupidity of the decent. All day they'd accept bank compounded interest or whatever. But offer one of the mothafuckas the same blood drenched money as loot and what does she say?

"Exactly how much dough are we talking about?"

Guess I showed my surprise, 'cuz when Milagros looked at my gaped opened mouth she said,

"What did you think? I would decline?"

I am somewhat abashed. "Most of you law abiders would," I mumble.

Mila shrugs that away. "All money's dirty, Jack. Given the prerequisites of capitalism, the best one can hope for is a livelihood that only indirectly exploits.So—" (she smiles radiantly) "—how much have we got?"

"Roughly four hundred thousand."

Baby drips sarcasm. "That's all?" She sucks her teeth and pouts prettily. "And I was so hoping for a million."

I laugh. "Greedy mothafucka. Actually it's half a million but a hundred grand is for Magdalena and Lizette."

THE BEGINNING OF ALL POSSIBILITIES

Mila touches my face. "That is such a dear thing." Then overwhelmed by my magnanimity, I guess, she inclines to put a hugging to me. I grimace. "What's wrong?"

"Splinter in my butt." I kind of smile. "From when I made my own great escape."

Milagros slips nimbly to her feet and tries tugging me to mine.

"What?"

"On your belly," she instructs.

"But—"

"Will you *cooperate*?" She sounds exasperated. Probably 'cuz she was pulling and tugging her determined self silly and I (my *chi* sunk like stone roots in my lower *tan tien*) hadn't budged.

"All right." I un-relax and let the adorable mothafucka stretch me out like a flapjack—jack-side down, of course.

Partly I cooperate because I do love to accommodate a lady. But mostly because I'd at last remembered that, yes, I had in fact lotioned thoroughly when last I showered. Laugh if you wanna,. but though I'd walk unselfconsciously butt-ass around a lady's bedroom, was no way I'd expose my rump if it was ashy—*dat* the fuck all. Laying widthwise across the bed, my overhanging arms pulling tuffs outta the carpet, I awaited my fate. Was only a moment, but just so I wouldn't feel so like I was waiting for a diaper change I decided to be pissed at Mila for something. Taking so long seemed good, so I zoomed in on that. I hardly got a good grumble going, however, when the diabolical mothafucka thwarted me by returning. Humming some fucking merry tune, her uncloven toes—like a vision appearing—appeared suddenly beneath my eyes.

I reached out to touch me someone.

"Stick 'em up."

My reaching hands (instead of stroking her calves as I would've liked) froze. I crane my head up. Past kneecaps, thighs and a *really* pretty *labia majora*. I smile. In one hand Mila holds a little wicker basket; in the other her infamous 'gun'.

"You look like a psychopathic chocolate Easter bunny. With braids."

The psychopathic chocolate Easter bunny with braids laughs gaily. "Fool. Taunting the doctor before surgery."

For a second time, the mothafucka 'shoots' me, a little flame jumping out of the cocked hammer. Speaking of 'cocked hammers', from my supine position, I throw up my hands, ostensibly surrendering in her little play act. Actually I'm debating if I should pull her close, the better to *really* blow out her flame. You know. Not the flame in her hand but the other one. The one that burns almost inextinguishably within women. But before I can decide whether or not to lay a grip on her, she's already plopped her ground-round down next to me on the bed.

I roll to my side.

Milagros holds the lighter-gun negligently on a thigh and putters around for something in her basket (which, incidentally, was not unlike what I still wanted to do. You know: putter around in her basket). She extracts a sewing needle and flicks her lighter, holding the needle's tip over the flame. Humming faintly, unaware of her nudity, the sense of things was frighteningly matrimonial. But bless my soul! For the first time in my existence instead of running to put my pants on I wanted to hang my hat.

Wasn't that a kick in the head? Just when I'm predisposed to set up shop, I'm on the most dangerous run of my life. Indeed, the plight so overwhelmed me I thought aloud. "Bad timing," I blurt, as though Mila knew the context of my thought.

Maybe she did. Leastways she came to a perfect standstill. Humming stopped. Lighter extinguished. And as if in metaphorical reply to my musing, the tip of the sewing needle she'd been sterilizing in the flame glowed molten-red briefly then died.

"Stretch out," she says.

I oblige. As baby prods my posterior, I'm prodded back to the urgency of the moment. "Mila," I say quietly, "if our association is established, some of the people interested in me might wanna question you."

"Where is that splinter?"

I reach back and point to the offending spot. "I cannot begin to tell you how sorry I am for complicating your life, but I think you might have to go away for a while."

Tenderly she rubs my ass.

THE BEGINNING OF ALL POSSIBILITIES

"You have such a nice butt."

I blink. Obviously we ain't watching the same program.

So as to fully cast my eyes on the mothafucka so intent on ignoring me I roll to my side. "Woman, are you hearing me or what?"

Milagros stares at me with something indecipherable in her eyes. Then she drops her gaze to the little basket she's pressed into service as a medical kit. Still without a word she douses a cotton ball in alcohol and wipes the soot from the tip of the needle. Looking at her, the word forlorn occurred to me. The poor baby. I didn't wanna burden her but I could not afford to not to.

"Woman, did you hear—"

"I *heard* you."

"Then act like it. I'm trying to tell you I've made us a problem and a damn dangerous one."

The lady shouts, "Don't you think I know that?"

"Hard to tell."

For a moment the lady glowers like a crazy, red-eyed dog. Then she visibly relaxes. Very dexterously, I must say, she holds the sterilized needle aloft in one hand and douses another cotton ball with the other.

"I'm scared, Jack," she whispers, her eyes avoiding mine. "I'm scared and I'm confused." Then she stares at me. "But more than anything I love you. So if you don't expect the door will be kicked off its hinges anytime soon," like a supplication, she holds out the doused cotton ball and needle, "can't we just be here now?"

Now that was so rending I immediately surrender. "Okay, *muneca*," (Okay, doll) I say to the floor, since I've already rolled bellydown. "But as a parting shot I've gotta tell you that the cops might connect us through the phone company."

"Really?" she says, but in such a way I know she ain't listening.

I proceed anyway. "Oh *really* really, mothafucka. The last half dozen calls I made were to you."

Milagros swabs my butt. "How sweet."

"Sweet? Woman, do you under—ouch! Okay okay." I make a display of relaxing.

"You're such a dear." Gently, now, the mollified sadist resumes her ministrations.

"Yeah, but—whether you stick me again or not—we've gotta figure what to do with you."

"So figure." I pause to assess.

"Well, there are three questions. One: will the cops seek to question you. Two: If yes, will they know that we're….." I grope for a description.

"Intimate." I raise an eyebrow.

"I thought you weren't listening."

"So what if they know we're fucking?"

In spite of my worry, I laugh. "Well, my unexpurgating love, that brings us to Question 3: If they know we're intimate, they will interrogate you intimately. But will it be about a murder suspect or about a vengeful mafiosi's drug loot?"

"Inquiring minds wanna know." Because bravery always makes me smile, I smile.

"Spoken like the roar of a mountain lioness. Nontheless, my courageous mothafucka, this is what we're gonna do."

READY. SET.

All pussy is not created equal.

Consider Denise's, for prime example. Many, many moons ago she was the most beautiful mothafucka in my high school, no matter whose eyes were doing the beholding. And I—with predacious intensity—ran her superlative ass down. For a while she did the customary thing and resisted. But when she at last yielded to my clutches. the little girl reveled therein.

Until she caught me in the school basement boning the guts outta Marjorie.

Naturally it hurt Denise to see me—her everlovin' boyfriend—in a sweaty, thrashing tangle with another. But what distressed her more, I am sure, is that the *Another* was plump and tacky and *ooglier* than four Sarah Jessica Parkers. Poor Denise was thus dumbfounded. Unable to understand how I could betray her choice tendercut for a side of fatback like Marjorie. Well, even though my pants were around my ankles I had enough presence of mind to not tell her: Marjorie had better pussy. Dat all. I mean Denise's was equally slick and cozy and warm as, well, ideal pussy. But Marjorie's was just...superior.

You had to have a dick to understand.

Which brings me nearer the point: the *ooglier* the girl, the *gooder* the pussy. Could be nature's way of compensating, I dunno, but that's the way that went. Consequently when you happened upon a beautiful woman who could pull your guts out through your dick you should run to give extra to your place of worship or convert to something, if you had none.

Hence, what I figured.

Milagros had depth and brilliance and virtue and beauty AND the best pussy I ever did have. Thus not getting her deluxe combo meal safe away somewhere was a sin I was not gonna commit.

Enter Marty, the way of my salvation.

Without question he'd agreed to cover for Milagros's disappearance by telling whoever asked that she was on vacation. Where? Why, driving cross-country with a friend. For *two months*. *Which* (he said he could really say with conviction) *was not long enough considering Dr. Dixon's tireless, exemplary service*, etc., etc.

Good old conspiratorial Marty did not know the reason Milagros needed to disappear was 'cuz I had wet a few cops. But whenever my APB was released I believed he'd still cover for Milagros. Yet even if he disappointed me, he didn't know where she was.

And neither did I.

I guessed that she'd gone to her mother's—or sister's. Or maybe to one of her gorgeous girlfriend's whose last names and residences I did not know. Hell if I knew. So even if the cops or the mob caught and interrogated me into a lifeless pulp...well, at least the money'd get away. Since white men *so* hated when that happened, it wouldn't be a bad last laugh. Thus I was content. Mila had already called, informing me that she'd touched down safely after giving Magdalena and Lizette that 100 grand. And I (barefoot, shirtless) had all of Mila's living room in which to do *Lan ch'iao wei*, Grasp Sparrow's Tail. Thus Grasp Sparrow's Tail I did. I'd just completed Embrace Tiger, about the middle form of a twenty minute *t'ai chi chuan* movement, when the beep came. I unclipped the mothafucka from my waist and checked the number just to assure myself it was Bakari. It was. So I moseyed to a window and checked the sky, just to assure myself it was dark. It was, Since there was nothing else to check, I commenced to getting dressed.

READY. SET.

Moments later—an anti-All-Points-Bullentin grenade in each pocket, pro-*Mind-Your-Own-Business* gats fully loaded—I shouldered my mojo bag and stepped.

*****

"Now say something in Rasta."

I look at the long tall mothafucka whose knees are damn near in his chest behind the steering wheel.

"Fuck you, *mon*."

Bakari laughs. "Well, you look Rasta."

Again I check my mug in the van's sunvisor mirror. Beneath the long, thick dreadlock wig Bakari's gotten me, I did look rather Rasta. Which is to say I looked like a black guy with dreads.

"Try these too."

I look. In Ba's extended hand is a pair of nominally tinted eyeglasses. I take them, plop them on; look in the mirror some mo'. "Yeah."

"They'll do for a ma'fucka giving you the once-over."

I agree by nodding at my reflection. "But lawd help he who gives me a double-take."

"Yeah." Ba says, but distractedly.

I look to him again.

He in turn is looking up and down the Brooklyn side-street through the windows, the mirrors. "Seems empty to me," he concludes aloud.

I take the cue and disappear into the rear. Like the last van we had, this one has no side windows. Bunching my dreads into a pillow, I lay me down so that only a low-down, tape-deck stealing scalawag would notice there was someone in the van,

"Be back in a flash," Ba says. The door locks.

I wait, expecting it won't be too long. Bakari, you see, is making an unannounced visit on Tim Dog, the close friend and top lieutenant of the still elusive bitch-ass mothafuckin' Skins. We'd both called upon him before, of course, but that's when we were looking for Skins. Now what we were looking for was to convey word to Vespucci. We wanted to deal: the loot plus interest in exchange for Bama. But of course, aside from threats, all we really expect from Vespucci is some inadvertent lead to where Bama is. Hence I wore a half-ass disguise and hid in the back of a van. Out of sight of my seekers; set to do the rescue thing if even half a chance emerged. About ten minutes pass when I hear the door opening. Automatically Lil Brotha comes to my hand. From my hidden angle I can see the driver's door open. Since I keep a round in the chamber, I thumb back the hammer and readied up. The Gods knew I wanted no innocents on my conscience. But since I would probably be murdered if I hesitated wrongly, if any unknown head appeared, I would pray the Gods forgave me and plug it.

But—save my soul—it's Bakari.

Without speaking he slips inside and folds his long self behind the wheel. Without speaking he starts up and pulls away.

Since I don't know if he's moody or being watched, I stay hidden and defer to his silence.

We've scarcely driven to the corner when at last he speaks. "They got Bama."

I take that as the okay to raise from my hiding place (which was getting decidedly uncomfortable, l can tell you). "That we know," Tucking Lil Brotha away, I slip into my seat. "What we don't know is where." Ba shakes his head.

"No where. I mean they *got* him, Jack. He's dead."

"*Dead?*" I repeat. Stupidly. As though the word is incomprehensible. As though the possibility had not occurred to me a thousand times. "Dead?"

Much too hard, Bakari brakes for a red light. "Yeah. Dead—and he was probably happy when they finished him."

Now that was so ominous the only reason I didn't shudder is 'cuz I don't shudder. I do, however, sigh. "Don't tell me they cut off his dick."

Bakari laughs. Or makes a noise that could've been a laugh had it not been crazed. "And crushed his balls—the mothafuckas."

Something something, he was saying they had done. But I heard only vaguely and from a distance. I was, instead, suddenly immersed in an image of the Frankenstein monster. Including his stitches—especially his stitches. In fact, *only* his stitches. The prominent zigzags on his neck and wherever tried to make an ungodly whole.

Ready. Set.

But I was seeing now that they functioned only to piece together irreconcilably disparate parts. The imagery was inevitable. Most folks, you see, think *Frankenstein*, or *The Modern Prometheus* was just a highly imaginative original tale.

It was not.

At least not in its mad scientist detail. All the author had to do to find her plot was look around at the London of her day. This Mary Wollstonecraft Shelly did; particularly at the Royal College of Surgeons, wherein anyone with eyes and an invitation could see the eminent white men of medicine experimenting with human body parts.

Which were often harvested from the living, who of course died in the process. Well, what did you think happened to the original population of Tasmania? Though, of course, the so-called Australian aborigine was not overlooked and in a pinch any black human being sufficed. Ain't that something? On and adamantly on whites went about how black folks were a subhuman species.

Except when the British medical schools wanted organs to examine so as to better understand human anatomy.

And with what frenzy did they seek to understand! My God! Someone once observed that the measure of a person's character is how he treats those at his mercy. Someone else said that character is what a person would do if she thought no one would ever know.

By either measure the white race fails.

We all know how it has consistently treated those militarily weaker than its warmongering self. Exploitation and brutality following conquest. Genocide through slaughter or assimilation. What is understandably less commonly known are the things whites have done in secret. Things they thought none would ever know. Like when they landed in what came to be called Tasmania. *Exterminate* is too clean a word for what happened there. Newborn infants literally roasted alive to feed the dogs of the (ha-ha) settlers. Young girls kept shackled as sex slaves. Men hunted for sport; boys used for target practice. Hellish depravity upon hellish depravity, committed not by individual whites but by whites in *droves*, whites by the *boatloads*, by whites as a business and pleasure. Thus to say that the Tasmanians were just exterminated cheats something. How many of them became specimens for white researchers is open to debate. What is unquestionable, however, is that one of the costlier Tasmanian samples in the human body parts trade was male genitalia. Yeah. Some things never change. The white male (and female) fascination and hate and love of the Black Bozack has a long (no pun intended) if scandalous tradition, and no doubt was a part (no pun intended) of the ten thousand Frankenstein archtypes Mary Shelly's pen was inspired by.

While I (in a rational leap of insanity) was reminded thereby of Bama.

"...just to send us a message—the mothafuckas."

"What?"

"*What?* Whaddaya mean *what?*"

I looked sharply at Bakari. He seemed quite ready to stop the van and endeavor to wring my neck, though of course it was not really me he wanted to kill, "I didn't hear that last thing you said. About a message."

Somewhat, Bakari relaxes.

"Yeah. T-Dog said the reason they killed Bama a hundred times was to send us a message. Give back the dough or else." Homeboy snorts. "Shit. We didn't have to come way out here to get word to V. He left word with everybody."

I almost laugh. Them crackers had to know that torturing Alabama to win our cooperation was utterly inefficacious. They just took that as an excuse to get their jollies. Word. That's one thing I really disliked about white folk. They couldn't even be honest about their virulence. They had to hide their racism behind excuses, like a kluxer hides his face beneath a sheet, instead of just admitting (like Popeye) I am what I am. Hm: maybe they couldn't admit it, because they couldn't acknowledge it. Hm...

I permit myself the slightest smile and try not to visualize the long last day of Joseph 'Alabama' Cofield. "Well, Ba, let us let Vespussy know that his message was received."

GO

GO!

Egregious as the comparison is, nothing better captures the spirit of the white race than the child molester.

Each does the same. Showing no regard for the innocence of its victim or for the unrighteousness of its act, all that matters is its own base gratification. Once that is accomplished we—like the violated child—are flung into the ditch, like so many gnawed bones or scumbags.

Why is this so?

The possibilities are two:

      a. The white race does not *recognize* our humanity;

      b. The white race does not *care* about our humanity.

Hence, for example, the double-standard and incessant hooplah about Kitty Genovese, the white woman stabbed to death allegedly by a black man while her entire community closed its windows or otherwise looked away.

Why, I ask, is it such a numbing outrage that someone, anyone, even I did not go to her rescue, yet when I would rescue *my* woman, *my* community, my *self* I am sentenced to a far flung prison, like a Sundlata Acoli, a Geronimo Pratt, a Dr. Mutulu Shakur; to be beaten, drugged, psychologically tortured, or (if I am lucky) *merely*

villified like a Dr, Leonard Jeffries? Why is not rescuing *Black* people not *equally* a crime and an outrage and a sin?

Because I have nothing they can see to rescue, is why.

No humanity, no worth. I exist only as a thing to serve, to plunder of ideas and wealth; to submit. Dat all. Whether they contemn my very humanness because they are intractably stupid or just irredeemably savage, I dunno, and frankly I no longer care. Too much time and hope and life has already been squandered in trying to understand the monster. I, for one, have ceased to bother. It is enough to accept that the only conciliation possible between us is the conciliation between the conqueror and the conquered. Dat all. That is all history has shown is possible and that is all I needs ta know. *Fuck* wracking your brain for an explanation or, for that matter, examples of how we've progressed. As the plantation proverb could've said: *De chops don't stank like de chit'lins but dey both pig.* In like fashion, white supremacy is white supremacy. The only difference between white trash racism and mainstream policy is attire. One wears overalls (or a hood); the other evening wear. But don't be fooled. Beneath the wingtip collars of one are the red necks of the other. 'Cuz, verily, chops don't stink like chitterlings but they're both pig. White supremacy (a synonym for brutal subjugation) is white supremacy is the sole thing whites can produce when they interact with those not stricken with melanin deficiency.

Let us extend this further: the only difference between whites of other ages and whites of today is that the current crop bathes.

Yesterday they kidnaped, tortured, raped and exterminated you and went unwashed to their beds with a clear conscience looking forward to another day's work. Now (whether or not they are separated from the blood and gore by proxies like 'foreign investment'), *now* they wash before retiring. But dat all. Wringing profits outta your misery is today like yesterday still all in a good day's work. Yeah. They no longer stink to the high heavens when they exploit your labor or your national economy at the start of the business day. They now primp and fuss and deodorize. They even do yoga! But dat the fuck all. And if the mutants occasionally seem not unkind it's for the same reason any overgorged dog seems not unkind. But dat all. Savagery can be sated for a moment, but not appeased. Let us not, however, mistake a pause for the digestive process for enlightenment. Once upon a European time child brothels were as commonplace as Mickey Dees. Today whites can love their children because they fuck yours. In Brazil, Haiti, missionary Africa, Oklahoma—the world over. That's when they're not *exporting* our children as sex slaves under the guise of enlightened interracial adoption to France, the Netherlands, all points USA. Ain't that a bitch? Whites create conditions that compel dark-skinned children into prostitution or sexual availability and now prattle about their precious own. Indeed, can it be mere coincidence that the "Age of Enlightenment" occurred during the *height* of colonialism and slavery? You know. When all the unenlightened things whites did to each other suddenly had other outlets. Inquiring minds oughta wanna know.

And, while I'm on it, there are two more inquiries to consider.

First, whites are tone deaf. They much prefer the lackluster and soulless imitation of a Barbara Streisand to the unsung plantation divas who are the archtype of Jewish spinoffs. But then a poor imitation is about all their spiritual wastelands can relate to, poor devils. I even heard one say that Mel Torme is the greatest jazz singer of all time! Imagine that. I guess he means after Al Jolson. Not that I'm mystified that they hype their inferior copies. See, I once thought that whites were a race of evil dogs from hell, I was wrong.

They are a race of *ignorant* evil dogs from hell.

They've so steeped themselves in fiction they think, for example, enslavement was nothing to be ashamed of. "Africans sold Africans into slavery," they say, so that is that. See? All the hellish tortures they inflicted on innocents are excused because they've reduced their crime to an obsfucation: *Africans sold Africans into slavery.* Never mind that for every African sold by a misguided Ashanti or a mercenary Tipu Tib, white hands snatched ten thousand. Never mind that Africans neither invited any one to buy them nor created the market to sell themselves. Africans sold Africans so that, de white man say, is that. Yet now after centuries of kidnapping whole nations of children, *now* kidnapping is an abominable crime and I'm supposed to be heartbroken when one of their kids gets his picture on a milk carton?

Kiss

my

ass.

ATIBA OMAR

That shit don't balance. Especially not when entire communities of *my* children are kidnapped by drugs, poverty and ten thousand other white piracies and nobody gives a damn.

Kiss my mothafuckin ass.

The second inquiry to consider (and you've absolutely gotta hear this) is that the white man is systematic. They started with the obvious stuff first: foods and goods and treasures and civilizations. And *people*—which can never be mentioned enough. Once they acquired enough to get their mange comfortably covered from the cold and their unhealthy bodies somewhat fattened, they turned their covetous attention to intangibles: Philosophy, science, religion, music—whatever the genius of the subjugated produced. Now—*now*—that they've filled their bellies and their catacombs to overflowing: *now* that they've wrested from the Original People the veneer of civilization, *now* the mothafuckas return to the well yet again to draw forth the mystery of spirit. Long they have usurped the trappings of spirituality, seizing our creeds and rituals as their own.

Now they got their paws on our soul.

Straight up. Now that they've stripped us naked of all our material achievements, now that they've made all our possessions their own, now they wanna rape what we're made of. Was inevitable. With all the wealth and leisure they've amassed, there was nothing left for them to do but discover spirit and—discovering it—want to possess it. Like, remember how they used to ridicule us for breast feeding? Talking about how it was savage and ungodly, they foisted all brands of processed garbage on us. You know. So all them millions of First World mamas would cover their tits in public. Now that we spurn nature (that is, are 'civilized'), now that *thousands* of our children are dead from using Nestle's infant formula, or are sickly from canned *Carnation* and *Klim*, now the whites coo reverentially about the *wondrous* spirituality of *white* babes suckling at *white* breasts and the wholesomeness of *white* mother's milk—the punk ass hypocrites. Now that the lack of material things to plunder has made our spiriutality conspicuous, meditation is no longer voo doo and hordes of rustic whites flock to African dance, discover yoga, chi.

It is the Case of the Vanilla Bean.

GO

Look at all the delicious recipes whites have with vanilla: cakes and cookies and yum yums galore. So many delightful, mouthwatering confections each of your ten million tastebuds salivates.

But how did whites come by the vanilla bean? And cocoa and sugar and chocolate and all the marvelously wonderful ingredients that flavor so many marvelous treats?

Through the destruction of cultures. Through mass murder. Through inhuman savagery. Through injustice. Through pillage. Through the extinction of entire peoples. Through the death of liberty. And for what?

So they can enjoy vanilla fudge swirl ice cream?

Kiss my ass. Kiss my *mothafuckin'* ass.

The price is too high. *The price of their delight is too high.* Centuries of death and thievery so they can have a happy mouth?

That shit don't balance.

Yet giving variety to their food supply is not the only thing that's too costly. The same monstrous price is paid for *all* their smiles. History is quite clear that they did not mutate their way into existence with cheerful dispositions. Rather they acquired emotional prosperity as direct result of material prosperity.

This must be said again: they acquired emotional prosperity as a direct result of material prosperity—and we all know how they acquired that.

Verily, their god complex is not entirely insane 'cuz they really have made us into their image. Africa, et al., is what Europe used to be. Poor, pestilential, war-torn. Europe is now Africa. And outwardly (and, alas, somewhat in our inner selves too) we are European.

We have traded places.

And they have acquired trappings. Conditional morality, superficial refinement. ritual compassion—the gesticulations of a civilization. Certainly there are those among them who have broken with their traditional Way and whose humanity thus runs deep. But the average honored blue ribbon patron of the arts, their most cultured and refined, is essentially a soulless savage who will do anything for power and wealth.

Like the honorable don Vespucci.

Wealth and power had draped him in social respectability. Yet what was the sum of his life but a single-minded pursuit of wealth and power at any cost? Measured on the scale where gold had weight, Vespucci's life was a great success. But on the Great Scale of Existence? Did his life add to Life or despoil it? Did he fulfill a righteous purpose or an unrighteous purpose in Creation? When the smoke of human accolades was blown away, the esteemed don was what he was: a worthless cracker who lived a worthless cracker life and would go to his worthless cracker grave a worthless cracker.

And I want to help him to it. "Here they come."

"I see," I whisper back.

Doc, I can feel, nods acknowledgment Seems the story of my life, but once a-damn-gain I find myself crouching in the darkness awaiting the arrival of a moment. A moment to pounce, a moment to flee, a moment to live, to die. A moment and a moment and a moment. On this occasion I'm at least waiting in style, albeit somebody else's. Indeed, at that moment, Somebody Else's speaks.

"*Please*--why can't you just let me go?" she asks.

I look on the floor behind the driver's seat of the customized jeep with—unfortunately for Somebody Else—curtained windows. The girl's university jacket is dirty, I'm afraid. And the crystal of her trendy designer watch is no doubt scratched from the handcuffs locking her wrists behind her back. Even though she is face down and has a paper bag over her head I am sure of what she's said—'cuz she's said the *same* damn thing twenty times already, for crying the fuck out loud.

"I told you we will." Then I put a little menace in my voice. "And I also told you to shut your mouth or I'll tape it shut."

"But please—"

"This is the *last* time I'm telling you," I say like I really mean it. I don't. The mothafucka has a cold, you see, stuffy nose and all. So if I taped her mouth shut.... I know. According to the movies and the heroic-cop TV shows I (the 'Bad Guy') should've just killed her outright. She had, after all, seen my face when she'd caught me stealing her jeep. According to the unwritten program, I was supposed to do her on the spot and then strip her corpse of identification. Instead, kindly, I kidnapped her. Everybody and his henchman was already looking to maim, kill, or imprison me, so if she lived to tell of her experiences it didn't matter—as long as it was *after* I was done.

But since she didn't know that, I lied. "In fact, bitch, one more sound outta you and you're dead."

Doc peeled his eyeball off his Starlite night vision scope and put it on me.

I winked.

Unmollified, homeboy assessed me. He was one of those triple black mothafuckas. Not in pigment but in heart. You know. Live for the people. Fight oppression. Self-determination, etc. Always after me to forsake my criminal ways and start a community takeover of a local school curriculum or something. George 'Doc' Epps was also a rather grisled Vietnam vet—which is why I had him sticking his 30.06 between the parted curtain of a carjacked jeep. During that infamous US aggression, Doc had been an unlegendary sniper. Seems like he could hit targets with monotonous regularity, all day and through the night. But when it came to hitting Vietminh, he was stupid. Guess despite that he'd been conscripted to save the world for democracy, he was really quite the humanist even then. Which, I suppose, is why he looked askance at my threat to kill homegirl.

And why for a fifty thousand dollar tax free 'contribution' to his organization's coffers, he'd agreed to kill Vespucci.

Eventually Doc's impassive eyes were satisfied that I was just scaring the girl 'cuz he turned his attention back to his scope.

Well, I say 'eventually' but actually only a couple of heartbeats had passed between the time the sedan pulled up to the vacant lot and Doc's eyeball protestation.

"Come on," he urged to whoever it was in the sedan he was eyeballing through the scope.

Because I too was wondering what the fuck was going on, I peered through the night vision binoculars the well-equipped Doc had so thoughtfully provided. We were two blocks away but the mobmobile seemed close enough to kick.

"Wonder what they're waiting for," I muttered.

Doc, I imagined, shrugged. "It's your party." Then: "You sure it's them?"

"No diggity."

And no doubt there was. It was the right time (1:30 a.m.); twenty minutes before the next pigmobile was scheduled to be in the vicinity. It was the right place: the wide ghetto expanse of Atlantic Ave. near the old Brooklyn Armory. So it had to be them, 'cuz in this deathtrap of a neighborhood traffic didn't just happen by in the high crime time of day.

"Guess they're sizing things up."

Doc *harumphs* agreement.

Another long moment passes in silence. Then: "Somebody's getting out."

I peek. "It's about time."

"Just confirm the mark when it shows."

I smile. Both at Doc's kinda formal lingo and the possibility that Vespucci's head might be on the verge of getting exploded. "Roger," I lingo back. "Roger and Wilco."

Wisely the car's occupants have turned off their car's inside light, 'cuz when the door opens its insides are unlit. Clearly, though, four *gumbas* are inside. Two exit. One from the rear, one from the front passenger side. Alas, from their blocky builds neither is Vespucci. Cautiously they head into the lot.

"They're going for it," Doc observes.

I nod. *It*, by the way, is the hundred thousand dollars in cash we'd hid in a clearly marked spot. Evidence of our good faith. Least that's what Bakari and I had conveyed to Vespucci. Tim Dog had given us the don's number, a number (said T-Dog) that had been so spread around for us we probably could've gotten it off the Internet. With a threat, of course: return the money or end up like Bama. Wasn't that funny? Like they didn't intend to do us like Bama regardless. But we played dumb. Dumb and stereotypical.

"Please tell don Vespucci we didn't do nothin'," I told the lackey who answered the phone.

"We was there—but we stayed in the truck the whole time. Bama and some other nigga robbed and killed everybody." Several times the lackey tried to interject, but I just jabbered on in terror. "Tell him we got most of the money and he can have it." (Ba rolled his eyes at that. *Stop jiggin'*, he mouthed, *and get to the point*.) "All we

Go

want is for the don to personally guarantee our safety 'cuz we ain't do nothin' and we sorry."

(You **are**, Ba had mumbled. *Sorry and pitiful.)*

"We'll even leave a hundred thousand of his money for him to pick up to prove we'z sincere. Once he personally guarantees our safety we'll give him the rest 'cuz—"

"Listen, nig—"

"—'Cuz we know we can trust his word, 'cuz he a don. The money will be. . ." And so here we were, watching the two flunkies scurry back to the car with the package we'd left.

"They got it," Doc says.

"Yeah."

"But they ain't him."

"Yeah," I say again.

The dude carrying the money had passed it to the dude in the back seat. "Should I do that one?" Doc offers.

"Nah. Might not be the don."

And it wasn't. For he emerges from the car and turns back to the lot with the first two. As if choreographed, they all unbutton their coats.

"Guess they're looking for you."

I lower the binoculars. "Yeah. To give me something. Here." I pass him his binoculars. "Get your gear together."

More the true warrior than good soldier, Doc instantly complies; stashing the glasses, dismantling his rifle, collecting his odds and ends. "Ready to roll."

"Go 'head," I say. "I'll be right behind you."

In very unsoldierly fashion, Doc hesitates.

I shake my head. "Don't worry." I incline my noggin towards the girl. "I won't. But do you want her to see your face?"

Doc nods, exits, moseys for the car he followed me in that's parked just around the corner. I wait till he's turned the block then climb over the back of the seat.

"Girl," I say, undoing one of the cuffs.

"Please don't kill me."

I laugh and pull her up into the seat.

"I'm not gonna kill you."

She whimpers. "Please don't rape me."

Courteously I suppress a chuckle. She sounds positively terrified and I believe she is, 'cuz even though one of her hands is uncuffed she's yet to take the paper bag –the used, slightly oily paper bag I got out of a garbage—off her once squeaky clean blonde perm.

I do the honors. "Don't believe everything you see on CopBitch."

The now not-exactly figuratively dirty blonde bites her lips and keeps her eyes downcast. Until I reach towards her. She starts. Recoils. Looks to me with fright.

"Sorry." I remove a shred of candy wrapper from her mane. "It was the cleanest bag I could find."

The fright (probably in spite of her stereotyped expectations) recedes somewhat. I guess 'cuz this ain't how the script's supposed to go.

"Wha—, what are you gonna do?"

I stretch her cuffed arm out and reach across the front seat with it.

"Hey!"

The other cuff I click onto the steering wheel.

"Hey!"

"It's a bit awkward, I know. But in a minute you can clamber over the front seat and make yourself comfortable. Right now I want you to look around."

She does. Almost instantly she's scared again. I could tell because her eyeballs were popping outta her head like a whiteskinned Stepin Fetchit.

"The desolation's almost predacious," I observe aloud. "Like any moment it may come to life and—"

"Oh *please* get me out of here." Half over the front seat, she turns her frightened face to me. "I swear, I'll *never* say a word."

"If someone from this neighborhood finds you alone and defenseless in this secluded place, I'm sure that will be true."

GO

Blondie moans.

"So you have two options. When I'm gone you can climb over the seat and honk the horn for help. If you're lucky some cops'll come. I mean, before the drugfiends and sex monsters. Or—" I whip out a cellular phone. Wasn't technology wonderful? I mean, when it wasn't destroying the planet or alienating humanity from Creation. Anyway, these days you could buy active cell-phones on almost any street corner, like a hot dog or a bag of dope.

"Or," I resume, "you may choose option two. Hide under the dashboard and wait ten minutes for me to call the cops."

She stares at me appraisingly. Then: "What about option three?"

I burst out laughing. Guess my not being a mad killer rapist has paved a path for her wits to return. "And what might that be?"

Her face is as straight as can be. "Just give me my keys and let me go."

Despite my effort to put her at ease, I guffaw. "Sorry. But that's a bit much." I put the phone back in my pocket and reach for my trusty bag. Not that they'll do me any good since the girl can I.D. me, but like Doc I'm wearing surgical gloves. "So what's it gonna be?"

Homegirl looks like she wants to haggle.

"This is *not* negotiable." I prepare to leave. "If you don't tell me you want me to call the cops for you, I'll just go and assume you're gonna honk your horn."

Resigned, her eyes do a quick *ping pong*. *Ping* to the environs. *Pong* to me—the personification of Option 2, to be precise. I know instantly what she decides because she almost kicks me in the face when she scrambles over the seat and dives for cover. "Be sure to lock the doors," she instructs from beneath the dashboard. "And close the windows."

I grin.

"Sorry for the inconvenience." Before she can bother to humor me with some mollifying bullshit I slam the door. Immediately I whip out the cell-phone. But not to call the cops. That I'll do at the allotted time, if for no other reason than so I won't get blamed for the rape and murder that'll happen if I don't. First I gotta call—

"Hello. Who's this?"

I laugh. "The only reason I don't go to your kitchen is 'cuz I don't wanna have to fight your long ass later. Who the fuck else could it be?"

Bakari laughs back. "Guess he didn't show."

"You guess correctly."

"So what's the what?" Cryptically I describe the car the hench-bitches are riding.

"Y'all en route?"

"I'm walking to Doc as I'm talking to you."

"Have a good night." That, for your info, meant that he would call me once he got on their tail.

"I will," I replied. Which meant only that. Not uncheerfully, I hurried to Doc and the waiting car.

*****

"You sure you wanna stay 'down'?"

Doc, sitting behind me in the four-door Bakari has been driving, checks the magazine on the silenced MAC-10 we'd given him that was one of the handiworks of the dead but never departed Alabama Cofield.

"Y'all say my people can have that 100 grand those dudes picked up?"

Bakari, never taking his eyes off the store front across the street, confirms. "On top of the 50 thou' you earned, plus whatever more tax free donations we can find in there."

"Then I'm down."

Both Bakari and Doc look suddenly to me.

Sheepishly I smile. The breath I hadn't even been aware I was holding had come outta me in the damn *tritest* sigh soon as Doc confirmed he was still with us.

All he'd been required to do was take that one aim at where don Vespucci might've, could've been and the fifty thousand was his. Hitting a mobster of Vespucci's stature put both Doc and the grassroots organization he worked with at great risk. There-damn-fore he deserved indemnity for just lending a conspiratorial ear to our plan. Hell. He could've quit right now and neither Ba nor I would've been mad. But me and Ba didn't have a choice. We owed

Go

Bama. Dat all. Now was the time to pay. Dat all. Hence my sigh. See, if three of us stormed the redoubt (as it was) it was daring; if two stormed it was suicide. And *that* wouldn't've been no fun.

But wouldn't you know it. Just so I wouldn't be too relieved, Doc has to qualify his commitment.

"But if the don ain't here I can't help y'all on the next one."

"He's there," Bakari all but decrees.

"He's there," I concur.

But was he? It was what we had played for. From the giddy-up we knew it unlikely that he'd personally show up to collect the dough or to (ha ha) personally guarantee our safety. What *was* likely, however, was that Vespucci would want to immediately get the money and details about how the dumb moolies had begged for their lives, etc. That's why we had set up shop where we did. If don 'Pussy didn't show to have his brains blown out, whoever picked up the money and took it to him had to take it via the Brooklyn Bridge. Didn't matter to where: Queens, Little Italy, or (the Gods help us!) all the way to Long Island. The point of departure from retrieving the loot had to be the Brooklyn Bridge. Thus like a big cat in a tree, all Ba had to do was wait at Fulton and Adams—and then follow the Mafiamobile I'd describe over the cell phone that would inevitably pass his perch. So here we were. Mercifully here was Canarsie. Parked across from one of the ubiquitous olive green store fronts the *gumbas* call 'social clubs', to be exact.

"Y'all about ready?" Bakari asks.

Doc kind of tucks the MAC under his jacket. "I am."

Reassuringly I touch the incendiary grenade I have in a pocket. "Me too."

"Well then." Ba turns off the car's overhead light. "Remember, Doc, all you gotta do is hold down the front so nobody gets in or out. Me and Jack'll blast our way to the back. And when we come out, if ain't no bullets chasing us, we *walk* to the car." Ba turns so he can look squarely at Doc. "You got that?"

Doc just nods, wise enough to not feel chided.

*****

ATIBA OMAR

"What the—" was all the first mothafucka said when I (or Ba? Doc?) shot him, his cue stick still in hand. Three others sitting around a card table said less. In fact, they just knocked their drinks over and died. The dude shooting pool with 'What-the—' was more of a threat, though. Since no one imagined anyone would dare break into don Pussy's, the flimsy door flew open just ahead of an effortless kick. Yet before we could even enter behind it, this dude had dropped his pool stick and was reaching for his gun, God bless him. I mean, a *thorough* mothafucka like that—*even* when he's trying to kill you—is admirable. *Him* I was sure I shot, thereby conferring honor, etc. And even as he fell under my admiring gaze, I shot him again. By then Bakari was halfway to the back and Doc (bless him) had closed what was left of the street door. I was dead on Ba's heel when he passed through the poker/poolroom/abattoir to the doorway of the back room. Only a few interrupted Italian phrases replied to his muffled fire. Guess they were unprepared.

Aln't that something?

The four dudes we'd followed there, I could understand catching with their drawers down because they were in-between modes. You know. No longer hyped to kill darkies/collect money, but not quite settled into the reclining gangster mode. So they had an excuse for dying easy. But the rest! Unless there was such a thing as just-a-bunch-of-dumbos-at-the-social-club mode, the *almost* utter failure to fight for their lives was inexcusable--though *much* appreciated. I say *almost* utter failure 'cuz when I went behind Bakari into what was a surprisingly modern office, a dude Ba had strode past but not adequately wounded had risen to his knees and (with blood drenching his left side from shoulder down) was pointing a 9 em square at me. Pretty 9 too. Indeed, it could've been the triplet to my twins.

"*Sonuvabitchinmoolie!*" he yelled and (goddamn it!) fired. He'd missed, of course. 'Cuz the half second it took him to yell was time enough for me to slip just-so and shoot him in the throat. Subconscious choice, I guess. A symbolic silencing of the noise his damn gun'd just made. I mean my guns had the noise quota for the night just about covered! Anyway, homeboy keeled over near the office's small conference table, overturning a chair as he fell.

And that quick we were done.

Vespucci, you see, had also been seated at the conference table. No doubt he'd been being briefed by the dude who'd placed the bag of money before him and who now lay dead in his service. I knew he was one of the four who'd just arrived 'cuz unlike the die hard I'd just shot in the throat, he'd died with his coat on. Not that attire mattered. Not the henchmen who died in a coat, not Vespucci in his five-thousand- dollar suit. Once again death cheated me. I didn't bother to rationalize that it was because Vespucci died too easily. Torturing him would've been ideal. But he was so difficult to get at we were lucky to get a shot at just killing him. I'm sure the exactingly practical Bama understood. Yet even had we been able to ideally right the scales, no amount of pain, however meticulously inflicted, could undo a feather of Bama's agony or snatch his stout heart back from the grave. And that's all that would've made the carnage uncheating.

"I said get the money and let's go."

"Huh?" Ain't that something? A time like this and I'm silk reeling (which is kinda how you wool gather in t'ai chi.) Hurriedly I tuck Lil Sis in my waistband. "Gotcha." My free hand scoops up the bag. I turn for the door.

And see Die Hard going for his last hurrah.

But—damn me, damn me, *damn* me—just as my attention had a split second lapsed into musing about the inefficacy of Vespucci's death, I again got stuck in a gear. *Bakari!* part of me wanted to shout, while yet another part commanded *shoot!* Thus I did neithe.

Until Die Hard (with what seemed only a shredded neck to hold his head on) shot off the back of Bakari's skull.

Then irrelevantly I did both, yelling "*Bakari!*" as I fired.

Or had I fired then yelled? I don't know, I don't remember. Perhaps I'd done both at once. In hindsight I see that I just could not accept the moment and so the part of my cerebral cortex that makes sense of moments went someplace else. I mean, when that trigger got pulled on Bakari I had been ice, outwardly. Yet inside—*inside*—a primordial *NO!* had resounded inside me categorically rejecting the unacceptable, the inconceivable, the *impossibly* wrong: Bakari the immortal was dead. Within the reverberations of my emphatic denial, a little voice sought to be heard: *not your fault you hesitated had it been some new gumba coming onto the scene unexpectedly you would've got him without hesitation but this but this but* this *one was supposed to be* dead—*wasn't he?—'cuz you killed him—hadn't you?--and the dead ain't supposed to come back to life (at least not the soulless dead) so it's not your*

fault you hesitated because your mortal expectations did a doubletake when you saw 'dead' man who was not.

But a fuck lot of good that did anything.

"We gotta *go*, man!" I heard, but vaguely. It was only when Little Brotha was empty that I realized, *yes, Earl Ricardo 'Bakari' Moore was irrevocably dead and putting a thousand bullets in the equally dead gumba would not resurrect a thing.*

I kneel over my brother just long enough to confirm that his prodigious lifeforce had indeed skeedaddled to less chaotic climes. It had. So I take the car keys from his pocket.

And run like a jack rabbit. It's what I would've wanted him to do had his ass been still at risk and mine was just something to grieve over. So I run. Doc looks at me coming at then pass him.

"Bakari's dead," I explain.

Doc nods. "We gotta get outta here. I heard something outside."

I shove the bag at him. A hundred grand of dough ray me--and fa ti la dough. But even tallied with Vespucci's death, the night wasn't worth a damn.

Understandably, Doc is impatient. "We gotta *go*. I *know* mothafuckas is coming."

"Well, let's not keep 'em waiting."

In less than half a heartbeat I let Lil Brotha's empty clip fall to the floor, jam in a fresh one and after sliding a round into place—*presto!*—Lil Sis comes to my other hand. I start for the door but Doc beats me to it. He takes one step outside then ducks back in so abruptly I bump into his back. Lucky for him I had my roscoes skyward and my trigger fingers off 'hair.'

"Some dudes are coming!"

I don't hesitate to step pass him.

At sight of my unexpected black ass, the three *gumbas* who are hurrying to the rescue put on the brakes. It was an intrinsically human reflex. I mean, unless a mothafucka is *exceedingly* well-trained he's not gonna expect an instantaneous attack (me) forthwith after hasty retreat (Doc). I capitalize on that. A nanosecond after their brakes go on I put about one point five slugs in all three. You know. Like the 2.5 children we're always hearing about in the ideal American family. Anyway, I'd been rushing towards them as I

GO

salvoed, but now that I'd given them some distraction, I walked the last several feet and (a bit more leisurely) put two or three more full slugs into each.

As ever, there was the exceptional lad in the mediocre bunch.

Perhaps he was helped by the fact that the holes I'd put in him weren't as really bad as those I'd put in the two good (and dead) fellas sprawled at his either side. Whatever, this dude tried to do me from his knees., Least ways he struggled to raise his shotgun to an adequate height. Frankly, though, it wouldn't've mattered had he gotten off a round 'cuz I was full into the Fuck-You mode. Hell. I was Lawrence Fishburne in one of them stone cold killer roles he plays so fucking well. Thus the best the exceptional lad could've hoped for as I rushed to meet him with my bullet-eating soul opened wide was that perhaps I might've bled *after* I killed him.

"Good God-l-reckon!"

I turn.

Doc (bless him) had come to aid me. But since he's a tad belated, the bag and the MAC-10 hang limply in his hands. The grisled old warrior just kind of stands there, mostly unabashed eyeball.

I proceed to cross the street. "Let's go."

Doc jumps on my heels. We walk quickly but our heads whirl this way and that. Lights have come on, windows have opened; hostile Italian shouts are going back and forth. But what most concerns me is the cop siren. It's close—too close. Not that I'm surprised. As I never weary of pointing out, the Mafia is a rat society. Dat all. So almost as a reflex the glamorized criminals don't hesitate to dial 911 when someone commits a crime against *them*. Shit. Now I can see the flashing 'bubble gum machine' a-coming.

Thus midway in the street I turn and say to Doc what de white man said when the first Black astronaut got his token ride into space: "The jig is up!" Neck-in-neck we bum rush the last few strides to the car. "You drive."

Smoothly Doc checks his step and heads to the driver's side. Smoothly, like it's a tag team baton, he takes the keys.

"Drive where you want but stop when I tell you."

"Gotcha."

Doc revs up as the pigmobile screeches into the block just short of the social club. Their head- and bubble-gum lights catch us only incidentally.

But it's enough.

"Get gone, Doc!"

Doc obliges.

The pigmobile, now sure of its scent, u-turns to jump on our tail like ... well, like slave raiders and paddy rollers and parole officers and cops have always jumped on our tail. After scarcely two blocks they're just about kissing our ass.

"Doc."

"Yo."

"I'm gonna strap your seat belt on you."

"What?"

"I said I'm gonna strap your seat belt on you." Since time for elaboration was unavailable, I just got to it. Was quick and (mercifully) didn't much interfere with the bee-line Doc was steering down the street. Then I strapped myself in.

Doc glimpses in his rear-view. "They almost on us!"

"Step on your brakes a little."

"What?" Then his light bulb goes on. "Oh!"

Almost instantly the cops rear-end us and (thank the Gods our ride has no airbags!) we get jarred, but not too badly since we were as set as you could be.

The cops, however, were not. They didn't lose control (as I would've loved though did not expect) but they do fall back several car lengths.

Doc has long since accelerated. "That ain't gonna hold 'em!"

"Hit a corner."

Doc does. The cops, of course, do too. "Now what? We can't outrun 'em in this shit."

"We don't have too." I look back and, naturally, the cops are gaining.

"Just let him hit us again. But when they fall back, come to a full stop—and stay stopped."

Go

Doc flicks a glance at me. "All right."

I reload Lil Brotha, take out the incendiary grenade I'd brought for Vespucci's. Then I undo the shoulder strap of my seat belt.

Doc's lightbulb goes on again. "Aaaaah."

But there is no time to commend him for his realization. I told you Doc was a good soldier. That meant also he could do two things at once. So even as he *ah-ed* appreciation for my improv, he had been at his post, eyeing the approaching bitchmobile through the mirror. Almost before I knew it we were braking again. This time the cops alertly brake with us, fall a cautious three or four car lengths behind but keep coming.

"*Now*, Doc! Stop *now!*"

Doc responds instantly, perfectly. The cops' hasty response to avoid crashing into us succeeds quite well, I'm happy to tell you, because when I spring from the car and run behind it, the space they've left between us is just enough.

Bam bam bam bam bam. I shoot the cop riding shotgun and am close enough to see his asshole *this-ain't-supposed-to-happen* face get sprayed by the imploding windshield. Even so, when my gun segues to where the driver was, the driver's already ducked beneath the dash. No matter. I pull the pin on the grenade and toss it through the hole I'd just blasted. Too desperate to be aware, the momentarily surviving cop has (ha ha) 'cleverly' shifted into reverse and is steering blind.

I've already rushed back to our car. "Step on—" I start to say. But Doc has seen. Thus my ass barely hits the seat before he's gunned us away. "*Tur—*" *n* the corner, I was gonna say. But Doc has again recognized what the ass-saving thing to do is and has done it. We just straighten out after the turn when a wonderful *KABOOM!* and burst of light rends the night.

"That oughta take care of them other sirens," Doc observes.

Hm. I'd been so focused on the immediate result I'd totally overlooked that bonus prize. And from the sound of things the sirens did seem to be honing in on the barbequed pigs like flies honing in on shit. Wisely, Doc reduces our getaway speed to within the limit and zigzags his way away. I relax and extract the half-filled clip from Lil Bruhda. Relax? I merely shift to another distress. Now instead of stressing about holding onto my life, I'm free (free?) to stress about Bakari.

Doc, apparently, is 'free' too. "So how'd he die?" he asks, and wasn't that a bit uncanny? I mean, like he knew just what I was thinking.

To collect my emotions I retrieve my mojo bag from the floor and unzip a compartment. "He just died, Doc." I put the partially filled clip with my boxes of bullets so I'll know to reload it later 'cuz now I didn't feel like being bothered. A fresh clip I put into my gun. "The back of his head got blown to perdition and he just fuckin' died."

Out the corner of my eye I see Doc weighing me. *You all right?* he wants to ask. But however well meant, it was a lame question, even fraudulent to a degree. Doc has wit enough not to ask it. What was I to say, anyway? *Sure, Doc, I'm doing just fine. Still ain't over Julio and Lizette and Bama and my wrecked life and apartment—and Bakari gets the back of his head blown off for no other reason than that I get startled by a 'dead' man.* But there was no point in confessing guilt or acknowledging my ineptitude 'cuz not a sympathetic or scornful thing anyone could do would expiate Bakari back to life or erase the rest of my sorrows.

We pull up to the ride he and I had switched to from the jeep. "Thanks for your help, Doc."

Doc nods. Starts getting his stuff. By his choice, he's heading for the subway. "Gonna miss Bakari," he says, but as though talking to himself.

I force a semblance of a smile. I don't know why. To hearten Doc; to hearten myself. I gather my own stuff. "Yeah. Me too, Doc." Dejected, watchful, we part.

STRANGEFUL

I took a chance because chances are what I take. That is, when I'm not making my own.

This particular chance constituted driving straight from the scene of the crime to Jersey. On surface it may not've seemed a spectacular stab. To the contrary it was arguably dumb: a stolen car with my triple wanted ass at the wheel in the wee-est hours of the morning with a gillion red-alert cops on the prowl, and I head for the GW Bridge. Why?

In part 'cuz it was there.

After Doc left I just drove, concerned only about distance, and I ended up on the FDR. So I drove some mo'. And when I looked up, the GWB loomed before me, merely there. So I took it. The other part of why I risked the chance I realized only after I was on the overpass: Jersey (my subconscious had surmised) is where Milagros was. Dat all.

Dat *all*? Verily, *dat* was *every*thing. Problem was, I didn't know how to reach her. I had to wait, is all. Wait for her to get at me. Wait for the initial fever of the white-hot hot pursuit to cool. Once I clarified that this was my immediate problem, my aimlessness transformed into solution. I got off Route 80 West (which is where the GWB had taken me) at the first exit that had a name I'd heard of. Turned out to be Union City, but that's not important. I drove around the empty city streets, but carefully. Having avoided contact with the notoriously psychotic Jersey State Troopers, running into local racists would've been shameful. So every time I saw headlights I turned a corner. Eventually I found what I'd been seeking.

A PATH station.

The temptation to just jump outta the car was great but too stupid to succumb to. For one thing, the cops might not've connected the car I was driving to me—but they sho' as you born would've if I just dumped it higgley piggley in the street. And of course, had they found it parked near a PATH station, that would've been too bright of me. So just jumping outta the car in the middle of the street and running to the PATH train because it was synonymous with running to Milagros was an impulse I curtailed. Another thing that deterred me into good sense was the time. It was only 4:30 a.m., too early for what I'd planned. So I drove to a secluded area about ten blocks away and chilled a couple of hours. Seemed like an eternity. An agony stretched out for an eternity. The moment Lizette's face departed my conscious the back of Bakari's head appeared or Julio's closed casket or Bama's wrack, which was so excruciating I could see it. Minutes were a series of *I-should-haves* and rationalizations, as though I could philosophize Bakari's death away with *that live-by-the-sword* shit. I could not, of course. For though he'd been a sword wieldin' mothafucka who'd cut a wide and gory swath, he was *my* sword wieldin' mothafucka, swath and all. Scrutinizing shadows, hearing footsteps in every sound, I clutched one gun hard the entire time I waited and (without the least vestige of self-pity) cried.

At merciful last, a not too ungodly hour came. Action made time a whirlwind, a mercy. Plates came off the car and dreadlock wig went on my head almost at once and by themselves. Just as suddenly I was at the PATH and then in a cab in Randolph, NJ. because that's where I recall Mila's mama said she was from. From a local paper I'd gotten the address of some rooming houses. The Gods (to my grateful surprise) had not forsaken me. Least ways the first rooming house I tried gave me action. The manager or land lord or whoever the mothafucka was gave me the spiel about no drugs or violence on the premises and I gave him $600 cash. Four hundred deposit: two weeks in advance. About five hundred was in fifties and hundreds, but just so my ass would not be entirely without drawers, I paid the balance with crumpled singles, fives and tens and a mumble about how I'll always pay for two weeks at a time every time I get my check.

Four days had passed. I exercised, listened to a small radio I'd purchased, and went out a few times for appearance's sake so it wouldn't look like I was hiding. The room wasn't too bad. Half the size of a boxing ring. Had a bed and a dresser and a chair, You wouldn't let your mother sleep there without G.I.-ing it some, but it wasn't filthy, praze da lawd. I'd even made a 'friend.'

Knock knock knock. Knock knock.

That was him now—or had better be.

"Comin'," I responded instantly, even though I'd been sitting on the bed in a full lotus, digging on (believe it or not) how the vital pinpoint spark within and the Infinitude without are the same. Nonethe-spiritual-less, I stuck Little Brotha down the back of my pants and kept my hand underneath my shirt tail as I open the door.

And let go Lil Bruh.

"Hey, Jimmy." I step aside so my young white 'friend' can enter. Despite the fact that he would've gotten his brains blown all over his dingy brown ponytail had anybody resembling a cop been in the hallway, the skinny, pimply faced crackhead is cheerful. Being oblivious of his possible fate no doubt helped. The fact that I'd become his sugar daddy helped, I am sure, even more.

"Got everything, man. And here's all your change." Jimmy all but flaunts the $2.30 as evidence of his rectitude.

"Keep it, Jimdaddy." I take the small bag of vittles he's brought me and mosey over to the dresser. The chair and table are closer, just inside the door. But the faint stench arising from Jimmy encourages me to mosey, so I do.

He helps himself to the chair. "Good thing I hurried up like I did 'cuz I still got time to get to the movies before it starts."

Because my back is to him, I permit myself a smirk. "I'm with you there, Jimdaddy. Unless you experience the opening credits and theme music, you ain't experienced the whole show." I think I say this convincingly. Like I'm the regular American negro smitten by all things Hollywood.

But movies ain't really Jim-gamester's point. Yesterday he'd needed transportation money to see his mammy. He'd said. The day before he'd needed money for medication—which was as close to the truth as he'd thus far gotten: he *did* need money for medication. The kind he could buy from a thug on a street corner and smoke in a glass-tube pipe. From what I gathered, poor Jimmy tried to hustle all the chintzy building's newcomers and I was just the latest sucker.

I didn't mind. Being another notch on his gun was worth not having to go out when I didn't absolutely haveta.

"You did good, Jimdaddy my man." Not that this particular good was hard to do, but he was good at getting exactly what I ordered, be it navel orange or a brand of cheese. I hit him with a five spot.

"Did I say I was goin' with my girl?" He eyes me most beseechingly. "She's goin' with me, you know."

Thoughtfully I rub my chin. "I dunno, Jim. I gotta keep a few bucks for emergency." Of course, I had on my person enough for quite a few emergencies. But if I just shovelled dough at him on demand, even his dumb-ass crack brain might start to wonder. "Besides," I add, thereby throwing him a line with which to hook me, "I must've give you more than thirty bucks since the day before yesterday."

"And I appreciate it. But, I swear, anything else you give me from now on I'll pay back." Both his hope and agitation are palpable. "With *interest*, Ras man. I swear."

Thus out-haggled, I relent. "Well, since you put it like that, Jimdaddy." I hit him with a ten.

"Gee, thanks. man!"

Then three singles. "Put this with that grocery change and y'all can have popcorn."

"Rastaman!" Jimdaddy is on his feet and beaming; my mothafuckin friend for life—or until his crack jones comes down again. He is all but ushered outta my domicile.

And my beeper beeps.

Like a hound catching a scent, he halts (one foot in the hallway) and eyes me eye the number.

My face is impassive. "Well, Jimda—"

"You're not a drug dealer, are you?"

Strangeful

I force a scoffing chuckle. "I *wish*. But until I can afford a place with a telephone..." I shrug.

Hometown eyes me suspiciously—*hopefully*. I ain't worried that he might rat. Indeed, if anything, the possibility that I'm a *real* sugar daddy endears me to him more.

"Well, okay." He grins widely. One of them my-Lord-Jesus-I'm-about-to-get-a- jumbo-blast-of-crack kind of grins, then vamooses from my doorway. I close the door and get to collecting my things. The open bread and cheese and mayo and stuff from the day before, and even the fruit and juice he just brought, I leave. But my gats and mojo bag come with me. I expect after I call I'll return here, but was no way I was entrusting my supply line to this room. Trying to curtail my excitement, I go outside.

*****

"Another 'lite', please."

The oily used car salesman lookalike who is tending the rundown bar of the rundown establishment tears himself away from the tabloid he is reading and heads to me, snatching up what will be my second lite calorie, lite alcohol chaser. He pops and pours it into my empty mug. "Want me to top off that drink for you?"

"A little later, maybe. Just the beer for now."

He nods, scoops up my money and returns to reading *HOW I WAS SEXUALLY ENCOUNTERED BY MARTIANS*, or whatever.

I sip my beer. Of course I have no intention of getting my drink refilled. I just said later so he'd leave me alone. Indeed, that's why I'd guzzled my first beer. So I could order another and not seem like I was nursing my drink—'cuz I was. Hell. All I came in for was to use the phone. But it seemed like all the transients from all the rooming houses in the vicinity were cosmically in sync for the same purpose. Had the sky been just a bit more overcast I'd've tried my luck at one of the outdoor phones I'd noted when I'd first skulked my way into the neighborhood. But the gray afternoon seemed a spot light to my fake eyeglasses which saw cops and Mafia hitbitches ev'where. Besides, the locals knew the lay of their land. So if they were here to use the phones. . ...

I sipped my beer and from my perch near the end of the bar kept my eyes on things through the looking glass. I wasn't sweatin' missing the phone. There were about two dozen or so people in the joint. Out of this assortment of poor folk (which to my relief included some black males for me to sit among as camouflage) about half had unofficially picked a number and waited or were awaiting their turns. I was now number trey-ski on booth two. Thus far all seemed respectful of the order. In fact, a few times I heard strangers say to strangers, "Hey, Mister, it's your turn." Or, "The lady who next is takin' a piss," and what have you. So I wasn't worried about missing my turn. I just checked things out 'cuz checking things out is what I do.

That's how I noticed the dude clocking me. He didn't look like a cop. More important, he didn't act like a cop. And most importantly, he didn't act like a cop trying to arrest me. I confirmed and reconfirmed that by peeking over the rim of my Screwdriver whenever I raised it on high for a swig. If anything, he looked like a biker dressed like a pimp—or drug dealer, now that I thought of it. No doubt the three dudes who sat with him in the booth were his henchdogs. No. He didn't look at all like a cop (probably thought I was!). But these days you never know. Thus as he watched me, I watched him back, but discreetly.

Or so I thought.

Apparently our eyes had crossed one time too many when they parried each other in the mirror. Whatever. After one such crossing, Biker Pimp openly locked on me and muttered something to his companions. Two peeled themselves outta the booth and head towards me.

Nonchalantly I set my glass down in the exact center of the paper coaster. The Law of Interdependence was really amazing, I tell ya. Once you had attained ... spiritual equilibrium, let us say, all you had to do to center your inner power was to center your outer focus and—*heka*—your whole being was an empty hand with which to *experience, grasp,* kill.

The henchdogs close. My gaze lowers. But my *chi*—now awakened—ascends. Ascends and sees every nuance of the moment. Deluded, one dude stops on either side of me to box me in, I guess; never for an instant realizing that it is I who has *them* surrounded.

"You got a problem?"

I look up, 'surprised.' "Problem? I have no problem."

"Yeah you do—you just too dumb to know it."

STRANGEFUL

I shift to my right. Wouldn't you know it? The big black flunky would wanna make a ruckus. His less tactless white homethug seems interested in result. But insecure ass dumbo gotta prove something.

Nonetheless, I am reasonable. "Now why would you say something like that?"

Dumbo's face screws up, aghast, no doubt, by my impudent query—though he'd probably think you impudent if you asked him for the time. Anyway he menaces me with a glower, a scowl, a sneer and (unbeknownst to him) the stankmouth. Any moment (I imagine) he imagines he could just reach right out and break my back.

I suppress a smile. Mothafucka--I've fought barefoot and bare ass naked and empty-handed against multiple mothafuckas fully loaded with everything, and I'm still here to tell you about it. *You*, I really wanna tell him, *can suck my dick*.

For a certitude, however, that would've pulled Dumbo's hair trigger and I was no more interested in the counterproductiveness of whupping his ass than he was in hearing the litany of my deeds.

"Look." I spread my hands. "I don't know nothing about problems. I'm just here to use the phone. If I offended someone I'm sorry."

Dumbo looks like he wants to rub my face in it, but the senior henchdog forestalls him. "No harm then, buddy." He pats me on my back. "Enjoy your drink." He steps off.

But true to his dumbo nature, Dumbo just has to have the last word. "And don't be lookin' at us in the mirror no mo'—and I mean *no* mo'."

I raise my glass and tip my noggin to signify my obeisance. When he swaggers off in triumph, I tilt a few drops onto the counter. Libations, of course. Or, as the ancients yet say, *tua*. Thanks. In gratitude; *tua* for my people, for the Creation: *tua—thanks*; libations—for my spirit and myself. It was all a oneness anyway. I was just glad that whatever part of the Oneness that was in charge of the last few moments had quelled that bullshit with Dumbo. The last thing I needed was for mothafuckas to give me attention.

Except Milagros, of course, who was the mothafucka I had come to call.

ATIBA OMAR

I was sure it was she who'd beeped me. The Jersey area code gave hope to that. Besides, with Bakari dead and all of my remaining 'friends' too scared to know me, who else could it be but my beloved?

Hence why I was nursing a Screwdriver, Mila's drink of choice.

I'd ordered one to kind of celebrate our kind of drawing nigh. Yeah. Drinking my baby's drink was sentimentally right, but hell if I could figure what she saw in them. Vodka and orange juice did jack for me. Unlike cognac—or Jamaican rum. Now *there* was a drink! When I saw a couple splashes of Myer's over an ice cube I saw, well, the very very good friend who'd introduced me to her island's delightful beverage (and several other delights, I can tell ya). But when I saw a vodka and o.j. I saw... Hm? I looked down upon my Screwdriver to see what I would see. And (*whaddya know!*) like a zillion imbibers before me who looked searchingly into their booze, I looked into mine and saw the most fascinating thing. Was inevitable, I suppose. These days many whites drink soda or milkshakes or tofu juice with their breakfasts, because orange juice is O.J.—Simpson, that is. Which is too much of an association for most whites to swallow with their breakfast. Or for many blacks to swallow with anything, for that matter. Anyway, swallowing or shoving Orenthal J. Simpson down somebody's throat was epidemic these days, and I was not entirely immune. Inevitably, there-damn-fore, the o.j. in my Screwdriver reminded me of the O.J. drama—the synopsis of what was wrong with the world. Forget the delusion about racial interpretations of the evidence. The true racial divide had nothing to do with differing views of the evidence or, indeed, with OJ's guilt or innocence. The racial divide was over what it was always over: the *definition* of justice. Dat all. On the one side, the Strong Haired thought (but did not say) *Shoot! Whites have murdered us for centuries and got away with it! It's about time one of us got a break!* While on the other side of the chasm of perception, the Weak Haired thought (but did not say) *Goddamn it! Guilt or innocence is irrelevant! A black man is accused of doing something to a white woman! Justice—therefore—must lynch him.*

And what the o.j. in my drink avowed the vodka therein restated.

Never mind that the crap in my glass was probably made in Philly. Vodka was a Russian thang. And what was the Soviet Union now after the celebrated collapse of its communist pretensions? Why, *celebrated*, of course, because it pledged its allegiance to

STRANGEFUL

'democracy', the preferred euphemism for capitalism—which is the preferred euphemism for economic and environmental racism.

And what has democracy brought to the once fearsomely social welfare empire? Rampant drug abuse, organized crime, prostitution, homelessness, unemployment.... There's plenty of cake in the Moscovite bakery these post-state socialism days, but now there's no money for bread. Gone is universal health care and guaranteed higher ed. The Soviet peoples now have the privilege of paying for them, just like us long democratized mothafuckas over here. And those who can not pay, why, they are now free to beg in the streets, free to pass their begging bowls on to their children.

Neither should we forget the dozens of wars the blessing of democratization brought!

Bosnia, Chechnya, Armenia, Kosova. Oh happy mothafuckin' day! No longer must we in the west suffer the rights of democracy all by ourselves. The right to poverty, to hunger; the right to die prematurely in despair. Au contraire! The many rights we've endured so long and which are so basic to the American Way (the chronic financial insecurity and social injustice we take for granted) are now also the rights of the Russians.

And for what?

So a few elite-niks can get obscenely rich at the expense of the multitude. A multitude, it must be noted. which now clamors for a return to 'communist tyranny.'

If the Fondling Fathers (which is what they should've been called after the least of what they did to enslaved children), if the Fondling Fathers had lived in the more openly hedonistic times of today, instead of life, liberty and the pursuit of happiness, they might've written life, liberty--and *fun!* 'cuz fun is what the Fondling Fathers meant anyway.

Therein lies what the Screwdriver portends: whites are having too much fun with what they've made of the world. And since they think having fun is the purpose of life, they're not about to do a serious thing to alter the white fun status quo. Don't waste your time appealing to the big hole in their beings where a conscience is supposed to be. They're not even trying to hear that all this great fun they're having is made possible by the suffering of millions and the steady destruction of the earth itself. Such underlying truth would poop their party, thus that kind of talk ain't allowed. In fact, if you just *seem* to think that there just might possibly be some causality between their fun and all those hungry 'native' children they like to prostitute on TV, they get downright bellicose. Part of their lunatic morality, you see, 'cuz what the fuck good is fun if you can't think good about yourself when you're having it? The dumb mothafuckas. They think admitting the truth would demean them. You know: that to reject the rapacity in their culture is to reject themselves. And of course rejecting themselves is unthinkable since the only thing they sanctify more than fun is ego, the insecure ass mothafuckas. Again when the test of character is given they fail utterly.

This time in seeing that laws and cultural institutions are less often hallow and are more often only the errors of men.

Thus I looked into my vodka and o.j. and saw also room for pity. Poor crackers. They got life so backwards they can't even shit straight. I mean that exactly. To eliminate efficiently, naturally, one must squat and relax. But what do they do and teach others to follow? Grunt and strain on a commode. Verily, they make a mess of shitting and everything they touch turns to shit. Show them black powder, they make a bomb. Show them a camera, they make child pornography. Objectively assessed, there is almost no achievement in white culture which is not some other people's wholesome original turned to shit. I mean Jimi Hendrix strummed chords that still ain't even been invented yet, then whites—revealing their spirit—make heavy metal.

But I plumb too deeply in the glass.

My turn to call had a-come. So I take a farewell swig of my Mila mix and mosey over to the phone booth. I'm so eager to start dialing I drop my precious mojo bag onto the booth's floor without pausing to check for what ungodly thing might've congealed there. I punch the last number in and wait forever.

Actually it's all of ten seconds. "*Hola*," the most encompassing voice in Creation says.

So I tell her: "Your voice wraps around me."

"*Jack!*"

"*Si, mamita. Como tu?*"

"I was so worried when you didn't respond right away. I thought—"

"I just couldn't get to a phone is all."

"Oh, *Jaaaaack*….. I hope I haven't caused a problem by paging you."

I scoff. "You didn't page me soon enough."

"You really weren't definite on how long I should wait."

"You waited too long."

"Oh." She misunderstands me. "I'm sorry. I would've called sooner if—"

"No, *muneca*. You've done nothing to apologize for. I just mean I've been impatient to hear from you."

"So it's over?"

I can hear the hope in her voice; can almost hear her holding her breath. Of course much of what had happened could never be over because it could never be undone, would always be a heavy ball and chain on my life. But to hear such need from such a glorious one as she—*ah!*

"As over as it can be, my love."

"What does that mean?"

I sigh. "I'm gonna have to take very low for a very long while and—"

"I'll come with you."

"You don't understand."

"No, Jack—*you* don't understand. Your name and picture is in all the papers. They say…." She trails off. "It doesn't matter. But that's why I had to call: I wanted to warn you because I didn't know if you'd seen the news today."

"Thank you. I had not." In fact, I had planned to get the paper before I returned to my room. Twice already I'd had Jimmy Crackhead get it for me, and that was twice enough. Call me paranoid, but I hadn't asked him to fetch it again because I didn't want him to wonder what I was interested in. Just my luck. The first day I miss the morning edition is the day I'm the front page.

The concern in Mila's voice is heartwarming. "You've got to get someplace safe, Jack."

"That's what I'm trying to tell you."

"But you're not going without me."

"My heart thumps at the possibility—but we've been on this phone too long."

For the first time since too long, she laughs. "Relax. This phone is safe."

I raise a doubtful eyebrow. "Yeah? How you know that, my little secret agent?"

"Because I'm calling from a prepaid cell phone and from someplace no one knows, Jack. Neither the police nor anyone who knows me can trace me here. So my side of the phone is certainly not tapped and," she adds triumphantly, "you can stay here while we sort things out."

I shake my head. "I can't let you destroy your life."

"Fool!" She sounds rather angry. "Do you take me for a child? I know my own mind, Jack. I've had more than enough time to think it over and I'm decided: you are my life. Please, Jack, spare us the bravado bullshit and come on."

I laugh. "Well, I guess we do have enough money to give it a good try."

"We'll do better than that."

"Maybe. But you gotta agree to one thing or forget it."

She sounds annoyed. "You're being ridiculous."

"I'm tellin' you, Mila. Either you accept one condition or forget it. In fact, I'm hanging up now."

"Well then yes, damn you. Yes: I accept your condition."

I smile. "Yes? But you haven't even heard it yet."

"Well then state your damn condition."

"You must take this seriously, my love," I pause a moment for emphasis. "If we're caught, you must say I kidnapped you."

Silence. Though I can imagine what she's thinking.

So I say, "If that's what you think, good b—"

"All right, Jack. I promise."

"I'm not kid—"

STRANGEFUL

"You're wasting time. I said *yes*, damn it. *Yes yes yes*." As though that settled everything, she continued. Continued? She took charge. "Do you have a safe place to wait in?"

"It'll do."

"Give me the address and I'll pick you up."

I give. Ain't that something'? Without the slightest wag of my antennae (without the least fear of betrayal), I give.

"It'll take me about two hours to get to you from here, Jack—but stay put till I arrive." My smile broadens.

"Yes, General, sir."

The general laughs. "Is there anything I should bring?"

"Only thyself."

"Oh, Jack."

"Just proceed carefully. If things look funny—if you see anything that resembles a cop or Mafiosi back off and wait for my call. All right?"

"Yes."

"This ain't TV, Milagros. Don't let emotion influence your decisions, 'cuz there'll be no second chance if you decide unwisely."

"I hear you," she says, exasperated. "Just wait for me because I'm leaving right now."

"Just be sure to wear your seatbelt—and don't speed."

Mila laughs. "I love you. See you soon."

And I love you, I say to the dial tone. But that was all right, 'cuz that meant my baby was en route. Suddenly, life seemed like it had some promise again. With great effort I manage to get outta the bar without once grinning like the Cheshire Cat. I'm not sure why I felt it necessary to veil my elation. Fear of the crab-in-the-barrel syndrome, perhaps. In any case, once I stepped out onto the sidewalk I could suppress my smile no longer.

"You look like you won the lotto."

I turn suddenly. It is a Puerto Rican drug addict who shares this assessment with me. Ain't that something? I'd been so engrossed I had totally failed to notice the slim, somewhat grimy fellow standing smack up against the bar's facade.

ATIBA OMAR

"Not lucky with money, my friend. But love. . ." I smile hugely. "Love has not been stingy. Here." I hit him with a couple of singles, which is what I figured he was playing me for. Actually I was feeling so expansive I wanted to give him a hundred dollar bill. But that would've been a mite conspicuous.

"Gee thanks, man." Hometown takes the money. "And I promise not to buy no drugs with this neither."

Now you know I don't believe that. "Okay. Sure." I wave him off and commence to mosey the two blocks to my (ha ha) hideout.

I go only a few paces, however, when all the alarm systems in all of my molecules get to screaming on extra loud.

The one thing had led to another. You know. As in: First they asked us to pull our pants down.

"We just wanna see it," they said. "Just bend over and let 'em fall."

"Outrage!" some among us cried. "Emasculation, violation, buggery!"

"Well, I don't know about that," the appointed spokesnegro interjected. "Maybe our butt could use a little air-time anyway. Maybe this—maybe that! Maybe maybe." And he who had been entrusted with our belt buckle dropped our drawers.

Almost instantly a paw was upon us.

"Hey!" we cried. "You said—"

"We just wanna touch it, for crying out loud. "Where the world's the harm in that?"

"They'z white--I mean, right," the spokesnegro chimed in. "Besides, it just so happens that right where their hand is touchin' we feel a itch coming on. True, it don't itch yet—but it might!"

Thus, because he who spake had been authorized by Authority, we let the hand stay.

Almost instantly we felt our ass part. "Hey!" we cried. "You said—"

"Now what's all the ruckus for?" they indignantly inquired. "Y'all act like we was up to somethlng or something. All we wanna do is *see*."

STRANGEFUL

"That's right," the spokesnegro chimed. "Besides, an oh-ffi-shul inspection might do us good! Might discover some piles or something!"

Thus we submitted. And almost instantly felt a probing. "Hey!" we cried. "You said—"

"Checking your prostate," they said, all choked up.

"With that?!" we protested.

"It's only the tip," they said.

"That's white, er, I mean that's right," the spokesnegro agreed, was always agreeing because to agree was his function, his existence. "Besides, it ain't doing much more than resting there. So just quiet down and take it."

Thus we submitted further. Almost instantly our eyes were watering. "Hey!" we cried. "You said—"

"Shut the fuck up," they said. "We're too deep in you to care anymore, Mother Mary and Joseph. Fucking you is too good—you must be *crazy* if you think we're stopping now."

"That's right," the spokesnegro agreed. "You can't expect someone to give up such powerful pleasure just 'cuz it's hurtin' you! Besides, if we turn our head and look at the carrot, you really don't feel the dick—I mean the stick."

Thus we were fucked.

And they never did slap no grease on us. Hell, they ain't even showed us the jar. Just hard and raw nigga-broke us into accepting our unnatural status quo as reality, as reality right and proper. And the worst of it is—the *worst* of it is—we got used to it.

Most of us, anyway. I, for one, still do not accept getting fucked, no matter how circumspectly the dick sneaks up on me.

That's why the moment I saw in the 'dope fiend' outside the bar a figurative glint on a figurative zipper, I slung my mojo bag over my left shoulder as I strolled and (rather than wait for the dick to screw me) unzipped my jacket. To ready my hammers for exit, you understand. The footsteps approaching behind me were confused. They wanted to be stealthy but they wanted to be quick. What they therefore ended up being was hesitant. And a little noisy, of course; though that is not what had alerted me that I might get fucked.

ATIBA OMAR

I cut my eyes to the storefront without turning my head. In the usual trick of reflection, I can see several feet of the sidewalk behind me. The drug addict I'd just hit off with the two dollars is hurrying my way. And though I can't see what he's holding in his dangling right hand, 'cuz that side of his body is towards the street, I imagine it's not my two dollars he wants to return. You know what's funny? Although he was slimmer and shorter than I am, I kind of passingly thought the dude now endeavoring to bushwhack my lights out resembled me. That's really not much of a leap of perception 'cuz as a child I thought we all looked alike. You see the joke: when I used to hear white folks say *they all look alike* I took it as a compliment. 'Cuz every time I looked at a black person (or even a brown person like the one now following me) I saw myself and felt, well, just *every*where. And I thought that was just all right. It was only as I grew older and more American, more socialized (that is to say, more whitened) that I started seeing myself as different from my people, separate from my people; an Individual, in fact. Nonethemothafuckinless, some rationally inexplicable how I retained the jet black roots of my humanity. Like the baobob that during long periods of drought stands in meditation—shed and dry but undying—so too the vital essence of my original self—my ancestral self—remained within me, undying (perhaps imperishable!), despite the long white drought that would extirpate from my mind and spirit every vestige of my tradition, of myself. Thus even as I wound my stumbling path through life I had now and then been from within compelled to cast about for truth, for the soul of truth, for the naked face of Creation. My untutored eyes recognized little, but *little* was enough. Truth, I had glimpsed—transcendent Truth; Truth that explained life's purpose—was corny and unglamorous and ridiculously low-tech: accord with Nature.   Dat all. Dat simple, as de old folk used to say. Penetrate the multitudinous seemings of the daily treadmill existence and find the conduct of Nature. And in finding it, hold to it. But hold to it *now*, *this* time round, because now is your last go-round. Yet even if there were another, I would not trade a single regret of my life for a second chance. Who knew? Were it not for my life having been just-so, I perhaps would not have come to value the most blessed of understandings that whispered to me even when my mortal being was steeped in its worse: ultimately all we have is the truth of our own souls. What do we see there? What is it that we have made of ourselves? These are the questions. These are the measures. We come naked into the world and steep our flesh in things. But none of these attachments is anything else but that: attachment. In spite of the ten thousand things that insert themselves between us and reality—in the midst of a mountain of accumulation—we are still and only *only* what we are: a naked being surrounded by things surrounding a naked being. And always the same questions and measures apply. Thus I who am despised by everyone this society esteems look back on the road of my days and am overjoyed. Deed upon deed of unsung kindness follows me to this moment. Who was so low I would not help them? What have I not sacrificed for others? How often had I deferred my own yearning? Thus, without meaning to be, my spirit was ennobled and thereby—despite my alienation from the injunctions of men— closer to the One. So I was not among those who longed for all-over-agains, even though mistake and regret filled almost all the days of my life.

And right now threatened to rush me out of it.

The dude's fingernails had alerted me to that possibility.

My mistake was in not noticing right away. His nails were just too neat and clean. Less like a drug addict's needing two bucks and more like a prissy undercover cop who had regular appointments at a nail salon.

Maybe the bitch had been staking out the Biker Pimp. Maybe he'd just happened by. For a natural born fact he was a cop. How he'd spotted me didn't matter. What did matter, however, was that the mothafucka not get a promotion at my expense. I was almost to the corner. I don't know what the mothafucka was waiting for to make his move, but I wasn't mad. Indeed, I walked with my thumb hooked in the front of my pants and could've drawn and killed hometown several times over. Only reason I didn't was because I didn't need a swarm of cops in the area just now when Milagros was en route. For that reason I was glad he didn't force my hand by closing the distance between us. But what, I wondered, was he waiting for?

The answer came in the form of two cops wearing jeans and sneakers. They came from around the corner I was hoping to disappear around. And rather boldly they came too. I guess because the 'drug addict' behind me had reassured his back-up via his wire that I hadn't made him. Guess they knew they'd been misinformed when I drew Little Brotha and fired into their faces. *Bambambambam!* I spit so fast I'm sure neither of them had time to regret being greedy. You know. For not calling for more back up so they could keep the glory of killing me all to themselves. I was .just spinning around to deprive the third and equally undeserving mothafucka of said glory when suddenly I *felt* the brightest, most all-encompassing light in Creation fill my head. . .

BLISS

BLISS...

"...and that's how I got here."

The two suspended pans of the scale (which had begun with one low and one high) came even.

"THEY BALANCE."

jack turned towards the source of this pronouncement. It was the strangest thing. Although *THEY BALANCE* registered in his head as a voice so resonant and sublime his heart wept, he was sure his ears ain't heard a peep.

Then he saw. Saw the source of the pronouncement; the source of his achingly exquisite tears.

And both his eyeballs bugged out his head.

There (holding out the Scale of Truth in one gigantic hand, a single tall, proud ibis feather rising, it seemed, from the very crown of her head) sat the Keeper of Truth and Justice, Law and Order, the Preserver of Harmony: MA'AT.

"What the!" jack's head swirled at the impossible sight of the Keeper who—even though she was squatting on her robed haunches—was yet a full head taller than jack—and twice as wide as what he used to proudly consider his 'padded football jersey shoulders.'

And then his head swirled some more when all at once he realized he had been speaking for some lengthy time but only now saw to Whom. Panic threatened to overwhelm him. A million questions sprang to his mind. But irreverently (and quite in spite of himself) what he found himself saying was: "I thought those were Justice's scales. You know. Like in court."

Ineffably, jack felt someOne smile into his head.

"**ALL ROADS,**" MA'AT explained, "**LEAD FROM KHEM**."

At least the explanation, like the smile, came from MA'AT, *through* MA'AT, even though the not unsensual lips in the serene and gorgeous face had not once moved.

"**AND HE SPEAKS WITH** *MAA HERU.*"

jjack turned again. Another voice from another source had just as mysteriously, just as exquisitely been heard within him entirely without his hearing. Even more mysterious to him, however, was his reaction. He thought he should be terrified. He wanted to feel panicked. Yet the sweetest tranquility—sweeter than anything he'd ever imagined or heard of—embraced him and held him still.

Which was a whole lot of holding considering he was looking at a twelve-foot man with a bird's head. The long, black, curved billed head of an ibis, to be exact.

Well, bless my soul, jack thought. *Looks like somebody peeled his hieroglyph right off 'n a pyramid wall.* His gaze shot back to MA'AT. *Hm. Her too, now that I think of it but (*he deigned to approve*) at least her shadowed head is human—and fine, too.*

Unperturbed by the thoughts He heard clearly, DJEHUTI (THOTH), the giant 'man' with the ibis head, finished his mighty inscribing on the papyrus. "**HE SPEAKS WITH** *MAA HERU,*" DJEHUTI spoke—no: DJEHUTI *manifested* again.

This time jack understood. *Maa heru.* True voice. Honesty.

And then came a voice. *The* Voice. The Voice that jack knew must have resonated to the ends of time, to the beginning of time and from before all Beginning. The Voice that was OM—the First Photon—the Voice that was the breath in all things, spoke; loud and soft and all sound and soundless all at once. Just to hear it was benediction. And all that Jack was and had ever been was filled to sublime overflowing.

"**ATTEND ME,** *A' TE,* **YOU WHO WERE** *ANKHET.*"

jack craned back his head and with obeisance in his heart looked into the Eyes of AUSAR (Osiris), Lord of the After Life.

The looking was a crossing of a threshold.

"i attend your judgment, i who was a living being. i attend You, AUSAR."

Whence the words came, jack did not bother to wonder. But he knew that he had spake them. Not his conscious mind but *he*: the quintessential being which had now arrived—which had now *returned*—to the Threshold. Holding the sacred *ansate* cross—the ankh—against his breast, OSIRIS swept out towards jack with the flail in His other great hand and pointed it down at the supplicant. Was it accusation? Was it direction? The gesture was eloquent and infinitely silent; said all and nothing at all. Yet whatever it meant as verdict, wholly jack accepted.

"PASS," the God said, then (recrossing HIS outstretched eternal arm against HIS eternal chest) fell more silent than the statue of Ramses at Abu Simbel.

At that moment the *ba* (the soul that had been weighed in MA'AT's Scales and which jack noticed now for the first time) glowed black. *Brilliant* black. *Black* as the heart of Creation. *Black* as a newborn's soul. Then all at once—as though it had always been—the soul of the man became one with the Soul of Creation. Yea, itself became Creation.

jack wept. "i am unworthy." He felt himself being led away. "But i have killed."

"NEVER INNOCENTS", said a One.

"YOU DEFENDED INNOCENTS," said Another. And then what would have been a chorus had the many voices not been one paved his way with expiation.

"YOU DID NOT MISTREAT THOSE WEAKER THAN YOURSELF."

"YOU HONORED COMMITTMENT."

"DESIRED RIGHTLY."

"LOVED JUSTICE."

" SOUGHT TRUTH."

"COME NOW," said the Personification who led him. **"PAY YOUR FARE."**

As jack blinked away grateful tears, recognition shimmered. "i know you."

The giant Personification with the jackal head smiled without smiling.

"I AM ANPU. THE UNKNOWING CALL ME ANUBIS. PAY YOUR FARE."

jack cast about for his mojo bag. "But I have no money. Everything I owned was in—"

"EVERYTHING YOU OWNED YOU ARE. PAY YOUR FARE."

"But i'm telling You: *i ain't got no dough.*"

ANPU pointed. **"CHECK YOUR DAYU."**

jack looked down at himself. He found himself bare chested, in sandals, wearing the loincloth given to boys in ancient times as a sign of their rite of passage. In the knot at the waist of the dayu jack found a pearl.

He handed it up to ANPU. "I thought this was a Chinese thing, paying your way into the afterlife."

Dismissively, as though it was too obvious to mention, ANPU said what the Heavens knew but the earth had been taught to forget: **"ALL ROADS LEAD FROM KHEM."**

Suddenly they were at The River. jack's eyes widened. "But how can we cross? It overflows." And indeed the Waters awashed its banks like an ocean churning.

"IT IS ONLY THE WEIGHT OF YOUR SOUL THAT DISPLACES IT. COME."

Somehow a boat of reed had come to shore and (defying the turbulence that even then abated) waited like a faithful dog. ANPU stood at the stern and took the rudder.

jack hesitated at the bank. "Why can't i stay here?"

"HERE IS AMENTA. THE NETHERWORLD", ANPU manifested. **"YOU MUST GO TO AARU."**

To paradise, jack understood. But Atur (or Hapi, now that she was swollen) lapped at his feet on the near shore and jack felt loath to break away. "Why can't i just stay with *Y"ALL*?" Again he felt himself crying. "You are all so beautiful. i won't be a problem. Why can't i just stay among YOU?"

ANPU stretched out his hand. "**COME**."

Reluctantly jack wiped his eyes and boarded. Immediately the sailless boat cleaved the waters. jack sat upon the single bench between the feet of the Personification.

And sniffled. "Sorry i had forgotten your name."

"**THAT IS WHY WE SLEEP. OUR NAMES ARE NO LONGER REMEMBERED.**"

"Sleep?" jack was as nonplussed as a 'dead' man could be. "You DUDES *sleep*?"

"**WE ARE NOT PERFECT.**"

"But you are Gods!"

"**AND STILL WE** *BECOME*. **ONLY THE ALL AND THE ONE IS.**"

And what did that mean? jack wondered. He wanted desperately to ask—or to ask further. For his mere wondering had been a query answered with a silence that was Mystery.

The far bank drew too swiftly near.

"Hey!"

ANPU, without nodding, manifested a nod, showing that he was disposed to answer.

"Is that cross artist, rat Skins over there where i'm going?"

A weight descended on jack with the answer; a sense of cold desolation. "**HE HAD NOT EARNED THE FARE.**"

jack thought he should gloat but found that he was devoid of the desire. Yet a vestige of his puny self remained. Hence shrewdly, or as shrewdly as a 'dead' man could, jack raised an eyebrow. "But what about white folks? i always figured heaven would be any place them motha—, i mean, those people were not."

The bank had come. As smoothly as the boat had cast away, the boat was still.

"**FROM SEP TEPY** (the First Occasion, the Morning of Times: the Creation) **FROM SEP TEPY ALL WHO CAN PAY THE FARE ARE HERE. GO. SEE FOR THYSELF—HOMET0WN** jack double-took. Had that been a sly dog wink ANPU had just manifested at him? Stepping out of the boat and (pondering the decidedly human quirks of immortals) Jack returned among the Ancestors, the GODS…..

HEAVEN ON EARTH

…..except he did not quite.

"*What?!*" The undercover cop who'd just (he thought) blasted a new air hole into the head of the Most Wanted Nigger Alive was stupefied.

Terrified too.

"*Wh-wh-what?* What the *fuck!*"

A minute and an eon had passed since he'd shot the guy who he thought might be the perp who was the prime subject of the duty roster given at this morning's roll call. Not that he ever thought he'd actually lay actual eyes on Jack Kerwin (for God's sake) Moore when he left the precinct to resume his regular assignment, which was to tail, surveil and nail Irish Bob, a major meth producer and distributor.

That's why he'd been 'panhandling' in front of the bar, peeking through the window every now and then.

He hadn't given even a spittle of notice to the dreadlocked guy at the bar until two of Irish Bob's body guards approached him. Immediately he thought a connection was being made with a heretofore unknown player in Bob's network. Excitedly he then peered as discreetly as he could at the Rasta-looking dude, intent on getting a glimpse of his face. Right away (when the

'Rasta' turned to say something to one of the guns) the undercover knew that he knew that profile.

But from where?

Somehow it seemed important but he could no more conclude that the face belonged to the Most Wanted Nigger Alive than Joe Smoe could actually believe that the lottery ticket he just purchased was the gazillion dollar supermega jackpot.

Until Jack exited the bar and almost caught him with his mouth agape.

As much to cover his astonishment as to stay in role he blurted to the *very* happy-looking Most Wanted Nigger Alive, "You look like you just won the lotto."

Quite uncharacteristically, Jack was a little startled. That's why he kind of let slip, "Not lucky with money, my friend. But love….." He smiled hugely. "Love has not been stingy. Here." Jack hit the apparent druggie with a couple of singles, which is what he figured the dude had been playing for. Actually Jack was feeling so expansive he wanted to give the dude a hundred dollar bill. But that would've been a might conspicuous.

"Gee, thanks, man." The undercover takes the money. "And I promise not to buy no drugs with this neither."

Jack smirks a bit, not believing that avowal for a heartbeat. "Okay. Sure," he says and waves the dude off, commencing to mosey the two blocks to his joke of a hideout.

He goes only a few paces, however, when all of the alarm systems in all of his molecules get to screaming on extra loud.

The one thing had led to another. As in: First they asked us to pull our pants down.

"We just wanna *see* it," they said. "Just bend over and let 'em fall."

"Outrage!" some among us cried. "Emasculation, violation, buggery!"

"Well, I don't know about *that*," the appointed spokesnegro interjected. "Maybe our butt could use a little air-time anyway. Maybe this—maybe that! Maybe maybe." And he who had been entrusted with our belt buckle dropped our drawers.

Almost instantly a paw was upon us.

"Hey!" we cried. "You said—"

Heaven on Earth

"We just wanna *touch* it, for crying out loud. Where the world's the harm in that?"

"They'z white--I mean, *right*," the spokesnegro chimed in. "Besides, it just so happens that right where their hand is touchin' we feel a itch coming on. True, it don't itch yet—but it might!"

Thus, because he who spake had been authorized by Authority, we let the hand stay.

Almost instantly we felt our ass part. "Hey!" we cried. "You said—"

"Now what's all the ruckus for?" they indignantly inquired. "Y'all act like we was up to somethlng or something. All we wanna do is *see*."

"That's right," the spokesnegro chimed. "Besides, an oh-feesh-shul inspection might do us good! Might discover some piles or something!"

Thus we submitted. And almost instantly felt a probing. "Hey!" we cried. "You said—"

"Checking your prostate," they said, all choked up.

"With *that*?!" we protested.

"It's only the *tip*," they said.

"That's white, er, I mean that's *right*," the spokesnegro agreed, was always agreeing because to agree was his function, his existence. "Besides, it ain't doing much more than resting there. So just quiet down and take it."

Thus we submitted further. Almost instantly our eyes were watering. "*Hey!*" we cried. "You said—"

"Shut the *fuck* up," they said. "We're too deep in you to care anymore, Mother Mary and Joseph. Fucking you is *too* good—you must be *crazy* if you think we're stopping now."

"That's right," the spokesnegro agreed. "You can't expect someone to give up such powerful pleasure just 'cuz it's hurtin' you! Besides, if we turn our head and look at the carrot, you really don't feel the dick—I mean the *stick*."

Thus we were fucked.

And they never did slap no grease on us. Hell, they ain't even showed us the jar. Just hard and raw nigga-broke us into accepting our unnatural status quo as reality, as reality right and proper. And the worst of it is—the *worst* of it is—we got used to it.

Most of us, anyway.

Jack, for one, still did not accept getting fucked, no matter how circumspectly the dick snuck up on him.

That's why the moment he saw in the 'dope fiend' outside the bar a figurative glint on a figurative zipper, he slung his mojo bag over his left shoulder as he strolled and (rather than wait for the dick to screw him) unzipped his jacket.

To ready his hammers for exit.

The footsteps approaching behind him were confused. They wanted to be stealthy but they wanted to be quick. What they therefore ended up being was hesitant. And a little noisy, of course; though that is not what had alerted Jack that he might get fucked.

He cut his eyes to the storefront without turning his head. In the usual trick of reflection, he can see several feet of the sidewalk behind him. The drug addict he'd just hit off with the two dollars is hurrying his way. And though Jack can't see what he's holding in his dangling right hand, 'cuz that side of his body is towards the street, he imagines it's not the two dollars he wants to return.

The dude's fingernails had alerted Jack to that possibility.

His nails were just too neat and clean. Less like a drug addict's needing two bucks and more like a prissy undercover cop who had regular appointments at a nail salon.

Maybe the bitch had been staking out the Biker Pimp, Jack speculated. *Maybe he'd just happened by.* But for a natural born fact Jack knew he was a cop.

How did he spot me?, Jack momentarily wondered, then shrugged it off. *How* didn't matter. What did matter, Jack concluded, was that the officer not get a promotion at his expense.

Jack was almost to the corner. *What's the mothafucka waiting for?*

Not that he was mad. Indeed, he walked with his thumb hooked in the front of his pants and could've drawn and killed 'hometown' several times over. Only reason he didn't was because he didn't need a swarm of cops in the area just now when Milagros was en route. For that reason he was glad the cop didn't force his hand by closing the distance between them. But what, Jack wondered, was he waiting for?

The answer came in the form of two cops wearing jeans and sneakers. They came from around the corner Jack was hoping to disappear around. And rather boldly they came too. Jack guessed because the 'drug addict' behind him had reassured the back-up via his wire that the Most Wanted Nigger Alive hadn't made him.

Of course they knew they'd been misinformed when Jack drew Little Brotha and fired into their faces. *Bambambambam!* Jack spit so fast neither of them had time to regret being greedy. Greedy for not calling for more back up so they could keep the glory of the capture or kill all to themselves.

Jack was .just spinning around to deprive the third and (he thought) equally undeserving mothafucka of said glory when suddenly he *felt* the brightest, most all-encompassing light in Creation fill his head.. . ..

*****

"What the fuck! What the *fuck!*"

The undercover cop visibly shook; even spun frantically around. He'd just shot a cop killer. A *cop* killer and the Most Wanted Nigger Alive! He *saw* the hit. Even saw the body fall. Then suddenly the body was gone.

Gone!

As though Scottie had just beamed it up.

Where'd he go where'd he go where'd he go??????, the cop frantically wondered. Breathless, trembling, fearful eyes as wide as a house darky jigging for massa, he cautiously approached the impossibly *empty* patch of concrete between himself and the two dead cops.

*****

Jack watched the undercover approach.

His jaw hurt from hitting the concrete--but not half as much as his head. Desperately he wanted to raise his gun. Desperately he wanted to rise. But all he could do was lie there utterly helpless.

Well, guess my number had to play eventually, he thought as he watched the undercover draw closer to him. Jack smiled a little. Or thought a little smile. He wasn't sure if his face was quite cooperating with the emotion. *Faggot bitch. Here i am shot the fuck up and on the ground and you still come at me like you're scared to death. Ha ha--last laugh is mine.* Or so Jack perceived.

Through his right eye.

Through his *left* eye, however--as if on split screen--another milieu simultaneously unfolded.

He still saw the cop approach. But stiffly. Like a zombie completely enthralled; his mesmerized eyes staring blankly straight ahead as if in sleep walk.

And between himself and the cop Jack saw--through a shimmering haze--*multitude* of translucent beings. *Gods*, he thought, then knowingly qualified, *Spirits*, before the recognition finally distilled to a quintessence: **ANCESTORS.** From ten thousand nations across ten thousand thousand years--*Ancestors*.

Hosts of Ancestors surrounded him, cloaked him with their presence.

And their presence was chant and seed. *Your passage was to return*, dropped into his awareness just as surely as a sower plants a seed. *Work remains*.

Later the part of his mind that required logical explanation would decide that it was the metal cap in his Rasta wig that had deflected the grazing bullet. But for now he only watched. Watched with his right eye as the undercover knelt over his two dead comrades frantically searching for vital signs. Watched with his left eye as the undercover stood over his two dead comrades unmoving as a statue.

And then watched as an SUV slowed and then stopped in the street next to him. Parked cars prevented Jack from actually seeing the vehicle and its slowly opening door. Nor could his right eye actually see the person cautiously, cautiously emerging from it.

But he knew it was Milagros.

With his right eye he watched her come to the sidewalk; saw her hands fly to her mouth in shock and trepidation as she looked first to Jack and then to the man kneeling over two dead men with his back to her and Jack.

A cop, she surmised. *Has to be a cop*, and she was almost overcome with fear. Nonetheless (Jack saw through his right eye) Milagros moved steadily towards him, equal parts stealth and fear……

Heaven on Earth
...and audacity and perfect courage.

For she appeared (his left eye saw) not in an SUV but on a wave of light and sound. Approached not with guarded steps but boldly; all at once; an apparition appearing. The hosts and hosts of surrounding Ancestors parted before her advance; greeted her as if a favorite child. And familiarly she in turn greeted them and--

Thanks y'all. i really appreciate it because i really needed this guy, you know?

As if he had no weight at all, Jack felt himself being lifted and transported away.

*****

"You know this place started in Atlanta."

Jack (with difficulty) tore his attention away from a trademark Spicy Kale Wrap. "Really? And they're franchising even here?"

Milagros reached across the table in the artfully ethnic cafe to daub a mess of kale from Jack's mouth. "Obviously. Whenever i used to go to Atlanta for conferences or to visit friends, I *always* went to the West End to eat at Tassili's Raw Reality Vegan Cafe." She laughed, and Jack thought never had a more musical sound existed. "Some people probably went to Atlanta *just* to dine there."

Jack downed a swig of Spicy Sorrel. "Can't say that I'd blame them. Heck--" he chuckled. "--this food is so good it made even my cheese-loving ass a vegan."

"I'm glad, dear, 'cause you know you'll be needing your health."

Jack nodded. "I know. When I sleep my left eye is like a window and--I tell you--i keep

dreaming the strangest dreams….. In fact they sometimes feel" He smiled very sheepishly, though with a quizzical look in his eyes. "--they sometimes feel like portents of things to come."

LOOK FOR
R. ATIBA OMAR'S
SOPHOMORE NOVEL

DESCENDANTS
COMING NOVEMBER 2016

...suddenly the church doors crashed open.

"Somebody been shot!"

Everyone turned around, many seeming puzzled, unsure of what they'd heard.

Everyone but Miss Hattie. She was hurrying slowly from the stage, brushing off the hands trying to help her. Because (even before the obviously excited oldster who'd burst in clarified (*"The cops just killed somebody down the block!"*), she had already put the two and the two together. "Lawd, lawd, here we go again….."

The congregation swarmed forward and out like a single organism.

Hypatia turned to follow the crowd shoving past her.

Reflexively Leonard grabbed her arm. "Stay here."

Hypatia shook free. "Fuck that." She stared at him like he was crazy.

He stared back at her for a moment then shook his head at himself. "You're right. I just met you and already I'm getting selfish. Let's go." He extended a platonic hand. She hesitated a moment then took it. Together they streamed into the surging flood that was a community enraged.

*****

"Get 'em! Get 'em!"

"I'm warnin' you!" The two casually dressed white men brandishing cocked automatics were pressed back against the passenger side of a late model Ford sedan. A quarter moon sliver of concrete stood between them and the roaring crowd that pressed in on the cops from all sides.

In the sliver, a teenage girl in a bloody pool had stained the quarter moon red.

The cop nearer the front passenger door groped blindly for its handle as he, like his partner, kept pivoting this way and that, not daring to take his eyes off the crowd.

"You ain't had to *shoot* her," somebody yelled.

"She was a crack dealer!" one of the cops defended, protested, appealed. "She had a gun!"

"Yeah? Where it *at*?" someone asked and screamed and raged.

"That's Nadine—she don't hurt *nothing*!"

"But herself!"

The cop who'd been groping for the door handled finally yanked it open and dove inside for the radio. "Dispatch! Two-eleven! Officer assist....."

Wild eyed, his partner rushed in backward behind him and plopped heedlessly onto his legs, scrambled in, locked the door. The throng that had been in the street pressed against and pounded on the car. The mass on the sidewalk engulfed it too. People jumped on the back and stomped on the roof. Twenty hands rocked the front hood. Black faces and fists and feet were everywhere—*everywhere*.

Without the least trace of telepathy both cops simultaneously imagined themselves fish in an alien fish bowl surrounded by, well, aliens.

"Get us outta here!"

The cop in the driver's seat dropped the mike, ignoring the dispatcher's responses and fumbled the keys into the ignition. The other cop alertly hit the siren and the suddenly startled people on the car's hoods and roof jumped reflexively away. The engine roared and the car lurched forward. People screamed in panic and pain as the car gained more and more momentum as it snow shoveled the black mass out of its way. Finally (though assorted thugs and grandmothers, civil servants and homeless people jammed both sides of the street), the way was cleared and the cops were almost to the corner when some reckless hand stuck out from the crowd and (waiting for the car to come abreast) fired a gunshot into the car.

The driver slumped forward, blood and cranial matter streaking down the side of his head from the bullet splattered in his brain. Driverless, the car swerved suddenly left, penning a 12-year-old boy between its front fender and the last car on that side of the street. People mobbed the car again. Some tried to free the trapped child. Some tried to tear open the car. Panicked, the remaining cop fell with his back to his dead partner and fired a round through the passenger side window. Everyone fled. Miraculously the bullet had pierced nimbly through the crowd and lodged in the side of a building. Sirens shattered the night, grew louder, closer, pushing people into full retreat with their approach. The terrified cop looked up and saw a handful of people trying to get his car off a limp-looking marionette of a boy. With shaking hands the cop pushed his partner's remains off the wheel and shifted to reverse. Awkwardly he bent down and depressed the gas pedal with his hand. The car rolled back a few feet just as blue-and-whites started screeching to a stop from both directions of the one-way street.

Stop!

On the ground!

Hands on the wall! and other routine cop greetings were heard again and again in a continuous stream of violent sound as a dozen cops bailed out of their vehicles and bagged every black body in sight.

Those easing the broken but still breathing boy to the ground were thrown down beside him and cuffed. Even those who immediately submit were held down with a foot to the neck, a knee to the back, a choke. The headlines the next day would blare about an *Orgy of Mutual Rage. A Collision of Frenzy*, and the like.

Hypatia would write one of those articles, but without the pretense of unwarranted even-handedness. Just now, however, she wasn't thinking about writing. Currently, she was only aware that her lip was bleeding when the cop had pressed her face to the ground. Both she and Leonard were cuffed behind their backs lying scant feet from the dead Nadine. Indeed, when Hypatia turned her head to one side she clearly saw the dead girl's face. *So young*, she thought, *so young*. With a shudder she closed her eyes and waited for whatever would come.

Leonard could not begin to sort out a name for what he was feeling. But one thought was clear: *I guess that was A Sign this morning after all.*

CPSIA information can be obtained
at www.ICGtesting.com
Printed in the USA
LVOW12s2024070516
487196LV00001B/1/P